"YOU THINK I [...]
DON'T YOU? V[...]
VERY DANGER[...]
YOU LIKE THIS?"

Now she met his eyes and realized that he was young, certainly much younger than she. *Mysterious,* she thought. *And compelling. But not crazy.* With firm resolve she told him, "Let go of my hand and I will answer you."

"If I let go, you will run away." He smiled, but it was a smile without joy. It was a hopeless smile, utterly heartbreaking, and it shattered her firm resolve.

"No one is allowed to run in here. Or to run away. This is my restaurant and that is my rule." Why was she beaming such a reassuring smile back at him? She did not know.

However, she had enough presence of mind to know that if he detained her another second longer, she would have to break her own rule and run, after all. The table with the actress and her guests had expected her some minutes ago. And yet she lingered, hoping he would never let go of her because she was melting, melting, and the feeling was making her delirious.

"You haven't answered me yet—do you know how beautiful you are."

Her hand, she suddenly realized, was free, but imprinted on her skin was the impermanent outline of his fingers. *But if it's impermanent,* she thought, *why does it burn right down to the bone?*

SILVANA

Meg
Berenson

A SIGNET BOOK

SIGNET
Published by the Penguin Group
Penguin Books USA Inc., 375 Hudson Street,
New York, New York 10014, U.S.A.
Penguin Books Ltd, 27 Wrights Lane,
London W8 5TZ, England
Penguin Books Australia Ltd, Ringwood,
Victoria, Australia
Penguin Books Canada Ltd, 10 Alcorn Avenue,
Toronto, Ontario, Canada M4V 3B2
Penguin Books (N.Z.) Ltd, 182–190 Wairau Road,
Auckland 10, New Zealand

Penguin Books Ltd, Registered Offices:
Harmondsworth, Middlesex, England

First published by Signet, an imprint of Dutton Signet,
a division of Penguin Books USA Inc.

First Printing, June, 1996
10 9 8 7 6 5 4 3 2 1

Copyright © Margaret Burman, 1996
All rights reserved

 REGISTERED TRADEMARK—MARCA REGISTRADA

Printed in the United States of America

Acknowledgments

I wish to offer my deep appreciation and respect to the following "leading lights" of the culinary industry:

Pino Luongo, restaurateur extraordinaire (Mad.61, Le Madri, Coco Pazzo, etc.), who with utter graciousness and openness allowed me to pull up a chair beside him and observe the quotidian routine of a restaurant mogul.

Marta Pulini, executive chef, Mad.61 (former executive chef, Le Madri), who warmly welcomed me into her massive kitchen, which she runs with quiet grace. The same can be said of her supernal cooking.

Edda Servi Machlin, the quintessential Italian/Jewish culinary expert and author (*The Classic Cuisine of the Italian Jews, Vols. 1 & 2,* Giro Press), whose recipes and historical details provided rich background material.

Lydia Bastianich, owner, Felidia.

Andre Soltner, former owner/chef, Lutèce.

Sal Coppola, owner/chef, Coppola's, and the entire Coppola family, for their cooperation and friendship.

Catherine Alexandrou, owner/chef, Chez Catherine.

In addition, I found the following three books of great value and recommend them for further reading:

Benevolence and Betrayal by Alexander Stille, Simon & Schuster, 1991; *Black Sabbath: A Journey Through A Crime Against Humanity* by Robert Katz, Macmillan, 1969; and *The Jewish Book of Why* by Alfred J. Kolatch, Jonathan David Publishers, Inc., 1985.

I would also like to thank the following magazines: *Food Arts Magazine, Food & Wine, Gourmet,* and *Cook's Illustrated.*

Finally, two people who deserve the hugest portion of my thanks:

Eileen Weinberg, dearest friend, wisest counsel, sharpest critic, rarest woman.

And my husband, Sheldon, who makes it all possible with endless love, delicious wit, sagacious advice and unwavering, selfless support.

For Nicole,
a mother's dream

PART ONE

Silvana Levi's Prologue

1996

I hear giggling and on the street below my window I see three adolescent girls, New York girls, smartly dressed and pretty, who could pass for sixteen or seventeen. But I know they are probably no more than fourteen because your American girls develop early. I cannot stop staring at the tallest of the three, who reminds me of someone. There is something haunting, something startling in the familiar trill of her unrestrained laughter. And in that astonishing hair, so fine it pours like liquid sunlight down her back. I am jolted by those long limbs and that insouciant slouch of her hip. I recognize something, too, in her red, wide mouth and her enormous eyes but I am most sure that it is her nose I have seen before, her distinctive, unforgettable nose.

She leads me back, back to a time I have left unvisited all these years. It's as if she has taken my hand and mutely, helplessly, I must follow. I have no choice. To look at her is to remember.

Girasole! Like a sunflower she towers over the others. In my family I was called Girasole, as much for my golden hair and disposition as for my uncommon height. It was one of the many names they—all of them squat with stubby, chubby limbs and hair dark as morning espresso—affectionately called me. I looked like none of them; I looked like a stranger from up north. Silvana del Nord, they called me. And La Blonda. But like hers, my hair was not really yellow at all. Rather, it was the color of a fine grappa. What you have in your America that matches a grappa's chroma is your Vermont maple syrup.

"Mama, why do you persist in calling it *your* America? Haven't you lived here for forty years? Aren't you in fact an American citizen?" my daughter Elena always asks me with exasperation. I never answer her but I will tell you now that though I was born in Rome, Italy is not my country, and though I indeed am a citizen, America is not my country either. At fourteen, I learned that your country can betray you as heartlessly as a lover. And at twenty I had to learn it all over again. After that, I knew I'd never again belong anywhere. They'd never have my heart and my mind to twist like a rope of wet laundry. I became a woman without a country, but this I have told no one until now.

I dip the *biscotto* I baked yesterday into my espresso to soften it and suddenly the taste on my tongue is new, though I eat this same snack each day at four o'clock. It is as new as my first memory, which was of food. Food, always food. Perhaps, in the not too distant future, it will also be my last memory.

It is the girl, the girl on the street below my window, who makes me say these things. She makes me remember. Just now, as she laughs again, her hand cups her prominent nose. It is a Roman nose, a Jewish nose. It is mine.

Business is very good tonight at the newest of our five restaurants, Casa di Grazia, named for my granddaughter Grace. The first one I rather vainly named for myself, Per Sempre Silvana Ristorante, and the next three for my girls ("Women, Mama!" they always remind me). Big successes, all, but I can see that this one, packed from the minute we opened the doors one month ago, may prove to be the most spectacular of all.

Grace, of course, is the main reason. It is for a glimpse of her that these men in suits of weightless silk and women wearing chunks of gold at their ears and chunks of diamonds on their fingers wait, standing at the overflowing bar without complaint. Not only customers. Even her own stepfather, as long-haired as some rock star, stands at the bar and stares at her. Just stares and stares. If I could, I would pluck out his eyes.

Back and forth Grace glides from the narrow front desk to the edge of the large, square room with a stack of menus under her slim arm, seating customers, weaving around tables, bending over a laughing party of six, her skirt so short it barely covers her rump. With each shake of her head her hair follows in the slow-motion swirl of a shampoo commercial. She has my hair.

And my talent for cooking. She invents in the kitchen; she combusts. Oh, that Grazia! How she sniffs! How she caresses! How she chops, chops, chops! You can hear her imagination ticking as she slaps a slab of calf's liver down on the table, as she pounds a scaloppine of pale veal until it is no thicker than a business letter. Unfortunately, Grace is an artist. Unfortunately, I say, because nothing would please her more than to be banished to the Sahara heat of the kitchen where, draped in a chef's white jacket and toque, she could cook her delectable dreams all night long.

"*Nonna,* let me at least do the Pasta dalla Grazia. It's my creation, isn't it?" she begs, but how can I hide a beauty like this in the kitchen, even if it does have a glass window? I relent, of course, and allow her to prepare her special *farfalle* and artichokes in the Jewish style for those customers who specifically ask her to do it. It does, I admit, make for quite a spectacle: Grace, through the window, pressing down on the baby artichokes as they fry in hot oil; Grace deftly upending half the contents over a platter of hot *farfalle;* Grace, her elbows pointed like arrows, tossing the mixture as she flicks her hair from her radiant face, then pursing her bright red lips as she arranges the last of the crisp artichoke petals on top. Oh, the crowd does love it, but I fear they will all catch on and soon Grace will have to stand, wet and sweaty behind the stove all night long, as I once did.

Am I overly protective, do you think? But how can you judge until you know, until you understand the entire story? And then, when you do know, perhaps you will forgive me. Perhaps you will say, "There was nothing you could do. It was always there in the blood, in the genes ... in the flesh."

But how, I wonder, do I forgive myself? I, most of all, should have seen it coming. I, most of all, should have remembered how irresistible innocence is, and how overwhelming the longing to possess it. Instead, I denied my past and let disaster happen all over again. Now, I must live through it all once more—all the passion and the shame. But this time, dear God, I must put an end to it for good.

Chapter One

In the old Jewish ghetto, the streets are dark and narrow and Rome's golden sun, preferring church domes and open squares, rarely visits. There, in the city's once-gated quarter where Rome's Jews have lived continuously for over two thousand years, dawn is never radiant ... but it is often quite noisy. It is the swallows, those small, fork-tailed, swift-diving birds that arrive in the spring from the south who make morning's first racket.

But on the morning of June 8, 1937, it wasn't the squeaking and shrieking of the swallows outside Silvana Levi's window, unshuttered to catch the breeze, that awakened her. If anything, it was Silvana who'd been waiting for the birds. She'd been waiting, it seemed, the entire long, dark night. And with their arrival, she now had her excuse to get up and begin the most important day of her life.

Stealthily, with bare feet, she crept from her bed, which she had all to herself (because she was a girl), and squeezed past the bed of her two older brothers, still deep asleep. Wearing only a white cotton shift, she made her way to the communal kitchen her family shared with a neighbor. She knew her mother would scold her if she saw how scantily she was dressed, but this was how she liked to cook—barefoot and half-naked in the quiet semidarkness of dawn. Anna Levi, however, was forever cautioning her daughter to "cover up."

More and more often lately, Anna Levi would admonish Silvana with hushed exhortations. "Your breasts are showing. Remember your brothers. They're almost men now—"

"They *are* men. They've been bar mitzvahed."

"All right, they're men. Even more reason to cover up." Then, in exasperation, Anna would pull Silvana's robe more snugly across her daughter's chest and belt it tightly. "Already you've got the body of a woman. And then, with that blond hair and those long, long legs—oh, try, Silvana, try to cover up what you have!"

"But why, Mama?"

"Because everybody's going to be staring at you, wanting to take a bite out of you just as if you were a big, golden challah, that's why, *mia bella blonda.*"

Silvana found it hilarious to be likened to the holiday loaf of bread, yellow with eggs and olive oil and honey, that they ate on Rosh Hashanah. She laughed heartily at her mother. "You just always think people are mean. But they're not. People are so nice to m—"

"I'm just trying to protect you, Blonda," Anna would interrupt and almost sob with growing impatience. "But you must help me. Say you will, Silvana. Say you'll try. Please, my beautiful Girasole, say you'll try!"

But since Silvana was doing all the cooking on this, her most important birthday—her bat mitzvah—she hoped her mother would let her have her way just this once.

This exact day last year, when Silvana turned twelve, was to have been her actual bat mitzvah. Jewish boys are bar mitzvahed at thirteen, but Italian Jewish girls celebrate at twelve. That day, however, began not with joy but with tearful preparations for her father's funeral. Half the previous night, Umberto Levi had writhed in pain, refusing to waste precious money on doctors and hospitals. By morning, he was dead of a burst and bleeding ulcer.

"Don't try to find some ignorant black symbolism in this," Silvana's brother Eduardo warned her, trying to console her with intelligence and logic. "And don't listen to the neighbors—they're uneducated. Papa dying on your birthday was a sad coincidence, nothing more."

"Even Mama says it's as if I've got *malocchio*, the Evil Eye," Silvana argued miserably. "Maybe I really am doomed."

"She's just upset. She knows better than that—and so do you. Maybe we're poor but we're not like the others here. Papa gave us that. We could be scholars or bankers or rabbis—or anything—just like Papa's ancestors. There's nothing stopping us. The walls of the ghetto came down sixty-six years ago."

"Then why are we all so poor and ignorant?"

"Don't ever say the Levis are ignorant! And plenty of Jews in Italy have money and education. Jews in Turin and Venice and Ferrara. The Levis are not educated but we're not ignorant. We're the only family in this building with books. We read—"

"Raffaelle doesn't read," Silvana countered sulkily.

"Raffaelle doesn't have to read. He'll take over Papa's stall. He was born to sell. But, Girasole, Papa told me he had bigger dreams for you and me. And I mean to live up to them, in Papa's memory, may he rest in peace."

"What were Papa's dreams for me?"

"He was going to tell you at your bat mitzvah."

For two days Silvana had been cooking and baking. This morning she needed two more hours in the kitchen . . . alone. No one was allowed to see her final decorations—platters bordered with parsley and basil and rosemary and sage and wildflowers—until they returned from the synagogue. The neighbors had been warned. Even Anna Levi was banned from the kitchen; she'd taught her daughter all she knew and now Silvana's almond cakes and stove-roasted veal with rosemary and handmade *gnocchi* with Gorgonzola cheese and sweet noodle kugel with pine nuts and raisins surpassed her own. Even more extraordinary, Silvana actually loved to cook, whereas to Anna it had always been a chore.

Since the June weather was cool and the icebox was

full, the eggplant layers were marinating out on the shaded windowsill in olive oil, garlic, basil, parsley, and balsamic vinegar, along with the platters of cauliflowers, pepperoni, and *fiori di zucca* (squash flowers), all steeping in their own piquant dressings.

On the oilcloth-covered table, the sourdough Tuscan bread dough had spent the night rising. Now, throwing one of her brother's shirts over her, she carried the four loaves to the commercial oven of the bakery down the street and began preparing the rest of the cold salads to be served at the celebration lunch. By the time all the platters had been decorated, the aromas had awakened everyone and turned them irritable with hunger.

Suddenly the glass doors of the kitchen were flung open. At last they all could have their morning espresso—La Blonda was going to have a bath!

The dress, of Italian silk taffeta, white as a bride's, and the pure silk veil capped by a wreath of just-picked peach blossoms were each almost too fine, too beautiful, too valuable to wear. Silvana's mother Anna, an expert seamstress, had worked on the dress and Giuditta Carrara, a close friend of the Levi family, embroidered and hemmed the veil. Money had somehow been found for the costly silks—all Anna asked of Silvana was that she try not to spill red wine or sweet vermouth on her skirt.

"I'm not a dribbling baby, Mama. As of today, I'm a woman," Silvana argued, highly insulted.

"A woman," Anna sniffed. "Make me proud of you today. You can be more than just a pretty face with a shapely body that drives men crazy. Be a good Italian and a good Jew."

"Oh, Mama—"

"No, don't roll your eyes. If not for me, do it for Il Duce. So he'll continue to look with favor on us and have no cause to follow that hateful German, that Hitler."

"I'll do it for Papa, may he rest in peace."

For a full minute, Anna said nothing. Then, slowly,

she nodded her regal head of shiny chestnut hair. "Yes, do it for Papa. And tomorrow, at the cemetery, I'll tell him all about it."

"Mama, Papa's—"

"I know, I know. But he likes it when I go and talk to him. I know he does, even though he's ..." Suddenly Anna looked at Silvana as if she were seeing her for the first time. "What did you do, grow a foot in your sleep?"

"What do you mean?"

Anna pointed to the hem of Silvana's dress. "Look, it's shorter than it was last week, when I finished it." With eyes cast upward she prayed, "Signore, *per favore,* she's tall enough already. Thank you, Signore, but enough. Give some, if you wouldn't mind, to her brothers instead."

"What's wrong?" Silvana asked in alarm. "Do I look horribly ugly? Do I? Mama, tell me!"

Barely five feet tall, Anna had to point her chin in the air to meet her daughter's anxious eyes, but her own expression was serene. "Someday you'll understand why I worry so much. It's not because you're ugly ... just the opposite, in fact. But you don't see it yet, do you?"

"See what?"

Anna smiled and touched her daughter's cheek. "Who you are, you silly. Who you really are."

"Who am I, Mama? Why won't anybody tell me?"

"Someday you'll find out for yourself."

"How?"

"You'll just look in the mirror and ... you'll know. You'll know with such certainty that you'll never doubt yourself again." Then she raised her eyes skyward once more and clasped her hands to her small chest. "But I pray to the Signore that He make it happen soon, before she drives us all into the Tiber .. or something even worse! And now," she announced briskly, "everybody, *andiamo,* or we'll all be late!"

The synagogue, built near the Tiber on Via del Portico d'Ottavia in 1904, was an old and familiar friend

to the Levis, as it was to almost all the seven thousand
Jews still living within the ghetto or overflowing across
the Tiber into Trastevere. Friday nights at sundown
the Jewish community crowded into the synagogue to
kiss the silver-crowned Torah and to pray to the Signore. So its columns fluted in gold, its marble floors,
and its six menorah hung high on the wall were no
surprise to Silvana. She felt almost as warmly comfortable here as she did in her own home and sang out
boldly the *Baruch Abbah,* a hymn for festive
occasions.

After several more hymns and prayers the chief
rabbi gave a short speech, offering cautious gratitude
to Il Duce, their "duke," Benito Mussolini, for rejecting Hitler's overt anti-Semitic programs, a speech
that accurately reflected the congregation's identical
eagerness to believe that here in Italy—their beloved
land—they were safe.

Then, without her father to do the honors, her
brother Eduardo offered his arm and slowly escorted
Silvana to the front of the Ark, the *Echal,* where the
parchment scrolls of the first five books of the Hebrew
Scriptures—the Torah—were kept.

"Look at Raffaelle in his dumb Fascist uniform.
Why did he have to wear it today? It's so embarrassing," Silvana hissed to Eduardo as they made their
way down the center aisle, passing family, friends, the
two Christian neighbors who also lived in the ghetto
. . . and their eldest brother, Raffaelle.

"I hate it more than you do. I'll join the Resistance
and get shot before I join the Fascist Party, but thanks
to him we'll eat fresh bananas today—so don't criti-
cize Raffaelle."

"I know, but he just looks so stupid. Eduardo"—
she suddenly stopped and clutched his arm tightly—
"how do *I* look?"

Eduardo patted her hand and urged her forward.
He did not have to glance at her in that delicate white
dress and the translucent silk veil in order to answer
her. He knew how she looked; he saw her every day
of his life. But he didn't tell her the vision he had of

her, his sister, the image of an almost endlessly tall and straight stem capped by a yellow flower head that was forever turned to face the brilliant flame of light over Italy's sky. It was he who had nicknamed her Girasole, but even though she had taken it as an insult at first, convinced he'd purposely chosen a most ordinary plant, he never took the trouble to convince her that his vision of the sunflower was of the tallest and most radiant flower in the ghetto garden, maybe in all of Rome. And he did not do it now. She was his Girasole, but she was, even more, when all was said and done, still only his baby sister.

"You look nice," he said instead.

The apartment, packed to overflowing, was absolutely incapable of admitting even one more well-wisher. Everyone seemed to be screaming, in local Roman dialect, to be heard, and the noise and laughter rose up the old walls to the high ceilings and out the windows that had been flung open in the warm June afternoon. As Silvana squeezed past them, carrying platters of food above their heads to the long dining table, their eyes followed her ... and her meticulously decorated dishes.

"Look at Girasole, the angel, cooking and serving at her own confirmation!"

"Is there anyone in all of Rome who could do it better?"

"The way she sang today in the synagogue and that dear speech she gave—such sweetness! She lit up the entire *sinagoga.*"

"Is there anything she *can't* do?"

"She can't bring poor Umberto back. Oh, the thought of Silvana, fatherless, brings tears to my eyes."

"It's Anna I feel most sorry for. They say she goes to Umberto's grave and 'talks' to him for hours. What she needs is a new husband and a new father for those three kids."

"Oh, not Anna Levi. She's completely devoted to Umberto's memory."

"She loves her children, doesn't she?"

"*Certamente*. With all her heart."

"Then Anna Levi will marry again ... and if she's smart, she'll do it soon, before she gets too short and fat."

"Never! Not Anna."

"How long can you keep up a conversation with a dead man?"

At four o'clock, just as some of the guests began to depart after a final round of kisses and compliments and congratulations, one new guest arrived. He was tall—taller than most of the men there—and quite handsome.

Silvana, from across the room, immediately recognized something familiar in his strong nose and that crown of dark curls. At first, she thought the stranger looked exactly like some great Roman emperor, Augustus, perhaps. But then, coming closer to the door where he stood waiting, a suitcase in each hand, she realized that he had the face of a Levi, and that he had her father's nose. What he didn't have was Umberto's short, stubby limbs. Or the Levi potbelly. So who was he?

Only Anna knew. Rushing ahead of Silvana, she called out to the stranger, "No! Could it be? No! It's not possible! Benno? Is it really you, Benno?"

Shyly, Benno Levi smiled and dropped his bags.

"Benno, Benno!" Anna exulted, clapping her hands to her hot cheeks. "I can't believe it! Twenty years, and look at you—still as skinny as a boy!"

"Little Anna, dear Anna, how are you?" Benno asked, clasping her hand and bringing it to his lips.

"Ah!" the crowd sighed as they watched Benno kiss Anna's hand, making Anna turn the color of a Sicilian blood orange. This scene of reunion, they all agreed, was almost as delicious as Silvana's deep-fried, sugar-dusted jelly doughnuts, her *bomboloni,* which they ate with their hands while their eyes remained glued to the spectacle at the doorway.

"Everyone, listen!" Anna called to them over her shoulder. "This is Umberto's second cousin—"

"Second cousin once removed," he corrected softly.

"All right, second cousin once removed," Anna allowed. "Benno Levi. As children they played together. He was Umberto's best friend. And now, here he is again, all the way from"—she glanced at him— "Milan, yes?"

"Yes, Milan."

"From Milano. All the way," Anna repeated again, not quite in control of anything she was saying. All she knew was that she wanted, needed to tell everyone how honored, how pleased she was to see Benno again. The last time she saw him was the day of her wedding to Umberto, but she never forgot him. He was to her then the epitome of elegance and refinement. Memories of him, individually wrapped in softest velvet, memories of his voice, his manners, his hand-kissing, were all carefully folded away and preserved in her mind. Now, in the instant that she unwrapped the old images of him and compared them with the living, breathing Benno Levi standing before her, there was, she concluded with finality, no difference. No difference at all! Oh, perhaps a wrinkle or two around the eyes and a barely visible slackness to his square jaw. But essentially, he was still exactly the same handsome, soft-spoken gentleman she had known all too briefly before they lost touch when he went off to the north to work and later, they heard, to marry.

"Your wife!" Anna, remembering, cried out almost hysterically. "I'm sorry. Her name. I've forgotten. But you did bring her?"

For a moment a spasm of constrained misery contorted his smooth face ... then it was gone. "My Rosetta—" he began and then shrugged helplessly.

"When?" Anna asked, taking his hand in hers. The crowd looked on blankly; she alone seemed to understand.

"Two years now. The tumor was very large. In three months she was gone."

"Ah!" As Benno's personal tragedy became clear
to the others, they sighed sympathetically and pressed
closer around the door.

"So now you are ... alone ...?" The realization
turned Anna timid. She let go of Benno's hand and
took two tentative steps back from him.

"Anna, I only just heard about Umberto or I
would've come sooner."

Flustered, Anna's eyes filled with tears. Just a moment ago she was overtaken by maidenly shyness; now
she was once again a bereaved widow. But she shook
her head vehemently, unwilling to give in to her grief
in front of all these people ... especially this handsome stranger.

"No, this is a happy day. Tomorrow I'll visit Umberto—come with me, if you like—but today is my
darling Silvana's bat mitzvah. You didn't know?"
When he indicated he did not, Anna quickly twisted
around and searched the room. It was a relief to look
away. Once again, an unbearable modesty had overtaken her and it was a relief to look anywhere but at
him. "Silvana?" she called out. "Where are you?"

"Here, Mama!" Silvana answered from the kitchen
and made her way to her mother's side.

Planting Silvana directly in front of her, Anna hid
behind the human barricade that she'd made of her
daughter.

"Say hello—politely, the way I taught you—to your
father's best friend when he was a boy, Benno Levi,"
she whispered. Then, peeking over Silvana's shoulder,
she told Benno, "This is my youngest. Silvana."

Wordlessly Benno stared at the willowy creature
with the burnished hair for what seemed like a year,
an entire decade before any part of him unfroze and
began to move again. His eyelids were the first. They
blinked. But only Silvana saw it ... because only she
was standing that close.

Then his lips twitched and formed several words,
which he spoke in a whisper too low for most of the
crowd to hear. He spoke as if they were alone
together.

"I'm honored to meet you, Silvana."

"Thank you, Uncle Benno."

"Just ... Benno. I'm not really your uncle. And what shall I call you? Do you have a nickname?"

"Well, everyone calls me Girasole," she reluctantly admitted.

Benno pouted. "An ordinary sunflower for such a pink ... rosebud?"

Silvana flashed Eduardo a smug smile. "My brother started it. I told him not to"—she shrugged—"but it was too late."

"Is it too late for me to call you something else?"

"What, for instance?"

"Oh, let me see." Benno pondered for a moment, then he brightened. "Milano?"

"Why Milano?"

"Because you remind me of all the pretty girls in Milan."

"Oh," said Silvana, unable to hide a blushing smile of pleasure. Triumphantly, she glared at Eduardo. "Milano. I like it, Uncle Benno. *Si*, call me Milano."

Now the room broke into pandemonium.

"What did he say?" they called from the back.

"He says she reminds him of someone."

"Who?"

"His little girl in Milan," someone sighed.

"No, his Rosetta, who died."

"Oh, how sad!"

"No, it's a *mahiach*! At last, a man to save Anna and her family. This is truly a blessing."

"What about Umberto?"

"He's dead."

"Not according to Anna."

Up front, they were all tittering as they ushered Benno into the apartment, starting the party up all over again. One after another, the guests came forward to get a good look at him and then to welcome him. Anna remained in constant motion. First, she introduced her two sons to Benno, then she hurried to the cabinet and poured a large glass of wine for him.

No sooner had he taken a sip than she rushed to the table and loaded a plate with food.

From his chair, Benno looked up at her with soulful eyes. "For so long I've felt lost—like a stranger in my own land—but today you made me feel as if I've truly come home. Thank you, dear, kind Anna."

But it was simply too much! With cheeks flaming, Anna about-faced and retreated rapidly to the kitchen, followed by three giggling women. As soon as the glass doors were shut, they all gave in to a fit of hysterical laughter, shrieking and shouting so loudly they had to stuff towels in their mouths to muffle their sounds. They laughed until tears rolled down their cheeks. Then, just as suddenly as it began, the laughter ended, leaving Anna feeling vaguely embarrassed and self-conscious.

"I can't imagine what just got into me."

At that, the other women exchanged sly glances but, by silent agreement, managed to control themselves.

Again by silent agreement, the women gesturing to each other by barely lifting their chins, Giuditta was voted to begin trying to reason with Anna.

"Such a fine man, Anna. The way he shook hands with your boys. So . . . fatherly. And did you hear how nicely he spoke to Silvana? What words!"

Anna merely sniffed disinterestedly.

Now the others joined in. "It was pure poetry."

"Anna, how'd you like a poet for a new husband?"

Anna began fanning herself while denying to them all that she had any interest whatsoever in this stranger in her house.

"I had one husband and that's all I want," she insisted. "I could never love another man the way I loved Umberto," she said, suddenly turning serious. "Never!"

"Every love is different," they told her.

"For a woman, love comes and goes like the seasons. You had Umberto in the summer of your life. But now, Anna, it's winter."

"And you need someone to keep you warm."

Suddenly the expression in Anna's almond-shaped

eyes became frenzied. She pressed her hands to her breasts and squeezed. "And what do I do about these?" she demanded.

The women looked blank.

"They're Umberto's." She gave her breasts another squeeze. "No one else will ever touch them. He wants me to save them for him. Only for him."

The women sighed and patted her back.

"Anna, just give it some time."

"Just rest now. Don't worry about anything. Just rest," they reassured her while secretly exchanging worried looks.

"If she's lucky, it may all still work out in the end."

"Since when did we Jews get lucky?"

The only one who seemed to be forgotten at the party was Silvana. Out in the hall, at the top of the dirty marble staircase, she stood alone in her white silk taffeta dress, leaning against the banister and wondering what, exactly, the girls in Milan looked like.

Chapter Two

Eleven months later, Silvana listened on the other side of the door as Benno Levi proposed marriage to her mother for the third time. The first two times were not so much proposals as hysterical arguments, deteriorating as soon as Anna Levi heard the word "marriage" mentioned. They began well enough, with much hilarity and mutual enjoyment. In fact, Silvana could hear her mother giggling as if Benno were tickling her ... and perhaps he was. And when Benno recited, almost crooning, a list of Anna's superlative, enticing, irresistible qualities, Anna murmured something too low and husky for Silvana to hear.

But at the dreaded word, Anna shrieked in horror. She held her hands up to stop Benno and shook her head no, no, no. Both times, she refused to allow him to finish his speech, which forced the soft-spoken but exasperated Benno to shout at her. And that reduced Anna to a fit of tears. And then they stopped speaking for a week.

Not so the third time. The third time there was no shouting and there were no tears. Instead, there were long periods in which Silvana could hear nothing but Benno's barely audible, undecipherable whisperings behind the door.

Maybe, Silvana surmised, he was entreating her mother, and using the same words of urgency as her neighbors, her friends—even her sons—all of them begging her to be realistic, to be unselfish, to be a good mother, a devoted wife, a devout Jew, a loyal Italian, and just give in and marry Benno Levi.

Or maybe he is staring at her, Silvana thought, *his*

*dark coffee eyes percolating over her skin, making her
pores hiss steam . . . the way he sometimes looks at me.*

It was impossible to interpret the silence behind the
door with accuracy, but just when it had become unendurable, Silvana heard her mother sigh deeply at last.

"I'll marry you, Benno," she heard her mother tell
him, "for three reasons."

Silvana could almost hear Benno's smile of delight.

"No, no, Benno," said Anna. "For three good,
moral reasons. For Raffaelle, Eduardo . . . and, most
of all, Silvana."

There was a pause before Benno responded. Then,
he, too, sighed in resignation and said, "All right, my
dove, we'll marry for your three reasons now . . . and
for one hundred reasons more . . . later."

So it was settled. They agreed to marry in a little
over two months, on July 14, 1938, in the same synagogue where, the year before, Silvana had turned thirteen. And all those who had pressed Anna to remarry
during that long year now laughed out loud with relief
and immediately began chattering about the next potential problem—the wedding.

All except Silvana. Only she remained unmoved and
oddly mute during the general mayhem following the
announcement.

But it was for exactly that curious reason that Anna
Levi found herself turning to her young daughter for
advice. Anna may have sacredly pledged her troth to
Benno, but in her heart she was still far from convinced she'd made the right decision.

"Tell me, what do you think of him, *mia blonda*?"
Anna would ask, searching her daughter's face for a
sign. "Do you think he's a nice man?"

But Silvana would only shrug her shoulders
noncommittally.

If Anna persisted in this course of questioning, she
usually got nothing more than another shrug and
then another.

"What," for instance, she asked Silvana one night
after Benno had come for dinner, "did the two of you
talk about while I was cooking?"

"Flowers."

"Flowers?" Anna asked incredulously. "Why flowers?"

But Silvana simply shrugged. How could she tell her mother that Benno spent an hour describing the difference between a pink bud and a blossom in full bloom—"the exquisite promise in a taut, unopened flower versus the beauty of a ripe but no longer mysterious rose"? She herself didn't quite understand everything that Benno said to her. She only knew it was too embarrassing to repeat, though she couldn't say exactly why. So she shrugged and said nothing, leaving her mother to wonder helplessly.

Then, one evening Eduardo arrived home from high school with a bloody nose and a torn shirt. Anna was working on her wedding dress at Giuditta's apartment but Silvana was there to tend to him. When Benno arrived after work, his hands still stained from applying gilt to picture frames all day long, the three sat in the living room and discussed the incident. And that is where Anna found them. One glance at Eduardo's bloody handkerchief pressed to his nose and she staggered dizzily, her beautiful almond eyes becoming enormous with alarm.

"What happened?"

"It's nothing, Mama," Eduardo cautioned her.

"He's just trying to be brave. It was terrible, Mama!" Silvana insisted, holding a cold cloth to her brother's head.

"But what happened?" Anna asked again, almost beside herself.

Benno went to her side and tried to comfort her by stroking her back but she brusquely shook him off. Her wide almond eyes never left her son's face and Benno gave up and sat down again.

"Some hooligans knocked him off his bike," Benno explained, "and—"

"Fascist brutes, you mean!" Silvana interrupted heatedly.

"But they didn't get my bike!" Eduardo announced proudly. "I jumped on the backs of those two rotten

anti-Semites and beat them until they let go and then
I pedaled—"

"They were just hooligans. Why do you call them
anti-Semites?" Anna wanted to know as she took the
cloth from Silvana and sponged Eduardo's hot cheeks.

"Because they are," Silvana volunteered defiantly.

Anna shook her head. "You're mistaken. Thanks
be to the Signore, there's no anti-Semitism here in
Italy. None."

"That's what Benno says."

"Well," Anna argued, hands on her shapely hips,
"he's right, isn't he?" She even smiled at Benno, to
prove her point.

Silvana rolled her eyes. All she knew was what Eduardo told her; she, herself, became only more confused
reading the newspapers. For a sunny fourteen-year-
old in 1938, the volatile politics of the era seemed too
complicated to unravel. But she had complete faith in
her brother's intelligence; his was an informed and
pragmatic logic upon which she could rely in every
possible situation . . . except one. Romance. In matters
of romance, logic does not apply, of course, and therefore, Eduardo was no more help than a dunce.

"Eduardo says," she pointedly told her mother and
Benno, "Mussolini controls our Fascist newspapers.
Now that he's turned anti-Semitic, so have they."

"No, no, my darling girl, our Duce would never turn
against us," Anna protested. "Your brother couldn't
have told you such a thing"—she glared briefly at
Eduardo—"because he knows what every Jew in Italy
knows—our Duce speaks *for* us, not against us. And
in return, we're completely loyal to him and to the
Fascist cause. You see?"

Silvana hesitated, glanced at Eduardo, who was
glowering sullenly, and shook her head no.

Now Benno tried. "Actually, Eduardo is partly
right. But Mussolini isn't against all the Jews—the Fascists are just against the Zionists, those disloyal Jews
who want to abandon Italy and go settle in Israel."

Finally, Eduardo spoke for himself. "If we put our
trust in Mussolini, then we're more than fools. He's

slipperier than an eel. I predict he's going to make an alliance with Hitler any day now. And Hitler hates the Jews."

"But Il Duce loves us!" Anna insisted. "We've all heard him. The sincerity. So how can we not believe him?"

This time when Benno's hand traveled up Anna's back, she allowed it to rest for a moment on her shoulder. Encouraged, Benno smiled at her and stood up to make his point, agreeing with her not just to keep her affection. But for a kiss, he would have said Hitler was an angel, too.

"Your mother speaks from the heart and I speak from the head—but we both agree. Our Duce will never betray our trust because he's the Jews' greatest friend—an even greater friend than Julius Caesar!"

"What's he talking about?" Silvana whispered to her brother.

But Benno heard her. "Ah, my little pink bud, you haven't studied your history." He shook a teasing finger at her, making her blush and laugh. "In ancient Rome, there was no emperor kinder to the Jews than the great Julius Caesar." He paused. " 'How kind?' you ask." He stood directly in front of Silvana, who nodded to him as if she had, in fact, asked that very question.

Now that he'd captured her complete attention, he continued. "So kind that when Caesar died, the Jews asked permission to weep on his casket and keep watch on his tomb in gratitude. But I promise you we'll do more than weep when Il Duce's time comes. We'll build a monument to his great memory with our own hands, that we may never forget him."

Despite themselves, Anna and her children listened enthralled when Benno spoke—he was a mesmerizing speaker whose dark, hypnotic eyes held his listeners' attention even as he evoked occasional sighs of disagreement from Eduardo. But even Eduardo couldn't deny that Benno Levi's fierce loyalty and quiet confidence were both authentic . . . and impressive.

And as a result, Benno won Anna over at long last.

Two weeks before their wedding, he finally managed to pulverize the last of her doubts, hard as rocks, into sand. She could feel the tiny grains drain out of her pores, as if her skin were a *colabrodo,* a colander. And all that was left behind was relief.

Yes, now she was sure. No longer would she have to implore Umberto in his grave or her young daughter Silvana to tell her what to do. Now she knew. Benno Levi was indeed a good man and from this night forward she would give him her allegiance and her heart. Her body, however, she still held in reserve.

Her allegiance to both men—Benito Mussolini and Benno Levi—remained as unshakable as it had been to Umberto, her first husband. Perhaps even more so, for, on the day of her second wedding, when the news broke that her beloved Duce was indeed about to betray the Jews, she, like Benno Levi, refused to believe it.

"What is the matter with you boys?" she asked of her two sons who sat reading the morning newspaper in frozen silence, their tiny cups of espresso untouched beside them. "Not even a 'good morning, Mama' on her wedding day?"

Raffaelle and Eduardo exchanged looks of despair.

"Why such long faces?" Anna asked laughingly. "Afraid your mama won't care for you the same after she's married?" She ruffled Eduardo's hair. "Afraid you'll have to make your own breakfast in the morning, eh?"

Grimly Eduardo shook his head. "Your Duce has done it, Mama."

"Done what?"

"What we never dreamed in our worst nightmares—not even I." Then he read from the front-page article that a group of Mussolini's so-called racial scientists had announced that a pure Italian race had just been discovered.

" 'Jews, lacking the pure Aryan blood of our authentic Italian race, do not belong,' " he quoted with suppressed rage.

But Anna, who understood the gross fallacy of such a pseudo-theory, refused, nevertheless, to acknowledge its danger.

"Don't you see?" Eduardo argued. "Now that he's got his 'scientific' henchmen backing him up, Mussolini is getting ready to pass the kind of racial laws they have in Germany—the kind that will end the existence of Jews in Italy."

"It's not true!" Anna cried. "I'm a loyal Italian. I'm a loyal Jew. And I'm a loyal Fascist. So how can this be true? It's just a rumor, like so many these days. And I will not believe it!"

But Anna's sons, in accord for once, could perceive what Anna could not even imagine.

Even Raffaelle—who, because of his mother's wedding, closed the small souvenir shop for the day—agreed that this was the news they'd been dreading.

"It's the beginning of the end," he said darkly. "Now that he's got his scientific proof, what's to stop him?" he wondered, clutching the newspaper against his barrel chest as if to stem the actual pain he felt at having to worry his mother on this most sacred of days. Of the three Levi children, Raffaelle's devotion to their mother was greatest, perhaps because he was the oldest. Being the firstborn he had his mother, young and patient, all to himself for five calm and blissful years before the others arrived and distracted her. The hours he spent on her lap as she sang to him, her lips pressing warm kisses on his forehead, shaped him into an adoring, selfless son. Nevertheless, even he couldn't help himself.

"If today the Fascists say they've discovered an Aryan Italian race and that the Jews don't belong, then tomorrow they'll try to kick us out, just like they're doing in Germany," Raffaelle concluded, his dark, round face even gloomier than usual. "We may have to leave. It may come to that."

"What are you saying?" Anna cried, her small chest heaving rapidly. "Leave here, Rome? Leave my home? Are you out of your mind? And where would we go? Who has money for hotels?"

"Shh, shh, it'll be all right," Raffaelle told her, wrapping his short, heavy arm around her shoulder to comfort her. "Let's not think about it anymore."

"Leave your poppa's grave?" she persisted.

"Shh," Raffaelle said again and shook his head at the others to stop them from saying any more. "I was stupid, as usual. Of course we're all staying right here. You, Benno, me—all of us." And he glared at Eduardo and Silvana and repeated his words again. "All of us are staying right here, Mama. With you."

That Eduardo and Silvana did not jump in to agree, that they, in fact, said nothing, didn't seem to register. This was, after all, Anna Levi's wedding day and she was determined to be cheerful. And if the ceremony seemed to some slightly more somber than usual, Anna refused to notice that either.

At the reception, however, the mood was unmistakable. Guests gathered in gloomy clusters to whisper their shared anxiety about the impending political events, but Anna was adamant. She wasn't going to allow any grumbling or wringing of hands at her wedding—and she told everyone so.

"Drink wine!" she commanded and refilled her own glass. "Laugh! I promise you, tomorrow will be a new day, a bright day for all of us."

"Amen," said Benno and clinked his glass with hers.

Many who were there tried to mask their sorrow for the sake of the bridal couple. Like Anna, they refilled their glasses several times and grew tipsy or drowsy ... or both. They shouted toasts and whispered lewd jokes; they even sang a few songs.

Nevertheless, all the guests were gone by nine o'clock, including Anna's three children, who were doubling up for the night with neighbors to give the bride and groom some privacy.

"Benno, where are you?" Anna called from the bedroom some moments later. She sat at her dressing table in the pale blue slip that had rustled under her handmade pale blue dress that afternoon and that now clung to every curve on her small, round body. Looking at herself in the large, old mirror, she decided that she liked the slip more than the dress. The slip showed off her smooth shoulders and its naughty décolletage gave more than a glimpse of her abundant breasts. She unpinned her long knot of hair, silky as Silvana's, but darker, shook it, and peeked at herself again in the mirror. *Sexy,* she thought, and giggled tipsily.

But where was Umberto? Oops! She giggled again as she realized her mistake. "Benno," she told herself. "You're married to Benno now."

She found him in the living room, slumped in a chair, drinking wine. Wordlessly, she stood before him and pressed her breasts with her hands, thinking, *These are yours now*. Then she took his hand and led him to the bedroom.

For almost a year, Benno had pursued the reluctant Anna, begging, cajoling, caressing, even pinching her in the hope of gaining her concession. So hungry was he to feel a woman's soft flesh again that once he had actually sobbed in front of her. But in all that time she had never given him the fulfilling nourishment he craved and he slowly became inured to his hunger, living more in his mind than in his body. By the time he married Anna, he no longer desired her. Perhaps it was never the mother who he truly desired anyway.

Yet here she was, willing at last, pulling him to the bed, looking up at him with her sultry almond eyes, finally offering him all of her flesh to touch and fondle without restriction—but too late! He'd long since lost his appetite.

"Take off your shirt," his new bride directed. "And your pants. Put them on the chair. No, not that chair, the big one." She sat up in bed and pointed like a *maestra* to a wayward student. "Benno, can't you move faster?"

All at once, everything had reversed, he realized. And now it was Anna who was in control, directing, cajoling, pursuing ... him! Gone was the sweet, meek little dove he thought he had married. Instead, here was his wife, indecent under the sheets, bossing her husband around. No! This was too much. He would not stand for it.

He stood above her at the side of the bed. "Turn off the light," he commanded.

"Benno," she argued, "you're closer to the lamp. You do it."

Obediently, he reached under the shade and switched off the light, fuming inwardly.

"This is your side," she told him, patting his pillow.

He climbed onto his side of the bed and lay on his back, sulking.

Turning to him, Anna thrust her chest toward him and whispered, "Benno, don't just lie there in the dark. Talk to me. Tell me, what do you think of this slip? Do you think it's pretty? Turn on your side, Benno, so you face me. Good. Now go ahead, tell me, what do you think of my blue slip?"

Benno took hold of the slip. "You want to know what I think of this?" He grabbed it with both hands and pulled until it ripped right down the middle and Anna's breasts flopped out. "There!" he cried, triumphant. "That's what I think of it."

Then, as Anna gave out a startled gasp of delight and fear, Benno completed the job he had started, and tore the rest of the slip off her, aroused at last.

Anna, he could see, was about to laugh or to speak; he had to stop her. Roughly, he took her head in his hands and pulled it down.

"Benno, wait!" she managed to cry out, but he quickly silenced her, forcing himself deep into her mouth. But what Anna did to him then with her lips and her tongue could not reach him, could not reach his hunger, which remained unappeasable. And after a while, he lay back, thinking of ripe, full blossoms and pale pink buds, his mind a bouquet of roses. Lost in his nosegays, he barely seemed to notice that Anna had slowly drifted off to sleep.

But when Anna's breathing was finally locked in a deep and rhythmic snore, Benno rose from the soft double bed and lowered himself into the large, upholstered chair where his neatly folded clothes hung over one arm.

And there Benno sat, all of that night and on into the next morning, drinking the last of the wine. Occasionally he glanced at the ripped shreds of the pale blue slip that had fallen to the floor. But more often his gaze fixed on the bedside table where a vase of rosebuds, their immature petals tightly curled, gave off the faint but exquisite aroma of promise, of mystery ... of a deliciously girlish sensual scent.

"Good night, Milano," he whispered, not looking at the bed. "Good night, my little bud."

The marriage of Anna and Benno had its positive aspects, of course, and not the least of which was that it was legal. Because the racial laws—instituted as predicted that summer and fall—forbade a Jew from marrying a non-Jew (among countless other more devastating prohibitions), it was a relief to know that at least their union was approved of by the government. Little else in their lives was.

Benno lost his job, Raffaelle was kicked out of the Fascist Party, and Eduardo was expelled from the university. Now the little souvenir stall had to support the entire family, and the only customers were the visiting German soldiers.

A period of gloom and dread settled over the household all that year and the next, punctuated by erratic spasms of irritation and hilarity. Between the dreary lulls, bitter arguments—and, much more rarely, laughter—would break out, subside, and erupt again. Uncertainty about the future, the outbreak of war, and Mussolini's betrayal were heavy on every Jew's heart ... and on many non-Jews' as well. But for the Levi family, political discussions were superseded by the war of life itself, which was deteriorating into a daily, desperate struggle for survival.

Anna spent long days out searching for rations and waiting on food lines. Raffaelle managed to hold on to his shop, selling anything he could get his hands on—mostly thimbles, needles and thread, cast-off furniture, old clothes, and small souvenirs.

For Eduardo, a formal university education was now out of the question. However, because every Jewish professor in Italy had been fired, some, who didn't have the money to flee, established an informal study group that Eduardo joined. To pay the professors their fee of a few coins, Eduardo peddled rags on the street—virtually the only work left open for Jews. And at night he worked with the Resistance fighters, knowing this meant that someday soon he'd have to take his family with him to hide in the hills with the partisans. That was, if he could ever get his mother to agree to flee.

Benno, too, had to resort to peddling but he found it so distasteful that he often quit work in time to walk Silvana home from the Jewish school down the street. If at first she preferred to linger after school with her friends rather than keep her stepfather company, in time—perhaps a year of petting and patient coaxing in all—he finally won her over. Then, when he'd call to her, "Milano! Come to me, my Milano!" she would run to him eagerly and give him the smile she now saved just for him. For, despite herself, despite every teaching and moral principle in her head that told her this was wrong, he had won her. He was her father, he was her lover, and he had won all of her. What was more, he had convinced his little bud that this was good, that this was right, that this was love. She was fifteen, and she believed him.

And so, each day she would run to him and then the two would eagerly make their way to the silent, shuttered apartment where, for a short while, they were able to lock the cruel world out.

Chapter Three

It was time to get dressed and prepare dinner for the family, but Silvana lolled awhile longer in erotic languor on the rumpled bed. In an hour her mother would be arriving home with her few meager provisions, worn out after waiting on food lines all day. Then Eduardo would burst through the doorway, lugging with him a ragged, bulging book bag and an empty, growling stomach. Raffaelle would probably be late, as always, arriving just in time to eat and then go out again.

But Silvana gauged that there was still time. Just enough for Benno to tell her everything all over again—all the words that somehow justified what they were doing here together.

"Tell me again," she commanded in a lover's whisper.

Benno, of course, knew immediately what she wanted to hear. It was always the same; she could never seem to get enough, even though she had heard the same words a hundred times since he had first lured her into bed with him almost three years ago. A year of words had led up to that final act—a total of four years in all.

"I love you," was what she wanted to hear. "I love you more than life itself. And because this love is so powerful and so special, what we do here in this bed isn't a sin. It is really a blessed act. Blessed by our magnificent love."

That was what he told her the first time he slid his hand inside the blouse of her school uniform, almost four years ago. And when she tried to pull away, he said, "Don't be afraid, my Milano. I am your new father. Who else can appreciate you the way I can? Has anyone else ever noticed these exquisite breasts so carefully hidden under your uniform? I alone have discovered your beauty. Now all I want to do is help you appreciate your prodigious gifts. Trust me, my Milano. Trust me."

It took him a year before he finally forced himself inside her panties. And still, he had to force her that first time. Even after a year of entreating her, petting her . . . and tantalizing her. And murmuring those endless words of love—the same words she wanted to hear now.

"Has anyone ever adored you the way I do?" he said again for the hundredth time. "I am the only man who could—because only I can love you as both a father and a lover."

Silvana stretched her long, catlike body and stared dreamily at the peeling ceiling. The words were beginning to do their work. They were beginning to dull the shame of what he had just done to her . . . and what she had just done to him. The words were her opiate.

"And tell me about when we run away together," she beseeched him.

Benno sighed, bored with this incessant repetition that she kept insisting upon. Nevertheless he submitted to her demand, making his voice purr with tenderness as he stole a glance at the windup clock on the end table. "Someday we'll go away and live together. And everyone will understand because our love is so different, so unique that it defies ordinary rules."

"Yes!" Silvana cried and clasped her arms around his neck. "And they won't be angry. They'll be happy for us, won't they? Even Raffaelle and Eduardo. And even . . . Mama. Say it, Benno. Say it again so that I can believe it until tomorrow. And then tomorrow make me believe it again!"

Carefully, Benno pried her off him. He could feel the wiry hairs of her golden pubis tickling his hip. In another minute he would be aroused again. This blond vixen excited him like no other. Her skin had the exact same delicacy of rosebud petals. And now that he had finally convinced her of this, she had begun to enjoy rubbing herself up against him.

But there wasn't time for another round of love-making. Perhaps tonight, however. After Eduardo left for one of his political meetings and Raffaelle went out to woo a girlfriend and Anna began to snore after a fit of yawning, he could steal back into Silvana's narrow bed.

"And we'll be married," Silvana was repeating now in a mesmerizing mantra. "And they will be happy for us. And we will be together forever. And the rabbi will bless us. Because our love is like no other."

These were his words, his promises, but hearing them in her mouth made him uneasy. They had slid so smoothly and so often off his own tongue that he hardly gave their meaning a thought. The words merely served a purpose. Or rather, several purposes. They calmed her. They complimented her. They lured her. They aroused her. They opened her up.

But when *she* said them, he would wonder if he had gone too far. Now she hung on his words as if to a life raft. As if she expected the promises he had made to come true. As if they could.

It was time to end this with her, he knew. But how to endure this spare life without this one ounce of sweetness? Benno put off the unpleasant answer, not for the first time—and despite the mounting dangers—by closing his eyes and tracing her face with his fingers. Blindly, he found her lips and immediately covered them with his own—not entirely paternally. But instead of palpating her rump—which he would have preferred—he gave it a quick slap and ordered her to get up.

"Get your clothes on, my bud, and tonight be ready for me. I'll try to come to you late."

Reluctantly she rose and stood unself-consciously naked before him, no longer the cowering, tearful child he had first ravished. Back then he would have to insist with veiled threats and impassioned appeals;

now she willingly offered him her silken flesh. Because he had taught her the lust she aroused in him was called love.

As soon as she was out of the bed, however, he began smoothing the sheets, forcing his eyes away from her voluptuous form, and redirecting his thoughts to another appetite that demanded satisfaction.

"What are you making for dinner tonight, my plum?" he asked, following her into the kitchen where, nightly, he would sit and watch her as she cooked. There, while she performed a kind of magic, creating a hearty and delectable supper out of virtually nothing, he could inhale the aromas and enjoy her beauty all at the same time. No longer could he remember what had attracted him first—Silvana's luscious cooking or Silvana's luscious body. All he knew was that the combination was irresistible. Sometimes, the scents and sounds of the bubbling pots, combined with the sight of her rounded bottom as she bent over the worktable, got him so excited that he would have to get up and touch her. Despite—or perhaps because of—the risk, he would come up behind her and surreptitiously plant kisses on the warm nape of her neck or slide his hand under her skirt. He did so now, nuzzling her ear while one hand worked its way into her panties.

It was the faint noise—not quite a gasp, more like a short intake of breath—that made him turn. And there was Anna, his wife, at the doorway, clutching a sack of potatoes, a startled expression in her eyes.

"I was just asking Silvana what we were having for dinner," he said lightly, removing his hand so smoothly that it almost seemed as if it had never been between Silvana's legs at all.

"And how are you, my poor dove?" he continued, taking his wife's sack of potatoes and pecking her lightly on the cheek.

"*Va bene,*" Anna answered automatically, though she looked anything but "very well." In these last four years she had aged gently. But in these last two alarming minutes she had transformed into an old woman. All color drained from her face and even her dark, lustrous hair seemed to turn to ash above her sagging shoulders.

Yet, what exactly had she seen there in the kitchen? Already it was becoming clouded in her mind. A hand ... a touch. Yet Benno seemed normal. Could her eyes have been playing tricks? She did not know, but she remained wary.

"Does this mean we're having potato *gnocchi*?" Benno continued, eager as a boy. *"Il mio favorito!"*

Anna could not help smiling. Was there ever a man who appreciated a good meal more than her Benno? Every dish became his favorite. For him alone she had begun cooking again with pleasure, often with Silvana at her side.

Silvana! Anna stole a glance at her Girasole, who was setting the table in a clamorous frenzy, clattering plates and splattering utensils. *Why does she avoid meeting my eyes?* Anna asked herself. *And why such a racket?* Silvana's apparent nervousness could not help but provoke Anna to wonder again what exactly had been going on here.

But maybe it is only that she is unsure how to make the potato gnocchi, Anna reasoned with herself as she handed the Parmesan cheese and the grater to her daughter. Silvana had been making weightless ricotta and spinach dumplings all by herself for years now. But last week, with fresh green vegetables in short supply, Anna had taught Silvana to make *gnocchi di patate* and they had been received enthusiastically. *Yes, she is simply nervous,* Anna concluded, *to do them alone.*

"I'll help with the *gnocchi*," Anna offered, despite her exhaustion. "We'll make them just as we did last week, remember?" She joined Silvana at the sink and began scrubbing the potatoes.

Silvana looked at her mother and smiled. Of course she remembered! It had been such a rare, happy day. It was always comforting when her mother joined her in the kitchen and they cooked together. As a little girl, Silvana's first memories were of her mother's short arms, floured to the elbows, kneading a ball of dough for *pasta fresca*. In those early days, Anna taught Silvana not only to make fresh pasta, but all the delicate sauces that would go with it. Those were the days when they would work side by side, their contented silence punctuated only by Anna's occasional gentle instructions—"Like this, *dolcezza*. Yes, that's it, *cara mia*, press with the heel of your hand."

In the gloom of the last years, last week stood out like a beacon. They had hummed as they worked side by side, peeling potatoes, grating cheese, tearing off sage leaves from the plant on the window.

"Aiii!" Silvana had stopped humming and cried when she tried to peel a boiled potato, still hot and draining in a bowl. And suddenly her mother was kissing the burn on her hand, just as she had done when Silvana was a child with a *ferita*, a "boo-boo."

Such a tender kiss! Silvana had thought, and for a moment felt like a beloved daughter again with nothing to hide.

That was the day Anna had shown her the secret to peeling hot potatoes. "You wrap them in a towel and rub the skin off." Together they riced the hot potatoes and piled them on a board, making a well in the center.

"Beat in the flour, eggs, salt, pepper, and Parmesan cheese and knead the dough until it is smooth," Anna had directed. The dough, Silvana had remembered, was sticky and she automatically added some more flour, while her mother had looked on approvingly. How she had cherished that smile!

Now they were preparing the same dish, rolling out logs of dough and cutting them into one-inch pieces. But as they scored each piece with a fork and popped them into a pot of boiling water, Silvana wished she could turn the clock back to that day, one week ago, when for a brief time she forgot her shame and felt only contentment. Today, nothing was forgotten and a new question worried her: *What if Mama saw Benno touching me?*

As she sautéed chopped sage and black olives in olive oil for the sauce, she yearned to fling herself on her mother's breast and cry, "Save me, Mama! Save me from him!" Since that first night three years ago, she had often prayed for her mother to rescue her.

But by now, she mostly prayed that Benno would make his promise come true soon. Then, instead of rescuing her, Anna could give Silvana her blessing.

She drained the *gnocchi* and tossed them with the sauce. At the table, she shaved pecorino cheese on top, but neither she nor her mother could eat a morsel. They both sat in silence, watching the men clean off their plates, and carefully avoided each other's eyes.

Anna knew, even before she opened her huge almond eyes at ten-thirty, that Benno was not in bed beside her. Had it been a dream that awakened her? Or a noise? Sweat soaked her small, compact body, staining her nightgown under her breasts. She felt as if she had just endured the most terrifying nightmare, yet she had no memory of any dreams. Where was Benno? She wanted to ask him to feel her head. Perhaps she had a fever. Where was—?

And then, just as surely as she had known that Benno was not in bed beside her, she now knew where he was. It came to her as a completed puzzle, the pieces of which she had been trying to fit together for some time. Odd-shaped little pieces of suspicion, of dread, often nagged at her, but an empty hole remained at the center of the picture. Now, in one instant, the puzzle was complete.

She rose and went to the other bedroom. Her little feet barely made a sound. Hesitating a moment, she beseeched God, *"Per favore, Signore. Per favore."* Then she pushed the door open. And in that instant, her life—indeed all their lives—was changed forever.

The age of innocence had ended. Like a firebomb dropped from a warplane in the sky, it ended in an explosion, instantly shattering the sanctity of the Levi family. And afterward, all that remained amid the burning heat and the tragic wreckage was the continuous, searing pain.

Chapter Four

"What's wrong with her?" all ten men wanted to know, but particularly the partisan Paolo, who scrutinized Silvana up and down. "What's the matter with the girl?"

At the question, Silvana cringed. Even though she was now eighteen years old and a full head taller than Eduardo, she futilely tried to hide herself behind her brother. It had been that way from the moment she glanced up and saw the group of partisans waiting at the top of the hill. Immediately she cowered behind Eduardo, gripping the back of his belt, burrowing her head in his spine as she climbed in his footsteps. And when, sweating and breathless, they at last reached the top, Silvana continued to cringe as the ten men made a circle around her.

Behind them in the distance, the foothills of the central Apennines framed the horizon with their bare, lifeless peaks. Below them, the silvery-gray olive trees and the tall, slender cypresses spread luxuriantly over the plain. On the low hills were several ancient villages and towns, some with palatial villas and old farmsteads and churches with tall campaniles visible for miles. Just as in Rome, the air raid sirens screamed warnings of planes overhead. But up here, high in the hills of Umbria, they were safe. At least, for now.

"She's just shy. She's . . . had a hard time," Eduardo explained gently and put his arm around Silvana's shoulder.

"Is she ill? We can't accept the sick ones up here. There's nothing—no medicines—*niente*," Paolo, bearded and grim, told Eduardo emphatically. "And no women. You didn't tell me you were bringing a signorina."

"She's my sister. And a brave anti-Fascist. She has nowhere else to go. She's been wandering—" Eduardo stopped midsentence, hushed by a sudden distraction in the crowd.

The circle of men were staring at someone approaching behind Eduardo and Silvana. As he entered the circle, his presence seemed to make everyone stop breathing for one awestruck moment. Though they all knew Michele Bassani—even Eduardo recognized the tall, tanned, smoldering partisan leader though he'd never actually met him—something in his powerful presence made them momentarily speechless.

Paolo was the first to break the silence. "It's Eduardo, the Levi boy from Rome with the gift for words who I told you about. The one who writes the anti-Fascist pamphlets that have caused such a stir in the city lately. But he's brought the girl with him and I think she's sick, Michele."

"The girl is my sister, Silvana Levi," Eduardo said again, and looked directly at Michele. Silvana buried her face in her brother's neck as he spoke up. "She's become a bit skinny, that's true, but she's not sick. She's . . . just afraid. Of men." Eduardo knew it was not really that she feared all men. Just one man. Benno Levi. Her stepfather. Eduardo did not even know if what Silvana felt was fear. All he knew was that because of Benno, she had been driven almost mad. And that she would need a very long time to become well again. That is, if she ever did get over what had happened back there in Rome. But he did not tell the men that.

Michele sauntered behind Eduardo and looked Silvana up and down. As he neared her, she stole a glance at him. All she noticed was the pain in his dark and piercing eyes, glossy as black olives, before she hid her face again. But she could feel those eyes of his on her back, her neck, her hair, her legs, and they made her want to crawl underneath her brother's shirt.

Except that when Michele Bassani spoke, her eardrums began to pulse and tingle as if the sounds they were receiving were music. Indeed, his voice was a kind of music; it was like the deep, resonant strings of a viola, vibrating with infinite compassion, infinite sadness. Despite herself, Silvana stopped shaking and listened to the music of his voice.

"In these times, who among us is without fear?" the celebrated Resistance leader asked his men. "Haven't we all trembled as Italy approaches its blackest midnight?"

The men answered in murmurs of agreement.

"It's no sickness to be afraid," Michele continued, talking to his men as if before a battle. "For now, the Fascists are fearless. But soon they'll be shaking like this frightened colt—" He pointed to Silvana. "But they won't be half as pretty."

Everyone laughed—except Michele and, of course, Silvana.

Eduardo could feel Silvana beginning to tremble again at the men's laughter. To change the subject, he blurted out, "She can cook!"

Instantly all laughter ceased.

"Yes, my sister can cook!" he said again.

Food. The thought of it transformed the mood. Now everyone became intensely serious and the eager, expectant expression on each man's face was the same. It was as if, in the silence created by his announcement, Eduardo could hear all of them insisting, "Shh! Go on, Eduardo. Let's hear him out! Now, this—*this* is important. Did he say she can cook? Shh! Give him air. Give him space. Let him speak!"

Eduardo saw that he had no choice but to continue. So he said, "My sister cooks like a"—and he kissed his fingers—"like a dream."

But the men only grew more insistent. They were avid, rapturous. And at the same time restless, as well. For a moment they muttered, they shifted, they sighed, and then they stopped still. And waited. Intently. Not only did they expect to hear more, they absolutely demanded it—now. Thus Eduardo, who rarely—if ever—praised his sister out loud, was forced to find words to extol her—in detail.

"Like your mama," he said and then shook his head. "No, like your mama's kitchen. On Shabbat. Or on Christmas eve. Every meal a feast. Oh, the aromas! Chicken with garlic and rosemary grilling on a wood fire. Bruschetta—or what you men from Florence call *fettunta*—little rounds of toasted garlic bread topped with sweet peppers or chicken livers or ripe tomatoes and olive oil. Creamy fettuccine aromatic with wild mushrooms—"

"We've got wild mushrooms growing all over these hills. All she has to do is pick them."

"Does she make a good polenta?"

"Can she make a soup with whatever these farmers up here can give us?"

Dreamily, the partisan called Gianni said, "My mother used to make a soup with just bread and tomatoes."

"Mine, too!" said the skinny partisan Vittorio. Then he, too, kissed his fingers.

Eduardo laughed. "Pappa cal Pomodoro. *Sì.* My mother taught it to her. But Silvana adds—" He twisted around to face Silvana. "What do you put in your tomato bread soup that makes it so good?"

"Leeks. The white part sautéed until just golden. And hot red pepper flakes. And heaps of Romano cheese, of course," she said without thinking. For exactly one entire minute, she'd forgotten to be afraid.

"Leeks," Paolo said wistfully, no longer quite so grim. "My aunt Marcella used to make it for me with leeks when I visited her as a boy. I still remember." Paolo rolled his eyes in his head. Then he looked at Michele. Beseechingly.

Michele understood, but instead of answering, he gazed out at the sparse farms dotting the Umbrian hillside. There, most of his partisan force lived hidden in the barns that were offered as refuge by the poor but sympathetic farmers. Below him, sheep grazed and herbs grew wild and grapes for the great Rubesco wine of Umbria were cultivated. Somehow, all those

men and all the beauty of this landscape had become
his responsibility. He could not afford a mistake, not
even a tall, blond, ravishingly beautiful mistake. Least
of all a terrified Jewess.

For a long moment he stared at her. Then, one by
one, he searched the faces of the ten men in his inner
circle. Seven were nodding their heads up and down.
Two were grinning. One was smacking his lips as if
before a plate of steaming polenta that only he
could see.

At last Michele finally smiled. And instantly his
handsome but taut face was transformed. Even
Silvana, who stood bravely out in the open now beside
her brother, couldn't help but notice. For although
Michele Bassani would be considered a handsome
man in any light, day or night, the radiance of that
smile softened the sadness in his piercing charcoal
eyes and the sharp contours of tension on his extraordinary face. When he smiled, his face matched his
voice.

For Silvana, however, there was no man's voice, no
man's eyes, no man's smile that could lift the painful
memories of devastating loss that she carried inside
her everywhere now. A month ago her entire world
in Rome had blown apart, as if by a bomb. On that
dark day she had lost her mother's respect, she had
been ejected from her home, and she was abandoned
by the man who, for almost three years, had forced
her to love him. After that, nothing, it seemed, would
ever cheer her again, least of all a man's smile. There
was one man, however, who seemed to understand
that. Michele Bassani. And because he understood,
because he did not seem to expect her to smile back,
she trusted him. Without her even realizing it yet, she
trusted him.

"Silvana?" he inquired softly. "Would you do us
the honor of cooking for us?"

Silvana didn't speak but she didn't look away, either. Slowly, she gave him an almost imperceptible
nod. That was all, but it was enough to elate the men.

"Brava!" they cheered. "Brava, Silvana!"

* * *

Living mostly outdoors in the clear, wintry air, Silvana slowly began to heal. Perhaps it was the beauty of the scene—the panorama of the mountains, the blue, blue skies, and the lush slopes below. Or perhaps it was the silence. Unlike the teeming streets of Rome, filled with the noise of traffic and people, and, lately, the ever-present rumble of fear, here there was only the sound of a fire crackling, or a branch snapping, or a lamb bleating. Here there was no fear, only serenity, the kind of serenity that comes from the wind in the trees and the belief in virtue and righteousness that filled each man's heart.

Or perhaps it was the vigorous outdoor work—the lugging of pails of water, the hauling of sacks of corn-meal, semolina flour, and beans, and the stirring and scooping of fresh pecorino cheese made from sheep's milk—that strengthened her, body and soul. It was the constant transporting of precious jars of olive oil and the building of endless cookfires (hidden from the open sky by a lean-to), the serving of all the meals, and the always arduous cleanup afterward.

But perhaps, most of all, it was cooking for the men that brought the color back to Silvana's cheeks. The daily chopping, slicing, grinding, and stirring had a certain salubrious monotony about it. For the first time since Rome, since her world had split apart, the dark thoughts and lacerating regrets that had plagued her were stilled. She was as still as the landscape. There was no need to talk as she tended the fire and ladled out the soup. Mostly, she simply listened—to the wind in the trees . . . and to the men. To their plans of raids on Nazis and Fascist terrorists, their anecdotes about partisans and Jews they helped to flee the country, their memories of family and lovers they had to leave behind.

And all that fall and winter of 1942 and spring and summer of 1943, while Silvana grew stronger and the shadows of fear slowly faded from her eyes, Michele Bassani watched her . . . and said nothing. He asked her no questions about her past and told her little

about himself. Eagerly he accepted the bowls of soup
she ladled out to him, but with only the barest of
smiles. He ate everything with gusto—her polenta, her
pasta, her thick and hearty stews. He especially savored the tasty though rarely available side of veal
that she grilled and carved to perfection, but unlike
the other men who festooned her with wildflowers and
accolades, he made no attempts to win her.

But his eyes were always on her. The sight of her
was never enough. He always needed more of her.
More of the sight of her hair gleaming like liquid gold
down her back. More of her slender arms, taut as she
chopped onions or hacked up a chicken. And more of
that beguiling face with that strong, crazy nose and
those lips, round as a pouting cherub's, that never
smiled.

Oh, how he'd love to see those full, moist lips curl
up in a smile! And hear her hearty laughter. He'd give
almost anything just to make her laugh. But he knew
with an instinct borne of his own suffering that if ever
he was to hear her laugh, first there would have to be
tears. Her tears. And perhaps he'd be the one to cause
them. So he waited, not without a certain dread, for
the day of the tears ... and prayed that later he might
then hear her laughter.

The tears, however, came later than he expected.
They came almost a year after Silvana arrived at the
camp, a year of silent longing for her. Eduardo may
have brought on the tears, but Michele knew it was
he who really caused them.

He could remember that first day the two of them
arrived and all the days afterward: Silvana, magnificent despite the mysterious fear and pain that haunted
her, and her serious, devoted brother. Eduardo, it was
immediately apparent, had brought with him a wealth
of experience, for even before he came to their camp,
he'd been active in the Resistance.

Resentment against Jews—especially anti-Fascist
Jews—began to build in Rome the summer and fall
of 1942. Eduardo spent his summer writing pamphlets
for the underground where his gift for words and his

passionate commitment even stirred several Fascists to convert. Encouraged, he began knocking on doors and urging his ghetto neighbors to join the cause and resist Fascism.

"I saw a Jewish woman complaining to a shop-keeper about the spiraling prices," he told Michele. "All she said to the storekeeper was that a pair of stockings had gone up several lire in a week and the owner accused her of spreading anti-Fascist propaganda. He threatened to have her arrested. I met her outside and talked to her for a while. The next day I knocked on her door and invited her to one of our meetings. Now she is a loyal partisan."

By November of 1942, Eduardo's face and his politics had become too well known and if he didn't flee Rome, he himself faced the risk of arrest. But a startling, tragic turn of events held him in the city three weeks longer: Silvana was missing, and he would not leave without her. All he knew was that something had happened at home—something terrible, even catastrophic—and that his sister Silvana was gone. He could still remember his sickeningly empty feeling when he discovered she had disappeared.

"What happened?" he had asked his brother and mother over and over. "Last night I went to a political meeting and when I came home, Silvana was gone. And where's Benno? What's happened?" But Raffaelle knew nothing and Anna Levi, strangely bitter and tight-lipped, would say nothing.

For three long and dangerous weeks Eduardo searched for her until a sympathetic priest stopped him on the street and whispered, "Your sister was seen by one of my parishioners. She was searching for someone. She was heard crying out his name over and over. Benno. Benno." He pointed to a remote Catholic cemetery. "She was seen there two days ago."

Eduardo rushed to the cemetery and wandered in between the old headstones, calling, "Silvana? Where are you, Silvana?"

He heard her before he actually saw her.

"Benno? Is that you, Benno?"

"It's Eduardo," he answered, puzzled. Surely she knew his voice. Yet when he found her, hiding out in the open, unwashed and half-starved, it was *he* who hardly recognized *her*. She appeared like a specter from behind a stone burial vault and approached him oddly. He had the sensation that she might walk right through him.

"Benno, I knew it! You've come for me. I knew you wouldn't run away without me. I knew it!"

"It's me, Silvana. Eduardo. Your brother. Eduardo." He gripped her and shook her, shouting directly at her, until she finally realized who he was. Then her thin shoulders slumped in utter dejection.

"Oh, Eduardo. It's you." For a mere second her haunted eyes met his, then she squeezed them shut in anguished disappointment.

"Yes. I'm here. And I'm going to help you. But first tell me what's wrong? What happened? Who did this to you?" he demanded in a voice so shrill with shock and heartache that it seemed to hurt her ears, for she covered them with her hands.

In a milder voice, he asked again, "Silvana, tell me, what terrible thing has happened to you? And where the devil is Benno?"

But Silvana shook her head no and averted her face from him. From some deep, dark place within her, he heard her warn him in a kind of low growl, "Don't. Don't ever ask me for I can't speak of it. Ever. If you love me, never ask. Not now. Not ever."

"All right," he relented. He'd do anything never to have to hear her sound like that again. And though he was desperate to help her, to hold her and comfort her, he sensed she might jump at his touch, so he kept his hands at his sides as he spoke to her.

"Come, Girasole. I'll take you with me," he offered tenderly, but it was she who grabbed his arm.

"Not home! Not there!" she screamed. "Not ever again."

"No, not home," he agreed immediately, although he was shocked that she felt she could not return to

her home ever again. But he knew enough now not
to ask why.

"Where then?"

"We're going to the country."

"Will men be there? I don't like them." Then she
softened and touched his cheek. "Not you, though.
Never you."

"Where we're going there will be others ... and
some men, yes. But it will be peaceful and safe and
you'll have me. And I promise you, Girasole, no one
will ever hurt you again. Come." Then he placed her
hand in his and took her with him that November to
the partisans in Umbria.

In the beginning, Silvana clung to Eduardo, but as
she recovered, Eduardo was sent with the men on
more and more frequent forays. Michele went north
with several men to his hometown of Florence, while
Eduardo went south to Rome. With an equal mixture
of bravery and anxiety, Silvana managed to endure
their separations. The anxiety, however, was kept well
hidden, locked away in her heart.

By spring of 1943, Eduardo was gone from the hills
much of the time as Mussolini's regime encouraged
angrier and more violent expressions of anti-Semitism
in the cities.

"What do they want from the Jews?" Eduardo
would ask, more exasperated each time he returned.
"They're not allowed to serve in the army, yet when
Jewish young men are seen on the streets of Rome
without a uniform, they're routinely stopped and arrested by the police. They're becoming virtual prison-
ers in their own houses."

"Anti-Semitism has no logic," Michele agreed.
"Why do they force out-of-work Jewish professors,
doctors, and scientists to do useless manual labor for
virtually no pay? It's irrational. And a stupid waste."

"It's not just stupid, it's also violent," Eduardo
added bitterly. "In Rome I saw bands of Fascists
roaming the ghetto, looting and beating Jews. It's getting too dangerous to check on my own mother."

After Eduardo reported to Michele, he had to do it all over again for his sister. Because Silvana hungered for news of home, no matter how depressing, she begged Eduardo to tell her everything he had seen, as well. She'd listen silently, shaking her head helplessly at the grim tales. Then she would always ask him the same two questions. And Eduardo would regretfully have to give her the same two answers.

"And what of Mama?" she'd ask.

"She still says she won't leave, even if the Germans come and march right down Via Arenula."

"Did she speak—did she ask about me?"

Eduardo would have to shake his head no. "Maybe she will next time."

"Yes, maybe next time," Silvana would agree, although they both knew that it was becoming increasingly dangerous for Eduardo to slip back into Rome, even with the help of several kind priests.

Eduardo made his last foray to Rome in the fall of 1943, and afterward Silvana's tears came. It took Eduardo a month after the Germans occupied Rome in September of 1943 to get anywhere near the city. He never did get all the way home; he didn't have to. What he saw stopped him from ever going home again. From now on there would be no reason to return; his family was gone.

Then, as if that were not enough misery, two Nazis surprised him with drawn guns as he set out on the arduous journey back to the partisan camp in the hills. Running for his life, he managed to escape, but one of their bullets caught him in the arm, splintering the bone.

The blood was not what brought on Silvana's tears. The dark, wet blood on Eduardo's arm almost made Silvana happy. Somehow it proved that he was still alive, even though he fainted and had to be carried halfway up the hill.

No, it was later, when Eduardo had been bandaged and she was about to ask him the two questions that were, for her, always the same. Except that as soon as she asked the first, "And what of Mama?" she could tell that she would have no need of asking the second. This time she wasn't going to hear the same bitterly disappointing answer. She could tell. And dreading what was to come, she almost yearned to be merely bitterly disappointed again. Suddenly the past, however painful, was infinitely preferable to the unknown horrors the future now held.

Michele and the grim Paolo sat with her at the side of Eduardo's cot, but she did not look at them. Wincing once in anticipation of what she was about to hear, she gestured to Eduardo to begin.

To delay the worst news for last, he told her first of the harrowing events preceding the German roundup of one thousand two hundred fifty-nine Jewish citizens—about a tenth of the city's Jews—for deportation to a German concentration camp.

"It was horrible. The Germans surrounded the ghetto and demanded one hundred and ten pounds of gold from all the poor Jews. If they didn't get it, the Germans warned they would take two hundred hostages."

Eduardo was weak and he kept his eyes closed as he spoke, but he could see every image he was recounting as if it were happening before his eyes all over again. Someday he knew he would write of this event. If he ever survived this dreadful war, he would write about all of it—the Jews, the Fascists, the partisans. And his family. Most of all, he would write about his brave mother and brother Raffaelle. Lest he ever forget, he would write a book about them, and thereby keep their memory alive.

"Word of the ransom spread quickly," he continued. "Silvana, you wouldn't believe the throng of people—the whole of Rome, it seemed to me!—that crowded the square. Everyone wanted to express his disgust with the German occupation, to rise up in defense of the Jews, to make a personal contribution. Some gave gold watches, some gave rings or coins or cuff links and even cash. Every Jewish woman in the ghetto, it seemed, gave up her wedding ring that day.

"And you know, it forged a new solidarity between

we Jews and Christians. So many Christians gave—
often anonymously—that we all stood around hugging
and crying."

Silvana nodded, moved by the stories of generosity
and kindness. But she could not smile. She dreaded
what was coming too much.

"So the sum of gold was quickly collected." Now
Eduardo opened his eyes. "But to everyone's horror,
it did nothing to appease the Germans or to prevent
the terrible events that followed." He took a deep
breath before continuing.

"The Germans ordered a roundup."

Silvana gasped and shook her head no, but did
not interrupt.

"Oh, Silvana, the panic! The pleas and the attempts
to escape. It was like one loud, collective scream,"
Eduardo reported dully. His wound, and what he had
heard and seen finally drained him of all emotion. But
with Silvana's eyes upon him, he had to continue.

"Entire families jumped out of apartment building
windows and some mothers handed their babies to
strangers on the street before being dragged off."
Then Eduardo paused before telling her the worst.

"Silvana, they took Giuditta, wheelchair and all.
She'd had a heart attack the week before."

"And Raffaelle?" Silvana asked in growing alarm.

Eduardo nodded yes.

"But they didn't take Mama, did they?" Silvana
cried.

Eduardo said nothing. He stared at her without
moving. He did not blink, he did not sigh. He did not
tell her that their mother and brother were dragged
onto one of the trucks and that their brother kept his
arms around their mother the whole time—even as
Raffaelle pleaded with them to take his mother off
the truck. Even when they hit him with a rifle butt.
And even as the truck, filled with crying, screaming
Jews, pulled away. But in his empty, motherless eyes
she found her answer.

"No, Eduardo, don't tell me that. Not my mama!
They didn't take my mother from me. I needed to feel

her arms around me once more—just once more. Oh, please, no! Not yet! How can I go on without her? Oh, how I need her. Mama! No! Eduardo, I never got to hold her, I never got to kiss her, I never got to ask her—oh, dear beloved Mama—to please, please—forgive—her—Girasole!"

Then, finally, came the tears.

But Eduardo collapsed back on the pillow of hay and his eyes closed. He had no strength left to comfort anyone, not even his bereft sister.

Michele, whose eyes were always on Silvana, saw her suddenly rise and clutch her throat. He could see that her despair was drowning her, suffocating her. She had to get out of that barn. So he was not surprised when she suddenly bolted, running wildly, as she sobbed, out into the night. He was there, right behind her.

For some time, he let her run and followed without trying to stop her. But when she fell to the ground, he fell beside her and pulled her into his arms.

At first, she hardly knew he was there. He was just someone to cling to as she sobbed her heart out. Which was all he'd intended to be. But slowly, as her tears subsided, he increased the pressure of his arms around her. It was impossible not to. Lying there under the stars with her magnificent body next to his, it was impossible not to press her closer, tighter. It was impossible to stop.

"Tell me not to," he whispered. It was almost a plea. "Tell me to stop and I will. But, Silvana, please let me. I'm so sorry and"—he stopped to kiss her wet and swollen eyes—"this is the only way I know to help you. Please let me help you."

Again, he kissed her, this time on her wet, soft cheeks. Again, she did not stop him. He kissed her ears, which were wet with her tears, and her strong Roman nose, and finally he kissed her lips. He had never kissed lips quite like hers. They were like the flesh of a ripe peach. From the first taste, he knew he could dine on the fresh fruit of her lips for the rest of his life and never, ever be sated.

But he didn't want to rush her. And he was unsure
of how to make up for the hurt he felt he'd caused
her. So again, he pleaded with her, "Please, Silvana.
Lose yourself in me. Just forget, for now. It was my
fault for sending Eduardo one more time and bringing
all this pain back to you. Now let me do this for you."
He was almost rambling now, but even as he said this,
he was touching her. It was impossible not to touch
her. And just as impossible for her to stop him.

She never thought she'd ever feel like this again.
She had thought her body was as dead as a burned-
out lightbulb. Much too young, she'd learned the devastating lessons of passion and betrayal. Now, at
nineteen, she felt used up ... and entirely unprepared
for Michele Bassani.

At first, it was his voice—a voice that, for her, was
like music—that reached all the way to her soul and
saved her. And then, it was his eyes. All that year,
she was aware of his penetrating eyes. And for a few
brief seconds, whenever she'd catch Michele staring at
her, she'd suddenly feel warm and young and beautiful
and alive again.

But tonight, of all nights—what was she to make of
this? Of his hands tenderly touching her breasts, and
then her hands covering his, pressing them harder and
harder into her? Was the magic in his hands making
her hands bold?

He had told her to stop thinking, to just give herself
up to him. But she couldn't help wondering, how did
he know? How did he know this was what she needed,
she who thought she would never want the touch of
another man again?

But his hands seemed to know more about her than
she did. It was those searching, sensate hands of his
that found the place she thought was dead between
her thighs ... and brought it keenly back to life.

It was then that she stopped wondering why she
was letting him pull off her sweater and slide off her
wool skirt. She did not ask herself why she was reaching out to him with both arms, pulling him down onto
her, into her. Or how she could be smiling.

For now, for tonight, she was finished asking questions, finished asking why. He made it impossible for her to think at all. Each touch, each thrust, silenced every doubt. Therefore, all she could do was feel. Feel the rapture that had replaced the despair. Feel it in her hair wet on the grass, in her thighs wrapped around him, in her back arched with ardor, in her heart.

He was right. For now, for tonight, only this mattered. Only this—her body and Michele's body—and this one long, ecstatic night in the moonlight that joined them.

A year ago she first saw something in Michele's eyes and heard something in his voice that moved her. She hadn't known then what it was. Now she did. It was trust. And because she could trust him, she let him into her heart. And found bliss. Bliss, not just for this night, but to last a lifetime. Bliss to make her whole at last.

Chapter Five

They had become inseparable. Ever since that first
night of tears and of bliss, Michele and Silvana became
spontaneously—and permanently—entwined, like two
separate climbing vines that had knotted together and
then grew as one. Except for those times when he
went off on sorties with the men and they were sepa-
rated for several days and nights, some part of his
body was forever encoiled around hers. That is, when
she wasn't clinging to some part of him. Often, he
could be seen rubbing up against her as she worked
at her cookstove, one hand snaking up her skirt, the
other wrapped around her waist. Or she would stand
behind him while he held his meetings with the men
and rub her knee up and down his back or fold her
arms around his neck.

The men, uncomfortable at first, grew to accept
their open lovemaking because of the changes in Michele. They had never known him to sing with them
before or to laugh. A somewhat somber loner in the
past, now he sat with them and shared jokes and anecdotes from their recent battles and even long ago
memories of home.

But most important of all, they, who relied on him
to lead them, who put their lives in his hands, actually
felt more secure now as a result of the changes in
Michele.

"Not only has he opened his heart to us, he's
opened his mind to us, too," they told each other.

"And his mind seems clearer, sharper than ever before," they agreed. "What a thinker!"

"The way he plans the raids—with such meticulousness, such detail, such precise information and timing, that I feel safer than if I were sitting in Mussolini's living room!"

For such security, the men could endure the sight of those two lithe, young lovers kissing out in the open with utter joy and abandon.

To Silvana, the changes in Michele were most apparent on the outside—in the sharp angles of Michele's face and the piercing pain in his eyes that seemed to soften almost overnight. And the words, the torrent of words he now eagerly shared with the men and with her.

But only he knew why all those words he now spoke came so easily to him. Only he knew the depth of the change within him. For that, however, he needed only one word: Silvana.

Each night with Silvana beside him, he felt his very soul open up, his soul that he had always kept hidden—even from himself. And a shower of words would pour out of him, drenching them both with his ardor.

Each morning, he'd awaken early just to be able to stare at her freely, without interruption, for as long as he liked. It was then, with his eyes upon her as she slept, that the words would come, words of longing and passion and humor to describe to her how beautiful she was, how happy she made him . . . and how much he loved her. A flood of heartfelt words that he saved to tell her in the velvet darkness of their long, languorous nights together.

And because the words were to her like poetry, they entered her as he entered her—pulsing through to her core.

They would lie naked beside each other in the barn, and Michele would murmur his words of love until he had covered her body with a cashmere blanket of words. Only then would he begin to touch her.

He told her, "Before you, I never really laughed. Now, sometimes when I'm creeping through the woods with the men, and the German guns are cracking in the air, I begin to laugh to myself, thinking of you. Of the funny way you scrunch up your face as I take the first taste of your meal. Like a Catholic praying to Jesus with her hands clasped and her eyes closed. Yes, a Catholic! And then how you look up at the sky and thank *Him*—not me—when I say your food is delicious."

"My mother used to do that, too," she told him, her words tinged with nostalgic melancholy, but he knew not to press her to tell him more ... because she simply wouldn't speak of her past. So it was he who spoke to her from his heart, and silently longed for the day when she, too, would come out of hiding.

One night, her foot in his hand, he told her, "It is for this perfectly round little toe"—and he sucked it— "for this slim ankle"—and he kissed it—"for this tender thigh"—and he playfully bit it—"that I lost my heart to you the first time I saw you."

"You fell in love with my feet?" she teased, goading him to tell her more.

"Your feet, your calves, your long, amazing legs. When I saw them I thought, 'She's got the legs of a young filly. A prancer. They're legs made for running ... or for dancing in red satin slippers out on a terrazzo in the moonlight.' "

"I don't own a pair of red satin slippers," she pouted. "No slippers at all. Just those old boots Vittorio gave to me because he wears a small size for a man, and because he's kind."

"You will. Someday, Silvana, you will have a closetful of satin slippers. You'll slip these sweet feet into leather shoes from the finest shops in Florence. And drape this eternally tantalizing body of yours in dresses of the smoothest silk. You'll have a kitchen with a fine new stove and shiny new pots to cook your delicious meals for me. You'll have everything, Silvana, everything you ever wanted," he promised her with complete certainty. More certainty, in fact, than he had about his own future.

Once, Michele had dreamed of becoming a lawyer, but the war had interrupted his plans. Once, he'd even had another love, but her family refused to permit her to marry a Jew.

"For a long time afterward, I was consumed by bitterness and shame," he told Silvana one night in the dark barn.

"Why shame?"

"Because I felt a kind of self-contempt. I somehow thought her family was right to reject me."

"They made you ashamed of being a Jew," she concluded.

"Perhaps, but until you, I was always wrestling with my Jewishness—with my very soul, I suppose."

"Until me?" She knew what he meant, but she wanted to hear it anyway.

"Until you, my *amore*, I was always in some kind of torment. In a way, I was almost grateful to the war for showing me an example of suffering deeper and of more importance than my own personal pain."

Now, the war no longer made him grateful; it made him afraid. But he did not tell her that. He told her instead, "But you set my soul free. YOU!" And he took her into his arms and whispered, "You, you, you!" as he buried his face in her breasts, then her belly, and finally in the warm, moist place where he could make her moan.

She was his wife even before the partisan Ettore, a former judge from Turin, married them on a hill in the sunlight. In that brief, sunlit ceremony on a chilly February afternoon in 1944, they were formally united. But Silvana always felt she had become Michele's wife that first night, the night he carefully, delicately, compassionately collected all her broken pieces and put her back together again.

But the Silvana who emerged was not the same Silvana. She was no longer a lost and frightened girl; she was a woman. And always afterward, she would remember it as the night she became whole. And the night she became his wife.

Except, of course, that she wasn't entirely whole at all. A part of her life still lay buried and smoldering beyond her conscious memory, like the charred remains in a pot that had sat too long on the coals, its lid too hot to lift. As long as she did not lift that lid and look inside, as long as she avoided remembering the day her world had gone up in flames, she felt whole. It was only when she thought of that shattering day, and the desperate time afterward living in that forlorn cemetery until Eduardo found her, that she remembered all that she'd lost. Then the blistering memories would begin to crackle and burn inside her again and she'd have to scream out loud until Michele could calm her.

To avoid the scathing pain inside that scorching cauldron, she knew she must never lift the lid. For the year that she spent at the camp before she and Michele fell in love, she broke her own rule only twice. But on one of those occasions, neither Eduardo nor Michele was there to hold her and she writhed, tormented and inconsolable, until they returned, four days later. In the five months since she and Michele had married, she had broken her rule not at all.

But Michele wanted her to break it. Though he did not press her, she knew he yearned for her to trust him enough to confide what, in her early life, had caused her so much pain.

"I do trust you. Completely," she often told him. "When I was a young girl, I was so happy and sunny that they nicknamed me Girasole. Then came the time of which I cannot speak. And after that, I believed I would never know such innocent trust ever again. But with you, Michele, I'm happier than I was when I was Girasole. I love you and trust you completely, my *amore*."

"Not completely," he couldn't help saying. "But it's all right. Someday, you will. When you're ready. And even if it takes you an eternity, I will continue to love you every single hour of that eternity—so long as you continue to feed me."

Weeks later, she laughed to herself, squatting over the makeshift latrine in the woods, remembering how he'd made her laugh with relief the first time he'd said it. Then she wiped herself with one of the soft leaves and torn rags she'd gathered in expectation of a bloody menstrual flow. But the leaf was clear. Again, she wiped herself. Again, nothing. It was puzzling. The same thing had happened last month when her breasts had become tender and she went to the latrine with a bundle of rags and the same expectation. But there had been no blood.

Then, as she hoisted up the worn pants she wore every day but Saturday, the Sabbath, her hand glanced over her smooth, hard belly. And in that moment, she knew. She knew with complete certainty though she could not detect even the slightest bulge in her abdomen, even the merest thickening of her slim waist. Yet she was sure, all the same.

And her first thought, as soon as she knew, as soon as she was sure was, *Now, I will tell Michele!*

Yes, now she would tell him. But not of his baby that she now carried inside her. No, that marvelous news would have to wait. For even though she was certain it would delight him, and that together they would rejoice in the miracle their love had created— defying a world torn by war and destruction—this was not what she would tell him first.

"My *amore*," she would begin, "I believe I am ready for you to know all of me, even that part about which I could never speak." She knew he would nod then, eager for her to continue. And she would.

"Always before, I thought I could hide the burning embers of my painful memories here—" and she would point to her heart. "Under a tight lid too hot to touch. But this morning a miracle has changed me and cooled the fire. Later, I will tell you of this miracle. For now, let us sit on a rock, and I will lift the lid and together we will revisit the time of all my heartache."

Oh, yes, she would tell him at last. Tell him and be free. Free of all the nightmares and pain. And the fear. And free at last to give him all of her trust, all of herself.

She hurried back to the camp to wait for him. This

had been their longest separation—more than two long weeks without being able to touch or kiss or talk or just gaze at each other silently. More than two long weeks of danger and waiting. Fighting had become so fierce that she could hear the boom of mortars and the crack of rifles miles and miles away. But always, Michele came back, and this time, their reunion would unite them in the closest, most permanent bond of all.

She had no satin slippers to wear, of course, but she could go barefoot, the way he really liked her best. And she could wash her glorious golden hair in a bucket of spring water and dry it in the sun. And fasten wildflowers behind one ear, as she did when they had married five months before.

She did not own a lipstick or a vial of perfume or even a mirror. So she was unaware that the pale bronzed apricot of her skin, the golden flecks in her hazel eyes, the dark sable fringe of her thick lashes, the high arch of her wide brows, and the pale peach tint of her lips were all the cosmetics she needed. At that moment, hers was a face kissed by such beauty and radiance, makeup would have been excessive, no matter how lightly applied.

But because she was unaware of her own loveliness, she primped and fretted. In 1938, when she was fourteen, her country had betrayed the Jews, and she had cursed the government for its politics and immorality. Now, as a wife, as a lover and a mother-to-be, she cursed her country anew, this time in behalf of all Italian women, Christian and Jew alike. For all women who, like herself, were forced to live a life of austerity, devoid of aesthetics and grace.

"Duce!" she cried. "Look at us. You did this. You, with your lust for power and tyranny. Look how you've stripped us of our femininity and allure. Look how you've ruined us!"

Once, several months before, giving in to a moment of self-pity, she'd complained to Michele, "I've forgotten the way stockings used to feel on my feet. I've forgotten what perfume smells like. I've forgotten how to wear a dress. Yes, that's right. I've forgotten what it means to be a woman. How can you love such a wretch?"

Waiting for Michele to return, she remembered his response and, for a time, his words calmed her.

"It's true that it isn't easy loving such a tall, ugly wretch," he'd said with a wry smile, "but whenever she seems too frightful, I console myself by remembering that at least she has the legs of a prancer and the rump of a summer melon. And if that doesn't console me, then I remind myself that her skin is like a satin sheet pulled taut over the soft bed of her body. And that her breasts are the only two pillows where I will ever want to rest my head.

"Her face, of course, is a horror, but at least she has eyes the shape of two huge almonds. Ah! Her nose! It's unforgettable! And don't forget her lips, I tell myself. As if I ever could. Such lips! Like two pulpy sections of a tangerine pulled right from the fruit. Lips to feast on whenever I, her poor, unlucky husband, need sustenance."

But even the memory of the magic of his words could calm her only for a while. She had so much to tell him! By midnight, she was frantic. At least, if Eduardo had been in the camp, she could have turned to him for comfort. But he, too, was away leading a group of poor Jews to safety.

There was, of course, the gun. Michele had given it to her on the day they were married. "For your safety, for your peace of mind," he had said. "I want you to keep it, always." It was her gun now, intended to calm her fears. But when she had looked at it and felt the dull, black weight of it in her hand, she had asked, "How will this bring me peace of mind?"

"If not for yourself, then for me," he had told her, his mood abruptly darkening. "Knowing that while I am away you sleep with this weapon under your pillow will bring *me* peace of mind. Take it, Silvana. Please."

And so she had accepted the gun and for an hour on the next three days of their "honeymoon" he had taught her how to shoot. Then she placed it under her pillow, but it never brought her comfort. Thinking of it now only increased her agitation. Michele's gun was here in her bed, but Michele was not.

Yet, somehow, she knew that tonight was the night Michele would return. Though she never had any warning, she always knew when he was close. It was as if she could hear his heart beating down below in the valley, beating more and more loudly as he made his way back to her.

The sound of his beating heart awakened her at three-thirty in the morning. Dozing off for a half hour, she suddenly sat up, wide awake, the beating loud in her ears. Then, just as suddenly, the beating stopped. And she heard nothing more at all.

"Michele?" she cried in a tense whisper as she ran barefoot from the barn to the path at the edge of the steep cliff. Over her shift she had pulled on his old sweater and as she peered into the darkness below, she sniffed the sleeves, infusing the scent of him into her veins, into her memory. It would be her very last memory of him and she would take it with her to her grave. The sweater, the scent of him in its sleeves and circulating through her veins all the long years of her life.

He was dead by the time they dragged him over the top of the cliff and onto level ground.

And though she had not yet seen him, she knew it. She knew that Michele, her husband, her love, her life, was dead. She knew it first when his heartbeat stopped and panic had gripped her, sending her out into the night to the edge of the cliff.

"I heard it. I know I heard it. And then it stopped. What happened? Why did his heart stop beating?" she wanted to ask, though even then she knew the answer.

But she also knew it when she saw the tears. So many men, so many tears. She saw the tears of Paolo first, and she knew. Then the tears of Vittorio. Out of the darkness the two loyal partisans emerged, panting and bleeding and sobbing. As they staggered toward her, dragging something behind them, she knew.

Then came more men and more tears. Never had she seen so many tears.

Then the thing that they had been dragging was set down on the dry earth, and she knew.

But though she knew and she knew and she knew, she would not believe it.

"No. No tears," she insisted, robotlike, slowly shaking her head at the men. "He is alive. So do not cry for Michele."

"Silvana, I'm so sor—" Paolo began but Silvana silenced him.

"No! No sorrow! No tears. Not for Michele. Because he's alive. Isn't he alive, Paolo? Oh, please, say he's alive. Please do say it."

"Down there"—and he pointed down at the blackness below—"he still had a heartbeat and we thought if we could just get him back up here, back to you—" Paolo told her, wiping the tears from his eyes. "But we lost him on the way. Silvana, we have all lost him. He was loved. He was much loved."

Though his wounded and tired men had fashioned a gurney to carry him, Michele still was soaked with mud and with blood. *So much blood,* Silvana thought, *but none of it in his body.* All of it rushing out, gushing out. Mixing with the mud.

Stop! she wanted to cry out. *Stop the blood! Put it back in his body, where it belongs.* But her mouth would not work. Her lips would not move. Her voice made no sound. And only she heard the dry, silent scream that rose up from her womb until it pierced her brain, where it echoed endlessly in every dark chamber of her memory.

One month after the death of Michele, Eduardo made plans to escape north through the mountains, into Switzerland, and finally to America. Through the Italian underground, he'd been given a German uniform and a new identity. Silvana hardly recognized him in his dyed blond hair and his new blond mustache.

"Now I finally look like your brother," he joked lamely but he was not surprised when Silvana did not smile. For the second time in her life, his sister had lost all capacity for joy. In her eyes there was only sorrow and in her new, slow gait there was a certain dread, as if she feared disaster might once again tap her on the shoulder at any moment. Only when she thought of her baby did her face come to life, but even that joy was tinged with loss.

"Michele!" she would cry out to the ghost of a husband only she could see. "How could you leave us? Now I have no husband and our child will have no father. We miss you, Michele. We both miss you unbearably!"

"Come with me," Eduardo implored her. "The trip will be arduous but you're strong. You'll make it. And then you can have your baby in the New World. It'll be an American."

The look she gave him made Eduardo wonder if he'd ever again see happiness in his sister's eyes.

"Eduardo, don't be foolish. I can't climb mountains and I'd only slow you down. No, I must have my baby right here. But you are wanted by the Germans and the Fascists and it's best if you go now."

"How can I leave you?"

"You're not leaving me. You're going to America to find a new life for us, the last of the Levis."

"You mean you'll come to America?"

"Do you think I mean to remain here? Here, where they killed my husband, my mother, my brother, and betrayed all of my people? Certainly, I will come to America."

"When? Oh, tell me when, Silvana!" Eduardo was jubilant.

"When this hateful war is finished and you are settled, I will bring Michele's child across the sea to you."

"Promise?"

Silvana clutched her brother's shoulders. "First promise me."

"Anything."

"Promise me you will not die. Eduardo, you are all I have left. You ... and what is growing in here." And she made him touch her belly. "We need you. So, just ... don't die. You must promise me."

"I promise we will grow old together in America. The three of us. As soon as I get there, I'll send word."

Then, in the silence that began to grow between them, he saw a wistful smile transform her face for a moment.

"What is it?" he asked gently, but still she hesitated.

"I—" she began and then stopped, blushing with girlish embarrassment.

Then she bravely met his eyes. "Say it," she said in a hushed whisper.

"Say what?" he was about to ask, and then he remembered and his eyes filled with tears. He took her pained but still beautiful face in his hands and stroked her cheek and brushed back all the blond tendrils until the years of war and loss and betrayal melted away. Until he could see again the sunny young girl of his childhood.

"Girasole," he said hoarsely. "Good-bye, my dear, sweet Girasole."

PART TWO

Prologue

1955

I am swaying. I am rolling and swaying and sliding with the swirls of the waves on the sea. Out on the deck of this big ship I see nothing but a gray mist, as gray and dense as my memories. But I do not think of them, neither the bitter nor the beautiful. I think only of Elena, who looks at me with her father's eyes, shiny as black olives. And of Eduardo who, after these ten dry and difficult years, will at last see her, my daughter, for the first time. And see me, whatever it is I've become.

"I would have come sooner," I tell my brother, "if there had been passage."

I would have come when my Elena was born in January, but the war continued on until May 1945. And then it was as if the war had not ended. There was no food, no work, no place to live. And no family. So, of course, I would have come.

And I would have run to you when Elena was three, and I had to cook and scrub for a rich family outside Florence. Gladly would I have braved these high seas than endure the patron's nightly attempts to seduce me while Elena slept beside me in my bed. Oh, yes, even after I escaped that household and began cooking for another family, large and demanding—but not unkind—I would have gladly come. For it was there that I slowly saved money for the ticket. But still there was no passage!

So I come to you now, ten years after our last tearful good-byes.

Do you remember your Girasole, Eduardo? Or

have you become such an Americano that Elena and I will embarrass you with our Old World ways?

I warn you—I am thirty-one now. Do you think I am old? I have been told by some that this is still a pretty face, that the years of hardship are reflected as only mere moments of time on my skin and in my eyes. But since the war, I am not in the habit of looking in the mirror, so I cannot confirm this.

But Elena, as you will see, is a real beauty! She has Michele's charcoal hair and our mother's almond eyes but, alas, no gift for cooking. Instead she has her father's mind—systematic, organized, precise. I dream that she will one day study at your American university.

I promise, Eduardo, we will not be a burden to you. I come with a little bit of money and a willingness to do almost any kind of work to survive.

You say in your letters that your "nightclub" is doing well. I do not know what this is—a "nightclub." What does a manager do? Somehow, with your gift for words, I thought you would become a teacher or a journalist. I suppose that is why you work on your novel in your spare time. Someday, you will finish it and receive the praise you deserve.

But meanwhile, tell me this—do they eat at your nightclub? If they eat, then there must be a kitchen. And is it there, in that kitchen, that, perhaps, I can work? I'll wash dishes, anything, and while I wash, I'll watch and I'll learn. You'll see. I'll learn fast. *Rapido!* Just like America.

You must not think me vain but I can't help wondering, What do the girls in Manhattan look like? Are they tall, like me? Are their clothes very smart? And why have you not captured one of those Manhattan girls and married her? We need to rebuild the Levi family. This we must discuss when I see you.

The truth is, I have discussed much with you already. Like Mama, I, too, talk to ghosts. I talk to Mama, I talk to Michele, and I talk to you. I always see your face before me. You look just as you did the day you called me Girasole for the last time. Young and dark and serious. But you are no ghost, Eduardo. You are alive!

Alive! You, Elena, and I. We have survived! And as I sail across this enormous ocean to be with you, to begin my life yet again, I practice my English with Elena, who is already far beyond me. But I now know three words and I will say them to you when I see you.

Hello, brother. Hello, darling brother.

Chapter Six

"Silvana, what's this about throwing out the lettuce?" Eduardo demanded, bursting through the swinging doors of the Club Midnight kitchen. Folding his arms tightly across his barrel chest, he tapped his patent leather shoe, waiting for an answer. He was dressed in his usual tuxedo, but because it was only six o'clock, he was tieless. Nevertheless, the white pleated shirt and black jacket and pants made him look surprisingly svelte and sophisticated. At thirty-nine, even the premature touch of gray at his temples had become an asset to his looks and Silvana, unfazed by his imminent scolding, gave her brother a smile of approval.

"It was iceberg."

"Iceberg," he repeated uncomprehendingly.

Silvana nodded and added scornfully, "No flavor, no vitamins, no ... crunch." She liked the word "crunch." Four years in America, and every day she learned a new word. Today it was crunch. She said it again. "A salad should have crunch. This iceberg was like a soft polenta. And as yellow. When a customer dines here, he expects quality."

Eduardo exploded with exasperation. "You still don't get it. Customers come here to do two things: to drink and be entertained. They do not—I repeat—they do not come here to dine. This ain't no French restaurant."

"This *is not*."

"Is not what?"

Silvana sighed. "This *is not* a French restaurant." His job, she knew, often required him to sound tough. But when his speech became filled with American slang, it was time to remind him of the Levi family's high standards.

The English lesson was not lost on him but he chose to ignore it. His head chef Lenny had threatened to quit today because Silvana had taken it upon herself to throw out the case of lettuce that had been delivered yesterday morning.

"It's either your sister—or me!" Lenny had insisted. "Who does she think she is—the Countess of Rome? She looks at the lettuce and says, 'Inferior.' And then she dumps it. Am I the head chef—or is she?"

He had to buy Lenny a box of cigars and a bottle of brandy and sit drinking with him for two hours at the bar before he could persuade him not to quit.

And he had to promise, "I'll talk to my sister. You're the boss in the kitchen and if she defies you one more time, she's out. I'll ... fire her."

He said it, but whether he would be able to stand by his words, he did not know. With a daughter to raise, how would Silvana survive without this job? Now that she'd been promoted for the third time— first from kitchen helper to assistant grill chef, then to salad chef, and now to chef, she was able to save, he knew, some money every week. How could he fire her just when she was beginning to stand on her own two feet?

If Silvana had only confided in him her grandly ambitious yet plainly practical plan for her future, she might have saved him all this endless fretting. But Silvana told no one—not even her brother—her strategy for opening a restaurant of her own, and Eduardo would remain ignorant for three more months, until she planned to announce, "You don't have to fire me because—I'm quitting!"

In three more months she'd have five thousand saved—enough to go to a bank, go to Eduardo, even go to Club Midnight's owner, Mr. Joey Rizzo himself, in order to launch her dream.

She even had a name for her *ristorante: Per Sempre Silvana.* The unspoken hope, of course, was that by calling it "Forever Silvana," it might indeed last forever.

She had scouted a location, too. In her wanderings with Elena on her day off she had discovered a small restaurant that had recently gone out of business on a quiet eastside street. Peering through a clear spot in the soaped-up window, she told Elena, "Yes, this is it. *Perfetto!*"

"It looks so small," Elena whined.

"Better to start small, my darling. Once, you, too, were a baby, small as our new *ristorante*"—and she cupped Elena's face in her hands—"and I cooked for you and fed you and soon you grew big and tall, just like our—"

"It's not our restaurant," Elena interrupted. "It's yours, Mama, all yours."

"I do this for you. For your future, don't you understand that?"

But Elena was adamant. "I want to go to college. I don't want to cook at a hot stove and carry heavy trays and grate parmigiano cheese on other people's spaghetti. I want to be an economist or a mathematician."

"You have a good head for numbers. You'll be in charge of the cash register. I'll put you up front."

"But I want to go to college!"

"And I want you to have an education, too. But when you're eighteen, *mia dolcezza,* my sweetness. For now, we will work and save to send you to school. Now I must write down the telephone number of this rental agent and call him."

"What if we go out of business?"

Silvana took her daughter's unhappy face in her hands again and kissed the tip of her nose. "You have your father's brains. And you have the brave Michele Bassani blood in your veins, too. With such brains and such courage, how can we fail?"

For the next three months Silvana did not throw out any more lettuce and was careful not to openly defy Lenny again. But when he caught the flu and was out sick for five days, she was put in charge of the kitchen, and those were her five most glorious days in America.

"Tonight," she told the staff, "we will add two specials that are not on the menu, so be sure to tell the customers before they order their steak and potatoes. We have a special pasta—"

"Pasta?" they asked blankly. The word, in 1959, was entirely new to them.

"*Pasta asciutta. Sì,* you know, dried spaghetti, linguine, and so on. But tonight I make *pasta fresca,* homemade ravioli filled with spinach and cheese, topped with butter and wild mushrooms."

"Wild mushrooms? That sounds exotic."

"Here, come and have a taste," she told the waiters. "That way you will know how to describe it to the customers."

"Lenny never lets us taste the food. Just the leftovers that he feeds us."

"I know, but Lenny's sick and tonight I'm head chef. Taste."

Deftly she scooped four ravioli onto a hot plate, topped it with the mushrooms sautéed in butter, and grated some fresh parmigiano cheese over it all. Each waiter cut into a square, pillowy ravioli with his fork, brought it to his lips, and inhaled. They all chewed in silence. Then they went back and finished off their ravioli.

Silvana waited, but finally she could not help asking, "Well then, so what do you say?"

The four waiters hesitated, exchanging looks before answering. Then the first, the oldest of the four, spoke.

"Do you think we might try one more of those wild ravioli?"

It was not the ravioli that took Warren Nachman's breath away, but the other special, the fish stew, cacciucco, fragrant with wine and lemon rind and toasted garlic bread soaking at the bottom of the bowl. Sitting at a front-row table for which he'd had to slip the maître d' a twenty, Warren Nachman, New York real-

tor and most eligible bachelor, could hardly breathe.
He barely heard Bobby Darin singing his spirited fi-
nale six feet away. Had Warren ordered the ravioli
special, too, he might have expired altogether.

Beside him, Sandra Block, his blind date for the
evening, had, in fact, ordered the ravioli, but she was
on her feet, applauding wildly with the rest of the
audience, her dinner untouched. Not that it mattered.
Warren Nachman knew that whoever had prepared
this dinner was not just a chef, but an artist, a genius!
An investment.

"Waiter!" he called, futilely waving his hand while
everyone, including the staff, listened immobilized and
transfixed to Bobby Darin's encore, the rousing, show-
stopping "Mack the Knife." When it was over, he finally attracted his server's attention.

"I would like to meet the chef," he said as he carefully counted out ten singles. This evening was costing
him a small fortune and though he could well afford
it, parting with his cash was, to him, always a sad
farewell. "Would you ask him to come out here so
that I can thank him personally for this inspired
meal?"

He placed the money in the waiter's hand. Then he
sat back, drumming his long, slim fingers on the table
as he waited. Thin almost to the point of gauntness,
Warren Nachman often forgot to eat, though he took
great pleasure in good, fresh, well-prepared food. The
difficulty was in finding it. Ever since his mother had
died, he was sure he wouldn't find a meal to equal
any of hers. Until tonight.

"Sandra, how do you like your ravioli?" Warren
asked the petite, not quite young brunette who, until
seven o'clock this evening, had been a complete
stranger. And who, after more than three hours now,
still seemed to him an uninteresting mystery. Conversation between them had been forced and halting, no
matter what they talked about. Even this last stab felt
like it was doomed from the start. The problem, he
knew, was that there was no chemistry between them.
Warren Nachman strongly believed in chemistry. He

could look at a particular piece of real estate, and if the chemistry was right, he bought it, held on to it, and eventually sold it at a profit. Making a profit was easier than explaining his particular definition of the chemistry that drove it. All he could say was that he knew the chemistry was right when he heard a high-pitched ringing in his ears. It happened every time and it never failed him.

"It's really too fattening for me. I'm on a diet," Sandra admitted with an embarrassed giggle. "Want some?"

And that was why Warren Nachman did not see Silvana approaching his table, still as tall and regal as a sunflower. Although she was wearing her chef's uniform, a shapeless white cotton jacket and baggy checked pants, and although her long, burnished hair was hastily pulled back in a ponytail, everyone stared at her as she passed. She was still that beautiful.

Everyone stared, that is, but Warren Nachman. He remained hunched over the table, reaching across to Sandra's plate for one more forkful, then another, and another of Silvana's supernal ravioli. This dish, of course, bore no resemblance to his mother's noodle kugel except in its creamy delicacy. Yet—dare he say it?—it was better. Fresher, lighter, newer. Yes, it was true. Mama Nachman had at last been surpassed.

"You wanted to see me, sir?" Silvana said in her sultry, accented voice after standing directly in front of Warren Nachman for several moments.

It was not a pink rosebud nor even a sunflower that Warren Nachman saw standing before him. He was a city boy, brought up in a world of concrete and contracts, and he knew nothing of flowers. But he knew a good investment when he saw one, and this one was solid gold. He knew because the moment he looked up at Silvana, his ears started ringing.

"I didn't expect you to be a girl," he said, rising from his chair to shake her hand.

"I'm hardly a girl. I'm thirty-five," Silvana said matter-of-factly.

Warren Nachman was dumbfounded. All night long

he had been trying to guess Sandra Block's age. The two friends who had arranged this date knew he was eager to settle down and have a family at last. "This Sandra had better be under forty," he'd warned his friends, and they had assured him, "She's young enough to bear you ten children." Warren, however, was not so sure.

At the Waldorf-Astoria bar where they'd begun their evening, he told Sandra his age, thirty-nine, hoping that his forthrightness would encourage her to do the same. But Sandra refused to return the confidence. At the very mention of the word "age," she grew restive and asked to change the subject. Yet here before him was perhaps the most beautiful woman he had ever seen, who cooked the best food he had ever tasted, and she had just unself-consciously volunteered her age as if it were anything but a shameful secret. As if it were merely a . . . number! Warren Nachman loved numbers.

"You look much younger," he told her quietly. "Not that thirty-five is not young . . . because it is. Extremely young." Suddenly he was rambling, scrambling to think of something to say, anything, just to keep her there. "I myself am thirty-nine and look it, but you, if I may say so, look like you're in your twenties." Too much about age, he told himself. Change the subject! But it was Sandra Block who did it for him.

"If you'll excuse me, I think I'll make a visit to the powder room," she announced frostily and hurriedly left the table.

As soon as his blind date was out of earshot he said, "May I ask your name?"

"Silvana Bassani."

"Oh, an Italian," Warren said with obvious disappointment.

Silvana understood and smiled. "My maiden name was Levi."

Warren brightened. "Levi? An Italian Jew?"

Silvana nodded. "There once were many of us before the war."

"So, you're married?"

"I was."

"I'm sorry. I am asking you too many personal questions. It's just that I want to keep you here, talking to me."

"I'm afraid that is not possible. I must get back to the kitchen, Mr.—?"

"Warren. Warren Nachman," he told her as he rose to shake her hand. Then she was gone, before he could tell her that he loved her cooking, that he loved the way she looked, that he, in fact, loved . . . her!

He did. He loved her. He was sure of it. But it was too early, of course, to discuss such matters. First, he would have to convince this regal Roman beauty to spend a night with him . . . alone. And that, he could see, would take all of his persuasive charms, for Silvana Levi was not going to be easy to capture. Unlike the anxious husband hunters he was usually introduced to, she had none of the desperation and loneliness he so often recognized in their eyes. Indeed, she held herself entirely aloof and it was he, returning to Club Midnight the next evening and the next and the next, who experienced for the first time in his life the churning anxiety of the desperate suitor.

After two weeks of a pursuit that included three dozen long-stemmed roses, a box of fine chocolates, several handwritten messages, and a gold watch— which was promptly returned to him—Silvana finally agreed to meet him for lunch on her day off, Sunday.

Wearing a black and white polka-dot dress and a black straw hat, black patent leather heels and white gloves, she was a chic vision of springtime in New York. But to Warren's dismay, she was not alone. At her shapely side stood her fourteen-year-old daughter, Elena, short and dark, entirely unlike her mother, and certainly not nearly as beautiful.

"I hope you don't mind," Silvana said as she introduced them, "but this is the only full day Elena and I have to spend together."

"No, no, of course not," Warren insisted, but his disappointment was palpable. To hide it, he turned to

Elena with excessive politeness. "What would you like
to drink? Coca-Cola? Ginger ale? Milk? They have
everything here." He swept his arm to encompass the
formal, French-paneled room. "Be my guest. Order
whatever your heart desires."

But Elena had caught the look on his face when he
first saw her, and because of it, because of that one
naked look of startled displeasure—which she received as the sharp slap of total rejection—she vowed
she would always hate him. Not that she did not resent
this usurper, this intruder, from the very first moment
her mother had laughingly announced that she had a
"suitor." Before she even met him, she knew she
wouldn't ever like this Warren Nachman. But at least
now he had given her a convenient excuse for her
feelings. *He hates me,* Elena reasoned with fourteen-
year-old logic; *therefore I will hate him.*

They were waiting for her order.

"Acqua," she said in Italian though she knew the
English word for water. Indeed, she spoke English
fluently, and no longer spoke Italian at all. Until now.

"Elena, why are you speaking Italian to Mr. Nachman?" Silvana asked, perplexed. "You know he can't
understand you."

"Acqua," was all Elena would say. And despite
Warren and Silvana's attempts to include her, and
then to ignore her, Elena's sullen behavior cast a pall
over the afternoon. For that reason, Silvana agreed to
let Warren take her to dinner the following night after
work—alone.

"But I warn you," she told him, "I begin the yawning every night at eleven, like clockwork!"

To sit beside this magnificent creature, even if she
yawned in his face, was so thrilling for Warren Nachman to contemplate that he almost threw his arms
around her and hugged her. But the daughter was
standing at the door as he said good-bye, her eyes so
cold, her manner so resentful, that she forced him to
control himself.

To his surprise, he was again forced to control himself the following evening, although in truth, he could

not remember ever enjoying himself more. This was a first "date" unlike anything Warren had ever experienced. What he anticipated was the usual sexual fencing. To his first suggestive thrusts, he expected the usual parries of giggles and mild demurrals. Instead, Silvana responded with no-nonsense ripostes that totally disarmed him.

"I don't mind telling you, Silvana, that I have lost a considerable amount of sleep over you," he began.

"Take a sleeping pill," she told him.

Laughing, he tried again. "I really can't stop thinking about you. Yesterday, at a meeting, I kept seeing your silky, golden hair—"

"This?" she interrupted, running her hand through a lock of her hair. "It needs to be cut, but there is no time."

"Oh, you mustn't cut it!" Warren protested, imagining her hair spread out on a pillow beside him. "Promise me?"

"This is an insignificant thing, what I choose to do with my own hair, yes? When I make a promise, I hope it will be for something more ... fat." She couldn't think of the word "weighty" or "important," so she used the one word that came to her—fat. And that so delighted Warren Nachman that it became a secret code between them, making both of them laugh whenever he said, "Make me a fat promise."

And after that, after he laughed heartily and noticed that she was distinctly bored with this empty flirting, he asked her a real question, and from then on, he was sure he understood her and understood how never to bore her again.

"Did you ever think of opening a restaurant of your own?" he asked. Then he watched Silvana's reaction.

Suddenly she came alive. She tossed her hair from her lovely face and rolled her almond eyes heavenward. For too long she had kept it a secret, telling no one but Elena. Yet day by day it was coming closer to reality and she longed to speak of it, to hear how it might sound to say, "Yes, I have thought of it. I have thought of it and dreamed of it and saved for it.

And soon, very soon, I am going to do it. I will have
my own restaurant and it will be called Per Sempre
Silvana."

Then she did say it. And having begun, she found
she could not stop. For the next three hours she told
him everything, every detail of her plan. She described
the menu and her ideas for the decor. She calculated
the expenses and the rent and subtracted them from the
possible profits. She described the space she had her
eye on and explained that because it had been a restaurant, it already conformed to building and city
codes and contained much of the necessary and expensive equipment.

Fahrbrent, Warren Nachman thought, listening to
her. *She's completely fahrbrent.* His mother had taught
him the Yiddish word; it meant "on fire."

This was a new experience for Warren. The women
he'd known had no interest in his work. When he told
them of a property he was interested in buying, they
yawned. When he told them about a business he was
thinking of investing in, their eyes glazed over. But
not this one, not this golden goddess. She was as interested in his business plans as he was in hers. She was
eager to understand everything about the real estate
business, and so, after she finished telling him all her
restaurant plans, he told her all his real estate dreams.

At her door after their long evening, however, she
couldn't help cautioning him. "Everything I've told
you is a secret. No one but my daughter knows. So I
must ask you to promise—to make a fat promise—to
tell no one."

"The same is true for me, Silvana," Warren admitted. "No one else knows about the three buildings I
just told you I'm interested in buying. Or the wine
importing business I've just invested in. Only you. So
we're both obligated to honor each other's secrets."

"I would honor your secrets even if I did not tell
you mine," Silvana said sincerely.

"I know that," Warren agreed.

"How did you know?"

"Because my ears rang."

Silvana laughed.

"No, it's true. My ears ring whenever I see the genuine thing. The minute I saw you, my ears started ringing and they haven't stopped. Which is why I could tell you what I've told no one else. There's an alarm going off in my head because I've hit the jackpot, I've grabbed the brass ring, I've discovered gold. Silvana, do you understand what I'm saying?"

"Yes, you've got wax in your ears."

"Oh, kiss me, Silvana. Kiss me or I'll stand here all night."

Reluctantly Silvana closed her eyes and allowed Warren to take her into his arms. It had been an unbearably long time since she had been kissed and the sensation was not unpleasant. But it wasn't thrilling, either. Nor had she expected it to be. She knew what she felt for Warren, and it wasn't passion.

"Spend the night with me," he murmured, surprising her.

"Are you completely *pazzo*?" she whispered, reddening.

"I mean it. I want you, Silvana. I've never known it could be this intense. I want you, all of you." His hands were all over her, squeezing, pressing into her breasts, her back, her rump, her thighs. The minute she peeled one hand off of her, the other hand grabbed her. "Come back to my apartment and spend the night."

"Have you no respect?" she couldn't help blurting out. Didn't he understand what he was asking of her?

This stopped him momentarily. "Silvana, we're not children," he said.

"But I could only do that if I loved you."

"And ... do you?"

"I only just met you."

Here it was. For two weeks he had burned with desire for her. More than desire. Love. He was sure it was love and just as sure it was undying. It was a love so immediate and intense that it completely overwhelmed him. And not once had he really stopped to wonder if she felt the same. He thought only of clasping her to his heart. Now, however, here it was—the unbearable agony of unknowing. Did she? Could she? Would she? Ever?

He sighed and took her hand in his. "I'm going to tell you something and you're going to tell me I'm *pazzo* and maybe I am crazy but I must say it. I must because I'm not a patient man. When I invest in a property, I have to hold on to it, sometimes for years, before I sell it. But until I sell, I am a nervous wreck. I can't stand the waiting."

Silvana yawned.

She had warned him, but still, it cut. Nevertheless, he had no choice but to continue. "If I have to spend months, maybe years, waiting for you to make up your mind about me, I'll—I don't know—jump out of my skin, jump out of my window. Anything might happen!"

"But I don't know! What do you want of me?" she asked helplessly.

"It's what you want that I need to know."

Silvana shrugged. "I want to bring up my daughter and open my restaurant."

"Let me help you."

"With Elena?"

Warren nodded. "With Elena. With the restaurant. You could use some financial help. Silvana, let me into your life. This is very new for me, this desire to give. I used to be known as a tightwad, but you—I'd give you everything. Let me, Silvana. Let me help you!"

Warren's words were like an echo in time. She could hear Michele saying almost the same words—"Let me do this for you. Let me help you." But somehow, it had felt different then and she did not know exactly why. All she knew was that she was too exhausted to resist. And why should she? Here was a perfectly nice man who wanted to take care of her, to help her. Since the death of Michele, all she had done was struggle alone.

Wouldn't it be comforting to share the burden with someone at last? she asked herself.

But for some reason, it didn't feel comforting. The thought made her anxious, uneasy, as if she were being asked not to rest her head on Warren Nachman's shoulder, but to hand him her head, as well as her heart and her fiercely independent soul.

"I don't know!" she shouted, exasperated. "It's too much, it's too soon, and I'm too tired to think. I must go to bed." She turned her back to him and shoved her key in the lock.

Moving quickly behind her, he grasped her shoulders, stopping her from escaping quite yet. "Thank you," he whispered into the nape of her neck. "Thank you for not saying no. All right, you didn't sign on the dotted line but at least the deal is still on the table. So, I'll wait. Maybe not patiently, but I'll wait. Here." And he thrust his hand in his pocket and pulled out a wad of bills. "Do you need some money meanwhile?"

Silvana whirled around to face him. "What are you doing? Put that money away. How dare you!"

"What did I do?" he asked innocently. He thought he knew her, he thought he understood her. She was, he had thought, a no-nonsense pragmatist. So what was all this?

"You have insulted me," she said, completely baffling him. But then, she miscalculated. Intending a total rebuff, she told him, "I am not your wife. How, if we are not married, could you think I would ever accept money from you?"

The end. Finished, she thought. Instead, she was to learn that she did not know him, either. And that her scruples, far from stopping him, had actually brought him one step closer. One enormous step.

Chapter Seven

Now that Warren Nachman thought he finally understood Silvana, he moved into high gear. If he had miscalculated at first, if he had mistakenly assumed she was primarily a practical, if impecunious, businesswoman, forgetting that she was, above and beyond all that, a romantic, creative, and cultivated woman of principles, then so much the better. For now he was sure he truly understood Silvana and his admiration and respect for her only expanded as a result.

And the intensity of his courtship of her now became positively frenzied. Roses, candy, love poems, champagne and cookies arrived at her door daily. Twice a day he called her. Every night he escorted her home from work in his huge, black limousine, chatting sprightly despite her yawns of fatigue, holding her hand in his, touching her nowhere else. He was attentive, he was persistent, he was ever present. And throughout it all, he was the complete gentleman.

After a month of this, he could wait no longer.

"I want you to see where I live. Come to my house Sunday, Silvana. Come alone," he told her. "Later, I'll ask your daughter over, too, but for the first time, I want it to be just us."

"If Eduardo is free to have dinner with Elena, then I'll come," she agreed hesitantly. "If not ... well, I don't want her to spend the afternoon and the evening alone."

He wanted to say, "Doesn't that kid have any friends?" He wanted to tell Silvana, "You baby her. She's fourteen. She won't die of loneliness, believe me." But he wisely held his tongue and prayed Eduardo was free.

Silvana, of course, knew why he wanted her to come to his home. The attention he had showered upon her this past month left no doubt about his intentions. Much less clear, however, were her own feelings.

When she looked at herself in her bathroom mirror, her hands would automatically grasp her breasts. *What am I supposed to do about these?* she would ask herself. Dare she violate what, even now, she still considered Michele's private domain? Like her mother before her, the deep and passionate love she had felt for her first husband hung like a garrote of guilt around her neck, choking off all tender anticipation about a possible second husband.

But it was not only the memory of Michele that made her hesitate about Warren. Often, this intensive wooing produced in her a sense of panic, the opposite effect of Warren's aim. And though she knew this, knew his aim was to please her and shower her with attention, she felt suffocated and struggled against an urge to flee or scream or gasp for air.

"He's just ardent . . . and impatient." Eduardo, who was eager to see this union, eager to see his sister comfortably settled down with a man of wealth, encouraged her to understand Warren, to forgive Warren, to accept Warren.

"If not for yourself, then do it for Elena," he said, grimacing, not for the first time, at Silvana and Elena's wretched living quarters.

But Elena overheard him. It would have been almost impossible for her not to hear them in the one large, ugly room that had to serve as kitchen, living room, and bedroom for both mother and daughter.

"Don't do it for me," she protested emphatically. "Uh-uh. I want no part of this."

For a moment Eduardo glared with impatience at his niece, then his face softened. He sat down beside her at the rickety little kitchen table and asked tenderly, "Don't you want your mama to have someone to love her and make her happy?"

"Yes, of course, Uncle Eduardo," she agreed.

"And someday wouldn't you like to have a nice, kind stepfather—"

"Not him!" she interrupted. "Not that Warren Nachman! I hate him!"

"But why, Elena?"

"He's rich, yes. And we're so poor. Mama has had to struggle and slave, to scrimp and save while we live in this dark, tiny room with peeling walls. I know all that. And I know Warren Nachman seems nice. But it's all just an act. I see through him."

"You see through him?"

"Yes. He would never be sweet to me the way you are, Uncle Eduardo."

"Why not?"

"Because he thinks I'm a spoiled, ungrateful baby. He hates me. And I hate him."

Eduardo raised his eyes to meet Silvana's, imploring her wordlessly to say something in Warren's defense. But Silvana, leaning against the grimy little refrigerator opposite the table, remained mute. She could not find the words to persuade her daughter to soften her feelings about Warren. And after several minutes of silence, Eduardo realized that Silvana never would. She preferred it this way. And he, without asking, without ever really having been told the details, guessed why.

On the other hand, Silvana was not entirely immune to Warren's ardor for her. The flattery and attention were having an effect, even if it was mostly secret. But despite the fact that Warren had behaved like a perfect gentleman ever since the night of her outburst, she remained in turmoil about him. Was he really mean-spirited and selfish, she wondered, or was that only what Elena saw? He himself had admitted he had always been known as a tightwad, yet he had been a most generous suitor. Which was the real Warren Nachman? Bowing to pressure, she finally agreed to come to his apartment, but arrived even more confused than ever about the man himself.

It was his apartment, she knew as soon as she saw

it, that finally won her heart—not the man. Never in her life had she seen such splendor and she was unprepared for the effect it had upon her. The entry foyer alone took her breath away with its floor of black marble and its lighted center wall niche in which an imposing, seven-foot marble Roman figure welcomed with a beckoning, sculptured hand.

Silvana allowed Warren to lead her by the hand into all nine rooms and four bathrooms of the palatial apartment, gasping here at an extraordinary carpet, sighing there at a garden view from a window.

The kitchen, of course, made her flush with the heat of cooking fantasies that immediately began to simmer in her brain. Oh, the meals she could concoct on that up-to-date stove, the ingredients she could store in that huge refrigerator and those endless cabinets! There was enough counter space to prepare and roll out ten pounds of fresh pasta, with room at the fine old wooden table to sit and peel a barrel of tomatoes for the sauce.

But perhaps it was the fourth bedroom, small—small, that is, by the standards of the dimensions of the other rooms—that most won her heart.

"Elena's room!" she almost cried out loud, hardly able to keep herself from voicing her rapture. But from the moment she saw the room's sunny yellow walls with white trim and the lacy white curtains billowing cheerfully in the afternoon breeze, she knew that she wanted this most of all for her Elena ... and that Warren must never know.

There was ice, frozen solid, between Elena and Warren. Ice so cold and hard that it might never melt. *And so much the better,* Silvana thought, though she could not tell either of them why. But it was the ice, she knew, that would keep her daughter safe.

Nevertheless, she wanted Elena to have this pristine room with its very own private white and lemon-yellow bathroom, this enormous living room with a separate study off one end and a dining room and library off the other end. She wanted Elena to see her cooking in this gleaming kitchen and she wanted to see Elena proudly inviting her friends to her new "home."

Silvana wanted this, all of it, all the quiet elegance and all the rich promise of ease echoing through every one of these rooms. She wanted it for herself, and even more, she wanted it for Elena. Ever since Silvana had been the very age Elena was now, fourteen, her life had been a desperate struggle for survival. And it was that penniless, rootless desperation, she was sure, that had turned Elena into an unsmiling and resentful child. To make up for all that, Silvana was willing to do almost anything.

But she would not give up her soul. Never that. Somehow, she would have to find a way to keep Warren Nachman from enveloping her completely. It would have to be soon, she knew, but she never expected to discover the answer right here, just two hours later, in Warren Nachman's bedroom.

Warren had saved the master bedroom for last, and it was to this hushed and lushly carpeted sanctuary that he now brought her. He stood in the center of the pale aquamarine room and looked at her with such longing that she felt a sudden rush of tenderness for him. Tenderness ... and something more, something so emboldening that she immediately removed her jacket and handed it to him.

But for a moment, he could only stare at the bare flesh of her shoulders, and the teasing décolletage that the strapless dress under the jacket suddenly revealed. Then gratitude widened his smile. Grandly now, he flung open one of the many mirrored and paneled doors, revealing a closet the size of a small room, and hung her jacket on a padded hanger.

And Silvana gasped. More than any other room, the closet filled her with awe. She could not resist, and entered it.

"It's like a clothing store in here," she marveled as her fingertips grazed the rows of hanging suits, the built-in mahogany drawers with brass pulls, the folded shirts on pull-out shelves. Watching her, he was unable to remain on the outside, and entered the closet with her.

"There is a companion, just like this one, right next to this closet ... completely empty," he whispered, although they were entirely alone.

Silvana continued her inspection and said nothing.

"In every room there are empty closets just waiting for you .. and for all of your things."

Again Silvana said nothing, and turned her back to him in order to admire the racks of his well-polished shoes.

"Silvana, do you understand what I am saying to you?" While his fingertips began tracing the outline of her ear, her nape, her shoulders, her fingertips traced his shoes, his ties, his vests.

"Yes, of course," she answered brusquely, trying to hide a puzzling trembling she felt when he touched her. "You are the only person in New York who actually has too many closets."

This time he did not laugh. He pressed his lips to the bare skin of her shoulder blades. "I'm serious," he insisted, and to prove it, he slowly, carefully began to unzip the back of her dress.

She had warned him, had she not? Therefore, she would be justified in forcing a halt to his lovemaking once again, wouldn't she? Yet she hesitated. It was his longing for her that stopped her, she told herself. *It's only sympathy that I feel,* she insisted. For how was it possible that her own body could hunger for a man she did not love? Impossible, she concluded. Yet the sensation of his lips on her bare back was sending shock waves down to her belly and knees, making her want to cry out, "Take me. Take me now! Here, Warren. Here on the closet floor!"

Unaware of the extent of her arousal, of how very close she was to acquiescing, he grasped her shoulders and tried to reassure her.

"It's all right. I'm not going to touch you. I just want to see you—all of you—when I ask you to marry me." Then he continued to zip down her dress. "I have to see you. I've dreamed of it for so long. Please?"

Wordlessly she allowed him to slip off her silk dress and gently turn her around to face him.

"Let's get out of this closet," he suggested and took her hand, but she stopped him.

"No, please. I—I like it in here."

"You don't want to come with me into the bedroom?"

She shook her head no, though she saw his angular jaw tighten with anxiety. Then, in one swift motion, she dispelled his fears. Her full-length slip slid to the floor.

When next she unsnapped her bra, his eyes glanced heavenward for a moment, as if to give quick thanks for this miracle without wanting to spare more than a second from the sight of her. Then, from deep in his throat a small "oh" escaped as she unhooked her garter belt and rolled down her stockings. After that, there were several more "ohs" while she took an eternity to remove her panties, bending over demurely to hide herself.

But when she finally stood up again, head high, her body gleaming in the overhead light, he made no sound. He hardly dared to breathe. Before him he finally had his goddess in all her bare and silken splendor.

"I tried to imagine you—you know, to picture you. But nothing I could imagine ever came near the real thing. You're—" He hesitated, at a loss for words. "You're—so—gorgeous. You're regal." Now the words flowed out of him. "You're like royalty. I kneel before your magnificence."

At last he made *her* laugh. It was a hearty, throaty laugh, so infectious that he burst out laughing, too, while still kneeling before her. But once on bended knee, he discovered that he was where he'd intended to be—albeit not in a closet!

"Silvana, please, can't we go into the bedroom now?" he pleaded.

But the thought of her nakedness in that huge, open

bedroom made her self-conscious. Here, however, in this small, contained space, she felt free. Free of all embarrassment, free of all doubt. Here, she could obey the impulses of her love-starved body without censure. Slowly she closed the door behind them and lowered herself to her knees beside him on the floor.

"If you have something to ask me, Warren, do it here."

"Here?"

"Here. Because here anything is possible. *Anything!* Out there"—and she pointed her chin toward the door to the bedroom—"well, I just don't know. Now, do you understand what *I* am saying to *you*?"

Warren nodded, comprehending her meaning, and pulled a small box from his jacket pocket.

"I'm not a man of words," he said, thrusting the box at her. "Marry me, and let this ring speak for me. Marry me, Silvana. Today! Tomorrow! Better yet, yesterday!" Then he took the box from her, opened it, and slid the ring on her finger. The ring consisted of one diamond, cut square, that covered the entire first knuckle of her finger. Staring at the four-carat diamond, she mused at the surprise of its weight, or lack of it. Strange, that something so large and imposing could feel light as an ice cube—and as cold, she thought to herself. And for some reason, that reminded her of the gun Michele had given her, which she kept wrapped up in his old sweater in a drawer. There had been surprise then, too, when she felt the weight of the gun, when she first felt the cold metal in her hand. But if the gun and the ring were linked, she could not say exactly how.

Meanwhile, Warren was becoming exasperated.

"Don't you like it? I could exchange it for something else, something—I don't know—different. Whatever you want, Silvana, it's yours. Just tell me you'll marry me."

Now Silvana gazed at him. Still in his suit, he was almost comical in contrast to her nakedness, and she had to smile. Without directly answering him, she reached over and undid his tie, which he allowed with a puzzled expression that changed to a small smile of total comprehension as she undid his shirt and then his belt. Watching her undress him, he became passive before her, mesmerized by her deft and delicate movements. Finally, when he was completely undressed, he took her in his arms and heard her sigh.

"Now you have my answer," she whispered. "You have my yes. Now take all of me."

And instantly the shock of her words and of her silken flesh against his electrified him. He was unleashed. Toppling her, he raised his body over hers, his mouth desperate to kiss every inch of her. But by the time his lips reached her breasts, he was so overcome with desire that he pushed himself into her. As she cried out in surprise, he jolted her with a loud groan of shuddering release.

There they lay on the closet floor, he in rosy reverie, his sinewy, hairless thigh flung across her belly, she in silent gloom, her mind and her will locked in a struggle to halt the tears of frustration that were welling up and threatening to slide down her still inflamed cheeks.

"You were right as rain about this closet," he murmured drowsily. "Better than the bed. From now on, this will be our special love nest. Our 'closet of love,' okay?"

From now on ... and on, she thought miserably, ashamed of the hunger she'd felt and, even more, her disappointment that it hadn't been satisfied. But to Warren she nodded yes.

"After we have a little nap, let's drive over to our new restaurant. I want to have a look at the space you picked out. It sounds awfully small. I might want something bigger for us," he said and yawned.

She sat up. "Our restaurant?"

"Yours and mine," he said, patting her leg. "Now that we're going to get married, I can put up the money, can't I? But don't worry. With you doing the cooking, and me running the operation, I don't expect to lose a penny on my investment." Satisfied, he closed his eyes.

Again she felt that urge to flee or scream or gasp for air. Time raced forward in her mind and she could almost see Warren hovering over her, taking charge, "running" everything, ruining her dream. "No!" she cried. "No more owners. Just me. I want Per Sempre Silvana to be mine, just mine."

"Be practical, Silvana," he urged, his eyes wide open now. "With my help, you could have a restaurant serving one hundred meals a night. A big, shiny—"

She shook her head no, stopping him. "I don't want it big and shiny like America. I want it warm and cozy, the way it would be in the old country. I want Americans to feel as if they are in Italy when they come to Per Sempre Silvana. And I want them to taste, for the first time, the Jewish dishes of my Italian ancestors."

"You're going to serve Jewish food?"

"Italian cuisine in the style of the Jews of Rome, of Venice, of the cities and small Italian towns where they settled," she corrected. "Jews have lived in Italy for over two thousand years and—"

"It won't make money."

"Why not?"

"People aren't interested in eating Jewish food. I didn't realize you were going to serve Jewish food."

"But this isn't the heavy, bland cooking of the Middle European Jews," she said with mounting exasperation. Still, as she quickly pulled on her clothes, she continued to try to reason with him. "This is Jewish only in the sense that milk dishes and meat dishes, as in kosher cooking, are never mixed. But it is the light, Mediterranean cuisine of Italy."

"Like what?"

"Artichokes Jewish style, deep fried like the Roman Jews have always done it. And Passover chicken soup with rice and Passover matzo omelets and the spinach ravioli that we always ate at Purim. All the dishes you love. Just as I explained to you that first night."

"But now we're talking money, so I'm listening more closely. And I can't see putting up money for a restaurant no one wants."

"Just because it's Jewish? Most people won't even know—they'll just think it is Italian."

"They'll know. And they won't like it—because it's Jewish. Neither will I. I don't like the idea of a Jewish restaurant, even if it is Italian."

"You're ashamed of being a Jew, aren't you?" When he would not answer her, she stood up, towering over him. With her hands on her hips, her chin in the air, she told him, "Now I know why I was afraid to let you invest in my restaurant. But I always thought that you at least believed in my dream. Now that I know you don't, I don't feel guilty for keeping you out. I'm glad!"

"Silvana, be reasonable," he entreated. "You're an artist, not a businesswoman. I know what's best. At home, you can cook anything for me that your heart desires. But when it comes to our restaurant, you'll listen to me."

"Is that an order, signore?"

"It's a command. You're too damned independent!"

"*Sì!* Yes, I am independent. I thought you Americans like independence."

"We do," he allowed. Then he could not help adding, "But in a woman, only so far. And you've gone far enough."

"Who will stop me?"

"I will, because what does a woman who has never been in business know?"

"Only this—what is in her heart and her mind, what her life has taught her. America is a land of dreams, is it not? Soon, Warren, I will make my dream come true. I will do it even though I am only a woman. And I will do it without you!"

She stormed out of the closet and opened several mirrored closet doors, looking for the bathroom. Finally, she opened a door that led to a long foyer, near the end of which was the white and lemon-yellow room . . . Elena's room.

Again her clothes came off as she stepped into the white tiled shower. *No!* she told herself, scrubbing her scalp furiously. *I can have nothing to do with this man. Nothing!*

Rubbing herself roughly with a thick, white towel, she continued to rail against Warren until her golden skin turned red and the tingling became almost painful. It was as if, angry at Warren but even angrier at the weakness of her own flesh, she were trying to thrash the two of them with one terry-cloth towel.

Even as she pulled her clothes back on once again, she still fumed inwardly. But then she left the steamy bathroom, entered Elena's crisp, yellow room . . . and her heart melted. All the anger and insult flowed out of her as she remembered who this was all for: Elena. Elena, who had to endure living in their wretched, one-room hovel while Silvana saved every penny for her restaurant. Elena, who could never invite a friend over after school, who could never have a moment of privacy. Perhaps that was why Elena was always so miserable. Here Elena would be happy at last, home at last.

For Elena, she could not give this up. For Elena, she would have to forgive Warren . . . and, yes, marry him.

But she would not give him her restaurant. Per Sempre Silvana was hers—it was her link to her past, to her heritage, to the land she had once called home. Even more, it was a bridge to her future—hers . . . and Elena's. For if she let Eduardo lend her some money and if they succeeded, Per Sempre Silvana would be only the beginning. Night after night, dreaming what she thought was the same dream, she had not noticed its subtle changes and additions. But over time, the dream had grown, enlarging in her sleep, encroaching on her wakefulness, consuming her. Why stop at one? Why stop at two?

It had become that grand and that immense.

Now it was time to take the first step to make the dream come true. Tomorrow, she would sign the lease and tell Eduardo and ask him for his help. But before that, there was still tonight to set right. Warren, she knew, was waiting. She had given him her promise; now she would do everything in her power to honor it.

Mrs. Silvana Levi Bassani Nachman. Her name, she mused, was becoming longer and longer. She took a last look at Elena's room.

Soon! she decided. *We will be married as soon as possible.*

Elena was still up, studying at the kitchen table, when Silvana, with a curt "good night" and no kiss (to which Warren, whose ears were ringing like sirens, was too startled to complain), let herself into the apartment. She sat down on a chair beside her daughter and took a deep breath.

"Elena, I want you to be the first to know. You are going to have a father. We are going to be a real family at last."

Elena whirled around in her chair to face her mother. "Mama, you're not!!"

"*Sì*, Elena," Silvana said, nodding. "I am going to marry Mr. Nachman."

"But I hate him!"

So much the better, Silvana thought, though she could not tell her daughter why. *So much the better, my darling. For your hate will keep you safe.*

But what she said as she took Elena in her arms was, "It will be all right. You'll see, it will be *bene.*"

Chapter Eight

"What happened to the five ricotta cheesecakes I baked? Elena, go look for them. Where could they be? And then go out front. If an early customer comes, run back here and tell me," Silvana commanded, fanning herself. She was so excited and so overheated in her crisp new chef's jacket and pants that sweat slid straight down her body from her forehead to the high-arched soles of her feet.

Opening night was not turning out to be the experience she had hoped for. After months of scrubbing and painting and decorating her new restaurant, after buying the dishes and flatware and pots and light fixtures, then arranging for the phones and the electricity and the gas to be turned on, then testing recipes and practicing cooking them in large quantities, after establishing credit lines with wholesale meat and produce suppliers, hand-lettering menus and business cards, she thought she was finished. So much preparation, so many details, but finally, surely, there was nothing more to do except . . . cook!

But she was wrong.

"Look at the time!" she said to Warren, pointing with dread to the clock on the wall. "Five o'clock on opening night and everything is *pazzo*!" Though she had vowed to keep Warren away from her restaurant, here he was, sleeves rolled up, so eager to be useful that after six months of marriage she finally felt a moment of complete satisfaction with her new second husband. Even if his shoulder was hard and bony, she would risk leaning on it just this once.

But she decided not to complain to him of her physical condition, of the nausea that had been awakening her for the past week, and of her exhaustion. She knew what he would say: "I told you the strain was too much for you. Let me take over."

It would never occur to him there might be another reason for the nausea. And if he even suspected what to her was now a certainty, he would not permit her to stand for twelve hours over the hot stove, nor heave the huge pots or pound slabs of meat or bend over and slide heavy baking pans into the oven. In the hills of Umbria more than fifteen years before, she had done all this and more while carrying Elena, and no one had thought to stop her. But this was not wartime Italy; this was 1960 in New York. Now she was married to Warren Nachman and if he knew she was pregnant, he would never let her continue working. And that would be the end of Per Sempre Silvana, and the end of her dream.

Therefore, she told him only of the problems that could be fixed. "The toilet has overflowed. The laundry service still hasn't delivered my tablecloths and napkins. And the waiter I hired hasn't shown up! Elena can't handle the room alone, even if it is only twelve tables."

Warren sighed but he held himself back from gloating "I told you so" at her. Since he was convinced this fiasco would burn itself out soon enough, he could afford to behave like a gentleman. Even roll up his sleeves and help the little lady out. Soon she would be sobbing on his shoulder. Soon she would have to admit, "You were right," her baby restaurant stillborn, doomed, as he had predicted, from the moment of its conception. Soon he would hear her say, "Oh, why didn't I listen to you?" Then he would have his satisfaction.

So, he fixed the toilet and called the linen service but before he could phone the new waiter, the young man arrived, saving Warren one more useless chore.

Instead, Warren broke out a bottle of house champagne—for why, he asked himself, waste a vintage bottle on a venture that was clearly a lemon?—and gathered everyone into the dining room.

At first, Silvana resisted, saying, "I can't leave my sauce." But Eduardo had just arrived to wish her luck before going to his own job, and pulled her into the front room.

Then she said, "If a customer comes, I don't want to be seen in my whites. I have such a pretty dress—the color of *una pesca*—"

"Peach," Elena corrected.

"*Sì, pesca,*" she said again, so nervous she did not hear her daughter. "Later, I'll wear it and come out." Later, when the front room, she hoped, would be full and she could greet all her patrons like a lady. Perhaps they would even applaud! But now she had no patience to sip champagne. There was too much yet to be done.

"Silvana, sit down," Warren commanded. "It's still early. Relax for a minute. I want to make a toast."

But to Warren's chagrin, Silvana would not obey him. "Thank you, Warren, but save your toast for tonight. Gino"—she indicated to the new waiter with her chin—"the glasses, please."

Gino gave Silvana a nod to show he understood that she wanted the glasses cleared, pleasing her immensely. *At least, this one is alert,* she thought to herself. In a professional kitchen, as she well knew, few words were necessary; if everyone understood his role, only nods and gestures need permeate the quiet, smooth-running hum. This was the atmosphere she hoped to achieve with her staff in her kitchen. But the thought made her eager to return to work. "*Allora,* everybody. Thank you and now, back to your stations," she said crisply, clapping her hands once. Then, before Warren could stop her, she disappeared behind the swinging doors into the steam and sizzle of her rightful domain.

Automatically, Elena began helping Gino collect the champagne glasses. Grateful, he flashed her a smile and in that instant took notice of her for the first time. Small-boned and dark—the opposite of her mother—

with eyes like two black olives, Elena suddenly came alive before him. It was as if a heavenly light had washed over, bathing her in a warm Tuscan glow.

A living saint! he said to himself, seeing in her an exquisite sweetness that no one else—except, perhaps, her mother, Silvana—had ever glimpsed. Not just sweetness, but saintliness. Yes, saintliness! He alone was able to detect it in Elena's eyes, in her face, and in the tilt of her head. It was the look of Saint Theresa, the look of passionate devotion ... the look for which he had been searching with secret longing ever since he was eighteen. It was then that he had received a picture postcard of Bernini's "Ecstasy of Saint Theresa," and fell in love with a statue. Now he had found a living replica of his fantasy. And although he was Catholic and Elena was Jewish—her mother had emphasized this at his interview—he would forever after struggle against the impulse to call her Theresa, Catholic saint of his dreams.

Warren watched with distaste as Gino gazed at Elena, making her blush and flutter like a gawky bird in front of him. How, Warren wondered, could such a good-looking, if somewhat short, young man find such a surly creature as Elena attractive?

Elena! To Warren, his wife's only imperfection was her sulky, impossible daughter. Silvana's fierce independence, for instance, was not seen as an imperfection, merely a charming trait that ran to excess; in time, it would be controlled. He would rein it in. But Elena was like a dark mole on his wife's otherwise faultless skin.

Oh, how he yearned for a child of his own! Child of his blood, child of his brains. And of Silvana's luminous beauty. If he had a son, he would send the boy to college, then take him into the business. If he had a daughter, he would buy her pretty dresses and give her lessons in refinement and elocution. One day, she would make a good marriage and make her father proud.

But how was Silvana supposed to have any energy to give him babies when she expended every last ounce of it on her nutty restaurant? It had to fail! It had to, for his sake, and the sake of his future children.

Morosely, he poured another glass of inexpensive champagne for himself and watched the two young lovebirds circling each other.

"Want me to help you?" Elena asked Gino, already unwrapping the package of crisp white tableclothes and napkins before he could answer.

"Sure." Gino shrugged noncommittally, but there was gratitude in his eyes. As they spread a cloth over a round, eight-seater tabletop, he stole furtive glances at her. Finally, he managed to ask, "Where do you go to school?"

"East Side High."

"How old are you?"

"I'll be fifteen January seventh."

"I somehow thought you were older." He was unable to hide his surprise.

"Oh," she said, and dropped her eyes.

"No, no, it's all right. It's just that you're very mature for your age, that's all." To prove it, he reached across the table and touched her arm. "You're more serious than most girls."

Instantly Elena's drab cheeks burst into flame. He of course could not know how she hated the word "serious."

"I'm twenty-one," Gino continued rapidly, the hand that had touched hers throbbing like a heartbeat. "I'm in school, too. I wait tables to pay for cooking school. My plan is to become a great chef before I'm thirty."

"My mother also says I'm too serious."

Instantly Gino moved to her side of the table, determined to console her, but unsure if he should dare. He gave her one final stolen glance. And there, on her face, was a look of utterly sweet, utterly silent agony. He was convinced. "Did you ever hear of Saint Theresa?" he whispered.

"No," Elena admitted miserably.

"You look just like her."

Slowly, Elena lifted her eyes to meet his.

"She was exquisite. And very serious, like you, but no one complained. She became a beautiful saint."

"Jews don't believe in saints."

"I do." Then he paused before adding, his voice breaking slightly, "I believe in miracles, too."

Eduardo reluctantly returned to Silvana's restaurant at eleven o'clock that night, after the last show at Club Midnight had begun and there were no more people to seat or tips to receive. His sister had insisted he come early, but like Warren, Eduardo believed Per Sempre Silvana was doomed to fail, and he did not want to sit around all night waiting for customers to show up.

"What are you doing in this sardine can?" he had asked in shock when he first saw the tiny space Silvana had chosen for her restaurant venture. "Tell Warren he can afford to pay more rent and get you a showplace."

"Warren isn't paying the rent. He isn't paying a penny," Silvana had told him then with an odd, fierce pride in her voice that confused him.

"Is he so selfish? I always thought Warren would be more generous to you than that."

"He's generous, *sì*," Silvana had sniffed. "But with this restaurant, there were—how do you say?— strings." And she made her hands flop like a marionette's.

"What strings?"

"Oh, Eduardo, everything. He wanted a big place. And he didn't want my kind of food. He wanted to change it, to run it—and if I took his money, I'd have to say '*arrivederci*' to my dream. So, I take no money from my husband and I do it small—but I do it my way, and I do it all on my own. You think I am right, don't you?"

Eduardo sighed, secretly convinced not only that she was wrong, but that this would be her greatest fiasco. But despite his belief in the doom of her venture, he offered to lend her most of his savings. "Without strings," he said. "Because you'll need it." And because, he did not add, he would do anything—even lose money—to keep his sister happy.

But he so dreaded returning to the scene of Silvana's crushing failure that he begged Mary Catherine McGee, the new cashier at Club Midnight, to accompany him. For a month he had been meaning to ask her out. Perhaps he had even hired her because he had been pierced by the Irish lilt in her voice and the whiteness of her skin and the tomato-red of her hair. All month he felt sexual stirrings whenever he came near her. But he hesitated asking her out because of her name—Mary Catherine. Was there ever a more Catholic name, he wondered.

Now, however, her name, her religion, her crucifix on a gold chain that she wore around her neck, no longer mattered. He could not face Silvana alone.

"Do you like spaghetti, Mary Catherine?" he asked, leaning so close to her chair that he could smell her scent, a clean combination of mint and lavender.

Mary Catherine shifted in her tall chair to face him and smiled wryly. "Why are you asking, Eduardo? Are you doing a survey?"

Eduardo shrugged. "No, I'm serious. Just before you came here, my sister was the head cook. You must've heard she left to open her own restaurant."

"I heard."

"Well, tonight is the opening. And I'd like you to go with me, but on one condition." And he pointed a warning finger at her.

"What is the condition?" She understood that he was playing with her, but her intelligent blue eyes became slightly wary.

"You have to like spaghetti. Otherwise, I can't take you to my sister's. You have to be what we call *simpatico.*"

Mary Catherine gave Eduardo her wry, knowing smile again, the smile of which he was growing extremely fond. "After potatoes, and rice, and then corn, spaghetti is my all-time favorite," she told him dryly.

"Naturally." He nodded. "Potatoes first, pasta fourth. I wouldn't expect anything less from a McGee.

Okay, you pass the test. So, Mary Catherine, will you
go with me now to my sister's?"

"But I can't!" Her high, white brow wrinkled with
distress and her long, slim fingers spread in a gesture
of helplessness. "You know I have to stay until closing
and add up all the cash and receipts."

Eduardo had thought of that and had arranged for
the owner, Joey Rizzo himself, to take over.

"Listen, I offered to give your sister a little loan, a
little advice, but you know your sister," Joey had told
him the day before, and indeed, Eduardo knew just
what his boss meant about Silvana. Nevertheless, Joey
had spelled it out. "She's beautiful, she's a great cook,
but she's too independent. She wants it her way or
not at all. She's gonna take a big fall."

"I know."

Now, as Eduardo prepared to leave, Joey was more
conciliatory. "But I understand—you gotta stand by
her. Anyway, I sometimes like to take a look at the
receipts myself—you know, to keep my fingers in the
pot. So get out of here and take Mary with you—if
she'll agree to go with such a sourpuss. Smile, for
chrissakes!"

Unable to smile, he nevertheless thanked his boss
and then told Mary Catherine, "It's all arranged. Let's
get your coat." But as he helped her off her high stool,
holding her under the arm, he felt a sudden urge to
laugh. Oh, wait till Silvana saw him with this redheaded shiksa! If anyone could make his sister forget
all her own troubles, it was Mary Catherine McGee.
Now Silvana could worry about this new "trouble" on
her brother's arm—this Mary Catherine, with hair the
color of a San Marzano tomato and eyes the blue of
the Mediterranean and a name that spelled enemy.

They walked slowly as they neared Per Sempre
Silvana. Eduardo was in no rush to see his sister's tiny
restaurant filled with empty tables and silent gloom.
The October night was cool and crisp and, with Mary
Catherine beside him, he would have been happy to
walk all night or to duck into that cute and crowded

place across the street, Perfetto, and clink glasses with lovely Mary at the packed bar. Instead, of course, they walked on, until a group of loud and laughing late-nighters blocked their way.

"Excuse us, please," Eduardo said to the revelers and, holding tight to Mary's elbow, gently tried to push through and enter Per Sempre Silvana.

"Hey!" someone protested. "Can't you see this is a line? Take your place at the end of it, buddy."

"No, you don't understand." Eduardo pointed to Silvana's charming hand-painted sign. "We're just trying to go to this restaurant."

A sleek blond woman in the group nodded. "So are we. And we're finally first on line, after waiting out here for an hour."

Still uncomprehending, Eduardo repeated, "You've been waiting on line an hour to get in?"

"You should've seen the line an hour ago. It's finally thinning out," the woman told him. "Our friends made a mistake and thought this was Perfetto." She motioned with her chin to the restaurant across the street. "They both start with Per. Perfetto. Per Sempre."

"They said it was the best mistake they ever made," the first man jumped in. "We were waiting to eat over there." He, too, motioned with his chin while he warmed his chilled hands in his pockets. "Our friends said this place is better. A crowd of people overheard and rushed across the street . . . and we wound up last in line."

"Until you, that is. Ha ha." The blond woman next to him laughed.

"Oh," said Eduardo, dazed. He peeked in through the window, and although he saw it—the bustle, the crowd, the trays of food, the buoyant, rosy faces—he simply could not believe it. But suddenly the door opened and two couples filed out, enthusiastically addressing the crowd as they squeezed their way through.

"Have the ravioli!"

"You'll love it."

"Worth the wait. Incredible food!"

Eduardo looked at Mary Catherine, too stunned to speak. But she threw her arms around his neck and kissed him on the cheek, as if he were somehow responsible for this miracle.

"How glorious! I'm so happy for you and your sister," she cooed in his ear.

And then it didn't matter if he had been wrong, if he had lacked faith. Mary Catherine was in his arms, her cool, soft cheek was next to his, a bright yellow moon appeared in the almost-midnight sky . . . and he had never known a happier moment in his entire life.

Silvana turned off the gas under the now empty pots, put the leftover ingredients away, and motioned for Enrico, the dishwasher, to begin washing the last of the pots. Then she stole into the bathroom with her peach dress on her arm and locked the door behind her.

A half hour before, Elena, smiling mischievously, had called into the kitchen, "Last deuce for dinner," without mentioning that the last two diners were Eduardo and Catherine. She merely added, "It's midnight. I'm locking the door and hanging out the closed sign."

But now Silvana, staring at her face in the bathroom mirror, wondered what had happened to Eduardo. She could not wait to tell him of her triumph. Not a single empty table the entire night! And the food! Elena and Gino kept carrying messages back from the patrons— "Best meal in my life!" "I didn't know Italian food could be so elegant." "Italian-Jewish cuisine is too good to be kept such a secret. I'm going to tell everyone I know!"

She washed and dressed quickly, wishing she had the money to install a private shower room for nights such as this. Money again. Oddly, the need to earn enough money for Elena's future—and for her own— weighed just as heavily upon her now as ever. For despite her marriage to the enormously wealthy Warren Nachman, Silvana did not feel rich. Or safe. Would she ever, she wondered, suddenly exhausted.

In her condition, fourteen hours of standing, stirring, slicing, sautéing, simmering, bending, and lifting took a toll on her legs and her back; they ached with the strain.

Her face, however, was magnificent. Here, no shadow, no sag, no strain, was visible. All was smooth, taut, unblemished. An apricot glow, matching the color of her dress, rose high on her prominent cheekbones. And her blond hair gleamed beneath the overhead light.

Silvana smiled at her reflection in the mirror and spoke to it. "They thought you couldn't do it. Warren, Elena, and yes, even Eduardo. But you did! Now squeeze your swollen feet into your high heels and go out there and let Warren make his toast. Now you've earned it."

Patting her hair, her right hand stopped in midair. Slowly, it traveled down from her shoulder to her breast and finally rested on her deceptively flat belly. Only she knew what lay hidden, secretly living and growing, inside her. Soon, the others would have to be told. Soon, she would no longer be able to hide it. But by then, they would not be able to stop her.

"*Sì*, soon." She nodded at the mirror. "But not tonight. Forgive me, my darling one, but tonight is for me."

Chapter Nine

There were dozens of pages of Eduardo's writing on his desk—short stories, single sentences, even one book-length manuscript—but Mary Catherine did not dare to do more than merely peek at them. The only time her father had ever slapped her was when he caught her reading the pages of poems on his desk that he wrote every night after work. Here in Eduardo Levi's apartment for the first time, she was not about to risk another stinging slap. Yet she wondered why Eduardo had never told her that he was a writer. She had thought she could trust him. She had thought he trusted her. She had thought this relationship was distinctly different from the others she had known. Now she was not so sure.

It had seemed different—and intoxicating—from the very beginning. Late that first night at his sister's restaurant, Eduardo had become quite tipsy and whispered, "I think I love you, Mary Catherine McGee. I think I hired you because I fell in love with you. I think we'll have to get married."

"Eduardo, I think you think too much." She was amused, perhaps even entranced. Yet not for one minute was she going to take him seriously. So she teased him lightly and attempted to change the subject. But to her surprise, he insisted.

"No, I don't think; I know. I know I'm in love with you. And I know, as sure as the sun rises, that we—you, Mary Catherine, and I—will be married. I don't just hope it, or wish it or think it ... I know it, Mary Catherine. I know it!"

He said this with such intensity, such seriousness,

that although she laughed, although she scoffed, and although she would not admit it, even to herself, she secretly believed him.

After that, they had been on three dates, necking and eating and talking all night. He said she now knew every detail of his life. But he had not told her about the writing. And discovering that he had kept this secret from her was, in its own way, a kind of a slap in her face, after all.

The sound of ice cubes tinkling against glass preceded Eduardo into the room. He carried the drinks on a tray, along with a small bowl of giant green Sicilian olives. One was already in his mouth, held between his teeth, his playful offering to her. But when he got close enough for her to bite into the exposed half that he was thrusting at her, she turned away from him.

"What's wrong?" he asked, placing the uneaten olive on the tray. He had known her only a short time—less than a month—but he understood her well enough to see that something had made her angry. Never before had she turned away from him. Indeed, despite the fact that they had not even been to bed yet, this he could say without hesitation: she was the warmest, most responsive woman he had ever known.

But now she stood with her back to him and when he pressed up behind her and began nuzzling her ear, she shook him off.

He should not have pressed his body so close to hers. When mere thoughts of her could arouse his most intense passions, the actual touch of her lithe body became almost uncontrollable. How he wanted to take her right now, right there, standing up in the middle of his living room! Yet she wasn't even speaking to him. And soon, they would have to leave for the restaurant across town where he had made an eight-thirty reservation. Monday was their day off and they had arranged to have a drink at his apartment before going out to dinner. Afterward, he had hoped that they would return here and finally, ecstatically, make love. But now she would not even look at him.

Sipping at his drink, he waited, watching her stand at the window with her back to him, a long, slim stalk in a leaf-green knit sheath topped by a cascade of cayenne curls. He ached to grab a fistful of that hair, making her head snap back, exposing her perfectly white neck. Then, like a vampire, he could devour her until he made her moan, breathless, bloodless, "I'm yours . . . for eternity!" Instead, he continued to sit on the sofa . . . and wait.

Finally, she turned from the window and looked straight at him, her azure eyes like blue ice. "Why did you lie to me?"

"I have never lied to you," he answered calmly, but his heart raced with both relief and fear. It was a relief that she thought he had lied to her because he knew he had never been more truthful, more open with any-one, and all he had to do was convince her she was mistaken. But it was alarming to see her eyes turn to hard, blue ice. Alarming . . . and unbearable. He had to go to her and melt the ice in her eyes! But she thrust out her hand to stop him. Then she pointed it toward the desk.

"You're a writer. Why did you lie to me?"

Again, Eduardo felt a rush of relief, and because it was not tinged with fear, he even managed a small smile. Despite herself, that rare smile on his usually somber face warmed her, touched her. This time she did not try to stop him when he came to her side at the desk and took her hand.

"I never lied to you—I just didn't tell you. I was going to—tonight."

"You said I knew everything about you. Everything. That was a lie." Her eyes were turning to ice again.

"You do know everything about me. You're free to read any of this"—he gestured toward the desk—"and if you do, you'll see it's all stuff I've told you. My writing is extremely autobiographical."

This surprised her. "I can read it?"

"All of it. It's an homage to my whole family before the war, but especially to my mother and brother, may they rest in peace. They died in a German camp."

Like a child given free rein in a candy store, her eager arms gobbled up piles of pages. Then she glanced at him once more, suddenly unsure he had really meant what he had said.

"I am going to read everything I have in my hands," she announced, daring him to stop her. "Right now."

"Okay," he said, shrugging. "I'll cancel our reservation and run out and buy us some steaks. While you read, I'll cook."

"You can cook?"

"I can broil a steak, yes."

"That's something else you didn't tell me." But she was smiling as she said it. Nevertheless, he took her face in his hands and scrutinized it with his dark, sad eyes for some time before he spoke. When he did, he won her heart all over again.

"Look, Mary Catherine, we have known each other only a month. We still have much to discover about each other. I hope that when we're old and hobbling around on canes and our children are all grown up"— he paused to watch the ice in her eyes melt into tears—"we'll still be discovering new things about each other. But you now know all the essentials about me. All. And everything I've told you is true. Including what I said to you that first night."

"You remember what you said?"

"Every word."

"I thought you were drunk," she admitted tearily. "I thought you'd forgotten. And part of me," she suddenly could not help confessing, "was glad!"

When he looked at her, puzzled, she repeated it again. "Yes, glad. Because then I didn't have to trust you. I could think of you as just another guy with a 'line.' As long as I believed I really couldn't trust you, I was safe."

"Safe from what?"

"From being hurt!" she sobbed. "So don't say those words unless you mean them . . . because, dammit, I'll believe you."

"I love you."

"I'm warning you!"

"We're going to get married and have kids and grow old together."

"We're not the same religion."

"You'll read every word I write and I'll grill all the steaks. You'll go to church, I'll attend synagogue, and our children will decide for themselves. Settled?"

Through her tears, she tried to protest one more time. "We've never even made love!"

"You have something there," he agreed and removed the pages from her hands, one by one, until her arms were free to hold him. "First things first."

What was strangest to Mary Catherine McGee as she stood in the center of Eduardo's living room was that she felt no shame. Always before, there had been shame. At the first instant of sexual arousal, shame would wash over her, scrubbing her clean of all excitement. Then, lifeless as a bar of soap, she would endure what had been begun, but without pleasure, with only her shame.

This time it was different. She was different. As Eduardo clasped a fistful of her hair, pulling her head back, exposing her neck, her fingers weaved through his hair, urging his head down to her lips, down to her neck, down to the erect nipples of her swelling breasts.

She was naked and the window shutters had not been closed and she was holding her breasts with her own hands for Eduardo to kiss and to bite . . . and she felt no shame. She moaned with pleasure, and hearing her own moans, she felt no shame.

How had her clothes come off? And his? After he had taken the papers from her, he had shoved his body roughly against hers and held her so tightly enfolded in his arms that she had neither the breath nor the room to resist. She could remember feeling as if the ground had given way—a kind of erotic earthquake—as his hands kneaded her buttocks, sending shock waves to her groin. And she remembered the feel, the taste of his tongue, wet and taut and salty from the olives, as he drove it into her mouth. But from then to now, perhaps some fifteen minutes, all was blank. There, in the center of the room, in the center of his arms, she had lost her shame, lost her memory, lost her consciousness. And for the first time existed entirely in the realm of pleasure.

Nevertheless, it was not difficult to surmise, from the clothes strewn about them on the floor, that they had undressed themselves—or each other—right there, and that was how they had become naked.

And then she no longer cared how her clothes had come off, only that they were off, leaving her body free to be kissed and clutched and stroked ... and finally, ecstatically, to be joined with his.

He had her. He had her, at last. He had her exactly as he had fantasized having her. Or was this still a fantasy? He did not know. All he knew, as he slowly pulsed in and out of her, standing face-to-face, a mass of her hair in his hand, was that one minute she was real, the next, a dream.

Holding her in his short, powerful arms, he bent her back, back, farther, farther, and entered her deeper, faster. He could hear her, he could feel her, he could see her, taste her, smell her. Still, she was like a dream, like an imaginary desire.

"Are you real?" he cried out, wild with passion. "Will you be here when I wake up. Will you? Will you?"

"Always, Eduardo. Always."

"Oh, Mary, I love you. Mary, be here! Oh, be—here—with—me!"

"For all eternity," she promised, gripping his shuddering shoulders. "Feel me. I am real! And this is really happening. Yes, to me. It's happening to me. Too. Oh, dear God in heaven, yes, to me!"

He could hardly hold her as she pulsed and undulated beneath him. Her back was only inches from the floor. Still, he held on, panting and exhausted, until she finally opened her azure eyes and smiled.

"I didn't know this about you, either," she whispered breathily as she stroked him between his legs. "It was a rather huge discovery."

"Amen," he sighed, and lowered her to the floor. Then he stretched out beside her, at peace for perhaps the first time in his life.

An hour later Mary Catherine curled up on Eduardo's bed and began reading his book-length manuscript while Eduardo clattered in the kitchen, the aroma of grilled steaks and onions floating through the apartment.

"Supper's ready!" he called to her and set a newly bought loaf of bread on the small dining table. On a high closet shelf he found two unmatched wineglasses, washed them, and set them, along with a bottle of Rubesco, on the table, which, for some reason, still looked bare. The plates! The forks! The napkins! Unaccustomed to entertaining, he kept forgetting the details. Or perhaps he was simply nervous. Mary Catherine had been reading for over an hour. Once, he had gone to the doorway, but she waved him away. Now that the food was ready, she would have to come out and talk to him. And tell him what he both yearned and dreaded hearing—what she thought of his writing.

When he had completed the table setting, he called to her again, "*Andiamo.* Let's go! Or the steak will get cold." But still there was no answer.

The apartment was small and it took Eduardo no more than fifteen steps to go from the kitchen to the bedroom doorway. It would have taken him another seven steps to reach the bed, where Mary Catherine sat propped by pillows, reading, but he stopped at the doorway.

"Supper's ready," he said again. "Didn't you hear me call you?"

At last, she looked up. Then, slowly, her arms reached out for him, but he shook his head no. "First tell me, what did you think of the book?"

Her expression was so serious that panic seized him. No longer did he yearn to know her opinion; quite the opposite, in fact. He did not want to hear it. The expression on her face told him all he needed to know.

He turned on his heels, went back to the table, and poured a glass of wine for himself.

Well, now you know, he told himself with finality. *Count yourself lucky. Otherwise, you could have wasted the rest of your life pouring your heart out on paper. She just saved you the effort. With one look, she saved you from making a greater fool of yourself than you already are.*

He did not hear her come up behind him and when he felt her arms clasp his neck, he jumped, startled. Neither her laughter nor her kisses could console him, and the lavender scent of her skin, which always drove him wild, now almost sickened him. Everything was suddenly distasteful to him—the platter of steak and sizzling onions, the desk in the far corner of the room with all his useless stories piled on it ... and even Mary Catherine.

He unclasped her arms from his neck and tried to pull away, but she clung to him, her cheek pressed to his.

"I loved it," he thought he heard her whisper, and his irritation only mounted. He knew she loved the sex they had shared; she did not have to tell him again, as if that would make up for his failure as a writer. As if anything could.

"I was there, in Rome when the widowed mother and her son were deported and killed, and then in the hills of Umbria. I was there with the men and the brave, romantic leader of the partisans. What was his name again?"

Automatically he answered, "Michele."

"Yes, Michele. You brought me right there, into the hills, into the fighting, and I didn't want to eat, I didn't want to stop reading—"

"*Allora,*" he said, returning to his first language because he was so excited. "*È vero?* Then it's true? You really liked it?"

"No, I didn't like it," she said, taking a chair beside him. She was wearing his old bathrobe with the sleeves rolled up to her elbows. Carefully, she served herself from the platter, keeping him in agonized suspense while she spread the napkin over her lap, cut the meat into eight little squares, stabbed one, and brought it to her mouth.

"So you didn't like it?" He knew she was playing with him, teasing him; he was sure of it. Nevertheless, he had to ask.

Chewing with excruciating slowness, she shook her head no. Finally, she swallowed and broke into a huge smile.

"I told you. I didn't like it. I *loved* it."

"You loved it," he repeated, watching her meticulously chew up all eight little squares of steak, but now he was grinning. "You loved it," he said again, as if only by saying the words out loud could he begin to believe them.

"The steak was great," she sighed, dabbing at the corners of her mischievous smile. "But your book was better. And that's saying a lot—because the steak was really, really delicious and I was really, really famished." Then she rose from the table, neatly replacing her chair.

Eduardo caught a glimpse of her white breast beneath the oversize robe as she stood up, and felt a stab of desire so sharp that it made him wince. Just a short time before, he had thought he could never want anyone more than he had wanted her. Now he knew that this time his passion was even deeper, even more acute. This time, he knew it was real. He reached for her bare thigh but she pulled away.

"I'm afraid you'll have to excuse me. I want to get back to your book." Turning to him as she reached the bedroom doorway, she said, "My father was a poet. But his was a small talent compared to yours. Because of him, however, I admire people with talent. And yours is major. I'm impressed. Eduardo, I'm so impressed."

In the space of two heartbeats, he was beside her. For the second time that night he removed his manuscript pages from her hands.

"You can read later. I have something huge to discuss with you and it can't wait."

"Your talent?"

He pulled off the shirt and pants he'd worn to the store.

"See for yourself."

"I see," she said, "that you're a man of many talents."

"The more, the merrier."

"Let's count them."

"I can grill a great steak," he offered as he undid her robe.

"And you can write."

"I have another talent—" he murmured and then his mouth was on her white breast at last.

"I forget. What was it?"

"Here, let me show you."

"Ah, yes," she sighed, "now I remember. Huge."

Chapter Ten

"You don't want that striped bass." Sloane Harding, a stranger to Silvana, nevertheless gestured to the striped gray-blue ten-pounder laid out on a bed of shaved ice, and pointed his thumb downward.

"And why don't I want this one?" Silvana asked, her arms crossing her chest and her chin pointing out at this rude stranger who dared tell her her business. "I think I do."

Sloane Harding shook his head no. "Look, lady, they're all premium bass. But the one next to it is brighter, shinier. See its eyes? I should know. I'm in the fish business. I have a fleet of fishing boats out in Montauk and I sell to these guys. All this fish is mine," he said proudly, extending his arm to encompass several rows of tables packed with ice and layered with fish.

"So you think I don't know what I'm doing?"

"I didn't say that." Sloane Harding looked like he was growing sorry he had ever begun this. He was not even sure why he had. All he knew was that he was killing some time, waiting for Henry Wade to bring him a check. Henry liked to pay as soon as he received Sloane Harding's shipment. Because of this, Sloane often personally accompanied his order to the downtown fish market. To be paid immediately—and in person—was worth the predawn trip. He was an early riser anyway.

"My mama, may she rest in peace"—Silvana was fuming, her hands balled into fists at her hip—"taught me how to pick a good fish. And let me tell you something, signore, you would never say that my mama did not know what she was doing. Because my mama was a fish expert, she was a—"

It was then that their eyes met. And held. It was then that they both really noticed each other, really looked into each other's eyes. And after that, everything stopped and began again. Everything was new, as if the sun had broken through after a rainstorm. Or as if a new day had begun, a new day for the both of them.

"I'm Sloane Harding." He held his hand out to her. "I'm sorry. It was presumptuous of me to barge in like that and—"

"No, no!" she protested. "You were right. This one is fresher. I suppose I am a little—how do you say— *nervosa*? I have a new restaurant, you see, and I want so much for everything to be—um—*perfetto*—" Looking into his eyes, she could not remember the English word for anything! Looking into his eyes, she could not think at all, only feel. And this feeling had a name—Sloane Harding. She shook his hand. "I am Silvana Levi Bassani Nachman."

"I know what you mean. I feel that way about my business, too," he agreed. "I want everything to be perfect. Everyone in Montauk calls me 'Mr. Perfectionist' behind my back."

Silvana laughed. "And in my kitchen they call me Signora Perfetta!"

Their hands were still joined. Awkwardly—and with secret reluctance—they pulled apart just as Henry Wade arrived with Sloane's check. Almost immediately, Henry went back to his office.

Sloane patted his wallet, satisfied. "I have to pay my men when I get back to Montauk this afternoon. But until then, I'm a rich man. So how about letting my buy you"—he looked at his watch—"breakfast?"

She had been up since dawn and had only grabbed a quick espresso before coming here to the market; now she was starving. But she knew that even if she had been full, she would have nodded yes just the same. For it was not the breakfast; it was him. It had been so long since she had felt like this . . . she could not let him go quite yet.

They sat opposite each other at a nearby coffee shop, wolfing down eggs and toast and marmalade and muffins and coffee, laughing and talking as if they had known each other for years. Yet each time their eyes met, all conversation would stop. And again everything would begin anew, as if another new day had dawned, only fresher, warmer, and even brighter than before.

"So, tell me about Italy. And tell me about your restaurant. And tell me how you became a restaurateur and chef. And how long have you been married?"

"Which do you want to know first?" She knew he had seen her diamond ring, just as she had noticed the gold band on his left hand. Even more, he could see that she was pregnant. Nothing was hidden. She just hoped he would not ask her to talk about it.

"Tell me about your restaurant." Even a lifetime did not seem long enough to find out all he wanted to know about her. Which was odd, considering her condition. And her marital status. And his, for that matter. Yet when their eyes locked, it did not feel odd at all. It felt exhilarating and magical. He was attracted to a married, pregnant woman with a strong Italian accent. *Am I losing my mind?* he wondered. *No,* he concluded, *only my heart.* "Tell me how you got started."

She sighed, relieved, and told him every detail about Per Sempre Silvana, from the dream she had on the ship crossing the ocean to its successful outcome today. "It took many long years, and the work is hard, but now my dream is a reality . . . and it is mine."

"Yes, that's the best, isn't it, when you can achieve your dream?" He told her he, too, had had a dream. "It's in Montauk." He told her all about the old former whaling village at the southern tip of Long Island where he had been born and raised, and his fishing boats and the business he had slowly been building into an empire. And then, in less than an hour, it was over. They both felt their lives pressing in on them.

"You must get back to your Montauk and I—"

"And you must get back to your kitchen," he said, finishing her sentence. He took her hand. "When is the baby due?" It seemed like the most natural question in the world.

"Soon. Two and a half months." Somehow, holding his hand despite being married and pregnant did not seem wrong. It, too, seemed utterly natural . . . and right.

"I'll never see you again, will I?"

She shook her head no.

"And if I am in Manhattan, I must never drop in at Per Sempre Silvana for your famous Jewish artichokes . . . or just to hold your hand like this?"

"Never," she sadly agreed.

"And I must never phone you or write." It was not a question; it was a statement. He did not have to ask; he understood the situation.

She withdrew her hand and placed it on her belly. "We meet with—how do you say—bad timing?"

He fingered his wedding band and nodded. "Still, I wouldn't have missed it for the world."

She had not expected him to say that. And she had not expected his words to have quite such an impact. She heard them echo inside her hauntingly.

"*Grazie,*" she thanked him and rose from her chair. Again their eyes locked but this time there was no new beginning. This time it was the end. "*Arrivederci,* Sloane Harding. I like you too much and I must say good-bye."

He watched her leave and vowed that he would never forget her, but in time, he did. For he believed he would not ever see her again.

When Silvana arrived at Per Sempre Silvana, she heard shouts coming from the kitchen and as she hurried into the fracas, Sloane Harding was erased from her mind. She would not recall him again for some time . . . for years, in fact.

It was Gino who was shouting. "Dammit, I said faster, and I mean it. Wash those dishes now, or you're fired!" He shoved Enrico the dishwasher with all his might. Enrico reeled and half fell against the sink.

Immediately Silvana stepped in. She took Gino by the elbow and led him into the empty front room. "In my restaurant we do not scream and we do not put hands on anyone."

"He's slow and lazy," Gino insisted.

"Enrico is a good dishwasher. I like him. And in my restaurant, I do the firing."

Gino shrugged sulkily. "You're the boss."

"*Sì*," Silvana stonily agreed. "I am the boss."

This was not the first time Gino had had a violent rage. But this time, she almost did not mind. For it made her forget Sloane Harding almost immediately and forced her back where she belonged—here in her kitchen. A moment later she felt her baby kicking inside her and silently she cooed to it—*Shh*, cara mia, *Mama is here. Do not worry, Mama is here.*

Sloane Harding became less than a memory, more like an unrecalled dream.

Chapter Eleven

Anna Michela Levi Bassani Nachman was born on May 7, 1961, after three rapid hours of labor. Which made her arrival a double blessing, said Silvana. "She tried to make it easy because she knew her mother has to get back to work right away."

"What are you doing, Silvana?" everyone said. "Let Warren get someone to take over the restaurant permanently."

"Stay home with your baby."

"For the sake of your new child."

"For the sake of your husband."

Privately, they whispered, "It's not like she has to work. Warren must have millions. So what drives her?"

And oh, Silvana was tempted! Cradling the newborn Anna Michela in her arms, surrounded by bouquets of flowers and crisply uniformed nurses, Silvana was tempted to sink back on her hospital bed and extend her stay another seven days. Just to lie there like a lazy queen. To do nothing at all but rub cocoa butter on her stretch marks and her brown, erect nipples. To wait until she began leaking pale blue milk from her near-bursting breasts, the signal that it was time to feed Anna Michela again. Then, perhaps, to nap for an hour until the whole delightful process could begin all over again.

It was tempting, but, of course, impossible. Because Silvana's other infant needed her, too. Not Anna Michela, but Per Sempre Silvana, the newly born restaurant that Silvana first conceived six years before on the windy deck of the *Christoforo Colombo,* the ship that brought her to America. Five and a half years of gestation. And finally, six months ago, a birth! But the fledgling enterprise needed her. Already, after only two weeks without her, it was beginning to languish.

Preparing in advance for her delivery and hospital stay, Silvana had put Gino in charge of the kitchen, entrusting him with her secret recipes of the Jews of Italy. And although she had trained him, tested him, and pronounced him ready to take over for her, business had fallen off when her chic, status-conscious clientele learned she was not there.

How she had attracted such a clientele was a mystery. Silvana suspected that it all began that first night. Word spread rapidly and within a month limousines were lined up along the block while industrialists, movie stars, producers, publishers, and models dined at the twelve tables that had become the most coveted reserved seats in the city.

All night long the phone rang with eager callers demanding reservations. When asked, "How did you hear of us?" the answer was always the same: by word of mouth or from newspaper gossip column items about famous people seen dining there.

Not one serious restaurant review had been printed during the six months of Per Sempre Silvana's astonishing popularity and success. Which was not surprising. In the New York of 1961, Italian restaurants, even one serving the novel cuisine of Italian Jews, were considered a poor culinary cousin to French fare ... and, consequently, were ignored. Still, they all called.

"I am so sorry, but we have no openings for a month," Elena would tell them, flicking through the reservations book.

"Not for a month? All right then, one month from tonight," they would say, sometimes ebulliently adding—"At least, we're in. Thank God for that!"—prizing their reservations as if they were the very last tickets on the very last train to paradise.

"So you see," Silvana explained to her distraught husband, "I must return or business will dry up—just like these!" And she pressed her hands to her breasts, which were bound up in tight bandages now that she was weaning Anna Michela to the bottle.

"A nanny is not the same as a real mother," Warren argued weakly after Silvana hired Mrs. Milgrim, a short Jewish widow, to care for their child. He argued without force because in the year that he and Silvana had been wed, he had come to know his wife, at last. And what he had formerly called her "adorable streak of independence," he now bitterly described as her "damned, obdurate, absolutely inflexible *indipendenza!*"

"She has a will of her own and she won't bend to mine, even though I'm her husband," he finally complained to Eduardo, emptying a glass of aged scotch with alarming speed.

"You knew she was independent."

"Yes, but I thought this restaurant business would fizzle and then she'd stay home and have babies."

"To tell you the truth, so did I," Eduardo admitted. "But aren't you happy for her?"

"Why should I be happy? If she's not at the restaurant, she's playing with the baby. Or she's arguing with Elena about her school grades or about Gino. By the time I get to see her, she can't keep her eyes open."

Eduardo could hear squeals of laughter coming from the kitchen where all the females—Silvana, Elena, Mrs. Milgrim, baby Anna Michela ... and Mary Catherine—had congregated. Part of him longed to sneak up behind Mary Catherine and carry her away from that bubbling epicenter of laughter and soup pots. To steal with her down the long foyer to one of the empty bedrooms. The mere sound of her laughter made him ache to have her alone, naked and flushed, beside him. It has been that way for the past six months; this, he now knew, was no fantasy. It was real and it was permanent. He had even written a short story about his feelings for Mary Catherine, "Passion for a Catholic with Red Hair." When she read it late the night before, she agreed to be his wife.

"Maybe the answer is to have another child, and another, as quickly as possible," said Warren, thinking out loud. "If I can keep Silvana so busy having babies, she'll have no choice but to give the restaurant up. What do you think, Eduardo?"

Eduardo shrugged. "I can't really say."

"Well, I think I'm right. Get Silvana pregnant—and keep her pregnant."

Eduardo did not like the sound of this. Carefully, he asked, "What if Silvana won't cooperate?"

Ignoring Eduardo, Warren refilled his glass and stared into it as if, in that amber liquid, a sign, an omen had been unveiled, like the portent tea leaves are said to reveal. When he finally spoke, it was in the hushed tone of a whispered secret.

"Now that we have Mrs. Milgrim, maybe we'll take a trip, a vacation. Just Silvana and me. I own a vineyard in Italy, did you know that?"

Half listening, Eduardo shook his head no, waiting to hear the trill of Mary Catherine's laughter again. But it was Silvana's voice, low and throaty, that broke into his reverie, calling the family to Sabbath dinner. "Warren! Eduardo! Come sit down. Everyone, *mangia!*"

As the women carried in the first course, two steaming bowls of Silvana's cauliflower and bread soup—one of the many wartime recipes she learned from Italian peasants—Eduardo and Warren assembled at the baronial chestnut table.

Like Gino's adoration of Elena, Mary Catherine had become the object of Elena's idealized worship. To Elena, Mary Catherine was the angelic embodiment of all that Elena could never be—tall and stunning, cheerful and witty ... and the passionate lover of her handsome uncle, Eduardo. Waiting nervously to see where Mary Catherine sat, Elena made a noisy spectacle, knocking against two chairs in her scramble to secure a place beside her. In her desperation to sit as far from Warren—and as close to Mary Catherine as possible—Elena's awkward movements drew everyone's attention to her.

"These chairs cost me close to a thousand apiece,

Elena," Warren joked with a tight jaw. "At the rate you're going, I'll be bankrupt by the end of the meal!"

Then Eduardo said, "Aren't you going to let me sit next to my own fiancée?"

"No, Eduardo! What are you saying? You are engaged?" Silvana cried. Then she turned to Mary Catherine, whom she had welcomed into her heart after only a moment of shocked hesitation ever since that first night. "It is true? We're going to have a wedding?"

Laughing, Mary Catherine motioned to Eduardo to take the empty chair on the other side of her and pressed Elena's shoulder to keep her seated where she was. Grateful, Elena gave her a worshipful smile.

"Yes, it's true. I'm afraid you're going to have a shiksa in the family."

"Not for long," said Eduardo.

"I'm converting to Judaism before we marry."

"I didn't ask her to—"

"I want to," Mary Catherine interjected.

At this news, Warren's glum expression turned positively sour. While everyone kissed and hugged the betrothed couple, Warren stared into his drink, thinking, *He didn't even have to ask her. She wanted to . . . for him.* He wondered why Eduardo deserved someone so sweet and pliant. *So devoted, so adorable!* Didn't he deserve a sweet wife, too?

"Warren, why are you sitting there? Aren't you happy for them? Come kiss Mary Catherine before the soup gets cold," Silvana implored him, baby Anna Michela in her arms.

But Warren remained seated. An idea had been forming in his mind. By the time he emptied the last of the scotch in his glass, he was decided. Since Silvana would not come with him into their love closet anymore, he had to get her away. Far away from her damned restaurant, from her glowering daughter . . . and even far from their new baby, Anna Michela. If he could get Silvana off alone with him, he would find a way to possess her again. Four more weeks, and she would be able to have sex again. And more babies.

He rose and tapped at his glass with a spoon to get everyone's attention.

"Congratulations, Eduardo and Mary Catherine. From my heart, I wish you what you already possess—happiness."

Everyone clapped but Warren remained standing. When they quieted down, he continued, "I, too, have a joyous announcement. Silvana, come stand here beside me."

Regretfully, Silvana gave the baby to Mrs. Milgrim and went to Warren's side, watching him with curiosity. But Warren gave her no hint of what he was about to say. He simply—and dramatically—made his announcement.

"I am taking Silvana back to Italy. For a second honeymoon. We leave next month and we'll go wherever you want"—he turned to his wife—"to revisit all your memories. You'll show me where you lived in Rome and where—"

"No!" Silvana gasped, sinking into a chair.

"Now, now, Silvana, it's going to be just fine," he assured her, chuckling as he patted her hand. Having anticipated his wife's reaction, he was confident he could quickly calm her fears. "We'll get help for Gino in the restaurant. And Mrs. Milgrim will take very good care of Anna Michela. And—"

"Never, never, never!"

"And before you know it," Warren calmly continued, ignoring her outburst, "you'll be standing right here again, telling everyone what a terrific trip you had, visiting the sights and the memories of your youth."

It was not Warren to whom Silvana turned, but Eduardo, her brother. Beseeching him with wild and terrified eyes, she reminded Eduardo of some beautiful, pitiful animal—a deer, perhaps—caught by a hunter's rifle, its muzzle aiming straight for her heart. Eduardo knew she looked to him to help her, save her, but before he could react, she bolted, rising up from her thousand-dollar chair like a submerged swimmer bursting through the surface of the water, flailing and gulping for air. Then she fled, her eyes still hunted, terrified, leaving behind in the stunned silence of the room the echo of her throaty, tormented apologies, "*Mi dispiace,* I'm sorry, I'm sorry. I cannot bear it. No! I cannot. But I beg you, forgive me. Please forgive me!"

Silvana sat all alone at the huge country table in the kitchen, trying to regain control of her emotions. Blaming herself in the tone of an exasperated parent, she wondered with annoyance, *Why are you behaving like this? Can't you see he's only trying to be kind? So why can't you say yes and give your husband a big kiss?*

As if she did not know the answer. But it was the answer—not the question—that caused the pain. For to answer herself, she had to admit her feelings, and she had not done that for some time . . . in order to avoid the pain. Now Warren gave her no choice.

How could he know the agony he had caused her by wanting to take her back to the country of her burning memories, the place she had once called home? He could not know because she had told him nothing . . . and she never would. All he knew were the bare facts: that she was born in Rome; that her mother Anna and her brother Raffaelle were deported to a concentration camp where they had died; that she spent the war in the hills and married the partisan leader Michele Bassani, who was killed before their child, Elena, was born.

"Such an interesting life," Warren had often told her. "So rich, so full."

"Yes," she would nod agreeably, with hardly a whisper of bitterness on her breath, "such an interesting life."

"Then why won't you talk about it?"

"Because, *caro,* dear Warren, it is better, is it not, to look to the future than to dwell in the past. I am happy when I think of the future."

She was not lying—not to him, not even to herself. It was as if another Silvana, separate and remote, had

lived her past while she went on to live her future.
This other Silvana held all her secrets, and all her
memories. Only in this way, unburdened of her sorrow
and her searing pain, could the present Silvana live
and laugh ... and go forward. The trick was never to
allow the other Silvana to catch up.

Now Warren had the ludicrous idea of bringing
Silvana back to Italy. *Italia!* Where the other Silvana
dwelled. *Italia!* The journey back to her worst
nightmares.

Everyone thought she should go back. No one understood why she avoided the old country. Even Eduardo had once wanted to make a trip back to Italy
and had gingerly asked Silvana if she might like to
accompany him.

"Back there," she told Eduardo, speaking of her
past, speaking of her country, her city, and her youth,
"there is only betrayal. Nothing else. I will never go
back. Never ask me again. Never!"

Now it was Warren who had asked her. No, not
asked; announced. And here he was, entering the
kitchen, sitting down at the table opposite her, glowering at her. He, who wanted to lead her back to all
her sorrow.

"Silvana, why are you making such a *mishegoss* over
this? I'm sick and tired of your refusals. First you
refuse me in bed. Now you refuse to go on vacation.
What is it this time?" he asked with a sneer. "The
restaurant?" He prayed she would not say yes, but
she did. She nodded her beautiful head up and down.

"*Sì*, the restaurant," she eagerly agreed, grasping
hold of the excuse he threw out to her as if it were a
life raft. "I can't. It is too soon to leave it."

"And what about me?"

"You, Warren?"

"Me! Yes, me!"

"We'll go ... somewhere, I promise. Just don't
push, Warren. And don't shout. Please, just be
patient."

"I warned you, I'm not a patient man. You're my

wife. You're supposed to give me sex. Instead you say, 'Wait.' "

"Because you're so fierce in bed. You always rush, rush. And even though I've asked you, begged you to wait for me, to go slow, you never do."

"Why should I? You owe me! Why should I have to wait for it? And why can't I just take you away with me?"

"You are a father now. You have responsibilities."

Suddenly Warren buried his face in his hands. "Too many responsibilities. I'm in trouble, dammit."

"What's wrong? Tell me." At last, Silvana relaxed. The focus had shifted from her to Warren. And although the subject was trouble—it was *his* troubles, not hers, and that, despite her husband's gloomy tone, was relieving.

"I've held onto several properties too long. Office buildings. Half empty. I can't fill them and I can't sell them. The mortgages, the taxes, the fuel and electricity bills are eating me up alive. Everyone thinks I have millions. But every month, more goes out than comes in. At this rate, I could go bankrupt in six months."

Often, Silvana had cautioned Warren, "More real estate? How much do you need? Slow down, Warren. You buy buildings like they were—*caramelle*—candy." Which only made him glower, "I know what I'm doing!" And buy more properties, she suspected, just to spite her, just to defy her.

But now, this disheartening news elated her. Yes, elated! "You see?" she cried, trying to unclasp his hands from his face. "All the more reason to stay close to home and work the restaurant. Thank God for Per Sempre Silvana! It, at least, is making money. It can support us."

Warren's hands dropped from his face, baring the sullen, brutish grimace that is the universal mark of badly bruised male pride. And although he was not a "physical" man, his hands now formed into tight fists. First with one fist, then the other, he pounded the table, punctuating each of his words with a punch to the solid wood.

"When are you going to face reality, you stupid Eye-tal-ee-ano! Your pathetic little restaurant can't even support your miserable daughter. She doesn't like me, does she? But she sure likes those cashmere sweaters. I support her—not you—and not your ridiculous restaurant." He was livid.

"Warren, I didn't mean—"

"Oh, you meant it. Wouldn't you just love to see me fail so you could support us all! What a joke. Why, I could close down your pathetic restaurant with one phone call."

"No, Warren, don't say that."

"Why the hell not?" Abruptly he rose from the table and marched back into the dining room where everyone sat miserably picking at the traditional roast chicken of the Friday Sabbath meal. Without a word he poured a drink for himself at the bar and returned to the kitchen, oblivious of the eight distraught eyes that followed him and the pitiful cries of his new baby daughter, Anna Michela.

"What a joke," he said again when he was back in the kitchen. "Do you have any idea what I pay in rent here?"

"Not exactly, Warren."

"Not exactly, Warren," he repeated mockingly. "But somehow, you and your teeny-weeny restaurant will save us?"

"I only meant that I wanted to help."

Slurring heavily now, he vented a final blast of vitriol at her. "You really want to help? Then take off your clothes and lie down right here." He slapped the center of the table. "Let me do it to you the way we used to do it in the closet. When was the last time? So long ago, can't even remember now. Did I ever really make you pregnant with Anna Michela? Named her for your dead husband—don't think I didn't notice. Michele. Michela."

"And for my dead mother, Anna," Silvana could not help adding.

"Get on the table, Silvana. Let's make another one." He reached out to grab her breast but she pulled away. "We'll name this one for my dead mother. Debora."

"Warren, please, everyone can hear."

"Ah," he sighed with disgust, ignoring her. "Why bother? You'll just give me another daughter. More cashmere sweaters!" He slumped down into his chair, spent. Then he managed to lift his head and point a warning finger at her. "Just remember, with one phone call . . ."

"He's had too much to drink," they said.

"He's upset."

"He's overtired. Don't take it to heart," they told her as they hurried out the door.

"Tomorrow, he won't remember a thing."

But she would. Silvana knew she would never forget his words, not the coarseness, not the threats . . . and not the cruelty. If asked, she would have said she had always suspected this streak in him. She noticed it most in their intimate moments. That was when she saw the clearest signs of his gross insensitivity and selfishness. And that was what turned her from his bed.

How thrilled he had been at first with her pregnancy. A carton of cigars arrived, which he proceeded to distribute to everyone he knew—even the doorman of their building. He'd puff away on those putrid cigars, beginning right after breakfast, and although they made her sick, she knew they were a symbol of his pride, and she'd silently endure the smoke and the nausea for him.

"What shall we name the baby?" she had asked him.

"Whatever you want," he told her expansively.

"Are you sure?"

"Sure, sure, whatever name you want." But he disliked every name she chose. She wanted to name the baby for his father if it was a boy, but he said, "I don't want a son of mine with a name like Yankel. Too Old World."

"We could pick a different name that begins with Y," she offered. "In his memory."

"Forget it. I don't like any names that start with Y.

Or with D, for that matter, so don't name the baby
for my mother. Pick a nice romantic Italian name."

Finally, they settled on Anna Michela and Federico.
At the time, he seemed satisfied.

Then he began to change. Working a six-day week
at the restaurant, she'd arrive home very pregnant and
very tired, and find Warren in the library, sullenly sipping on scotch.

"Did you eat?" she'd ask him.

"There's nothing in the damned house," he'd always complain.

Sometimes she would ask, "Why didn't you come
down to the restaurant? I could have fixed you a beautiful roasted veal with rosemary and baby potatoes—
we had it as a special. Or your favorite—*gnocchi* with
Gorgonzola cheese." She never waited for the answer.
She knew the answer: he hated the restaurant and he
hated sharing her with it.

And so she would trudge off to the kitchen and
prepare a late meal for her sulky husband—a risotto
with chicken livers, perhaps, or a simple linguine with
fresh tomatoes and basil.

Of course there was no time to sit with him while
he savored her hasty but succulent spread; the menus
for the next day had to be planned, as well as a list
of the fresh produce and ingredients that would have
to be purchased. All this, however, was subject to
whatever was freshest and cheapest at the wholesale
markets. Often, she would have to revise her menu
and lists when she arrived at the markets at eight
o'clock in the morning. These days, she took Gino
shopping with her, but he still did not know how to
pick out the ripest, shiniest, heaviest eggplants or the
leanest, whitest veal in the showcase.

"When you come here," she would tell him, "you
must look not just with your eyes, but with your nose,
your ears, your fingers .. and your heart. You will be
a fine chef, Gino, but a great meal begins right here,
with perfect raw ingredients. So, you must feel the
food, smell it, touch it, shake it, pinch it ... and love
it. You must love this, Gino"—and she would spread

her arms wide—"love it with all of your heart! And from that love will come the *abilità,* the know-how."

Then there was Elena to see to. Did she do her homework? Was she talking to Gino on the phone again? Didn't she realize that Gino had to be up early? As did Elena, for that matter. For school.

Still, every night Silvana entered her daughter's crisp white and yellow bedroom and snuggled with her, just as she had done when Elena was small. Kissing her daughter's sweet neck, she would ask the same questions every night that had become over time a kind of nightly lullaby.

"Did you wash your neck and ears?"

"Did you brush your hair?"

"Did you brush your teeth?"

"Did you finish all your homework?"

And now that Elena was what they called in America a teenager, a new question, "What is that book on your bed? A diary? What is a diary? And why is it locked?"

Wasn't Elena safe and secure now? Silvana wondered. Hadn't she become a real American girl with American friends and schoolbooks in English and this big, bright, clean room of her own? Everything new and modern and shiny. Nothing stained by war or tragedy ... or shame. So what secrets could she want to lock away in a book?

Silvana ran the household, ran the restaurant, cooked for Warren, snuggled with Elena, cuddled Anna Michela in her arms most of the night, and still she drove herself to work harder, do more, keep striving. It was not safe to let up for a moment; it was not safe to stop. Because behind her she could always feel that other Silvana catching up, calling to her, trying to force her to remember what lay back there in the ruins.

Even with Warren she never found the security and tranquillity she had hoped a life with him would offer. It was not that Warren was a bad man, merely self-absorbed and selfish. In his way, he loved her, she knew. And it was not just that he had so thoroughly disappointed her in bed, although that was certainly a

factor. For whenever he touched her, it was always
for his pleasure, never hers.

"I adore you," he told her. "I crave you all the time."

He told her he desired her so much because he
needed her so much, but somewhere long ago she had
heard those words before, and the words had made her
feel then as they made her feel now—used. In time, she
no longer saw before her the lean, angular face of her
husband, Warren, but the blurred face of another man
whose haunting specter turned her body rigid with fear.
For this reason, she turned from Warren in bed.

But it was power, not sex, that most prevented Warren from winning his wife's heart. For though she
longed to be held in a passionate caress, though she
yearned to be kissed until she was breathless, most of
all she wanted to feel safe and free. With Warren,
the issue was always reduced to power and obedience.
There had always been the hint of a threat behind all
his actions. And tonight, that threat had been voiced.
"With just one phone call . . ."

At least now, Silvana told herself, *you know you're
not crazy.* Now, he had said out loud what she had
always feared. He said he could close her restaurant
down, take it away. And with it, take away the one
source of her independence. Without it, she would
have nothing of herself to leave to her daughters. And
no way to keep far ahead of the other Silvana who was
always behind her, straining to catch up. She would be
dragged down again, overcome. Helpless and depen-
dent, she would once again feel used, betrayed, and
discarded like an old rag.

No! Never again, she had vowed long ago, and she
remembered her vow now. Here in America she had
become a new woman. She had become a chef. She had
become a restaurant owner. She had become a success.

Now it was time to gain power. For without it, she
saw, she would never be safe.

Chapter Twelve

Dear Diary,

Today Gino gave me a picture postcard of Bernini's "The Ecstasy of Saint Theresa." I keep it hidden in my panties drawer because if I taped it to my mirror, Mama would say, "This is a Jewish house. What is a Catholic saint doing in this house?"

But I love to look at Theresa. I love how her taut marble toes and her limp marble fingers peek out from the intricate marble folds of her gown. Her beautiful, draped head is uplifted, tilted toward her tense left shoulder. I like to think that the Cupid beside her has already pierced her heart with his bronze arrow. And that explains why her eyes are closed and her mouth is open and the expression on her perfectly chiseled face is one of sublime ecstasy. She has been pierced by the arrow of love. So have I.

I practice by sitting on my pillow (instead of a cloud of marble). I am draped in a white sheet and I close my eyes, open my mouth, and squint at myself over my left shoulder in my mirror across the room. I feel the prick of the arrow. As it thrusts all the way into me, I cry out, "Gino! Gino, my love!" Then I fall on my bed and grab my pillow and try to muffle my giggles. I know I'm ridiculous, dear Diary, but I cannot stop. I pretend I am Theresa a hundred times a day. Well, maybe not a hundred, but you know what I mean.

Mama is so embarrassing. "Why do you hang around the restaurant so much?" she says, right in front of Gino. "I don't need you at the cash register until seven-thirty."

She wants me to go home after school, do my homework, then take a taxi to the restaurant, eat dinner in the kitchen, take over the cash register until ten-thirty, and then go home by taxi again. But then, when would I see Gino?

After school, when the restaurant is empty and Gino is just coming on duty, there is time to talk and joke. Oh, dear Diary, Gino is so funny! He's always saying things like, "You're wearing two different colored socks," or, "Your sneakers are untied." I know he's just teasing me, just trying to make me look, but I can't help it; I have to look! And when I do, he laughs and then I chase him around the empty restaurant, and when I catch him, he tries to kiss me. I only let him kiss me once, I swear!

Not that Gino would ever take advantage of me. He says his feelings for me are so serious, he's willing to wait until I'm older to speak of them. All he'll say now is that he respects me. And the kiss? It was on the lips, but he kept his mouth closed and so did I. So you see, dear Diary, he means it.

The best is when Gino sits with me while I do my homework, and he tells me all his plans and dreams for the future. Someday, he's going to be a great chef with his own restaurant. The problem is that he's so grateful to Mama for giving him a chance to be substitute chef that he obeys her without question and follows her recipes slavishly.

"How are you supposed to become a real chef if she won't let you try out any of your own ideas?" I ask him.

"I'm lucky just to be able to watch and learn from your mother," he says. "She's my role model. And if someday I can learn to cook half as well as she does, I'll be proud."

I hate when he says that but I'm not sure why. But I just hate it!

Of course, not as much as I hate everything about W.N. You know who I mean. And now, in addition to every other disgusting thing about him, he's become a drunk! It's true! Even my mother knows. They fight all the time. The other night, I heard her say something about a divorce. I heard her sobbing. I was standing outside their bedroom door. I was about to go in. But then I heard him begging. Something about wanting my mother to get into the closet with him. She kept saying no, that she was finished feeling sorry for him.

"Have you forgotten what happened Tuesday night?" she asked him. "When you begged me and begged me until I finally gave in and then you locked me in the closet and wouldn't let me out?"

Then she told him she would never forget that Saturday almost a year ago when he'd gotten drunk and said all those horrible things to her and the whole family heard him.

"You said you were sorry. You said you'd stop drinking. I waited, but nothing has changed. So from now on," she said, "I'm on my own."

I had to clamp my hand over my mouth to keep from cheering.

Speaking of cheering, by the way, I just made cheerleader! As you know dear Diary, cheerleaders are the most popular girls in the school. And the prettiest. I still can't believe they chose me to be one. They must've needed a "brain" because it wasn't for my looks, that's for sure. But now that I'm in, I have to attend practice three times a week after school. And I have to go to all the Saturday night games. When will I see Gino?

Saturday night is the busiest night at the restaurant. Do you think Mama will hire a cashier and let me go to the games? I'm worried because now that she's expanding the restaurant, she says she's using up all the profits on the renovation. Maybe there won't be any money left to hire a cashier.

Of course, she can't count on disgusting W.N. to help. He has so much money, but he's cheap at heart, always reminding me how much he paid for everything. Mama says he wanted to give her money to start her restaurant when they got married, but "the price was too high." I'm not sure what she meant, but

I know one thing—now he hates her restaurant. And I hate him, as you know.

I never heard the end of their argument. Anna Michela woke up for a bottle and since I was awake, I told Mrs. Milgrim I'd feed the baby. Despite the awful fact that W.N. is her father, I love my half sister. She's so adorable. Sometimes, when I play with her and hold her in my arms, I imagine that she's my baby. Too bad she didn't have a brave, handsome partisan leader for a father like I did, even though I never knew him. It is Anna Michela—with W.N. for a father—who I feel most sorry for. I vow to you here and now, dear Diary, that I will always love and protect my little sister, Anna Michela.

Oh, dear Diary, why can't I be eighteen instead of sixteen? At eighteen, you're an adult. You can go to college. You can even get married. Ugh! Two more long years. How will I bear it?

After Gino Bracca had given Elena his picture of Saint Theresa, he could no longer gaze at that chiseled ecstatic face over his bed. But he did not have to. Now it was Elena's face he saw before him each night. All he had to do was close his eyes and Elena would appear, dark-eyed and serious, her lips whispering secrets only he could hear.

She was too young for him, of course. Sometimes he asked himself what was it that he, a man of twenty-two, saw in a girl of sixteen. That she was mature beyond her years did not mitigate the fact that Elena Levi Bassani Nachman was still in high school. But oh, that brain of hers! How quickly she understood all of his ideas, often even before he had finished laboriously trying to express them. And her sweetness and purity! Always volunteering to help him or listen to him or encourage him.

He had told her, "I'm serious about you, Elena," knowing that these words to a dreamy young girl were like chains of gold. Just when she should have been dating and partying, he said the words that would keep her willingly bound only to him. But how else to prevent her from some high school boy's eager mouth and hands? How else to keep her pure until she came of age?

It was not that he was asking of her more than he expected of himself. From the day he told her of his serious intentions, he had taken a voluntary oath of chastity so that their wedding night could be the ecstatic explosion of two expectant, eager virgins. Not that he was technically a virgin. But of the four sexual encounters he had experienced so far in his life, none had been thrilling.

"Remember Millie," he reminded himself with distaste. "Millie and her dirty pictures." To his horror, Millie Jones, his first "crush," had revealed that she was not the quiet, good girl she had pretended to be in their high school English class. When he came to pick her up at her substantial brick house for their first date, she took him by the hand, pulled him inside, and led him upstairs to her bedroom.

"Guess what?" she said, her green eyes bright with intrigue.

"What?"

"My parents went to the movies. It's a double feature. We're alone."

"Oh," he said dully, watching her bounce on the bed. It was to that same movie he had planned to take her. By the time they were watching the second feature, he had thought he might be able to carefully place his arm over her shoulders. Almost as pleasurable as the anticipation of his arm resting on her soft shoulders was the anticipation of her refusal to allow him to touch her. For then, of course, he would know with certainty that Millie wasn't "fast."

Instead, she had lured him to her bedroom of ruffles and stuffed animals and before his very eyes—with all the lights blazing!—began unbuttoning her demure white blouse. He stood helpless and agape as she stripped down to her white bra and panties. But the worst was yet to come.

Patting the bed, she coaxed him to sit down beside her and told him she had something to show him.

From a quilted box kept locked and hidden in a drawer, she pulled out a stack of old black and white photographs, some yellowed and torn with age. She placed them on his lap.

At first, the photographs of naked, bearded men and women wearing only black hose baffled him. Were they art? Were they old prints taken by a great photographer? But then he saw it. The bare, erect penis. And then, he saw it all—the masses of genital hair, the woman's legs spread open, the copulating couples curled around each other. He saw a woman buried between the legs of another woman, and he hurled the picture across the room. He saw two men penetrating a woman front and back at the same time. He saw five naked bodies all sucking on each other in a circle. There were perhaps fourteen photos. After he had examined them all, he did not have to look at them again; he knew he would never forget them. But oh, how he wished he could!

Out! He had wanted to run out, run away from those filthy yellowing pictures but Millie was smirking at him, asking, "Are you shocked?" as if she knew the answer.

"Of course not," he had to reply. "I've seen all this—and done all this—before. Many times."

And then he had to do it, do it with Millie to prove what he had said. But not like the pictures. He would not do it like that—bare and shameless and frozen in time. He would not remove his clothes. He did it fast, he got it done. And although he could never again face Millie (he even turned his back to zip up), he remembered his manners as he walked out.

"Thank you for a nice time."

Millie was forgotten but the pictures stayed with him, burning a hole in his sleep, igniting his dreams.

Over the next four years there had been three more sexual fiascos, but his greatest failure was his inability to forget those shameful photos. They awakened him in the morning and tormented him at night. Then he received the picture postcard of Saint Theresa, and found he could dream of her instead. At last he found peace. His soul had been saved from eternal damnation. And now, with Elena, his future promised to become a miniature heaven here on earth. Chastity was a small price to pay for such bliss.

Mark Kroll, the hat designer with a storefront adjacent to Per Sempre Silvana, had always promised Silvana a hat. Not that she had ever reminded him. But now that he had moved to a larger storefront and workroom on Fifth Avenue, he recalled that in all the excitement of his move and Silvana's renovation of his old space, he had forgotten to give her the good-bye gift he had promised.

They had become friends even before Silvana's restaurant had actually opened, when she was still readying the interior—three weeks of painting and scrubbing and polishing. Taking a break one warm afternoon, her glorious hair wrapped in a scarf, her long, lithe body hidden under an old shirt and paint-spattered dungarees, she ventured out onto the street and stretched her graceful but utterly grimy arms. Stepping back to the curb, she allowed herself a few proud moments to admire her hand-painted sign, and then wandered over to the enticing window of her next-door neighbor, Mark Kroll. Enchanted, she pressed her nose to the glass, craving everything on display—the hats made entirely of ribbons and the hats made entirely of rhinestone-studded veils and, most of all, hanging from braided satin ropes, all five of those chic little pillboxes that Jackie Kennedy had taught American women to love.

That was how he first saw her—with her face pressed to the glass. And despite the ridiculous kerchief on her head, despite her baggy, spattered clothing, Silvana nevertheless reminded Mark Kroll of some marvelous, mysterious actress in disguise standing at his window. Staring circumspectly, he had the feeling he had seen her before, probably in a recent movie or play. With such enormous almonds for eyes, with such prominent cheekbones, such flawless, golden skin, and such long, long legs, she had to be either a model or an actress. It bothered him that he could not place her. He prided himself on knowing most of the beautiful women in New York.

Women were his world, his universe. He lived openly with a spectacularly handsome and talented jewelry designer, a young man who went by only one name: Fabian, but women were his inspiration. For the love of women he designed not only their hats but virtually every object that might enhance their appeal and their femininity. At different times, for different favorite clients, he had been known to create entire wardrobes—coats and suits, evening gowns and, with Fabian's help, their jewelry. Recently, he had even custom-designed the entire interior of his most famous client's thirteen-room apartment.

"I want a house that feels like one of your hats— soft and elegant and subtly flattering," was the grand, enormously rich Sophie de Marchant's only instruction to him. Then she left him on his own. "I am off to the south of France for nine months. Surprise me on my return."

So he gave her sofas of brushed, velvety felt, like the hats he designed for her, and chairs upholstered in satiny leathers that he then hand-painted with zebra stripes or leopard spots. He converted an entire small bedroom into a dressing closet and lined it in the palest, softest, costliest pink suede on the market. Even the mirrors were tinted a flattering pink. And Fabian did a collection of pink jewelry to match the dressing room, using rare, gigantic pink pearls, pink quartz, and dozens of pink baubles.

To his women, he was their darling, their cherished, secret "find." When lunching, they would whisper his name in hushed tones, lest someone overhear and— God forbid!—catapult him into the noisy public spotlight. No, they wished to keep him for their very own, and they were willing to pay the price to keep his name quiet.

They telephoned him, their voices dripping with gratitude and hints of material homage:

"Mark, darling, may I come by today around three? I have something for you that I want to drop off."

"Mark, I just received your bill and I know I sound mad, but I actually think it is too low! Perhaps you forgot to add another zero. Do your arithmetic again and then call me later. Don't be afraid of zeros, Mark, dear. Zeros are my favorite number."

And they praised him:

"How did you know? I can't believe you've given me just the look I wanted. First, the gray suede cloche. Then the cape to go with it. And now the shoes! You're a genius. How did you ever learn to design shoes?"

"Divine, simply divine!"

"When you die, I will cast your hands in gold and mount them on a pedestal and I will say, 'These are the golden hands of the most gifted genius in the world, greater than Einstein!' "

But they hated his new workroom. "Too big." "Too commercial." "Too midtown!"

However, it was long before he had moved to Fifth Avenue, when his shop was still on East Ninety-fourth Street and the new workroom was only a secret yearning shared exclusively with Fabian, that he first saw Silvana. And although pushy salesmen revolted him, he could not resist such a beautiful mystery; he called her in with a wave of his hand.

Standing at the door, neither in nor out, she was all apologies. "As you can see, I am not dressed for shopping. But I did want to meet you, because you are my closest neighbor—I own the restaurant next door—and because your hats are simply *bellissimo!* Do come have dinner some night as my guest. We open in two weeks."

So that was how he knew her! He'd seen her, baggy and dusty, hauling barrels of plaster and trash to the curb on several occasions. But this was the first time he had really seen her face. Oh, God, he thought, what a face for hats!

She would not let him shake her soiled hand, but her smile was embracing, glistening, all teeth. Later, he would learn that her perfectly square teeth, white as a porcelain sink, were her proudest feature. "So many during the war suffered from rotting teeth. That I have all of mine is a *miracolo*," she would tell him, grinning broadly to show them off. "See? *Trenta-due*."

They became friends instantly. Often, in the late morning when business was slow, he would stand with her in the kitchen and sip espresso and chat for half an hour. At least once a week, he and Fabian would have dinner at Per Sempre Silvana, and if it was not too busy, Silvana would come out in her chef's uniform and sit with them over coffee and dessert. And occasionally, she would wander into his store in the late afternoon and try on hats, though she never bought one.

"You're not a customer; you're a friend," he insisted. "I don't sell to my friends. Any hat in the store is yours as a present from me." But she could never choose between them—she loved them all.

From the beginning, theirs was a friendship without sex—her first with a man and Mark Kroll's first with a woman. True, he adored most of his customers, but they had become his good friends partly—or mainly—because they were his good customers. With Silvana, there was no commerce involved. It was a pure friendship—pure respect, pure sharing, pure support. And pure hilarity. Rare was the day that Mark Kroll and Silvana did not begin by discussing something serious and end up doubled over in laughter.

"Hats are like eyeglasses," he had once told her. "There is an ideal style, an ideal shape for each face, and once a woman finds hers, she should stick to it."

"What is mine?" she asked him.

"You are the exception."

"Why?"

"Because you look magnificent in everything."

"Really? Even in this?" Smiling mischievously she pulled her white cotton chef's hat from her pocket and plunked it down on her head. Made for a man— as were all chef's uniforms in those days—it was oversize, and slid down below her eyebrows.

"I am lucky I can make pasta with my eyes closed. With this hat, I have no choice!"

He burst out laughing as the hat slid down over her nose and she just stood there, arms stretched stiffly in front of her like a semiheadless ghost.

"Veal marsala? *Pasta fresca?* Coming up!" she joked.

By the time the hat dropped to her chin, he was doubled over in hysterics and she was chuckling loudly inside the hat.

Now, two years later, he remembered that he'd designed a custom chef's hat for her out of stiff white organdy, and then another with a huge high crown, but he'd never given her a good-bye present. He wondered if it was because, like her, he could never find a favorite—they all looked equally lovely on her.

How he missed her! It had only been six days, but already he missed their morning espresso, their intimate chats, their easy laughter. Since he had helped her design the expansion and renovation of her restaurant, he decided to see how the project was progressing. He called out to Fabian, who worked in an anteroom in the back, "I'm going to visit Silvana. Want to come?" In a moment Fabian was at his side.

"Are we going to be very naughty and take the whole afternoon off?"

"No, just an hour or so."

Fabian's darkly tanned face drooped.

"Don't sulk," Mark Kroll scolded distractedly. He was searching for something to give Silvana. Several women sat at a long table, embellishing his spring collection of straw hats with flowers and ribbons. Hesitating before a navy-blue straw picture hat with an enormous brim, he glanced up at Fabian for his approval. Explanations were never necessary with Fabian; he always knew what Mark was thinking. But perhaps because Fabian was indeed sulking—and not a little jealous of Mark's friendship with Silvana—he vetoed the striking hat with a curt sniff and a roll of his eyes.

Had it not been for Fabian's sulk, Mark Kroll might

never have discovered the one gift of such monumental meaning to Silvana that she would cherish it for the rest of her life. But of course, he could not know that then. All he knew was that the huge yellow silk sunflower on a green satin stalk had proved too large to adorn any of his hats. Now it lay alone on a hatbox, almost larger than life—like Silvana herself.

Even now, though somehow he knew the single sunflower was perfect, he had to glance once more at Fabian for confirmation. Over the seven years of their combined business and personal relationship, virtually all decisions touching on design—even this one—were shared between them. They were that close.

And because they were that close, Fabian rose to the occasion, exchanging his pout for a wide smile of approval.

"Oh, yes, Mark! It's perfect. It's so ... Silvana!" Though neither of them could say exactly why.

Chapter Thirteen

"Keep it subdued. Soft lighting. Creamy beiges and flattering pastels—a barely apricot tint, perhaps—and pale, paint-washed woods," Mark Kroll had told Silvana, and he was right. "Then your food becomes the bright spot, the focal point."

But now, surveying Per Sempre Silvana's new room, formerly Mark Kroll's hat store, Silvana felt a tightness in her chest, a sinking sensation in her stomach. It was not the room, however; how could this splendid, inviting dining space cause her such anxiety?

The walls were washed in a pale terra-cotta and reminded her of an old Roman villa. The cream-and-rust-striped upholstered chairs that Mark had found for her were handsome and practical. On tiny wheels, the chairs rolled smoothly and quietly over the imported terrazzo floor. A tall vase holding the single, spectacular satin sunflower that Mark Kroll had given her sat on a pedestal at the archway connecting the new room with the old one. Its position allowed Silvana to see it from any corner of the room, to glance at it and smile. Even at tense and rushed moments, a glance at those brilliant yellow satin petals almost unfailingly brought her a small spasm of inner joy. The first time, however, the sunflower reduced her to tears.

"*Girasole!*" she had gasped as if she'd discovered a long-lost friend as she unwrapped the sunflower from its tissue and ribbons. Then she burst into sobs. And although she told Fabian and Mark Kroll, "You'll never know how much this means to me," she could not explain to them why.

Now, of course, the sight of the sunflower in its elegant vase warmed her, reminding her of her very best memories. The others, the scorching memories that still could cause biting burns, only the other Silvana remembered, the Silvana of her past. But that Silvana was not permitted in this room.

Along the wall opposite the sunflower, a marble counter displayed the evening's tempting Italian-Jewish desserts—a walnut and honey *torta*, dripping a honey-sweetened walnut glaze down its sides, and a meltingly creamy cheesecake laced with rum and vanilla. Platters of cinnamon turnovers and buttery almond cookies from Siena sat high on stands, their white doilies peeking out like imported lingerie. A pinwheel fruit tart and a rich chestnut pie, its surface a swirl of whipped cream, completed the table's offerings. And even Silvana had to admit that everything looked splendid.

So it was not the room that filled her with anxiety. And it was not even the expense. Silvana calculated that her brother's loan would be paid off in less than a year from the profits of this venture. And this, despite the three new waiters who had to be hired to service the sixty-six extra customers at the twenty new tables (ten deuces, seven four-tops, and three six-tops)!

With the renovation of the room, an expansion of the kitchen had also been necessary, but that only improved the overall efficiency of the operation. Now, at the new salad and vegetable island, one man simply peeled and chopped garlic and onions all morning and washed vegetables and salad greens all afternoon. And a new oven was installed exclusively for the baker who was hired to make fresh breads and desserts every day, according to Silvana's precise, well-tested, secret recipes.

Gino was now more indispensable than ever. Promoted to head chef, he did most of the on-line cooking, leaving Silvana free not only to supervise the expanded kitchen staff, but to venture out into the front rooms. Now she could greet diners, accept special orders and requests and survey the quality of service, roles she discovered she enjoyed almost as much as cooking. It was refreshing to get out from behind the hot stoves, out of her comfortable, clunky clogs, out of her shapeless uniform ... and into high heels and soft, clingy dresses again.

"The proof is in the pudding," Silvana liked to say, using one of the few English expressions that made complete sense to her. And indeed, every night Silvana got her proof—when the large, new room would fill to capacity with curious, jolly ... and satisfied customers. The expansion of her restaurant and kitchen clearly was a financial—and an aesthetic—success.

Yet anxiety gnawed at her. And a persistent feeling of nausea had begun to sour her mornings. Yet, though she refused not only to give into her discomfort, but even to acknowledge its cause, she knew. She did not speak of it, much less complain of it, but in the silence of her heart where pure truth dwelt, she knew.

For a few months more she was able to pretend she did not know and to keep it from everyone else. She could dress for work in her stylish wardrobe and enjoy the fruits of her success as she made her rounds. But as soon as she returned home, anxiety and despair descended like a sudden downpour, soaking her with sadness.

"What's wrong, Ma?" Elena would ask, a mixture of concern and annoyance on her face. "You're not sorry you kicked him out, are you? You don't miss him, do you?"

Immediately Silvana would begin twisting the two rings on her finger—the plain gold band and the four-carat diamond ring. "Oh, Elena, your mama is—how do you say?—all mixed up."

"I knew it! You're going to let him live with us again, aren't you?"

"No, no," Silvana tried to insist but she did not sound certain. How could she be? Pulling at the hem of her dress was Anna Michela, two years old, and demanding to know, "Daddy home?" And growing inside her now was a new child, destined, she sadly realized, to be fatherless like her other two.

This was a baby she did not want.

"Forgive me," she would pray silently, "but no, this one should not be born. This one was made without love."

Child of her blood and Warren's, it was conceived one terrible Tuesday night four months ago when Warren was still living in the house. She had just arrived home from work when drunkenly he beseeched her, "Come with me into our closet of love."

"Look at you. Warren, you're killing yourself," she said at the sight of him, ignoring his request.

"Help me. Aren't you my wife? Then help me."

"For two years that is all I have tried to do. I have begged, I have fought, I have talked, I have cried. And I have given you the child you said you wanted so much. When you broke promise after promise, I forgave you because I hoped, with all my heart, that we could be a family. But I cannot help you anymore. I am worn out. *Finito!* I am finished. *We* are finished."

"Oh, Silvana, my darling, don't say that! Give me one more chance. Please, I beg of you."

"Why, Warren? You don't want me. You want your bottle of scotch. You feel sorry for yourself for losing so much money. You don't feel sorry for what you are doing to me and to our family. So why should I believe you this time?"

"For the sake of Anna Michela."

This made her hesitate. Never before had Warren invoked the interests of their daughter as the primary reason to go on, though it had always been her first thought. Warren saw that he had her attention, and although he slurred, he drove his point home.

"Let me show you I can love you and Anna Michela—and, yes, Elena, too. Let me show you I can be a good husband and father. You're so beautiful, so wonderful. I don't want to lose you. And I don't want to lose our daughter. Please, Silvana, I want to hold you, feel close to you. Please let me."

His words made her cry despite the fact that she

had vowed never to cry over him again. But his words were exactly the words she had wanted to hear. It did not matter that she had heard words like them a hundred times before. It did not matter that all they had been was just that—words. For Anna Michela, she chose to believe them. It would be the last time she ever would.

But as he led her into their "closet of love," unused for more than two years, she could not quite stifle a wide, shuddering yawn. All the emotional tension here at home had caused it. She yawned when she was tense—as well as when she was tired. But Warren took it as a sign of disinterest, of boredom.

"All right, let's get this over with, since you clearly couldn't care less," he said, angrily slamming the closet door behind them.

What Warren failed to see was that beneath Silvana's yawn was a genuine yearning to be touched, to be held, to be loved. Deprived for too long of romance and tenderness, almost anyone caressing her flesh—even Warren—would have been welcome that night. So it was with a certain unadmitted eagerness that she followed her husband into the closet.

But Warren, his pride once again bruised and his brain blurred by alcohol, could not sense Silvana's throbbing heat. He saw only what was on the surface—that damnably insulting yawn. He grabbed Silvana gruffly and forced her down to the floor.

"No, wait!" she cried. "Warren, not like this."

"Wait?" he repeated, ripping off her panties. "I warned you, didn't I? I'm not a patient man." Then he forced himself on top of her.

"Stop!" she screamed, beating him on the shoulders with her fists, scratching his face with her nails.

He grabbed her wrists and held them over her head as he thrust himself into her. In that moment, their eyes locked.

"If you do this, Warren, you will be raping me. Raping the mother of your child!" she hissed breathlessly, her chest heaving with fear and rage.

For a moment Warren, stunned by her words,

seemed about to withdraw. But suddenly he cried out, "Oh, God!" as his neck stiffened, his jaw tightened, and he ejaculated his milky semen into her.

"It's your fault, goddamn it," he said as he rolled off her. "All your goddamn fault."

She did not know whether he blamed her for his raping her or for ejaculating prematurely, or both, but she did not care. Until this moment she would have said it was impossible, yet once again in her life she had trusted a man who betrayed that trust, who betrayed her.

Warren was right. It was all her fault. For being so blind, so utterly, stupidly blind.

In total despair, she curled into a ball on the floor, weeping soundlessly.

After some minutes Warren stumbled to his feet, looked down at her, and commanded drunkenly, "You stay in here. And in the morning, after you've thought things over, I expect a change in your behavior." He locked the closet door behind him.

As soon as she heard the click of the lock, a part of her yearned to pound on the door, cry and beg him to let her out. But what he had done to her tonight convinced her that she must not plead for her freedom; she must take it.

In a week, Warren was leaving on a business trip to check on a property in Florida. When he came back, he would find the locks to the apartment had been changed. He had asked for a change in her behavior, and he would get it. She was filing for divorce. By imprisoning Silvana in the closet all night, what Warren had not anticipated was the dark, silent opportunity for Silvana to think .. and to plan.

Put into action, the plan had gone so smoothly, despite the unbearable week of fighting before Warren left on his trip, and despite Warren's phone calls and telegrams afterward begging to be taken back, that Silvana began to believe she was at peace. The breakup of her marriage threw her emotions into turmoil, yet she now slept soundly in the big bed each night, no longer dreading Warren's demanding touch.

And gone was the endless bickering, the shouts and hollering, the stifled tears, the churning anxiety in the pit of her stomach.

Then nausea awakened her one morning, and the anxiety and the tears returned.

Now, as she gazed fondly at her daughter Elena, she struggled to find the words to explain her predicament.

"Elena, it is not that I want Warren to come back. It is just that I am so . . . *bound* . . . to him. Now, even more than ever."

"Why? You locked him out. You told him you want a divorce. He's living in a hotel. You're apart now, aren't you?"

"Yes, but even if he does not live with us, I will never be free of him."

"Why not?"

"Because Anna Michela is his daughter." Then she paused before adding, "And because I am going to have another child of his."

Elena, usually so quick, looked at her mother without comprehension. "You mean me?"

"No, not you, *cara,*" Silvana almost had to laugh. "You are not his. Your father was a *gigante,* a giant. This one"—and she pressed on her belly—"will have the same father as Anna Michela—a drunk."

Elena was appalled. "You did it with him and got pregnant?" She made a disgusted face and underlined it by graphically exclaiming, "That's disgusting!"

Without thinking, Silvana grabbed Elena by the shoulders and shook hard. Shook and shook until Elena's head bobbed back and forth like a rag doll. "Never, never speak to me like that! You are a child. You know nothing. Nothing!"

Abruptly she let go of Elena but she could not let go of the insult. She folded her arms across her chest and fumed.

After several minutes Elena took her hand. "I'm not such a child, Mama. I'm sorry I said you're disgusting. I didn't mean it. Not about you. Only about him."

"He is Anna Michela's father. In this house, we will speak of him with respect."

"Just promise me you won't take him back."

Silvana sighed and nodded. "*Sì, sì, sì,*" she agreed impatiently. "But without a man in the house, it will be hard on us."

"Not so hard. I'm used to it, remember?" Elena reminded her mother, making her smile ruefully. Of course Silvana remembered. Sixteen fatherless years. Could a mother ever forget such a sad fact? Yet Elena added, "Mama, it was much harder for the two years when he was here."

Again Silvana sighed. Elena was right, of course. Everything was so much easier now that they didn't have to deal with Warren. Her daughter's dislike of Warren had been perfectly obvious from the very first, but now even Silvana detested him. That he had brought it upon himself no longer seemed important, however. Certainly he was almost entirely to blame. Certainly his behavior had deteriorated over the course of their two-and-a-half-year marriage, sinking from mere selfishness to unforgivable cruelty and abusiveness.

And certainly she was finished with him.

But she was finished with anger and blame, as well. When her marriage had gone up in flames, so did her rage. Now, all that was left were the ashes. Gone were their dashed mutual dreams and whatever love or affection they had ever felt for each other. Gone, all gone. Except for the ashes, and the sorrow ... and, fruit of their short union, the children—Anna Michela and this new life growing inside her.

Elena, despite her insistence that she was grown up, was much too young to understand Silvana's complex feelings. To Elena, it was simply a relief to be rid of Warren. But to Silvana, beneath that relief was a thick layer of sadness and fear. Sadness at the failure of her marriage—and fear for the future of her unborn child. Now, because of that failure, and even more because of the new life growing inside her, an umbrella of sorrow hung over her life, blocking all sunlight and shading everything a dull, sad gray.

Even the glowing success of Per Sempre Silvana did nothing to lift her dark and anxious mood. That she could now afford to pay the apartment rent entirely by herself—and might soon have to if Warren continued to drink and to lose the remainder of his fortune—only reinforced her feeling of aloneness. Where once this financial solidity, for which she had worked so hard and so long, might have thrilled her, now it merely reminded her that once again she was on her own, and that her children would be without a live-in father.

Since she was fourteen, she had never known a truly and completely secure moment again in her life. Was this to be the destiny of her children, too? she wondered miserably.

"Mama?" Elena gently shook Silvana's shoulder, startling her. Silvana, who had been deep in thought, jumped several inches out of her chair, bringing a rare smile to her daughter's face. "I caught you daydreaming."

"What is this daydreaming?" Silvana wanted to know, smiling back at Elena. Then she immediately proceeded to drift back into her thoughts, missing Elena's explanation.

"It's a kind of deep thinking or dreaming, but while you're awake." Noticing her mother's glazed eyes, again Elena shook her. "Mama?"

"Yes?" This time, Silvana did not jump.

"Mama, why don't you just marry Mark Kroll?"

Now Silvana might have jumped from sheer shock at the question. Carefully she peered at her daughter to see if she was joking. But Elena's eyes stared back at her with curiosity and innocence. She was not joking. Nevertheless, Silvana burst into hearty, husky laughter.

"Ah, *mia dolcezza*, my sweetness, you made your mother laugh again. Thank you."

"But why? Mark is handsome. No, not handsome; *extremely* handsome," Elena continued with an intensity and singleness of purpose that could have won her a place on the debating team. "And you like him so much—you know you do, so don't shake your head. You two are extremely compatible. I've never heard you fight, only laugh and talk. So why, Mama?"

"Why what?" Silvana asked impatiently.

"Why won't you marry him?"

Silvana sighed with discomfort. This was not a conversation she ever envisioned having with her daughter. Just as she had never envisioned that Mark Kroll and Fabian would become her dearest friends. Yet they had, and it was time to explain who they were to Elena.

"Because Mark is already married, in a way," she said slowly. "To Fabian."

Elena was once again dense. "How can he be married to Fabian? Fabian's a man."

"Homosexuals can. Have you ever heard that word before?"

Elena nodded her head yes. "But I heard that homosexuals are perverted. Even Gino said so."

Irritated, Silvana snapped, "Gino doesn't know everything. If you would go out with someone else once in a while, you might discover that for yourself."

Elena was still pondering this perplexing news when suddenly comprehension cleared the dull film clouding her eyes. "You mean Mark is a homosexual? And Fabian? They do it together?" She made a disgusted face, the same as the one before.

"*Basta!* Enough! Too much talk about sex." Silvana, exasperated and exhausted not so much by the subject matter as by Elena's incessant disapproval, could not find the words to say so. "Let's—how do the Americans say it—change the subject."

However, Elena was now fascinated. "But I want to know how you found out. Did they tell you—or did you see them doing—"

"Enough, I said, and I mean it. Enough!" Silvana shouted, shaking with an anger she could not explain. At least, not to her daughter. But as she stormed down the foyer, as she slammed the door behind her, as she crawled wearily into her large, empty bed, she knew exactly what was plaguing her. Loneliness.

When had she last felt loved and desired by someone? When had she last felt love and desire for someone? Had she ever felt it for Warren, she wondered. Sadly, for no more than a minute, she had to admit. Then he destroyed even that moment of feeling.

Hysterically, she removed the two rings that had been symbol of her union to the once prosperous Warren Nachman and placed them back in their original boxes.

"Oh, Michele!" she whispered to the high, white, blank ceiling. "I still miss you. No one but you ever loved me so unselfishly. Michele, I miss you so!"

Chapter Fourteen

Most nights after work—and after he had stolen a few precious hours with Mary Catherine—Eduardo would labor over his novel—the tribute to his family and to all the Jews of Italy. This week he had gone back to an early chapter of the book in order to include some new material. Oddly, it was thoughts of love for Mary Catherine that had prompted the memory of a despised ancient site in Rome and the wish to write about it.

"I want to tell the history of a certain monument near where I lived in Rome—the Arch of Titus—which everyone in my family called the 'forbidden' monument."

"Why forbidden?" Mary Catherine asked with her usual curiosity about his work—what she called his real work—writing.

"Because my mother and father, may they rest in peace, would never let us walk under it." Then Eduardo asked uncertainly, "Did I ever tell you about the Arch of Titus?"

Blankly, Mary Catherine shook her head no. "If you did, I can't remember the details. Tell me again." Her mind was filled with so many of Eduardo's stories about the Jews of Italy that sometimes she forgot which ones she had heard before. Not that she minded hearing any of them again, for she found Jewish history fascinating . . . and almost always heartbreaking.

It was just that tomorrow was the wedding.

"Okay, I'll try it out on you," Eduardo quickly relented. She was his "test market," his sample "audience," and he would trust no one else with his new material before he sat down to write. Even now, despite tomorrow's big event, his mind was on his book and the new scene he wanted to add.

"That's your problem," Joey Rizzo, his boss at Club Midnight, would often tease, not without a hint of impatience. "Your mind is always on your book—but it should be right here, on the club. This is your bread and butter."

Nevertheless, Eduardo continued to write and dream, and slowly—for he wrote only three or four pages a week—the book took form. Sometimes he caught himself wishing for the impossible—not for fame or success but for Anna Levi, his mother, to rise up from her unmarked grave in the German camp and read every word. And then for her to kiss his forehead and say, "Eduardo, I'm so proud of you. You made all of us—all the Jews of Italy—seem so real and so touching. Even the worst of us. Through you, through your book, I feel as if Raffaelle and Papa and I have been kept alive ... forever." It was for her, most of all, that he labored so long. And of course, for Mary Catherine.

Stretching his short, muscular legs over the sofa arm in the apartment Mary Catherine shared with two roommates, Eduardo waited for her to look up at him from the floor where she sat with a jewelry box on her lap. From the box she pulled a black felt drawstring bag, tightly knotted, and set to work untying it. When, after some seconds, she still did not look up, he began his story anyway. If his sad tale could capture her attention on this, the day before her wedding, then perhaps it would hold the interest of every distracted reader. Even more important, she would then see why his love for her was connected, of all things, to this dark memory. And why he wanted to write it.

"It all began in ancient times. In A.D. 70, to be exact."

Still, Mary did not look up. But she nodded her head, encouraging Eduardo to continue.

"That was the year that Titus conquered Israel and destroyed Jerusalem. He returned to Rome trium-

phant, dragging thousands of Jewish slaves behind him
as the crowds roared."

"Jewish slaves!" Mary Catherine shook her head
disconsolately. "Every time I hear about Jews, Ne-
groes—*any* human beings forced into slavery—I get
furious and I get ill at the same time. For my two
weeks vacation, I want to go down South and volun-
teer to work for civil rights."

Eduardo smiled, not for the first time, at Mary
Catherine's good heart. Her compassion was one of
the reasons he was marrying her tomorrow. For her
compassion, for her beauty, and for her intelligence.
Then he smiled again, thinking to himself, *And let's
not forget her lustiness in bed. For that, alone, I'd
marry her.*

"I know. It enrages me, too," he continued. "But
when Titus marched his Jewish slaves before them,
the ancient Romans cheered. And when his father, the
Emperor Vespasian, held a victory pageant for Titus
upon his return, everyone cheered."

"But what does this have to do with the Arch of
Titus? And why are you telling me this story anyway?
Especially today, of all days." Didn't he understand
that today Mary Catherine needed happy stories, joyous stories? Or, at least, stories of love. Today she
had awakened in sadness and loss from a dream about
a hidden family jewel—a gigantic ruby the size of a
human heart—that she was trying desperately to find.
Though she searched and searched, the enormous
ruby could not be found. Once it had been a pulsing,
glinting gem. Now it lay lost and buried, gone from
her forever, its deep red color like dried blood inside
a petrified heart.

The dream had reminded her of the loss of her two
most beloved relations. And that tomorrow she would
not have them at her side. Neither her grandmother
nor her father. Both were dead, dead before their
time. Before *her* time. She missed them both today,
but oh, how she would miss them both tomorrow!

Eduardo knew nothing of Mary Catherine's dis-
turbing dream. Nor did he know the cloud of gloom

that had hung over her all day. But he recognized one thing, at least: that he had not yet gotten the point of his story across. Like most good writers, his stories, while always interesting—and at times even fascinating—often needed careful editing nonetheless. He told himself philosophically that like the rough diamond, his "rough" tale needed the same honing and polishing to bring out the facets of its intrinsic meaning.

And so he decided not to elaborate, for instance, upon the Emperor Vespasian. *Get to the point!* he chided himself, writing the story in his mind. Why recount the father's jubilation not only at Titus's conquest of Israel, at his bounty of Jewish slaves ... but also the valuable spoils Titus looted from the Temple of Solomon? This was not the point. Mentally, he drew a line through all the details he now considered superfluous. *Two pages,* he estimated he had cut. *Two wasted pages.*

Now he merely told her, "Titus's proud father ordered that his 'brave' son's entire triumph be recorded for posterity on the stone walls of the Arch of Titus in the Roman Forum. To us, this was no triumph; it was a shameful debacle. Which is why we Jews never walk under it. And the reason I thought of this was because I love you so much, I would do anything you asked ... even walk with you under the Arch—"

"Here they are!" Mary Catherine exclaimed, interrupting Eduardo. She held up a necklace of huge, lustrous, eight-millimeter pearls. When she was thirteen, her favorite grandmother, Grandmama McGee, had given them to her.

Deflated, Eduardo glanced at the pearls and looked away. Neither his story nor his message of love had held her.

"Bride's pearls," Grandmama McGee had called them then when she had placed them in the hands of Mary Catherine. "When *my* grandmama, bless her soul, gave these to me, that is what I named them. Bride's pearls. Now *you* take them, but promise me you will not wear them out in public until the day you are a bride."

After fifteen years, Mary Catherine again saw the pearls that would at last encircle her neck tomorrow at her wedding. It was the sight of them that had caused her to interrupt Eduardo's words of endearment.

For surely Mary Catherine had not yet had her fill of Eduardo's infinite variations, like a Mozart concerto, on the theme of his love for her. She would never have her fill. Today, she awakened needing to hear them more, perhaps, than ever. But at this moment, concentration on what Eduardo was saying was difficult, to say the least, knowing that their wedding was less than twenty-four hours away! She, who would always stop everything—anywhere, anytime—just to hear what new romantic "sonnet" he had composed just for her, was deaf to him today.

It's the wedding and the pearls and the melancholy dream, she told herself. And it was. But it was something else, too.

Religion.

Now that Mary Catherine had undergone the long and rigorous process of conversion to Judaism, she had become quite knowledgeable—and not only about the Jews. From volumes Eduardo had given her, she had been studying many of the world's great religions.

But a crushing burden of hidden feelings, heavy as a hundred-pound weight, pressed on her chest. What was so unbearable—yet so necessary—was keeping these feelings hidden. And the price was shame. Shame had become her new companion now that she had begun keeping secrets from Eduardo.

Deception. Oh, how she loathed lies! Hadn't it been she who had insisted that honesty must be the centerpiece of their relationship? Hadn't it been she who had warned him, "Never lie to me. Ever"?

Yes ... and now it was she who no longer told Eduardo the complete truth. There were things, she had come to realize, that he must never know about her.

For Eduardo, she had converted. For him she had abandoned Catholicism. But now that she had abandoned her old religion—and more painlessly than he would ever know—she slipped on her new religion as she would a coat. For protective covering. Nothing more. Only in silence, in secrecy, could she honestly admit to herself what she feared Eduardo might never understand: the truth. And the truth was that she was neither a Catholic anymore . . . nor really a Jew.

Carefully she retied the black felt bag with the pearls and placed it on the coffee table. Then, as she was about to close the mirrored lid of the jewelry box, she glimpsed the small gold cross and chain that, until a year ago, she had worn every day of her life. Now it lay at the bottom of her jewelry box, glinting brightly but almost entirely forgotten. She fingered it, allowing the fine gold mesh chain to drip over the side of her hand like precious water. When it spilled back into the jewelry box again, she closed the lid. She had felt nothing.

All those years of hurrying to church, of kneeling and praying and feeling shame for my sins and receiving the Lord's forgiveness. All those years! I loved every minute of it then, and yet I miss none of it now.

She, who had never missed a Sunday mass until she met Eduardo, no longer set foot in church. She had not lost her faith; she had given it up. Consciously. Intentionally. With the firmest inner resolve, she refused to allow herself to believe anymore. And it was this that she could not tell Eduardo.

Her disillusionment was not just with Catholicism; she had lost faith in all religions. Yes, she loved the stories the rabbi and Eduardo had told her. And she would always love reading the Bible, both the Old *and* the New Testaments. But belief no longer seemed possible. Not with what she now knew. That throughout history, all the world's great religions had been guilty, at one time or another, of flagrantly practicing the opposite of their own preachings. While preaching brotherly love, they had spread hate. While preaching charity, they had accumulated riches. While preaching tolerance, they had excluded, banished, even tortured not just nonbelievers, but many in their own flock, as well. And as far as she knew, no religion had ever publicly apologized for its sins of the past, much less made reparations.

It was too much! Too much suffering, too much pain. She wanted no part of it. Unlike all the passion and pain in the Levi family, her life had been comparatively dull. And although she felt enormous sympathy for the Levis' collective sadness and loss, she felt left out. How could she ever qualify as a real Jew—she who had suffered not at all?

Clearly, she could not. But she could not tell Eduardo. For Eduardo, if anything, was more devout now than ever. He clung to his faith, to his culture, to his rituals with silent but unshakable spiritual conviction. It was there on every line of the book he was writing.

Yet while Eduardo had renewed his faith, his sister Silvana had gone in the other direction. Something in her past had so pained her that she seemed to be trying to eliminate the memory of her roots. Silvana would not read the book, would not even hear of it. "All that is over," she would say emphatically. "All I want is to forget."

Therefore, Eduardo needed a spiritual ally. So much so, that he convinced Mary Catherine, without ever saying a word, that what he needed most was a Jewish wife. Which was why she offered to convert. For him.

For him she had become a kind of fraud. But somehow she would find a way out of this deception. Somewhere, she was sure, she would find her own sense of spirituality and identity. What she did not know was that it was always right there in front of her, waiting for her to see it.

"So this is what a Jewish synagogue looks like," Mary Catherine's Irish Catholic mother, Frances, whispered, peeking furtively from her upstairs perch. The bridal party was gathering in the upstairs room before the wedding ceremony commenced but Frances McGee could not help stealing a look below, noting with disdain the sleek teak walls, the modern light fixtures, the lack of gold and gilt. "It's so different. It's so . . . bare."

"Not bare. Simple," Frances McGee's brother disagreed. With his chin, and his knowing architect's eye, Kevin Garren directed his sister Frances to admire the unornamented, contemporary teakwood Ark of the Scrolls—the cabinet housing the Torah—that was directly ahead of them on what they, in their church, call Christ's altar.

"It's bare!" Frances McGee continued to insist. "Where are the saints? The marble and the saints? And the angels? Holy Jesus, forgive them, for they don't have even one wee angel!"

Frances McGee crossed herself and gave an exaggerated shudder. This was her first time in a synagogue, and even though it was a sacred place, her hands trembled and her eyes were wide with fear. She was sure that God was going to strike her dead any minute now for entering this alien house of worship. If only Mary Catherine had not converted to Judaism. If only this wedding were being held in a church. If only God would not punish them all!

To atone for this sacrilege, Frances McGee convinced herself she heartily disliked her surroundings. It was as if she were saying, *See, God? I may be sitting here, but at least I don't like it!*

"Oh, Mom!" Mary Catherine groaned, rolling her eyes. "The Jews don't believe in the worship of graven idols or images."

"Graven?" Frances was sure she had seen the word in the Bible, but its meaning escaped her.

"Sculptured. Like the sculptures and carvings that so richly decorate our Catholic and Protestant churches," said her brother Kevin. He knew this because, as an architect and a reader, he had studied the design of early religious buildings.

"Well, why not?" Frances argued, glaring at her daughter. Frances was still miffed at Mary Catherine for converting and could not conceal it even now, on her wedding day. "What would be wrong with just a wee angel or two here and there? Or the beautiful face of a saint?"

Patiently, Mary Catherine answered, "Because their God said they must not practice idolatry."

"Idolatry!"

"Yes, idolatry, the worship of 'false' idols." Mary Catherine was struggling to hold her temper, but her mother was beginning to irritate her. *Yet who am I to complain?* she wondered. *I, who believe in none of it, am the falsest of all, and my wedding, filled with religion and ritual, is a total lie!* She felt close to tears.

Seeing this, Kevin jumped in and led his sister to the railing, explaining, "In His Ten Commandments, God ruled that the Jews must pray to no other image but His unseen, formless spirit. He banned all religious idols. For that reason, the architecture of many of their temples is simpler than ours, devoid of any three-dimensional art at all. See, Frances?"

Despite herself, Frances studied the room with her light blue eyes, hoping to find an example that would dispute her brother's quiet certainty. Instead, she could not help noticing the multitude of windows, and how peculiarly high above eye level they had been placed. Hating to ask "Mr. Know-It-All" another question, she hesitated. Kevin, however, had been following her gaze and anticipated her query.

"They used to be set at eye level, but in the Middle Ages, non-Jews would look through the windows and mock and ridicule the worshipers. So that is why their windows are now placed high enough so that passersby can't see in."

Frances McGee merely sniffed. Why had she rushed in order to endure her daughter's exasperation and her brother's boring lectures? Yet this morning she had nagged and cajoled Kevin to set out one hour and thirty minutes earlier than was necessary.

"Pick me up in your car at ten," she had barked at her brother on the phone that morning. "The saints don't look kindly upon a mother late to her only daughter's wedding. Mary Catherine has given them cause enough to raise their eyebrows. So this is not a day for lagging."

"Lagging indeed!" her brother had harumphed. Older than Frances by four years, unmarried and childless, he had become his sister's "chauffeur" when Frances's husband Mickey died. Chauffeur, without ever so much as a how-dee-do or a would-you-mind? Nevertheless, Kevin met her outside her house at ten and brought her here to this almost-empty chapel. In less than an hour they would all march downstairs and down the aisle. But it was still too early. He just prayed that his suspicious and headstrong younger sister would hold her tongue and not ruin her daughter's most important day.

It was Mary Catherine's wish as well. Already they had been snapping at each other just as they had so many times since her father Mickey McGee's death. Except that today was her wedding.

Oh, Daddy! Oh, how she missed him. When he was alive, her father, among other things, had served as the referee between his wife and daughter. Now that her father was gone, Mary Catherine's Uncle Kevin had taken over the job. And he was almost as good at it, too, she had to admit. She suspected he rather liked his job, liked being chauffeur and referee ... and liked being of use.

"Thanks, Uncle Kevin." She reached over and kissed his cheek.

"For what?"

"For being here," she said.

Then she saw her mother's sulky expression and thought to herself, *Mom's jealous! Jealous of all this love!*

"You, too, Mom," said Mary Catherine, embracing her mother expansively. "You most of all." For a moment Frances McGee looked entirely pleased about everything.

Then Mary Catherine turned to her Uncle Kevin again. "We still have about fifteen minutes. Edify us, won't you, about something from your great store of knowledge while we wait."

The most edifying of subjects to Kevin Garren,
being a New York architect, was architecture. With
Mary Catherine's blessing, he was only too eager to
continue his talk on the history of the design of Jewish
temples. But he spoke mainly to his sister.

"Over the centuries, Jewish synagogues were always
being bombed, burned, or banned. Really, Frances,
the damage and destruction was on a level unlike anything that the Church has ever experienced. Naturally,
as a result, many of them never got to be old like
ours. Some, like this one, are brand-new and sleekly
modern in design." He deeply wanted to enlarge her
narrow tolerance. "Yet I do think it feels very holy in
here. Don't you?"

But his sister was no longer listening.

Frances McGee, wearing a pale blue lace dress and
a matching pale blue lace hat—designed by Mark
Kroll at Silvana's generous invitation—fingered her
rosary beads as she watched the chapel filling up
below. She wore a devoutly pious expression on her
still stunning face and her angelic, heart-shaped lips—
that she had genetically bequeathed to her only
daughter—pursed into a plump pout.

"How will we march in time down the aisle without music?"

Mary Catherine hugged her mother once more.
"There's an organ, Mom."

"Oh, there's an organ?"

Yes, Mary Catherine nodded. "And it will play the
'Wedding March.' "

"Well then, it won't be so bad after all," Frances
McGee allowed and at that moment the first triumphal
organ chords rang out.

Silvana's moist smile and even moister eyes only
hinted at the intensity of her feelings as she stood at
the back of the room, waiting for her turn to proceed
down the aisle. Big with child, big with maternal feeling, her thoughts were on motherhood ... and
mothers.

Oh, Mama! Mama, if only you were alive and here

*today. How I miss you! We all do. Especially dear
Eduardo.*

Eduardo. Silvana was his younger sister—his "kid"
sister, as he had learned to call her here in America—
but today she felt like his mother. *Mama, forgive me!*
Silvana counted the beats and followed Eduardo down
the aisle, gazing proudly at his straight back, almost
prouder than if she had birthed him. *Good luck, darling brother!*

Like Frances McGee, she, too, wore blue.

"But for you, Silvana, the color of bluebells." Mark
Kroll had begun imagining the dress he would design
for her the moment she asked him to be fashion coor-
dinator for the bridal party. It was Silvana's generous
gift to Eduardo and Mary Catherine. And immediately
Mark Kroll knew the exact color to bring out the vio-
let blue of her eyes.

"Bluebells? What are these bluebells?" She had
heard of them, of course, for the *glacinto di bosco* was
prevalent in much of Western Europe. It was just that
she had never heard the flower's American name
before.

"It's a wonderful blue. Sort of hyacinthy. Deep but
just a touch muddied. Ex-*treme*-ly romantic."

"With this one soon to be born," she mused,
spreading her arms across her belly, "and two more at
my side, I will look extremely romantic, *estremamente
romantica* in my bluebell dress, no?"

"Yes! *Estremamente,*" Mark Kroll adamantly insisted, refusing to smile at her droll self-deprecation.
He knew that it was her attempt to mask the guilt she
felt at bringing another child into a fatherless home.
And then, as if to prove his insight, she voiced it directly, her eyes searching his with naked intensity.

"Am I *pazzo*, Mark? Crazy for loving this baby
growing inside me though I bring it into a broken
home? A home where its Mama cries all the time, just
like a baby herself?"

"Silvana, it's not crazy to experience two opposite
feelings at the same time. People are complicated. Life
is complicated."

"But is it normal to love this baby one minute"—
she caressed her round belly—"and feel sad and sorry
the next?"

"In your case, it's understandable. Of course your
situation depresses you. Of course you cry. But it will
all work out. I promise you," he said with more conviction than he felt. "It's going to be fine."

"You're a good friend, Mark. You understand me.
And you always make me feel better. Always."

Not always. Mark remembered having coffee with
her one Wednesday morning at Per Sempre when she
vowed, in a dead voice, that her marriage was finished.
That day he could not help her; her depression was
too stark, too new. As she whisked a bowl of egg
whites, beating them fast, faster, then finally whipping
them furiously, she forced out the words.

"He raped me."

"Who?" Mark Kroll, with her first words, went into
a kind of shock. He knew who she meant, but he
could not believe it. "Who raped you?" he had to
ask again.

"My own husband."

"Warren?"

"*Sì*, Warren. Warren raped me."

"Oh, my God! The brute. The wicked, wicked
brute!" He had heard, in the dead dryness of her
voice, all the violence and all the horror of the night
before. He grimaced at the lurid picture she was painting, at her portrait in blood.

"And after he raped me," she continued in that
same voice, "he locked me in the bedroom closet for
the whole long, dark night."

He shook his head no, no, no, as if he could stop
the horrid picture from flashing in front of his eyes.
But of course he could not stop it. Just as he could
not stop feeling her heartbreak as if it were his own.

It was then that Silvana took a deep breath and
said it. "My marriage is finished. This time I will get
a divorce."

He could not look at her, but he reminded her,
"You have said that before."

"Before, for the sake of Anna Michela, I always felt I should try to forgive him for the many terrible things he has done to me and to our family. But last night was the end. That the father of our Anna Michela could do such a thing to her mother! That my own husband could rape me! No! It is finished. *Finito!* I can endure no more. I will see a lawyer tomorrow morning. I *will* be free of Warren Nachman!"

He nodded. This time he believed her. "And I will always be here if you need me," was all he could say.

"I know," she said and squeezed his hand, but he could do nothing to erase the anguish in her eyes.

Now, as he created in his mind the maternity gown Silvana would wear at her brother's wedding, he remembered that day, almost seven months ago. Since then, there had been more talks ... and more tears. But now Silvana was, if anything, even more unhappy ... for she was carrying a child she did not want. Warren's child: conceived in rape, carried in conflict, soon to be born into a world of rejection. Oh, the poor, poor child!

Bluebell satin. Bluebell silk chiffon. Bluebell matelassé. Inspired by Silvana's elegiacal loveliness, he flipped through a file of sample blue fabrics in his mind, fitting them against her. It had always been this way—the sight of someone—or something—beautiful gave him a jolt of creative current that sent spasms of colors and visions and ideas coursing through him. Inspiration. And no one inspired him more than the most beautiful woman of all, his best friend, *bella* Silvana.

It was the perfect friendship. From him, she got understanding and encouragement. From her, he got inspiration. Even her supernal cooking inspired him. When he tasted her pasta pudding Jewish style, he thought of ceilings painted with clouds and angels. Her roast leg of lamb gave him visions of ancient Rome. That was what he thought of now.

Graeco-Roman. Neoclassical. Statuesque. And with those three images, he found the look, the theme that would creatively link all the dresses in the wedding party.

For Mary Catherine, he fashioned a strapless, pleated column of white chiffon. And a rather virginal, translucent, tightly sleeved bolero jacket of the same white chiffon, to be worn during the ceremony. A satin cord crisscrossed the pleated column under the breast, Grecian style.

On her wedding day, this same satin cord would be braided with fresh flowers through her tomato-red hair. Over this, an enormous, transparent silk chiffon head "scarf," shot with hundreds of tiny, twinkling rhinestones, would take the place of a traditional veil. To hold the scarf in place, Fabian designed two enormous rhinestone hat pins. Later, the scarf could become a beaded stole, accessorizing and softening her rather revealing strapless gown.

Silvana, too, was draped like a Grecian goddess, but in a low-cut sleeveless gown and matching sleeveless robe of flowing silk jersey, the exact color of bluebells. It was not Mark Kroll's intention to design an outfit that would hide her pregnancy. He believed her pregnancy, like his homosexuality, was neither shameful nor shocking. For both, however, the prescription was the same: a teaspoon of discretion mixed with equal portions of good sense and good taste.

Fabian, however, called him hopelessly romantic and sentimental. Whenever Mark Kroll said something soppy, something like, "A woman with child is one of the more beautiful sights in this world," Fabian would tease him unmercifully.

"You're a contradiction," he would begin. "You're two opposite people existing in one person."

And Mark would play along. "I am?"

"Yes, on the one hand, you're a sharp businessman with a killer sense of competition and a fierce will to succeed."

"And on the other hand?"

"Cotton candy, marshmallow cream! 'A woman with child,'" he'd mock laughingly. "What a riot.

Mark, sometimes you're the sloppiest sentimentalist in the world!"

Nevertheless, Mark still thought that Silvana, in her silk jersey gown that molded to her breasts and her large belly and the matching, sleeveless overdrape looked both stately and yet utterly sexy.

Even Silvana loved her bluebell gown—for the soft, swishy sound it made as she moved. Like the sound of making love on the grass. A sound that reminded her of Michele.

Although the *huppah* of ancient times was a portable canopy under which the wedding ceremony was held, this *huppah* looked quite substantial. Its three trellised walls and roof were festooned with fresh flowers and ferns like a sturdy, blossoming bower.

Shifting his weight from one foot to the other at the front of the *huppah*, Eduardo waited impatiently to receive his bride and exchange their wedding vows and their rings. Once he had marched down the aisle and taken his place facing the rabbi, he could feel his pulse begin to pound against his wet temples. First he mopped his brow with his white pocket handkerchief. Then he pressed the handkerchief to his throbbing temples. Then he mopped his brow again. Yet the rabbi seemed completely unaware of Eduardo's agitation. And not only because his eyes were closed. He alone seemed transported to a sublimely spiritual plane. He alone was *davening*—bending his upper body back and forth in time to his serenely silent prayers.

Or maybe he's really worried. Maybe he's praying for me! For us! Eduardo thought anxiously. *He can foretell the future and he can see that Mary Catherine is going to tell me this is a big mistake. She's not even going to bother walking down the aisle.*

For one brief moment he smiled to himself, remembering how he had teased Mary Catherine that according to the Talmud, the *huppah* places the bride into subjugation under her husband's legal domain. He

remembered how Mary Catherine had argued back,
"That's why Jewish women have the *Ketubah.*"

"The *Ketubah?*" Mary Catherine knew more about
some of the Jewish lore than he did.

"The marriage contract," she said with a superior
smile. "It's true that Jewish women, like other women
in ancient society, were considered the property of
their husbands. But that's why the *Ketubah* came into
being—to give them economic protection."

"Do I have to sign it?"

"Absolutely!" Mary Catherine gleefully agreed.
"And in Orthodox ceremonies, the rabbi reads it out
loud. But I think we can forgo the reading of the
contract."

"Gee thanks," he remembered saying and then
smiling when she said expansively, "You're quite
welcome."

But now he began his worrying all over again. Was
there enough room for Mary Catherine on his right?
His "queen," according to a verse in Psalms (45:10),
stands at the "king's right hand in gold of Ophir."
Yes, he decided, there was room enough for his queen.
But where was she? It had been only thirty seconds
since he last looked at his watch, but it felt like
thirty years.

To Eduardo's left, Club Midnight's owner, Joey
Rizzo, yarmulke raffishly atop his slick black hair, was
"best man," and one of the two official "witnesses"
to the ceremony. As such, Joey Rizzo was entrusted
with remembering to bring the rings and to keep them
available in his jacket pocket. Then, after the rabbi
gave his invocation and blessed the first cup of wine—
signifying the betrothal—he would ask Joey to produce the rings.

Considering how nervous Eduardo was, entrusting
the best man with the responsibility of the rings
seemed to everyone a wise and sensible custom. Everyone except Eduardo. At this moment there was no
one Eduardo could trust, least of all himself. He certainly could not keep from motioning to Joey and ask-

ing in sign language, "You've got them, haven't you? The two rings? Are you sure you've got them?"

At first, Joey faked a look of alarm and slapped his forehead as if he suddenly realized he'd left the rings on his bureau back at his house. But when he saw Eduardo's face turn the green of a Sicilian olive, he knew that if he did not reassure him immediately, the groom might simply faint . . . or worse.

"Yes, yes." Joey nodded extremely vigorously, patting his pocket confidently. Then he shrugged apologetically at the rabbi because the rabbi's eyes not only were open now, they were attempting to follow the frantic, silent tennis match between the groom and the best man.

Eduardo could not wait until the rings were on his and Mary Catherine's fingers. And the benedictions had been chanted over the second glass of wine—the one which signified the marriage. Then the wine could be sipped again . . . His mouth was almost too dry to swallow.

However, even then, Eduardo knew, he still would not be officially married.

But at least then comes the fun part! he told himself, not entirely cheered.

The "fun part" was when he would then place the wineglass on the floor and shatter it with his heel. The ritual was often seen as a remembrance of the destruction of the Temple of Jerusalem. But the shattering of the wineglass actually originated much later—in the Middle Ages—when loud noises were thought to drive away evil spirits and insure good fortune.

And then, after he shattered the glass, and "Mazel tov!" rang out in a chorus by the audience, it would finally be time for the very best part—the pronouncement that they were indeed married. And at last . . . the kiss.

Ah! The kiss! Eduardo wet his lips, savoring the thought of Mary Catherine's mouth locked to his. Locked for all eternity. It was a lovely thought . . . but he simply could not stand still. Suddenly he became

aware of the organ music. *Grazie,* he sighed thank-
fully, and turned to watch the procession march down
the aisle, climb the two steps, and come to stand under
the *huppah* with him.

Silvana floated down the aisle on young chef Gino's
arm, then Kevin Garren and Frances McGee, then
Mark Kroll and Fabian. Elena and Anna Michela
wore matching flower girl dresses and stood with their
baskets at the back of the aisle, waiting to shower
the bride with petals. But where was Mary Catherine?
Eduardo was sure he was about to explode or to ex-
pire from the tension. Even Silvana's smile, as she
caught his eye across from him under the *huppah,* did
not help. Nothing could help except the sight of the
only person in the world who could save him now . . .
and forever . . . Mary Catherine.

And then, there she was.

Moving slowly, in measured, even beats, keeping
perfect time to the massive organ's melodic march,
Mary Catherine made her way down the aisle, her
proud, ten-year-old cousin Matthew at her side. The
guests smiled at Mary Catherine's unconventional escort. Then they gasped as they beheld her, or tried to,
half revealed yet half mysteriously cloaked in a glitter-
ing, translucent veil.

But beneath the headdress, she was not calm. She
still feared—dreamily—that she might be a fraud.
Never, perhaps, had she felt quite this dreamy, this
light. She weighed nothing.

Her feet, in white satin high heels, lightly touched
the ground and bounced off, like two party balloons.
Yet she did not fear she might fly away. As light as
she was, she felt grounded. Grounded to this aisle,
pathway to her heart. So how could this be a secret
sham when she felt so connected to this moment?

Then it came to her: she belonged! She was an out-
sider no longer. And to belong was to believe. Yes,
she did believe after all. She believed in all that was
here in this room—all the beauty, all the love, and,
yes . . . all the holy rituals. That was why she was here

today; that was what all this meant. She had not lied. She was not false. And there was no fraud.

Her belief began in this marriage and in the rituals of the ceremony. They tied her to Eduardo. Like the white satin cord that braided through her hair, they bound her to him. And to the Levi family.

Now at last she would be one of them. A new member, perhaps without their tortured history—but a true part of their clan. She had found the beginning of her new identity.

Relief slowed her heartbeats, quieted her pulse. At last she heard it: *Here comes the bride!* With each step the music in the room and the music in her heart became one.

She saw Eduardo step down and reach out his arm to help her. Behind her she heard the sighs and tears of the assembled guests. Vaguely, she sensed young Matthew stepping away, leaving her to the groom.

Then she saw his eyes. They were wet and full, but he was smiling. Her somber Eduardo was smiling! Grinning, really. Grinning with . . .

Anande.

Anande. The Sanskrit word suddenly came to her from deep in her memory, stored there years ago after she had read it somewhere. Bliss.

PART THREE

Prologue

1968

It is dawn and I am crying. Lately, I begin my days in tears. These early mornings are the only time I have entirely to myself, yet I spend them crying. My friend Mark says I am depressed. Perhaps I am.

"Who wouldn't be?" he adds. "I'd be depressed with three kids to mother, a restaurant to run and another about to open, a huge apartment to maintain—and no one to share my bed or my heart."

All that he says is true. Although I am busy from morning to night with my work and my family, I am lonely. Yet when my sorrow overtakes me, it is not a man's love that I most long to have. It is forgiveness. My guilt has stalked me all these years, and in the early mornings I am caught in its grip. That is when I think of you, Mama.

Mama, do you think, because I do not speak your name for some time, that you are forgotten? I do not forget you, Mama. Ever. You are always with me. Always, always. I see your face, just as it was that last day. Your eyes burn into me with their stare, sharp as pencil points. I hear your voice, hoarse, strained. "Why, Silvana?" you plead, as much with your shoulders as with your voice. Your shoulders flex up to your ears as they always do when you are filled with anguish or anger. "Tell me why because I still don't understand. Explain it to me because I cannot rest until I know why my daughter did this thing that tore our house down. But hurry, Silvana, because I am so terribly tired and I want to sleep. When will you let me rest in peace at last?"

Soon, Mama. But I am tired, too. I wish I could just

close my eyes and lie down at last beside you. But I must go on, for the sake of your beautiful granddaughters whom you did not live to see: Elena, Anna Michela . . . and now Debora. (Yes, Debora. I named her for Warren's mother, after all. He turned out to be a good-for-nothing, but his mother's name, his mother's memory deserve to be remembered and perpetuated with respect.)

You look at me with surprise. You look at me as if you are asking, "Respect? Is this my daughter Silvana saying this?" As if you still blame me. Do you, Mama? Do you? Don't you realize that your baby girl, your Silvana, was just that—a baby? And that I always loved you and honored you, even when I was eighteen, and you closed your eyes and your door to the sight of me. How I missed you then! And oh, Mama, how I still miss you now!

Millions of memories of you flood back to me, making me miss the parts of you I loved most of all. Like your darling little feet—your *piccoli piede*—in your little black Sabbath shoes with the little black bows. Exactly like doll's feet. Oh, how I loved to dress up in your dainty shoes! And your child-size hands! I close my eyes and I can feel them on my cheek. Such cool, damp hands. Always in a basin of water, scrubbing our clothes, or squeezing them dry.

Now I see your chubby little fingers (Papa's plain gold ring is so tight you cannot remove it), delicately pinching the ends of your homemade ravioli together and tugging a needle and thread through a worn-out sock. Such dainty, ever busy fingers. How I long to kiss each one of them!

No one believed that I, so tall and big-boned, could be your daughter, did they? You would tell them that I had been tiny like you, but that suddenly, overnight, I sprouted from a sapling into a tree. To me, however, it seemed that I was always big. By twelve, I had outgrown you. By fourteen, I towered over you—and over Eduardo, too. By fifteen, I looked eighteen. But at fifteen I had the heart of a child. Of a child, Mama!

When my Elena was fifteen, I would stare at her,

trying to remember what I was like at her age. And I would think, *Once, you were a baby like your Elena ... but you had the body of a woman.* Some men like that: a premature child with the tightly curled curves of seduction. A rosebud. I learned this at fifteen.

And I would tell myself, *Because your Papa had died and because you were so tall, so* differente, *so* blonda, *you prayed some boy would tell you that you were normal, that you were pretty ... that you were loved.*

Any boy. Instead, *he* said it. An older man. I did not pick him, Mama; he picked me. He said what we did was not wrong. None of it was wrong. And I believed him. For almost three years. But he did not tell me that the price was my youth. That I could never be a child again. That he would rip my innocence from me and that I would never again have a mother to sew up the wound.

Mama? Do you ever think of me? What do you remember of me as you rest uneasily in your cold, dark silence? Do you remember the daughter who loved you so ... or only the daughter who slashed your heart?

I always thought I would see you again, one last time after that final, terrible day. I prayed that you would ask for me, call for me. But then you were taken away and that day became our last moment together here on earth. And now I know why.

Because now I must go through life never, ever knowing whether you would have forgiven me ... if only I had been given the chance to ask.

I ask you now, Mama. Please, please forgive your daughter, your Blonda, your Girasole!

But always, it is the same. Silence. Silence for twenty-six years. And so, though I ask, I know I will never hear your answer and I will never receive your blessing.

This, then, is my punishment.

Purgatorio!

Chapter Fifteen

She did not really believe it was possible to do again, yet here she was, doing it! At forty-four, Silvana was certain of few things in life, but of this she was absolutely sure—that one restaurant was not enough. Not nearly enough. And so, she was doing it again.

The profits from Per Sempre Silvana, that had once seemed as wide and as thick as a tray of lasagne, had shrunk considerably—shrunk to no more than one slim strand of *capellini*—now that they were used to pay the rent on the luxurious Nachman apartment that Silvana had come to think of as her very own.

There had been a period when Warren, ordered by the court to help out—at least financially—contributed alimony and child support, but that had been a long time ago. "I can't afford this," he soon began complaining to Silvana's lawyer. "I've become a pauper." Then one day, he just stopped. The checks stopped, the phone calls stopped . . . *he* stopped. He vanished. And for more than three years, no one had heard from him or had been able to find him. He left no trace.

Overnight, he dropped everything, not only his few relatives and scant friends, but even his real estate business. Suddenly his three employees were left without jobs, without salary, without a "boss." And his smallish "bachelor's" apartment, where he had moved after the divorce, sat dark and empty for more than six months because his landlord was convinced "Mr. Nachman would never leave without paying the rent. He's just drying out. He'll be back when he's sober."

But of course, he did not return, to his landlord's dismay, either drunk or sober.

But most perplexing—and shameful—of all, was his absolute abandonment of his family—without warning, without preparation .. without even a good-bye kiss. One morning Silvana awakened to learn that from that moment on she would have to support and raise Warren's children entirely by herself. From that moment on they would no longer have a father, however imperfect he had been. Because Warren Nachman had simply—and ignominiously—left them all.

In a way, however, it was a relief. Now Silvana did not have to take anything from Warren, not even his check. And the link—their children—that she had feared would tie her to Warren for life had been severed. He was gone, vanished! Dead, she suspected. If not from his own uncontrollable drinking and self-abuse, then from an accident. It had amazed her how he had stayed alive this long, while growing ever more reckless.

Countless times she had been called by the sheriff's office or the highway patrol or the municipal courthouse.

"Your husband has had an accident while driving—"

"He is not my husband."

"He gave us your number."

"We are divorced. I am not responsible."

But she was responsible, no matter what the divorce papers said. It was she—and no one else—who had to come to the emergency ward of the hospital or the police station and take him home, sometimes bandaged, but always unshaven, unwashed and unbearably, blearily repentant.

"How are the girls?" he would ask, a sob in his voice. "Just tell me, how are my little girls?"

"They know you drive when you're drunk and they're afraid you won't be alive for Debora's first day of nursery school or Anna Michela's performance in her class play. They have nightmares."

"Oh, God! My little girls. I love them so much!"

"Then give them what they need most."

"What's that, Silvana?"

"A father."

After he was gone, the children said they missed him but everyone seemed slightly more relaxed, slightly more cheerful. No one jumped when the phone rang anymore. Nightmares became less frequent. And since he had not been reported dead, only missing, no one grieved excessively.

But Warren had not left Silvana entirely worry-free. In addition to the unshakable shame of marital failure, he had also left her with a problem that could still jolt her awake in the dark and fill her with more dread than a house burglar: bills. Bills, bills, mountains of bills.

"The cashmere-sweater-times-three factor," Warren had once rather wryly—and accurately—named it when he was still living close by and still writing checks. "One cashmere sweater for one daughter— well, you can almost afford *one* cashmere sweater. But now multiply the price times three. Pretty fancy, huh? Three daughters, three cashmere sweaters. It's that times-three factor that can drive you nuts!" (For the sake of argument, he included Elena as his daughter. Three daughters got him infinitely more sympathy than only two.)

To Silvana, of course, all three "little girls" really were her natural daughters, although Elena, at twenty-three, could afford to buy her own sweaters now—if they were orlon, that is. Not that she ever demanded that her sweaters be cashmere, but Warren was right about this—the price of any sweater, when multiplied by three, suddenly became a fortune.

So a second restaurant was not mere vanity; it was a necessity! But this time, Silvana had the experience and resources to do it grandly—grand right from the start.

"I shall name this restaurant for you, Elena," Silvana told her firstborn, expecting tears of gratitude. Instead, she received a cold refusal.

"No, don't. Thank you, but please, don't," Elena

implored her mother, though she could not tell Silvana why. Elena became red-faced and tongue-tied whenever she attempted to explain that she was torn between her love for Gino and her love of mathematics. Running a restaurant would mean the end of the hope of a math career. "Really, I don't deserve it, but thanks, Mama," was all she would say. And so, Silvana assumed that Elena's objection was based on mere embarrassment, youthful shyness, and went ahead and named the new establishment after her daughter anyway. She called it "Mia Elena." Elena was not at all pleased.

"I didn't name it for you; I named it for me. *Mia* Elena—'*My* Elena.' *My* daughter. You understand now?" Silvana pleaded, following Elena around the house while Elena fumed and slammed doors. "You see? It's not really named for you at all."

But Elena only rolled her eyes at her mother's facile argument.

"Or if you want, I go the other way. I make it just 'Elena.' No '*Mia.*' Nothing to do with me. Because, eventually, Elena, this one will be yours. Entirely yours. Nothing to do with me. *Niente.*"

For only the second time in the year since she had come home from college, Elena's eyes brightened with excitement. The first time was when she raced into Gino's arms again. Of course, she had seen him during every break and vacation in her four long years of study, but she was sure that when she arrived home, everything would be different. She expected it; she counted on it. She was convinced that Gino would have an important question to ask her, the most important question of her life. And that, instead of applying to graduate schools, she would be planning her wedding. "I doubt if I will go on to get a doctorate in mathematics," she told her professors. "You see, I'm getting married."

"A waste," they clucked and shook their heads, but she was sure she had made the right choice: Gino.

When Elena arrived home, bright eyed and eager,

she discovered that Gino did have an important question for her, but it was not the one she had expected.

"Will you wait for me, my Theresa? I can't afford to marry you yet," he admitted. "But you know I love you. So will you stay here with me and wait for me, my love?"

She supposed it was almost as good as the "real" question, but the light went out of her eyes. She could still apply to graduate school, but instead, she remained in limbo.

Now, hearing her mother's restaurant offer, Elena's eyes brightened with that same hope again. She had heard her mother's offer before, but this time she was sure she heard her mother say, "This one is yours. All yours." She was sure of it. Still, she pushed her mother to confirm it.

"Nothing to do with you? You really mean it's mine?"

"*Sì, sì,*" Silvana agreed, nodding enthusiastically, thrilled to be able to make her daughter smile at last. It did not seem worth the trouble to remind Elena that this second restaurant would certainly be hers ... but not yet. Not while Silvana was still young and energetic and determined enough to build an inheritance large enough for all her daughters. Nevertheless, again she nodded.

"Then, if Mia Elena Ristorante is mine, I make the decisions, yes?" She did not wait for her mother to answer, but she spoke clearly, reasoning with care, so that her mother would be sure to understand her meaning. "For instance, I can hire Gino as chef and let him cook whatever he wishes, can't I?"

Immediately Silvana's posture stiffened, and girding herself for an argument, she folded her arms across her chest. This was not a new or unfamiliar conversation. In the year since her graduation, Elena had argued forcefully for Gino many times. So many that Silvana said Elena should become a lawyer; she was that good.

This time Elena made a new plea—"Why won't you

just let him cook you dinner one night—just taste his recipes? That's all I ask, Mama—taste!''

But Silvana reacted by laughing out loud. She did not laugh to embarrass her daughter. She laughed to dispel the seriousness, the desperation in her daughter's request. Didn't Elena know that it did not matter what Gino cooked—or how well he cooked it? Because Gino wasn't Silvana's choice for head chef of her daughter's restaurant; Elena was. Despite Elena's love of numbers and her decided lack of interest in cooking, she was her mother's choice, her mother's dream. And all these years Silvana had been waiting, hoping for Elena to say, "I've thought it over, Mama, and I've decided that if I'm going to have a restaurant in my name, I'd like to be the chef. Will you teach me?"

So of course, the idea of Elena hiring Gino as chef struck Silvana as ludicrous, even hilarious.

"His recipes and his expertise aren't the point," she told her daughter with a short, tight laugh of impatience. "Oh, I'm sure they're delicious," Silvana hastened to add. "But sautéing an excellent veal and peppers does not make a restaurant great."

"Isn't that what a restaurant is all about? Food?"

Despite herself, Elena was eager for this argument. Although she always said she preferred high-minded theoretical discussions to practical arguments, when it came to restaurants, she could not help listening avidly to what her mother had to say. Her mother's earthy, tenacious grasp of the practical was unbearably unidealistic, but it was also, she hated to admit, extremely savvy. And that made Elena feel a certain grudging admiration for her mother, which she tried her best to hide.

And if, over the years, she had occasionally caught her mother trying to indirectly interest Elena in the field of restaurant cooking, she had never really taken her mother seriously. She would laugh scoffingly, and that would be the end of it. Until today, that is.

"Let's be honest, Elena. Why do I give you a restau-

rant in your name? So a stranger—who is not even a
Jew—can be the chef?"

"Gino's no stranger!"

"Okay, but he's not family either."

At that, Elena had to hold her tongue because it
was true; she was not yet even officially engaged and
Gino was still far from being family. Why was Gino
making her wait so long to marry, anyway? Was it to
torture her? Did he have a weird, cruel streak in him?
Sometimes, Elena had to admit, it seemed as if he did.

Silvana, however, was still gently pushing the idea
of Elena becoming a chef. "Food is important, *si*. But
it's not the only factor. And you possess all the qualities that can make for a great chef/owner. Besides the
cooking, that is."

"What else really is there?"

Silvana was aghast. "You ask me that, you, who
grew up behind the cash register?"

Elena only shrugged.

"And who made her mama very proud by distin-
guishing herself in mathematics at university?"
Silvana continued.

"Okay, but I think in large theoreticals. I never applied my studies to my own experience with restaurants." Elena knew her argument was weak, but
somehow, she was never her most brilliant when discussing restaurants. This was her mother's area of expertise, she had always assumed, not hers.

"Profits make or break a restaurant. You can cook
the most delicious food, but if your costs are too big
and your profits are too small, then you're in trouble."

"But isn't food the way a restaurant makes a
profit?" Elena argued.

"Yes, if the margins for food, labor, liquor are low
enough—as well as your fixed costs like rent, utilities,
and laundry. You have the *capo*"—she pointed to her
head—"for all of this. You, not Gino!"

Elena rolled her eyes.

"I mean it, Elena. Some chefs—well, all they want
to cook is expensive veal and steak. But you would
worry about profit and loss. You would worry if your

labor costs went over twenty percent, for example. And if your rent was more than four or five percent of your gross. And if your suppliers and your bartender were cheating you. And if your wait staff didn't make enough tips and quit. Or if they just grumbled their dissatisfaction to the patrons. You would make a great chef because you would be concerned about everything that makes a restaurant a success—or a failure."

"But, Mama, you forget one thing: I'm not a professional cook."

"You could learn. You have it in the blood. I'm sure of it."

Again Elena rolled her eyes. "Gino's the artist," she muttered. "I'm just a drudge. Isn't that what you're saying, Mama?"

"What is this drudge?" Silvana had never heard the word before.

"A drudge is someone who does tedious, menial work. And that's me!" Elena shouted and burst into tears. She was no artist; she was caught up in details: twenty-eight to thirty percent for food costs, four or five percent for rent. She liked quantities and percentages and specifics. She liked numbers. So much so that once, in a fit of extreme irritation, Silvana had accused her of being more like her stepfather than her real father, Michele Bassani. "You're just like a Nachman. You bleed numbers, preferably numbers in the black, of course. You don't bleed red blood at all."

It was not the worst thing she could have said to Elena. Aside from disliking being linked with a Nachman, Elena did admit that her mother's words had a certain ring of truth. She *did* bleed numbers. It was Gino, however, who was the genius. Gino possessed the talent; that was why she loved him. With Gino planning the menu, creating the recipes, and cooking the food, her restaurant could not possibly fail. All she could ever be was Gino's helpmate. She told herself she would be content with that because Gino would make Mia Elena a success. If she saw this so clearly, why couldn't her mother?

But Silvana knew that every year a plague of failure wiped out hundreds, perhaps even thousands, of New York restaurants, decimating its victims like a massive influenza epidemic. In the end, she knew, no restaurant was immune. Without hard work and constant attention to a multitude of details, even the most crowded of restaurants could become empty overnight. And yet, while she knew that no one was safe, at least her concept contained one important element for success: uniqueness.

Even in 1968, there were virtually no serious Italian restaurants in New York, aside from Per Sempre Silvana and perhaps one other. Being a pioneer of serious Italian cuisine—instead of the ubiquitous, Americanized "spaghetti and meatballs" or "veal cutlet parmigiana" dinner—alone made her establishment unique. But added to her restaurant's pioneering spirit was the fact that no one else in the entire city—perhaps in the entire country—specialized in the ancient cuisine of the Italian Jews—a fact that completely and permanently established its singularity.

It was Silvana who had developed an entire menu of fresh, succulent, surprising, delicious, complex tastes. And with her collection of ancient recipes, adapted, updated—and then cooked to her exact specifications—she was introducing Americans to a unique dining experience.

"Before Per Sempre Silvana, no one in America ever tasted artichokes prepared in the Roman Jewish style, or my Hanukkah rice pancakes," she often told Gino. "These recipes are what make us unique. That is why they must be followed exactly." Yet she was never sure that Gino understood this. Perhaps no one not of her blood could. For by preserving these recipes and presenting them in her restaurants, she felt she was somehow preserving the memory of her dead relatives—of her father, Umberto, and her slain mother and brother. Somehow, whenever she served Passover fish croquettes with pignoli nuts, her mother Anna's version of gefilte fish, she felt she was preserving the memory of her mother. And when she served what used to be Raffaelle's favorite, matzo lasagne, she felt she was saying a prayer to her fallen eldest brother. And when Risotto Coi Fegatini Dal Umberto was on the menu, she felt that the rice and chicken livers dish named for her father somehow kept him alive. How then could she entrust this mission to anyone who was not linked by blood to her, anyone who was not family?

Gino was a good chef. Had she not trained him herself? But he knew nothing of her family Passover seders, of the Hanukkah candles she lit each year, or of the hidden sacred memorial in all her restaurant menus. If she gave him his way, he would probably make pork a specialty!

But no, she had to admit it was not Gino's religion that she most held against him. It was something else—something strange, something cruel in his character. As yet, it was just a vague feeling she had about him, noticed in his brief but brutal outbursts in the kitchen, but it made her want to discourage Elena from loving him. Or from naming him chef of Mia Elena. However, the danger, Silvana well knew, was that in pushing Gino away, Elena might follow.

But what other choice do I have? she asked herself, sighing. And was forced to admit, *None. None at all.*

"Give Gino a chance," Elena was imploring, startling Silvana out of her private reverie.

"I will. But not yet. You are both still very young. It is best to wait. Many things may yet happen. Believe me, there is much time."

Elena wondered why her mother was making her wait, too. What things might yet happen? Then it became clear.

She hopes Gino will break up with me! That's what she hopes will happen. But she'll see. I'll show her. I'll win him. She'll see that finally someone does love me!

In a way, Silvana's words were what Elena needed to hear in order to break away. She had been unconsciously awaiting just this schism. Now she could shift her loyalties neatly—and swiftly—onto the other side of the line, where Gino waited. For she made the shift almost too eagerly, almost gladly, receiving her mother's words, without hesitation, as the final slice of a sharp knife that, forever after, divided mother and daughter into two separate halves of a former loving whole.

That night, Elena decided she would sleep with Gino—if he ever got up the courage to ask.

"She'll never give you independence. And she'll never pay you enough money to marry me."

As usual, they were arguing. About sex. But sex, the word, was never mentioned, and sex, the subject, hidden under a torrent of words, was completely disguised.

Needless to say, Gino had not yet gotten up the courage to take his beloved to bed, although Elena had hinted several times that she was as hungry for him as he was for her. But beyond that, she could do no more. She vowed to herself that she was not going to "wear the pants" in this relationship. And now, since no one would—or could—make a move, they were reduced merely to arguing about sex. They had stopped touching at all.

"The only way you'll ever be able to cook any of your own southern Italian recipes is to open your own restaurant—or sneak a dish in one night when she's busy with the opening of the new place."

Gino stared at Elena. "You want me to sneak behind the back of your own mother?"

Elena's shoulders curled in and she hugged herself, preparing for the peevish exchange that was now inevitable. In the year since she had been home from school, she and Gino still argued the same way they always had: by asking each other impatient questions and then answering with even more exasperating questions, while upping the volume and tension until one of them finally broke down—usually Elena, of course. Or gave in—usually Gino, of course.

This argument had not yet escalated to that point, however. Nor had the volume.

"Are you going to slave at Per Sempre forever,

dreaming of dishes you can never cook for anyone—except me?"

"Nag, nag! Are you the girl I once took for an angel—or are you really just a nag?"

"Do you really still think of me as your pure Saint Theresa? Your virgin angel?"

That question always got him. But today, he did have to pause and think for a moment because lately Elena was becoming more shrewlike than saintlike.

"Yes," he finally answered with all his old, hopeful innocence and reverence. "Aren't you?" And his own face, leaner and somehow more saintlike than hers, drooped with pure white dread. "Aren't you my perfect girl, my perfect Theresa?"

"First of all," she had to sigh, "I'm a twenty three-year-old woman, not a girl. And this is 1968, not the fifteenth century. And most important of all, a girl doesn't have to be completely, inhumanly pure for you to love her. She could just be . . . she could just be . . ."

"What?"

"Well, flawed."

"Flawed?"

"Yes. She could be flawed, but good deep down in her heart." She realized that she had stopped answering him with another question. She was speaking now from her heart—from the pure goodness of her heart.

Gino just listened. He, too, had stopped answering with more questions.

"She could hate her mother sometimes and push her boyfriend too hard sometimes and still be . . . well, good."

Gino nodded his round, boyish head. "I know that."

"Do you know it?"

"Yeah, I know you push me too hard sometimes, but I still love you, don't I?" They were back to answering in questions again.

"Do you? Do you really love the real me and not some ideal picture you have of me?" Suddenly, Elena was close to tears. "Sometimes I think you believe I really am Saint Theresa. And that you're shocked when I act well, act . . . normal."

"And sometimes *I* think you want me to get into a knockdown drag-out fight with your mother just to prove—what? What would it prove, Elena?"

"That you're a man! That you'll fight to win me! Even if it means toppling her, my mother, the giant! That you want me so much, you'd do even that," she blurted out impulsively. Immediately, of course, she was sorry, and clamped her hand to her mouth to muffle or stop the very words that she had already shouted out to him. But after another moment she had a change of mind.

Enough! She had had enough. Dropping her embarrassment and her hand from her face, she confronted him openly. Today, she decided, she was going to mention the unmentionable—sex—even if it meant "wearing the pants."

"I've been away four years and I've been back almost another whole year and though you say you love me, you've never made love to me. You've never even really tried."

Now it was he who looked embarrassed. "I thought we agreed to wait."

"But that was years ago!"

"I thought you keep to your vows."

"Keep to my vows?" she mocked. "I'm not a goddamned nun!" Then she took his hand and squashed it against her breast. "I'm flesh. Not pure, but not dirty, either. Just warm, human flesh."

His first impulse was to pull his hand away, but in spite of himself, his fingers palpated the pillowy softness of her breast. No zabaglione, no ricotta cheesecake, no béchamel-layered lasagne, had ever been so soft. This time, his other hand crept up her blouse and covered her other breast of its own free will. However, when her hands brushed against his as they traveled up her blouse to the top two buttons, he had to protest.

"We were supposed to do this on our wedding night."

"Jesus will forgive you."

"That's not funny," he said, but there was an unmis-

takable smile on his face. Usually, he hated it when
she teased him about his religion—but usually, he
didn't have both her breasts in his hands.

"It wasn't meant to be funny," she told him, but
she was smiling, too.

"Are you sure?" He didn't mean about not being
funny.

"How about you?"

"I am . . . if you are."

She took a deep breath and admitted, "I'm sure."
She unbuttoned her blouse—and noticed that he did
not stop her. Suddenly, wearing the pants in this relationship no longer seemed quite so odious. She pushed
him gently onto the double bed that occupied most of
the space in his tiny studio apartment. Then she
climbed on top of him and began unbuttoning his
shirt.

"If only I had known that all you needed was a
little push . . ." She bit his ear.

"I don't like to be pushed," he confessed. "Especially by a girl. But now that we're here . . ." He had
no need to finish the sentence. He simply rolled her
over and took her into his arms.

Chapter Sixteen

He was tall and dark tan with a face that was angular, striking, and exceedingly memorable. With eyes narrowed to slits, he kept shooting sizzling glances at her that bounced off her skin like hot grease. She felt singed every time he looked at her ... but who was he?

No one knew who he was. Elena, in her crisp white blouse with silver cuff links and her black tuxedo jacket with satin lapels, looking exactly what she was supposed to be—maître d' of Silvana's new restaurant—tried to find out, but got nowhere.

"Mama, no one knows him. All I know is that four weeks ago he reserved a table for the day after opening night under the name of Wolf."

"Wolf?" Silvana repeated, sneaking a glance at him through the small kitchen pass-through into the formal dining room. "*Sì*, he looks like a wolf—a very sly, very cunning wolf. *Lupo!* Yes, this one is a wolf, definitely."

What Silvana did not tell her daughter was the effect this Wolf's eyes were having upon her. Here it was, the night after opening. All the noisy hoopla and excitement had died down, and although every table was just as crowded, the front room of Mia Elena Ristorante bore no resemblance to the night before, when the crush and the noise of the crowds had been almost more than Silvana or Elena could handle. Last night seemed more like one hundred nights ago.

Tonight, happily, Silvana's brand-new second restaurant on posh Fifth Avenue already had the hushed, purring rhythm of a well-oiled, long-established operation. No dishes crashed to the floor, no goblets clinked and shattered, no entrées burned in the oven, and no customers laughed—or complained—too loudly. Instead, all was subdued, elegant, luxe.

Dark green, deep-pile carpeting covered the floors, velvet cushions softened the seats of the hand-painted green and gold chairs, and it seemed as if nothing could disturb the muted, refined tone of Silvana's restaurant ... but that Wolf man and his devouring stare!

Already those eyes of his had unnerved Silvana so thoroughly that she had burned her hand against the side of a pan in which she was sautéing minced garlic. She had just come back from greeting a table of six in the front room—the mayor of New York City, his wife, and several other well-known city politicians.

"How do you keep your whites so crisp and, well, so white?" the mayor's wife wanted to know. "I always get stains on my clothes when I cook—even with an apron."

"At home I do, too," Silvana confided, making an instant friend. "Tomato sauce and olive oil on all my clothes! But restaurant cooking is different—it's more organized, more precise." At that exact moment, she caught the Wolf man's eyes at the next table and her cheeks burst into flame as if from an inner explosion. But she forced her attention back to the mayor's wife and said, with determination, "You cannot afford to make mistakes or to have accidents ... and so you hardly ever do."

Yet here she was with a burned hand—a rare yet rather inconvenient accident, slowing her down and turning her irritable. And all because of a stranger's eyes.

It had been many, many years since a man had looked at her the way this stranger did, yet her body reacted as if she were still an adolescent, and not a forty-four-year-old woman nearing forty-five. Even when she wasn't sneaking looks, she could picture him sitting in the dining room, sipping his wine, his dark eyes searching, searching for her. And these thoughts of him sent her heart to a screeching stop like a sub-

way train, and then sent it lurching and clattering forward at triple the usual beats.

Oh, it was a jumpy, bumpy ride! Much too unnerv-
ing, much too unsettling! If only she could be guaranteed that she would never have to see those hungry
eyes again, and she would happily hide out here in
the kitchen forever, grilling the veal chops, stirring the
sauce, supervising the new cooking staff ...

But a half hour later, she was called out into the
front room again—this time to welcome a famous actress and several cast members of the Jewish stage
who were appearing in a hit show on Second Avenue—and her heart began to beat in triple time again.
This stranger, this Wolf man, was the cause of it all,
yet she could do nothing to stop it. Nothing.

And so, as she edged her way past the hot new
stoves and toward the swinging doors, an apricot flush
rose high on her cheeks. Her forehead and her upper
lip bubbled with sweat, but her hands were as cold as
a gelato. This was all because she could feel his eyes
on her body exactly like hot fingers. And because she
both dreaded—and yearned for—one more of those
looks.

With both reluctance and eagerness, she finally
emerged from the kitchen, leaving the cooking to her
new young assistant chef. (At Per Sempre Silvana,
Gino now ran the kitchen ... but still, of course, according to Silvana's exacting specifications and
recipes.)

Tying a new, clean, crisp apron over her baggy
checked pants, she silently rehearsed to herself the
special dishes on the menu that she would recommend
to the actress and the cast.

"Actresses are always dieting," she told herself, "so
suggest the spinach Venice style and the Roman vegetable timbale and the fillet of sole with lemon and
black olives."

For the others, she would offer to prepare a risotto
with three kinds of mushrooms or the baked fettuccine
with chicken, raisins, and nuts. Of course, they might
decide to order something else from the printed

menu—she was prepared to cook whatever they desired.

"Concentrate on the actress and her table, on all your customers. Don't look at him as you pass," she warned herself.

But as soon as she neared the Wolf man's table, he reached out and grabbed her wrist.

She stared at her hand in his dark grip as if this were a dream. It did not seem possible that she could be the owner and chef of this new, elegant restaurant and be handled like this, gripped like this by this strangely compelling man. And yet, at the very same time, it also seemed so familiar, so natural that she felt this actually might have happened to her once before, though she could not exactly remember when.

"I caught sight of you," he whispered, "when I first came in and now I've spent the whole night sitting here, just waiting for more chances to see you again."

His voice was deep, husky, and, yes, sexy, but she did not look at him as he spoke. She continued to stare at her hand, still in his tight, imprisoning grip.

"You're incredibly beautiful," he continued. "Do you have any idea how beautiful you are? Do you know how you look when you walk that way, with your chin pointing high in the air and the light bouncing off your hair and the strong planes of your face? And when you smile?"

Still, she would not look at him. She compared the skin tone of her hand to his: *We could be related,* she thought. *Mine is almost as tan as his—as tan as if I spend my days sunbathing!*

"You think I'm dangerous, don't you? Very crazy or very dangerous . . . to grab you like this."

Now she met his eyes and realized that he was young, certainly much younger than she. *Mysterious,* she thought. *And compelling. But not crazy.* With firm resolve she told him, "Let go of my hand and I will answer you."

"If I let you go, you will run away." He smiled, but it was a smile without joy. It was a hopeless smile, utterly heartbreaking, and it shattered her firm resolve.

"No one is allowed to run in here. Or to run away. This is my restaurant and that is my rule." Why was she beaming such a reassuring smile back at him? She did not know.

"Do you always obey your own rules?" he asked, his expression, though mocking, becoming slightly warmer. Just warm enough to shatter her resolve all over again.

She tried to nod yes coolly but she had no idea if she succeeded . . . or if yes was the right answer. However, she still had enough presence of mind to know that if he detained her another second longer, she would have to break her rule and run, after all. The table with the actress and her guests had expected her some minutes ago. It was always unwise to alienate patrons, but at a brand-new restaurant, it was positively suicidal. Silvana knew this in every cell of her body. Knew it and knew it. And yet, she lingered, hoping he would never let go of her because she was melting, melting, and the feeling was making her delirious.

"You haven't answered me yet—do you know how beautiful you are?"

Her hand, she suddenly realized, was free, but she was not sure when that had happened because imprinted on her skin was the impermanent outline of his fingers. *But if it's impermanent,* she thought, *why does it burn right down to the bone?*

"No, because I have another rule," she told him, pretending a coolness she did not feel. "I never look in mirrors. Ever." Then she spun around and, with her back to him, spent a ridiculous amount of time charming the actress and her party at the next able. When she finally returned to the kitchen, she was not surprised to see that he was gone. That even he had finally been chilled by her coldness. The only thing that did surprise her was the enormity of her sorrow— like a vast, empty crater—now that the young, handsome stranger was gone. For with him had gone the only chance for passion and romance she had felt in years—a feeling she'd long assumed was no longer attainable. It had been brief—indeed, merely an evening—but it had been as intense and as poignant as the flame of one candle illuminating the enormous dark and endless night.

Ever since the night she decided to switch from a skirt to wearing the pants, Elena had been living in a kind of stunned silence. Yes, she had coaxed Gino into making love to her. But once again, nothing, she had quickly come to realize, had changed. Gino still worked obediently for her mother and, she had to admit, so did she. *We're marking time,* she told herself. The only difference was that now she worked as maître d' at Mia Elena, the restaurant named *for* her but not yet given *to* her, and Gino remained at Per Sempre Silvana. It was enough, on the night of Elena's twenty-fourth birthday, to make her feel despondent.

"What did sleeping with you get me?" she asked Gino bitterly. "Name one thing."

"Are you serious?" Gino had been in a constant, steamy state of sexual bliss ever since Elena had finally seduced him into the act. All he could think of was when and where they would do it again ... and again. Therefore, her question was not merely insulting, it was entirely incomprehensible.

"Twenty-four years old and not even engaged yet," she continued. "I gave up graduate school for you."

Gino stared disconsolately at the book, *The Magic— and the Terror—of Numbers,* that he had bought for her and that now lay unwrapped and discarded on the floor. But he knew enough not to say, "You got the book you wanted on numbers." He knew enough not to say anything more at that moment, but inwardly he seethed. Someday she would pay.

It was Monday night, their one night off, and Elena had come to Gino's one-room apartment to receive her birthday present. Gino had asked the bookstore to adorn the gift with extra bows and ribbons, but as soon as Elena saw the bulky package, her face drooped and for a moment Gino thought she was disappointed solely with the gift wrapping. But of course, as soon as she asked, "What did I get for sleeping with you?" he understood that it was the gift itself that displeased her. He understood that he had not done the right thing; he just did not know what to do about it.

But Elena did.

Sliding her high heels back on, she stood up and pulled on her black tuxedo suit jacket, preparing to leave.

(Even when she was off-duty, Elena liked to be seen in the same outfits she wore as maître d': white blouses with pleats, French cuffs and striking cuff links, black suits with satin-lapeled tuxedo jackets.) She began collecting tuxedoes during her last year in college, after seeing a 1930s movie in which Marlene Dietrich wore her own exquisitely tailored but slightly naughty tuxedo. Completely captivated, Elena decided to adapt Dietrich's sophisticated style to her own wardrobe. The tuxedo, she resolved, would become her very own unique fashion statement.

The trouble, of course, was in finding a woman's tuxedo—anywhere in 1968; there were none. Ultimately, Elena was steered to a used clothing shop, where she bought men's secondhand tuxedoes that she then had tailored to fit her own short, petite body. The result, she knew, was worth the bother. She had achieved a distinctive look all her own; she stood apart. No one else dressed like her, least of all her mother, who said, "My daughter buys men's rags from old Jewish peddlers and turns them into fashions. Oh, *grazie*, Signore, for who—except You—knew that my Elena had eyes as well as brains!"

But now Elena knew she needed something more than eyes or brains; she needed courage. Courage to leave Gino in order to ultimately win him. But she would have to mean it when she left him, mean it when she said, "It's over." Otherwise, he would not believe he had really lost her. And if he did not know he had lost her, he would not be willing to do the one thing that could win her back—he would not be willing to marry her. Not immediately, at any rate. And immediate was the only way she would have it now; she was not willing to wait another second.

"What're you doing?" Gino asked when she had her hand on the knob of the door.

"I'm leaving."

"Why?" At this point, Gino seemed completely befuddled. "We haven't even had dinner yet, and I thought that later we might ... well, you know ..."

"I'm leaving because it's over between us."

Gino looked stricken. "What are you saying, Elena?"

"I'm saying good-bye. We're finished. I'm sorry, Gino, but I just cannot continue to wait for you to make up your mind. By the time you decide you really want to marry me—if you ever do—I'll be old and gray. I love you but I'm just marking time. I simply have to get on with my life. So, this is it. Good-bye."

Her hand was trembling as she turned the doorknob, but she was determined to walk out and not look back. She could not quite yet believe that she had said it all—and meant every word of it—just as she had vowed to do. And that it was not as heartbreaking as she'd expected. In fact, she was not even crying, although even she acknowledged that she might just be numbed with shock—and that the tears would come later.

At any rate, she managed to make it out the door and down the corridor without a sob, and was feeling rather proud of herself. But as she was about to enter the elevator, Gino, who was behind her in bare feet, grabbed her by the shoulders and pulled her back into the corridor.

"Don't go," he begged her in a broken voice.

She sighed but felt almost irritated by this interruption. Didn't he believe her? Couldn't he see that this time she absolutely meant it?

"Gino, I'm really sorry, but it's over."

"I can't lose you. I can't let you go."

Elena shrugged her shoulders. "Sure you can.

You've been doing it for the past two years. I've been sifting through your fingers like fine-grained sand ... and you've let me."

"No! I didn't realize. I didn't know!"

"And now that you do?" She waited a moment and when he had no answer, she turned her back to him and rang for the elevator again. Gino dropped to the floor on his knee, about to propose, when the elevator doors opened. As Elena was about to enter, Gino again reached out in desperation to stop her from escaping—but this time he threw his arms around her knees, tackling her to the ground. And as soon as she was down, he gripped her by the shoulders to hold her there, to keep her still.

"Marry me!" he shouted breathlessly into her face. "Yes or no. Put up—or shut up. Will you—or won't you?"

"When?"

"Why can't you just answer yes or no?"

"When?" she insisted.

"Tomorrow. Today. Whenever you want."

"Right now. Right this minute. That's what I want." Looking straight up at him, Elena repeated, "Now!"

"Be reasonable. It's seven-thirty at night. The marriage license bureau is closed. We'll go tomorrow."

Elena shook her head. "Tomorrow is Saturday. It's closed tomorrow and it's closed Sunday. No, if you want to marry me, it must be now. I'm not waiting until Monday."

"Be reasonable," Gino pleaded. "What can I do?"

"You can elope with me, that's what you can do."

"Elope? Elope where? Who'll marry us now?"

Elena's mind was suddenly as clear as a bare, black slate scrawled with only four chalk words: *Go to the judge!*

"Um, don't you have an uncle in New Jersey who is a judge?" she asked, assuming an exaggerated air of calmness while her eyes blinked nervously with suppressed anticipation.

Gino knew exactly who she meant—Uncle Tommy Calabrese, New Jersey federal judge. The first in

Gino's family to go to college, to receive advanced academic degrees, and to become a "professional," Uncle Tommy was the only relative Gino would ever boast about to Elena. He even told Silvana about Uncle Tommy, knowing she, too, would be impressed by Tommy's education and erudition.

"Just remember that I come from a family that values education, too," he would tell Elena and her mother. "My Uncle Tommy is an important federal judge. The entire family is hoping that someday he'll be named to the Supreme Court. In my family, you can attain no honor greater than being appointed Supreme Court Judge—except being voted President of the United States, of course."

So it was no surprise that Elena would remember his Uncle Tommy. What she was implying, however, made Gino wish he had never mentioned his uncle to her.

"Uncle Tommy is an appellate judge, an important jurist. He doesn't get involved in things like traffic tickets . . . or marriages," he tried to explain to Elena.

"But he could if he wanted to . . . as a favor, couldn't he? For his favorite nephew?" she persisted. "If you asked?"

Gino shrugged. "Maybe," he felt forced to reluctantly agree.

"Well then!" Elena clapped her hands delightedly, and then held them out for him.

Without realizing what he was doing, he took her outstretched hands and helped her to her feet. He could have remained right there at the elevator bay, holding Elena in his arms forever, with his lips transforming the short journey from her hot cheek to her sweet, pulpy mouth into a delightfully endless sojourn.

But Elena was all business now. She took him by the wrist and led him back to his apartment. Then she marched directly to his phone and handed the receiver to him. Never had Elena looked less like his Saint Theresa. In fact, her sharp, quick movements, the stiff way she held the phone out to him, reminded him exactly of his mother. Nevertheless, he had no choice but to make the call. His only hope was that his uncle was not expected home that evening. But when Tommy himself answered the phone, Gino knew that he was caught, trapped in a cage called marriage. And that his Saint Theresa had become his jailer.

There were times during their nine-year friendship when Mark Kroll had seen Silvana become so depressed that he had feared she might never laugh again. He had seen it many times during her marriage to Warren Nachman and on that day when she had told him Warren had raped her. This time, however, the depression was mixed with a new feeling—rage—but because of it, Mark Kroll was not as worried. Visiting her at her vast apartment, he satisfied himself that, this time, Silvana would certainly overcome.

"I suppose you're crying your eyes out over Elena and Gino going together, as usual," he asked Silvana directly.

"It's worse than that."

"What happened?"

"He eloped with her!" Silvana wailed. Then she raised her fists to the heavens. She cursed Gino in Italian for eloping with her daughter and denying all of them the pleasure of a proper wedding. And Mark contented himself that although it was loud, it was not necessarily serious.

Fabian, who could not join Mark at Silvana's because he had to complete a line of jewelry designs for a presentation the next day, arrived home tired—although he was never too tired to hear everything about Mark's "friend." In fact, he insisted to Mark, "Tell me everything. Leave out nothing," but they both knew that his interest was not entirely altruistic. It was, more accurately, jealousy.

"Silvana's my friend, my soul mate. But it is you I love, you I live with, you I sleep with." Fabian had heard Mark reassure him thousands of times. "She's only a friend—nothing more."

And Fabian would nod and smile and hold his hand

up as if to say, "No more. I really don't need any more assurances."

But he did. Because he lived with a gnawing, unrelieved fear that Mark Kroll would abandon him someday—perhaps for Silvana. To Fabian, that Mark might leave him for a woman was not outside the realm of possibility. He knew that Mark had been in love with a girl many years ago, when he was very young. And, "It happened once; it could happen again," he argued.

But Mark vehemently disagreed. "I was so young then and so confused about my sexuality. I thought I was straight—or, at the worst, bi. But after I met you, I became sure of who I am and what I want."

"What do you want?"

"You."

"Just keep telling me. Whenever I get afraid, or jealous, just tell me all over again that you love me." Fabian was sure that someday, if he heard it often enough, he might even believe it.

But tonight the fear had returned, and although he begged Mark to tell him every little detail of his visit with Silvana and the kids, his motive was to listen carefully to Mark for any secret hint of excessive affection for Silvana.

"Did Silvana cook dinner?"

Mark laughed, remembering. "We all did. She's teaching Anna Michela to cook—and Debora to help—and the kitchen, as you know, is so huge that she had us all working like assistant chefs in one of her restaurants."

"Were you helping the girls—or were you working next to Silvana?" He could not help asking, despite himself.

"Fabian! Do you think I can't see right through that question? Do you think I'm an idiot?"

"I'm sorry," was all he could say.

"How many times must I tell you before you will believe me? Silvana is beautiful, yes. But so are you."

Fabian could only sigh.

"She is a friend. But it's business, too. Because of her, we're in a whole new field. Did you ever think that after we did Eduardo's wedding, we'd wind up designing everybody's wedding? No. But she believed in us. And now we're wedding consultants, thanks to her. And we're more famous than ever before. So don't confuse things. Silvana is my good friend and trusted business adviser. You are my love and my lover."

"I know, I know," Fabian insisted shamefacedly.

"She is a woman with many more problems than you or me at the moment," Mark continued heatedly, "and I intend to be there for her."

Fabian changed the subject. "Are the kids okay?" In spite of himself, he did find Silvana's girls adorable.

"Anna Michela and Debora are gorgeous—and they know it, all right. It's a riot how they wiggle and giggle when I'm around."

"Flirting?"

"Yes, but when they're that age, it's easy just to laugh it off."

Fabian waited for Mark to go on, but after only a moment, he lost patience. "You said Silvana had so many problems. But it sounds pretty idyllic to me." And that was how he learned the news from Mark.

"Last night Elena eloped with Gino."

"No! You mean we can't do the wedding?"

Mark rolled his eyes. "What wedding? Silvana is so angry, she's not speaking to either Elena or Gino."

For some reason, Fabian was relieved. Perhaps because he hoped that Silvana would be preoccupied with her daughter and new son-in-law now ... and would have no time for visits with Mark. "How did she learn of the elopement?" he asked, and yawned, his interest in Silvana waning ... at least for the moment.

"Gino called her this morning. He had to. Not only to tell her he'd married her daughter, but to warn her to assign a substitute chef. Needless to say, he won't be cooking tonight."

No wedding to plan, after all. The story was getting boring. Again Fabian yawned.

But Mark continued recounting Silvana's problems.

"Did you know that Silvana's mother died in a concentration camp during the Second World War? She told me tonight that her mother and brother were shot and buried in a nameless grave."

Fabian shook his head no and began pulling on the silk pajamas Mark had designed for him.

"And that when her mother was deported to the camp, she had been angry at Silvana about something—I'm not sure what—and she hadn't spoken to Silvana in some time. Then she was deported and mother and daughter never got a chance to make up, never got a chance to say another word to each other. Her mother and brother were shot the first day. Isn't that sad?"

Fabian answered Mark's question with a question of his own: "Do you want to hear a really sad story?"

"What?"

"I'm tired of hearing about sad Silvana. Oh, how I want to wrap my arms around you while you slide my gorgeous pj's off—but I am so tired of hearing about Silvana that I think I'll just go to sleep alone tonight."

"No! Don't do that. That's truly the saddest story I ever heard."

"It makes you want to go 'boo hoo,' doesn't it?"

"Boo hoo, Fabian darling. Now let's see if we can rewrite the ending of that sad tale."

Chapter Seventeen

Silvana stood behind her pretty pastry chef, Fiona Woolcroft, a young British woman whose life was forever changed, at the age of ten, after watching a baker ice a four-tier wedding cake. By the time he had squeezed out the last pink frosting rosette on the top layer of the white cream cake, Fiona knew that pastry—and not nursing—would be her life's work.

Later, after studying pastry-making in France, she returned home and searched without success for a job in a restaurant or hotel. Women, she discovered, were not wanted in professional kitchens.

"Women are good for home cooking and home baking," she was told, "but they're too emotional for a professional restaurant kitchen. They should leave volume cooking to the men."

Just when she was about to give up, her family relocated in New York and she decided to join them. Only three days in America, she set out for her first job interview at Silvana's second restaurant, Mia Elena.

"Do you know how to prepare zuppa inglese?" she was asked as she was handed an apron.

"Certainly. I have a recipe for the original English version, which we call a trifle. And I have a recipe for the French version, called Charlotte Malakoff. And then I have a Sicilian—"

"Would you be good enough to prepare this recipe?" Silvana asked, interrupting her because it was clear she was knowledgeable. Now what remained was to see if she could perform.

Fiona scanned the recipe and commented, "I never

saw a zuppa quiet like this—with red cherry liqueur and cognac."

"It was my mother's recipe. We called it her 'Jewish Ransom' because she would give us this prized dessert after we not only promised to be extra quiet in synagogue—but after she made sure we kept our promise, too."

"A Jewish zuppa, eh? Interesting," said Fiona. "I never even knew there were Italian Jews—and I'm from Europe!"

"And so you had to come all the way to America to meet one." Silvana looked over at Elena. "I mean, to meet two of us."

But Fiona noticed that the beautiful Silvana smiled only at her—and not at her daughter Elena. Tension hung in the air. To avoid getting caught in it, Fiona smiled brightly and signaled that she was ready for the second phase of her "audition."

First, before assembling or measuring out any of the ingredients, she read over the recipe several times until she had it almost memorized. Then she lowered the temperature of the ovens to 350 degrees. Like most restaurants, the ovens had been lit and preheated early in the morning to be ready for the day's roasting and baking. Usually, the ovens were the first thing turned on in the morning, and the last thing turned off at night.

Now she assembled the ingredients for the basis of the zuppa, the sponge cake, next to a large electric beater. The liqueurs, the whipping cream, and the ingredients for the pastry cream went on the opposite counter, beside a second electric beater. Then she buttered the baking pans and read over the recipe one last time, beginning to fantasize possible variations and improvements she could make on the original.

Looking up at Silvana with her lively hazel eyes, she suggested in her clipped British accent, "Fresh cherries macerated in the liqueur would, I think, be even more smashing than just the liqueur alone. Don't you agree?"

Suddenly the kitchen became entirely, completely

still. Elena, who hired all the front-room staff and sat in on all the kitchen staff interviews, immediately glanced at her mother with avid curiosity. Chefs were her mother's domain. But how would her mother react to this one—this Fiona, who had the audacity to suggest an innovative variation on Silvana's sacrosanct recipes? Because it was exactly what she had urged Gino to do countless times—only to be sharply reprimanded for urging Gino to "deviate" from time-honored recipes—Elena waited, hardly breathing, for the form that her mother's disapproval would take with this new aspirant.

It was precisely this issue—whether Silvana would allow Gino to innovate or "deviate" in the kitchen at all—which had sent mother and daughter into storms of arguments this past year. Sometimes their irritation at each other dissipated as quickly as a small gust of wind, sometimes it provoked hollering loud as a hurricane at midnight. But always they made up, continuing to speak to each other, to communicate, their bond seemingly unbreakable—until Elena got married. After that, nothing was the same again.

"Our recipes are historically accurate," Silvana told Fiona coolly. "We are known for our uncompromising adherence to the original way this food was made. And, believe me, it has not been easy finding authentic ingredients here in America. Many Italian specialties—like true prosciutto from Parma, Italy, are not imported here yet. But still we try to do it here exactly the way it was done in Italy. We try not to change anything. Not ... anything." Only then did Silvana smile. "Can you accept that?"

Fiona nodded but she was no longer smiling.

"*Bene,*" said Silvana. "Good. You're hired. That is, if you don't burn the sponge cake."

At least she doesn't show favoritism, Elena told herself glumly. *I should be happy to see she doesn't treat Gino any worse than anyone else.* But she was anything but happy. Here she was, married at last ... and utterly miserable! Not only because of Gino. *Because*

*of Mama! She treats me like I did the most terrible
thing by marrying Gino.*

Then Elena had to admit what no one else could
know—*And she's right. But how was I to know it
would be a mistake? If only he wasn't so angry and
cruel. But it's not his fault—it's hers! Oh, if only I
could make him love me. Why doesn't he love me?
Why doesn't anyone?*

For two weeks now, ever since Elena and Gino had
eloped, Silvana had not spoken to her daughter, except when it was absolutely necessary. When Gino
phoned the morning after and told her that they had
run off and gotten married, Silvana lost all self-control
and cried out, "No! I don't believe it! I'll never believe it!" Then she dropped the phone and sobbed
inconsolably until Debora and Anna Michela began
to sob, too.

"Our darling Elena has run off and married Gino,"
she told them.

Immediately the two dark, pretty girls stopped their
sobbing and looked at their mother quizzically, as if
to say, "Then why are we crying?" They both loved
Gino.

As did Silvana. Which made it so difficult for
Silvana to understand her own feelings, much less explain them to Elena and Gino.

Who, for instance, had made her most angry—and
why? Gino, for his sudden elopement with Elena—
making final and absolute a marriage that Silvana had
been surreptitiously trying to hold off for years? Or
Elena, for shutting out her own mother from the
event? Or for marrying Gino at all?

It was not that Silvana disliked Gino. If anything,
she was closer to him than to anyone else on her staff.
From the beginning, when he was merely a waiter
dreaming of the chance to cook, it was she who had
recognized his potential. The timing, of course, could
not have been better. She happened to be in desperate
need of a subsitute chef to relieve her, and he happened to be attending cooking school several mornings a week. Almost immediately, she put Gino into

training. Advancing rapidly, he went from inexperi-
enced waiter to kitchen assistant to cook to chef ...
and finally to executive chef of the expanded Per Sempre Silvana. And all in only six and a half years! Certainly, he had talent, energy, and an appealing
eagerness. But without Silvana's blessing—as well as
her push—he still would be no more than head waiter
or at most junior cook.

Yet for all that, Silvana did disapprove of Gino—
as a husband for Elena.

"Why, Mama?" Elena was always asking her, from
the minute Gino first came to Per Sempre Silvana.
"Why don't you want me to talk to him? Why don't
you want me to like him? Because he's not Jewish?
Because he's Catholic?"

And Silvana would nod yes, though both of them
knew that was not really it.

"And because he's not a college professor?"

Again Silvana would nod, although both of them
knew that, too, was not really "it."

"Because he's a cook, like you?"

Silvana really could not say. Not then ... and not
now. All she knew was that this was not the marriage
she had wanted for her Elena, her firstborn. Not just
because Gino was not Jewish; not just because he was
not college educated. Something more, something
deeper concerned her about their relationship. It had
something to do with Gino's brutal outbursts in the
kitchen and his simmering jealousy. Oddly, as his
ardor for Elena was waning, his jealousy and posses-
siveness had intensified. (Oh, yes, Silvana had
noticed!)

Back when her Elena was a sweet, pure girl of sixteen, how Gino had adored her! He called Elena a
saint; he nicknamed her Theresa. But that was a long
time ago. Now it would not have surprised Silvana if
her daughter had to drag Gino to the altar! But although that would not in the least have surprised her,
it would not have pleased her. It would not have
pleased her at all.

No, this was not what she wanted for her daughter.

If asked what it was that she did want, she would say, "I want someone who will make my Elena smile all day long—or at least most of the day. Someone who will make her eyes light up like a lamp—or at least a candle. Someone with whom she can find the kind of happiness I once knew with her father. That is what I wish for my daughter."

Elena, of course, heard nothing of her mother's wishes. All that was apparent to Elena was Silvana's anger and disapproval, which manifested itself in a coldness so frozen that Elena yearned constantly not for her new husband, Gino—but for her mother to embrace her, to warm her . . . and to forgive her. Waiting for her mother to forgive her, however, had become an embittering experience. Each day that Elena waited, she seethed and muttered a little more loudly.

"She's always hated you, I see that now," she complained to Gino, her ordinary good sense twisted by hurt and resentment. "And how she hates me, too."

"That's ridiculous. Your mother doesn't hate me and she certainly doesn't hate you." But he secretly simmered over Elena's words.

"Yes she does!" Elena insisted, sitting in their tiny kitchen wearing a red satin nightgown. "Everyone hates me."

Gino glanced at his new wife in her bold gown. Then he quickly glanced out the kitchen window. Through a narrow window across the alley he thought he saw a neighbor looking at them . . . looking at Elena. The simmering came to a boil.

"Cover up, dammit!" Before she could move, he shouted at her again, this time even louder. "Look at you, asking for it. Standing at the window and just asking for it!"

Then he went in search of her robe, knocking over his chair, enjoying the sound of the wood cracking against the hard floor. *Crack!*

In one swipe, he whisked the robe off the bed and, returning to the kitchen, gruffly threw it over her shoulders.

"Everyone can see you in that red gown—it's as loud as a traffic light. Cover up!"

Despite herself, Elena reddened to the vivid shade of her gown. She blushed, yes, but not only with shame; with rage, as well.

"Ever since we got married, you've reverted back to being Mr. Pure. 'Good girl, bad girl. Pure, dirty.' I'm sick of it! Everything is black and white with you. Why don't you like your 'Saint Theresa' wearing a red satin gown?"

Through clenched teeth he told her, "You know why."

"Because I look like a slut?"

He would not answer but he glared at her sideways like an enraged bull in the ring.

"A slut," she repeated, taunting him. "You think your bride of three weeks looks like a slut and that's why you won't touch her, right?"

"Shut up!"

"To you I'm a slut. Right?" Though she taunted him loudly, unrelentingly, her eyes filled with tears.

He was bursting with anger he had been storing for weeks, ever since she pushed him into marrying her. Now Elena had pushed him again, and this time, she'd pushed too far.

"That's right! A goddamn slut," he agreed. "I know what you're doing at your mother's restaurant every night—how you're kissing every customer—every man—who walks in."

A part of her still thought she could reason with him. "But that's part of my job—to greet the customers warmly and—"

"And? And what else? To flirt? To wiggle your little ass? To let them touch you?" He grabbed her by the shoulders and before she could stop him, he pushed her back against the stove. Hard. Then he pushed his face into hers. "I hate you in red." With one hand, he ripped her nightgown. "Don't ever wear red again." He turned his face away so that he would not have to look at her again. But she would not stop talking or crying.

"Why are you doing this to me? You hate me in red, in white, in black. You just hate me, don't you? I knew it," she burbled between shuddering sobs. "I made my husband marry me and how he hates me!"

"Shut up! You didn't make me do anything."

"I made you! I made you!" she screamed hysterically.

Suddenly Gino not only could not stand her red gown, he could not stand her at all—just as she had guessed. Everything about her had become loud and ugly and enraging. And if she opened her mouth to him one more time—

"I'm right, aren't I?" she insisted miserably. "You can't stand the sight of me, can you?"

"I told you to shut up!"

"Why should I?"

His right arm tingled, his right hand vibrated. His right side was separate from the rest of his body. His right side had a mind of its own. When he reached out and cracked her across the face, it was his right arm, his right hand that did it . . . not the rest of him. His left arm didn't touch her. His left side just stood and watched as the blood began to trickle out of her nose.

"Oh, my God, my nose is bleeding!" she cried. "You—you hit me. You made me bleed!"

Crack! His right arm smashed into her face again. "I told you to shut up, didn't I?" He cracked her with the hard, bony side of his hand one more time. "Didn't I?"

This time she seemed to get it. Her right cheek was red and her eye was swelling up and blood ran down her face as she looked up at him from where she'd fallen to the floor—but this time she didn't say anything. She kept her mouth shut. He'd finally gotten through to her. Now she knew who was boss. Now she knew that if he said "Shut up," she had better obey or his fearsome right hand would smite her right down again. Smite. Just like it said in the Bible.

Saints and virgins, who needed them? If you had a righteous right arm, that was all that mattered.

He stretched and peered out the window. The sun was out and the bastard from across the way was gone from his window. Nevertheless, he felt like shouting, "The show's over. The bride will be wearing white from now on. So don't let me catch you looking this way or I'll—"

But it was time for work. He straightened up, pulled on his jacket. Then he leaned down and patted her on her sore cheek, but he avoided looking directly at her. His gaze went past her, to the wall behind her.

"Bye, honey. See you tonight around eleven. And don't forget, be good, okay?" He waited for her to answer and then he remembered that he had told her to shut up. *She's just obeying you,* he told himself, which made him smile. *It's good to be boss again,* he had to admit. Then he blew her a kiss and let himself out of the apartment.

Only when she was absolutely sure that he was gone did she risk moving, risk groaning. But every sound still frightened her. Was that him coming back to hit her again? Was that his key in the lock?

In this small apartment, there was only one place where she could feel safe—the bathtub. There she could hide, immersed in warm, soothing water behind a tightly locked door. There she could think. And cry. Cry for the brief and tragic mistake that was her marriage. And cry for herself, for the bloody, aching wounds caused by her new husband's own hands. Oh, yes, she had reasons to cry. And waiting behind her swollen eyes was an entire reservoir of tears, as if in preparation for just this event. Which was fortunate, for she would have use for every one of those tears today; she was going to fill an entire bathtub with them.

Despite a throbbing shoulder, she pulled herself to her feet and limped to the tiny, white-tiled bathroom, her mind filled with memories.

Once, for instance, when she was a girl new to America, she refused to go to school for several days. She was a foreigner with a "strange" accent and her classmates teased her unmercifully for that. Dreading having to face their taunts and rejection again, she announced that she simply would not be going to school anymore. But her Uncle Eduardo told her, "First, lick your wounds. Then go right back onto the battlefield again because this time you just might win."

Now, as she pressed a cold cloth to her bruised face, "licking her wounds," she stared at the damage in the mirror, remembering her uncle's advice. But return to the battlefield? And win? It did not seem possible. She stretched out her small, compact body in the tub and could still feel the sickening dread she had felt so long ago when she had finally returned to school and faced down her classmates. Yes, she had overcome that time but that dread had been nothing compared to what she felt now. The thought of facing Gino again made her almost black out.

"Mama. Oh, Mama!" she sobbed, yearning to be a little girl again and held in the comforting circle of her mother's arms. Then she suddenly sat up. *But it is Mama,* she instantly decided, *who is to blame for all this. Yes, Mama! Not Gino. How could it be Gino?*

Gino was her husband. He loved her. He married her. So Gino never meant to hit her. It was just that he was pushed, pushed beyond his limit. *Because of Mama! Because she stopped him—and stopped me. It's all Mama's fault and I'll never forgive her. Never!*

It was all perfectly clear now. She had it straight in her mind. It was all as simple and as elegant as a mathematical equation. She rose from the bath naked and dripping and smiled bitterly to herself. Now she knew exactly who was to blame and what she would do about it: she would call in sick.

"Mama, I think I have a stomach virus," was what she would say. "I'm sorry but I won't be able to come to work for two or three days."

From now on, she would tell her mother nothing. If her mother had not tried to stop her, she might have married Gino years ago. And then Gino would never have gotten so angry at her. Of course, he was sorry for what he had done. When he came home tonight he would feel terribly, horribly sorry. Already, she forgave him. Because now she knew who her real enemy was. It was Mama!

Sometimes it did not seem possible to Silvana that she still had the energy to rise from her huge—but empty—bed every morning and begin another day. Such full days ... and yet so empty! And so many responsibilities! These days, there always seemed to be two of everything—two restaurants to run, two husbands to remember, two little daughters to raise. Dear little Debora, especially. As soon as Debora was born, Silvana's heart had gone out to the unwanted child, and she had embraced her baby with a fierce maternal love.

Once, there had been three daughters—Elena, Anna Michela, and Debora. But Elena ran off and married. And now, though Silvana saw Elena six evenings a week in the front room of Mia Elena Ristorante, Elena seemed more like a stranger than a daughter. A wounded stranger.

Silvana noticed the faint black and blue bruises on Elena's eye and cheek immediately, even though Elena had not been to work for three days and was wearing heavy pancake makeup. But she said nothing. Because if she asked, Elena would not answer. Elena was barely speaking to her at all.

At first, it had been Silvana, shocked and angered by the news of the elopement, who was cold and distant. But Silvana could not remain angry with any daughter of hers, particularly one who looked as unhappy as Elena. When Elena spoke, her voice seemed like a hollow echo, with no real sound of its own; when she smiled, it was like a sheet of ice across her face. And Silvana's poor daughter's eyes! They looked positively haunted! Elena had become a living phantom, a breathing memory ... a flesh-and-blood ghost.

"My own daughter ... a complete stranger!" Silvana would sigh and shudder upon awakening. These days, it was always her first thought. Elena and her unhappiness. Elena and what Silvana could do about her. Elena. Elena!

And when she wasn't worrying about Elena, there was always Anna Michela and Debora to fret over. Now that Anna Michela was in school, for example, Debora missed her terribly. Mrs. Milgrim had told her that Debora often burst into tears when Anna Michela left for school in the morning.

"She's lonely all day long."

Silvana had to support the family; she could not stay home with Debora, yet she was ready to do it if that would make her daughter Debora happy again. But Mrs. Milgrim wisely advised a different course of action.

"I suggest a nursery school to occupy Debora for one year, until she, too, goes to school. She needs the stimulation of other children. She's too bright and friendly to sit at home alone all day."

Of course, Mrs. Milgrim was absolutely right. But Silvana asked herself, *Why didn't I notice? Why wasn't it me, Debora's own mother, who saw that she was so bored and unhappy?*

"You're such a wonderful mother, Silvana. The girls adore you and because of you, they're growing up to be fine young ladies. You have absolutely nothing to feel guilty about," Mrs. Milgrim told her whenever she gave into self-doubts.

"But my baby is lonely and my Elena is miserable."

"It's not your fault!" Mrs. Milgrim insisted firmly. "You did nothing to cause their unhappiness—and you can improve Debora's situation quite quickly."

Mrs. Milgrim was good for Silvana because she was older and spoke to Silvana not as an employee, but as a wise old friend. It was just what Silvana needed: a friend. As did the lonely Lena Milgrim. And so, with a deepening of their mutual need and respect over the years, their friendship deepened, as well. Now they were as close as two sisters—linked not, of course, by blood but by something perhaps as profound—mature affection and enduring devotion.

"But what about my Elena? How can I solve her problem?" Sometimes, because Mrs Milgrim seemed so wise, Silvana assumed that she could find the right answer to any question, the cure for any illness, the resolution to any dispute. Only when Lena Milgrim reluctantly admitted "I'm stumped!" was Silvana reminded that Lena Milgrim was only human.

"I'm stumped," was what she said now. If Gino had, in fact, once beaten Elena, then he could very well do it again. Maybe harder.

"I know," Silvana agreed miserably.

"Elena must leave him or get counseling."

"I know," was all Silvana could say.

They both knew that Elena needed someone to talk with about all of this. Because if Gino really was a wife beater, Elena could be in danger. "She can't keep all this inside."

Silvana knew all of this . . . and more. It was what she thought about every morning these days. But the problem was to get Elena to talk to her. "Why does she act like it's my fault her husband is hurting her?"

Lena Milgrim shrugged. She knew Elena, knew how she always blamed herself—and her mother—for everything. *Poor Elena! She can't admit Gino has turned out to be a rotten apple! She makes her mother the villain instead.* But though she tried, she could not put her analysis into words.

"I suppose," she said at last, "that we must wait a little while and hope that, in the end, Elena's intelligence and self-respect will win out." In the meantime, she would call Elena and try to get her to open her heart.

It was a small ray of hope, but Silvana clung to it and felt inexplicably buoyant and uplifted. An apricot flush returned to her cheeks and she smiled with genuine relief. Thus, when the phone rang, she answered it with a lighter heart than she had felt in weeks. Even her husky voice sounded uncommonly cheerful. Mrs. Milgrim noticed.

So did Gregory Wolf. He noticed it the minute Silvana said hello.

"You sound different, somehow happier. Are you?"

"Who is this?" Silvana demanded into the phone, but somehow she knew, even before he told her his name. And somehow, she recognized something different in his voice, too ... although she did not know exactly what it was. Only that it made her want to hear his voice again ... and again.

"It's Gregory Wolf. I'm the man at the table the night after you opened who held your wrist and—"

"Oh, yes, Mr. Wolf. How did you get my home number?"

"I promise to tell you if you promise to meet me for a drink."

She was about to say that was out of the question, impossible, ridiculous. She was about to hang up, to slam the phone down without another word. She was about to do all of that ... yet she did none of it. And when she hesitated, he knew that he had won her. That the hardest part was over. Now, all he had to do was keep her on the phone until she gave in and agreed to meet him. A piece of cake—and the rest would be the icing.

Chapter Eighteen

He had her by the wrist, holding her the exact same way he had held her the first time, the night he had singed her like hot grease by merely looking at her. But she told herself that she had no intention of falling under his spell again. She was here for only one reason.

"Who gave you my home phone number?"

She had it all planned. She would remain standing until she got her answer. Then she would twist her hand out from his grip and walk away. But he was staring up at her from his seat with an expression that was, at the same time, both bashful and bemused, and once again she was unnerved.

"Tell me, why is it so important to you to know who gave me your number?"

His manner was a baffling contradiction. Certainly, the way he spoke to her, the way he gripped her, the way he looked her up and down, was pure arrogance. He sported the kind of certitude and conceit that only the young and the spoiled possess ... and yet, he had a certain charm, too, which softened his edges. When he asked her, "Why is it so important?" it was as if he already knew the answer, or as if he really did not care. But nothing he did really hurt or angered her. Perhaps because she saw through him. Because she could see he was just trying to impress her.

Of course, she did not have to answer his question ... but she did anyway. In order to insist to him how important it really was. That she had agreed on the phone to meet him here today, at this small, dark bar two blocks from Per Sempre Silvana Ristorante, only to learn how he had gotten her number. She was here to prove she was here for no other reason.

She told him, "Because I pay the phone company extra money just to keep my number private." As she spoke she stared at her wrist, at his, at their matching skin. *We could be sister and brother,* she thought, *or even mother and son.* Their skin was that alike. "And because everyone who knows my number would never give it out to a—a strange man."

"Why not?"

"Because I am a woman who lives alone with her children. There is no man in my—"

He had her! And in the instant that their eyes met, she saw that he knew it because he grinned triumphantly. But then, to her surprise, the expression in his eyes quickly changed from triumph to relief. Relief that she was not married now. Which in turn suddenly transformed her own feelings. From irritation with herself for having unintentionally revealed to him her personal situation and marital status, now she, too, felt relief. And secretly even a bit pleased with herself for blurting out the fact that she was "available."

But what did she want with this ... boy? How old could he be? Twenty-nine? Thirty-two? In another three months she would be forty-five. This morning she had plucked a gray hair from her dark blond eyebrows.

As if he somehow knew what she was feeling, he let go of her wrist and began behaving with a new self-assurance and maturity. With a courtly grace he half rose and gestured for her to sit down. Then, without any further procrastination, he told her directly, "Gino gave it to me."

"Gino? My Gino? Elena's Gino?"

He nodded yes.

She was aghast. "How do you know Gino Bracca?"

He waited, politely holding the chair for her as she sat down. Without realizing it, she had slid into the seat beside him at the corner table. Just as unconsciously, she nodded yes when he asked her if she would like a drink.

"Scotch," he told the waiter without bothering to ask her what she wanted. So sure of himself. So in control.

Gino! No, it wasn't possible! And yet, in the silent corner of her mind reserved for nightmares and dread, she felt no surprise at all. Perhaps she had even suspected all along that Gino would turn out to be the one who had violated her privacy. If he had brutally violated Elena and invaded her safety, then she doubted if he would worry about the ethics of giving out a private phone number. Of course, she did not know for a fact that he had hurt her daughter. At their daily morning meetings at Per Sempre Silvana, where she always started her busy two-restaurant workday, Gino had behaved normally, giving no hint of anything awry. But after she had seen the covered-up bruises on Elena's face, she knew she would never trust Gino again. She could hardly even look at him. Perhaps that was why she had put off her morning meeting with Gino today and come here instead ... to hear her suspicions confirmed. To hear Gregory Wolf indict him.

Now that she had, she finally knew what she would do about Gino. She had been waiting breathlessly for just this kind of tangible proof. Now she could confront him ... not just about the phone number, but about Elena. She would do it today. But first, she took a sip of her drink because her knees, as well as her hands, were trembling with rage. Hearing her suspicions confirmed had only inflamed the anger at Gino that had been simmering inside her all along. Now she was afire, burning to save her firstborn child.

Gregory Wolf seemed to sense her extreme inner agitation and began to make a quiet but concerted attempt to put her at her ease.

"My mother and sister live in your building. I saw you twice when I came to visit them." When he spoke now, he was both clear and direct, surprising her by his open honesty. He was always surprising her, going from anxious little boy to self-assured adult in a mere but magical moment. But she could tell, just by the quietly mature quality of his voice that he would not be reverting back to the reckless boy again for now. And she found this so relieving that she could not help smiling at him.

"You saw me twice?"

"Once in the elevator. It was winter and you were wrapped in a huge mohair scarf. All I could see was a blond wisp of your hair and your huge almond eyes. It was all I needed to see. I never forgot your face ... or you. Then I saw you again a few months ago, on a hot summer night around eleven-thirty. As I came out of the elevator, you were just entering the lobby. You looked very tired; I think you'd just gotten home from work. But you were beautiful, nevertheless. I smiled at you as I left but just when you were about to smile back, you broke out into a yawn instead. It was a huge, exhausted yawn that made you throw your head back and made your eyes tear. You were very embarrassed and hurried into the elevator and I left the building, but I could not get you out of my mind ... because of that yawn."

"You liked the way I yawned?" She was incredulous. But she was also smiling.

"I know it sounds ridiculous but please listen."

She took another sip of her drink and motioned for him to continue.

"I come from a very tense, proper family. Too proper. All they do is worry about how their actions will look to everyone. They worry so much, they hardly do anything at all."

At that, Silvana had to laugh, and Gregory Wolf joined her for a moment. Then he turned serious again.

"That's why I don't live near them. After my father died, they moved to the city, but I stayed on in Montauk."

"Montauk?" She'd heard of it, but she did not tell him that. Montauk. *Oh, God, Sloane!* The longing, to her surprise, was still sharp. She hadn't forgotten him at all.

"It's at the eastern tip of Long Island. Used to be

a major fishing and whaling community in the last century. Even today, a considerable amount of lobstering and fishing still goes on. You'd like Montauk. It's quite picturesque."

"And what do you do in Montauk?" She was being entertained, charmed. She would not think about anything, least of all Sloane Harding. She wanted to be transported, to set all her worries and memories on the ground and float up above them, lounging on a pillow of air. The scotch, of course, was helping. Unaccustomed to alcohol in the afternoon, one strong drink was sufficient to calm her racing heart. But it was Gregory Wolf who was captivating her. As long as he did not mention Montauk. As long as she was not reminded again of her longing for the man she could never have.

"I'm a restaurateur," he answered her. "Like you."

She was dumbfounded. Her mouth rounded into an oh of surprise and remained a perfect oval for one full minute. It astonished her that she, who had struggled so hard and so long, who had cooked for partisans in the hills of Umbria, who had dreamed of a New York restaurant of her own for years before she finally opened her first, the tiny Per Sempre Silvana, was in the same business as this handsome, suave, spoiled, sweet, dangerous—and very young—man.

"I own a fish restaurant on the water. And I'm considering opening another one nearby. In my father's old fishing lodge. If I do"—he paused, observing her reaction—"I might want a cuisine featuring authentic Italian seafood."

No! She did not want to hear about his restaurants and his dreams. What did he know of dreams? Of longing? Probably his enormously rich father had given him this restaurant as a "present," a "toy" to play with, she thought somewhat cynically. A toy restaurant without the requisite years of working, of dreaming, of yearning. *For how else,* she wondered, *could he have become a restaurateur so young?*

As if in answer to her thoughts he told her, "I worked my way up, just like you, from kitchen help to chef and, finally, to owner. Years of hard work and long hours."

"But how did you know—?"

Before she had finished asking the question, he began answering it because he understood what she still wanted to know.

"I know all about you, Silvana. A month or two before you opened Mia Elena, there was an article— and a picture of you—in the paper. Of course, I recognized you. That's why I made a dinner reservation two months in advance. But the newspaper article also mentioned your other restaurant, Per Sempre Silvana. I decided to have dinner there in the meantime. I never saw you there, but that's how I met Gino."

"I see," she said, struggling to absorb all that he had just told her.

"He's a great chef. Really great. And a very nice guy. We had a drink together late one night."

Silvana said nothing.

"Don't worry. I'm not secretly scheming to steal him away!"

She almost said, "You can have him!" but she held her tongue and nodded as if she agreed.

"I never tasted anything like that rice dish—*risotto verde*—that he makes. All those herbs and spinach really do turn the rice a bright green—*risotto verde*. Did he create that dish?"

"That was my mother's recipe. She taught it to me when I was a girl in Rome and then I brought it with me to America and taught it to Gino," she told Gregory, pleased to be able to talk about safe subjects— cooking and recipes—again. "The problem is that here in America everyone loves long-grain rice and no one imports the unique Italian short-grain rice I need for this dish. I may have to start an importing company just to keep my kitchens supplied with authentic ingredients."

She did not notice how Gregory Wolf's gray eyes lit up at the mention of her starting up her own business. If she had, she might have realized that he was so smitten with her that he would have been happy

even to become her business partner—just to be near
her. But she could not meet his gaze because the way
he looked at her—even now, even when they were
attempting to talk about ordinary subjects—made her
lose her concentration. If she did happen to meet his
gaze, then, suddenly, she would stop thinking about
business or recipes ... or anything. Just him. Suddenly
she would marvel at the silvery gray of his eyes, as
bright as polished sterling. And everything else would
become unimportant and dull in comparison.

So she could not allow their eyes to lock. But, of
course, she did.

It was an accident. No, she tried to convince herself
that it was mere happenstance, but this was no accident. It was, if anything, unavoidable, even fated.

She was taking a last sip of her drink and as she
set her glass down on the table, her eyes traveled up
from his midnight-blue sweater to his strong, prominent chin. There, in the subtle cleft, her eyes rested
in that dark chin fold for a moment, as if making a
brief stop on an inevitable journey. For though she
willed her eyelids to close, commanded her head to
turn, nothing could deter her gaze from its ineluctable
goal. Onward, upward, her heart pumping unheeded
warnings, she made her way along his slightly imperfect nose, from the rounded, graceful tip to the bump
in the bone near the top. And then, suddenly, she was
there. She was at the bridge of his nose, where, span-
ning out from either side, were his charged, silvery
eyes. She had absolutely no choice; she met his gaze.
And then remained there, unmoving. It was as if he
drew her eyes to his like a magnet, locking her look
into his own. And once so locked, nothing else could
enter their field of vision; all they could see was the
deep center of each other's eyes.

Oh, she was sinking, sinking into his charged vortex.
Not only were his eyes a magnet, but all of him was,
really. He exerted an irresistible pull, and if she was
not careful, she would have no will left at all. Promising herself she would be careful—that in a minute she

would put a stop to this—she allowed his fingers to brush her fingers with the softness of a powder puff.

Was that really so dangerous? she asked herself, and not waiting for an answer, permitted him to continue, to trace the outline of her hand. By then he needed no permission to go further, to travel up her arm, pressing harder. Or to stop at her shoulder to caress it. Or to massage the back of her neck, digging into her flesh as if he owned it.

By the expression of rapture on her face he knew he could now go anywhere; he owned her flesh. Even her breasts were not out of bounds. He slid a hand inside her blouse and even his breath caught as he touched the warm, soft skin above her lacy bra. And when he covered her breast with his hand and squeezed, they both gasped.

Oh, yes, she was sinking. Once before she had felt like this, once long ago. And long before it was over she had wanted to die. To a great extent she was still recovering from that time when she was just a girl and she was petted and pressured into a kind of premature sexual madness. This time she knew she could not survive a repetition. But this time she had the will—and the maturity—to resist. This time she had the strength to end it differently, to just end it.

"In an hour Gino will be too busy with dinner orders to talk to me." She forced herself to look at her watch. Then she forced herself to look directly at him. "Thank you for the drink but I really am late for a meeting with Gino. I must go."

His smile turned immediately bitter and his eyes flashed a jolt of electric disappointment, sharp and deadly as lightning.

"Are you saying you're going? You're just . . . leaving me?" His palms lay up and open on the table, like flattened, incredulous question marks. "This is it, then?"

"I'm sorry. But I'm a busy businesswoman. I've got to see my chef before the dinner hour begins."

"What happens after?"

"After?" She wasn't following him. She was concen-

trating on pushing her chair back, standing up, getting
far away.

"After you see your chef."

"Then I go home and check on my kids."

"And after you check on your kids?"

"I go to my other restaurant, Mia Elena."

He almost knocked his chair over in exasperation
as he rose and followed her to the door. With one
arm he barred her exit.

"We're not finished," he said with menace. "Not
after what happened here today. You wanted me to
touch you." He sounded like a hurt boy again. "I
know you wanted me. I could tell. And I'm going to
have you."

She looked at his powerful arm blocking her way.
"Wanting someone . . . and having someone . . . there
is a big difference."

He dropped his arm. But as she pushed past him,
he whispered at her, "I know. But I'm going to have
you. We're going to finish what we started."

We already did, she said to herself. *It's finished.
It's over.*

But then she made the mistake of glancing back at
his face . . .

It was four-thirty and the momentum in the kitchen
had begun to build. Gino was supervising his chef and
three other cooks in the early preparation of the soup
stocks, sauce bases, and long-cooking roasts when
Silvana burst through the swinging doors, called out
"Gino!" once, and then turned on her black suede
high heels and left the kitchen. She was so sure that he
would obediently follow that she did not even check to
see if he was behind her. He was.

She was his boss, his mentor, his role model, so of
course he would follow when she called him. For
Silvana Levi Bassani Nachman he had only respect
and continuing awe. Yet it irritated him that she did
not smile, did not even hesitate, just turned on her
impossibly high heels, sure that he still was—and always would be—her obedient puppy. Everyone in the

kitchen saw it. Saw how she treated him. Saw that he was no more than a dog on Silvana Nachman's very short leash.

"Get back to work!" he yelled at them, red-faced. "What are you looking at?" The dishwasher, he was sure, was smirking at him. *Well, this dog knew how to fix that!* Balling his powerful hands into fists, he raised them threateningly. "Enrico, wipe that smile off your face before I—" He stopped himself just in time and punched open the swinging door instead, storming through it into the dark, neat, empty main dining room. Silvana sat alone at a table set neatly for a party of six.

"What are you so angry about, Gino?" she asked, throwing him off balance. This was not what he expected. Usually, Silvana wanted to tell him, "We have twenty pounds of good veal. Tell the waiters to describe tonight's special as 'veal softer than velvet in a sauce smoother than silk.' Or she wanted to complain to him that costs were going up or that a waiter's uniform was dirty. And occasionally she would reluctantly confer with him about raising the prices. Business. There was never any time to talk about feelings. So why today? *Out of the blue she suddenly asks me why I'm so angry. What did Elena tell her?* he wondered.

"Those fists look like dangerous weapons." She pointed to his hands, still balled up, still ready to strike. "What do you need fists for? Who are you planning to beat up?"

Oh, that bitch Elena! She told, she told!

He'd take care of Elena when he got home tonight. But here was Silvana and he had to deal with her first. He flashed her a huge, white-toothed smile.

"Everything's fine, Silvana. What's this crazy talk about beating people up? I'm for peace." And he held his hand up, palm uncurled now, fingers straight, as if he were making a pledge.

But because Silvana's frosty expression did not change, he could see she did not believe him. He had not gotten through to her. So he tried again.

"Really, Silvana, I don't know what you're talking about. Has someone complained about me? Said anything?"

Silvana continued to send looks of ice across at him but she assumed a studied—though convincing—off-hand manner when she asked, "Who would have reason to complain about you, Gino? Everybody loves you, *sì?*"

Almost laughing, Gino had to agree. "*Sì*, Silvana. *Sì!*"

"Enrico in the kitchen loves you." She smiled knowingly, ticking the name of the dishwasher he had just threatened off on her finger. "And Gregory Wolf loves you, and—"

At that, Gino's head snapped to attention.

"Yes, that's right: Gregory Wolf. He's so grateful to you for giving him my private phone number."

"Oh, no! Silvana, I didn't. I swear!"

"And I'm so grateful to you, too."

"Did he say I gave your number to him?"

She gave him a sharp look. "Don't try to deny it now. It's too late. And you know how much I hate lies."

"All right. But it was just that he was the last customer in the place one night and we got to talking . . . and drinking. Talking a lot about you, as a matter of fact. And I guess I had a little too much to drink because when he asked me for your phone number, I just gave it to him."

"Even though you didn't know him? Even though I told you my private number was to be kept private?"

He hung his head and mumbled something.

"What?"

A bit louder this time he mumbled, "I had to. He owns restaurants. He—uh—offered me a job."

But Gregory Wolf had just told her he wasn't planning on stealing Gino away. For a split second she hesitated, wondering who to believe, Gino or Gregory. One last glance at Gino's shifty eyes, and she knew, without doubt, who had told her the truth. *Oh, Elena, my child! Who is this beast you have married?*

"So, he offered you a job?"

Again Gino hung his head.

"And that's why you say you had to give him my number?"

Gino nodded woodenly.

"Well, did you take it?"

"Take what?" He was leaden, dazed.

"The job!"

Now he became jumpy, overwrought. His fingers drummed the table, his feet tapped the floor. "The job?" he repeated dumbly, trying to gain time.

Silvana simply nodded.

"Oh, the job. Well, Elena didn't want me to take it."

"Why not?"

Frowning, as if the effort to think of an excuse was painful, he finally brightened and said, "Elena doesn't want to move to Long Island." His voice contained a whine that made him sound more like a whipped husband than a wife beater. But this was her opportunity and although she dreaded it, she could not lose this chance to question him directly about her Elena. As a mother, she had no other choice.

"Gino, speaking of Elena, I noticed some bruises on Elena's face. How did they get there?"

"Bruises? What bruises?"

"Gino, didn't I give you your start? Didn't you say that I am like a second mother to you?"

Gino nodded.

"So tell me."

Gino's shoulders hunched and his palms opened in a gesture of helplessness. "It was an accident. Honest. We were having an argument. She was provoking me, and I admit, I pushed her—but it was no more than a tap. A tap, that's all."

"But the bruises, Gino."

"Yeah, but she tripped," he agreed, shrugging. "And in a way, it was her fault because she tripped on a pair of her own shoes that she should have put in the closet. The house was a mess. See what I mean?"

"Yes, I see. It was her own fault," Silvana repeated, seething.

"That's right." At this point Gino allowed himself a smug little smile, confident in the success of his ruse. He would not have been surprised if Silvana apologized. All the tension, coiled in the tight muscles of his compact body, flowed out. For the first time since he had eloped with Elena, he felt relaxed. He was therefore entirely unprepared for what occurred next.

Silvana rose slowly from the chair, but with a fixed determination, and circled behind Gino's chair. Then she bent in close to him so that her mouth was almost touching his ear and her cheek brushed the back of his head. Though her hands rested lightly on his neck, even he sensed something threatening in the gesture. But before he could move, her hands tightened, locking him in place.

"Gino, I want to tell you something but I don't want to look at you. And if the dear Signore wills it so, I will never have to look upon you again. So you do understand that if you so much as move your head, I will squeeze my fingers like this and choke you." And she pressed her hands tight around his throat.

"Good!" she said when he remained still, and released the pressure. But she kept her hands on his neck.

"A man who beats his helpless wife is lower than a worm. But a man who blames her for his brutality deserves a special punishment."

At that, she could feel him writhe slightly in his seat. And if this were all not so awful and painful and real, she might have enjoyed watching him squirm. Instead, she only felt bitterness and revulsion. And the urge to get on with this, get it over with, and be gone from him. Forever gone.

"Long ago I took you in—not just into my business but into my family. Now all that must end. *Finito!*"

She could feel the muscles in his neck and shoulders tense up at her words, contract and tighten like overcooked meat. She could feel his neck and his chin stretching up, up, as if he were wincing.

"No, Silvana!" he called out, still motionless and facing away, but there was movement in his voice—a sob traveling up into his throat.

"Yes, Gino. *Finito.*"

"But why?" he whined, as if he did not know—and as if she did not know, either. What would a psychiatrist call it, she wondered. Being in a state of denial, she supposed. Refusing to face what was in front of you.

"Because you hurt my daughter, my Elena. And for that you will never be forgiven. For that, you will never work for me again. For that, you cannot stay married to Elena. And that, Gino, is why it is over."

"I love Elena," he protested weakly, still staring out at the dark, empty room. "You can't make me give her up."

"The police can. If you ever hurt her again, I'll call the police and have you arrested."

He tried a new tactic. "Silvana, don't fire me. How can I find work if you won't give me a reference?"

"Take the job Gregory Wolf offered you."

"I lied about that."

"I know," said Silvana and let go of his throat. "You lied about everything. You ruined everything. Now, get out. Carmine will cook tonight." Then she lied, too, but she had to, to save her daughter. "And don't go home. Elena doesn't want you either. She told me all about it. She hates you for what you did to her. Just as I do."

Slowly, Gino rose, untied his apron, and let it drop to the floor. But it wasn't until he had walked to the front of the room and out the door that Silvana allowed herself to feel the loss. Walking out that door was a boy who had been like an adopted son to her, and the loss was as deep and as dark as an underground tunnel ten miles down into the earth. And yet it was nothing compared to the loss of her very own daughter—her firstborn Elena. For that is what she feared would happen when Elena learned what she had done today—Silvana would lose Elena, too.

And yet, how could she have done anything differently? Gino's behavior could be neither tolerated nor condoned. He had to be banished—for the safety of her daughter and for her own peace of mind. But Silvana knew the price she would pay for this. Knew it before and knew it even more so now. Because now, as she sat alone in the empty, unlit room, she could almost feel the gaping hole inside her that her daughter had formerly filled. Elena would hate her for this. Perhaps for a long time. But Silvana prayed that it would not be forever and that someday they would be reunited. But most of all, Silvana prayed that what she had done would keep her daughter safe and free of fear. Safe. In the end, it was what she had struggled for all her life.

Chapter Nineteen

No one knew she was here, rumbling along on this rocking, clattering, mostly empty train to Montauk Point, Long Island. She had told everyone, "I have some business to attend to for a couple of days. I'll be back Friday." Eyes widened, mouths opened, but no one questioned her, although she would read the surprise on their lips as, "Since when do you ever take a couple of days off from your two precious restaurants?"

Even Lena Milgrim said nothing when she saw Silvana packing a small bag. The rare sight of a suitcase, Silvana mused, probably stunned the poor woman into muteness.

"I have to go out of town for a couple of days on business," she told her long-time friend and caretaker of her children. Silvana folded clothes and packed them into the bag as she talked. "Not far, but don't ask me where and don't ask me why." She folded a cream cashmere sweater, a cream suede jacket, a pair of brown suede pants, and two sets of cashmere socks. Elegant but practical clothing. "And don't worry! It's nothing, really." Two extra pairs of panties. No, three. Two plain, one black lace. "Just tell the girls—" Hesitating as she pulled a drawer open, stared at a white cotton nightgown, then picked a gown of black satin that she quickly whisked into the bag, she finally finished her thought, "Tell them I'll be home on Friday and then we'll all sit down and I'll tell you about it."

But what exactly would she tell them, she wondered. That she was on her way to see a dangerous young man she had vowed never to go near again?

Yes, yes, business. She was seeing him about business. That's what she would tell them. That's what she had told herself. That's why he told her he had called again after more than a year. Business. For no other reason.

"I know our last meeting ended badly and I want to apologize even though I waited so long to do it. I had no right to speak to you that way. In fact, I'd like to make it up to you."

"That's not necessary, Gregory," she told him in a fuzzy voice. He had called her at midnight and although she had come home from work only half an hour before, she was fast asleep when the phone rang.

But he had insisted, "No, really, I want to make it up to you. With an offer."

Silvana lay in bed, the phone to her ear. On the dark ceiling she saw his silvery gray eyes flashing like the eyes of a wolf. They glinted at her as he talked, even when she closed her eyes. He was there inside her, under her eyelids.

"I am very tired," she protested, remembering last time and his bitterness at the end. Yet she could not do what her mind told her to do—just hang up. Her hand held on to the phone as if she were holding on to him.

"I know. And I'm sorry for calling so late. But this is the only hour you're ever in . . . and available. Anyway, I'll just be a second. Remember that fishing lodge I was telling you about?"

She yawned and shook her head no, as if he were right there in bed with her, as if he could see her. That was what it felt like to her—that he was there.

"Remember I told you I was thinking of opening an Italian seafood restaurant in my father's old fishing lodge in Montauk Point?"

He had succeeded in jostling her memory and although she kept telling herself that he was dangerous and to just hang up on him, she exclaimed instead, "Oh, yes! *Sì!* Now I remember. Your father's fishing lodge."

Her recall delighted them both, making him chuckle

quietly into the phone. "That's right," he said, laughing. "My father's fishing lodge. Actually, I call it my father's even though it's really mine now. He gave it to me before he died five years ago."

"Oh," she said, stricken. *Five years without a father!* Her eyes were wide open now.

"And now I'd like to sell it. And I thought of you. It's really a choice piece of real estate. Why don't you come out and take a look at it? This, of course, would be strictly business. You have my word."

Strictly business. It was because of those words that she allowed herself to be talked into taking this endless train ride out to the very tip of eastern Long Island.

"When you stand at the Point, you're closer to Europe than from anywhere else," he told her. "On a clear day you can almost see Dover. Honest," he joked.

That, too, had convinced her to come. To stand safely on the beach and look out over the Atlantic Ocean and know that on the other side was Europe ... Italy ... Rome. Just to stand in the sand and the wind and to call over the crashing waves, "Mama! Mama, have you found it in your heart to forgive me yet? Mama! Give me a sign!"

But she could not entirely fool herself. Business and proximity to Europe were two compelling reasons to travel out to Montauk Point, but they were not the only reasons. Even Silvana had to admit to herself that there was one other. And that it was perhaps the most compelling of all. Because it was not so much a reason as an anti-reason—an irrational passion outside her usual realm of good sense and sound judgment.

But whether she called it reason or anti-reason, she still felt a strangely passionate attraction to Gregory Wolf that she could not deny. It was a passion, however, that she was determined to fight off. Once she had met another man who also came from Montauk— Sloane Harding. She had felt passion then, too, but she had fought it off. She could do the same again now for Gregory Wolf was too young, too reckless, too unpredictable, too irresistible to be good for her. How could he be anything but harmful when the mere thought of him made her shatter her rules, abandon her resolve, contradict her own vows?

Yes, she was determined even now to fight this magnetic attraction. And so, though she knew that this trip was not wise, she actually insisted to herself that she could still make it a safe, uneventful, and businesslike odyssey.

Two days! she told herself. *For two days I can keep things in control. Two days is really not a very long time.*

For the last couple of hours of the trip, she had stared out the window at farms and barns and endless rows of corn and potatoes and tomatoes. *Where,* she wondered, *is the ocean?* Not that it was warm enough to swim anymore. It was late September, and although the days were not yet frosty, all of the oppressive August heat and humidity had been squeezed out of them like wet laundry spin-dried to a warm, parched crispness.

At the last stop, he was waiting for her, standing in the sunlight beside a car that looked like it had developed an allergic rash to the salty ocean air. She could smell the ocean as soon as she alighted from the train; she just couldn't see it. But she could see him.

"How was the trip?" His eyes were doing what they always did to her; quickly she looked away and shrugged.

"Just a ride on a train." How could she tell him she had loved it, loved sitting in peace for five hours, loved looking out the window at the flat landscape of endless farms, weathered English houses, and small, nondescript towns, loved daydreaming about what it would be like to see him again? If she told him all that, he might take it as encouragement. So, although she was here, she was determined to discourage him from assuming anything personal in it.

He loaded her small bag in the back and held the front door open for her.

"Is the fishing lodge far?" She sat so close to the passenger door that the handle dug into her arm.

"You've been traveling five hours. Don't you want some lunch first?"

She shook her head no. "After, maybe. First, the lodge," she commanded, trying to emphatically underline her reason for being here: business. *Nothing else, Mr. Wolf! So don't get any ideas!*

He nodded, started the car up, and drove for some minutes in silence. The sight of him—as well as the effort to resist him—had so rattled her that she was still staring into her lap, still trying to regain her equilibrium when he announced, "We're here." She had seen nothing of the hilly, twisty two-lane road that circled around the rather plain village and the long, low motels at the town's outer edges. And nothing of the view of the beach of pale sand that suddenly appeared as the road turned and began a long, slow climb up alongside the dunes. For the first time, she now looked out of the window.

They were on a hill and from the road he had pulled into the driveway of a long, bilevel, wood and stone structure. An old sign announced "Wolf's Lodge" with a faded picture of a wolf howling at the moon. The sign seemed to be suffering from the same allergic rash as the "skin" of Gregory Wolf's car. The lodge was closed and boarded up.

And that was when she heard it—the sound of the surf. It began as a low rumble, grew louder, and then erupted again and again in a pounding crash—exactly like battle fire. But the smell was different. This was a clean smell. The air had nothing of smoke or blood or gunpowder in it, only salt and mist and clams and beach rose.

Gulls circled above them, dropping clam shells from their beaks. Once smashed to the ground, the clam shells split open, providing a convenient dinner for the clever birds. The driveway was littered with them. And in the background was the continuous sound of the sea.

Pointing up at the gulls, Gregory joked, "They've

made a seafood restaurant of this place already! All you have to do is add the sauce and some bread."

"If it's so easy, why don't you do it, Gregory? Why are you selling?" she asked as he led her on a narrow path around to the opposite side of the lodge, facing the—

"*L'oceano! Finalmente!*" Finally, she cried, interrupting herself, the ocean!

Now, nothing else mattered. Nothing but the sea! She had not realized how she had been awaiting this moment. And not just because first she had been teased by just the sound of it out front. No, her eagerness went back, way back to when she was a child. Her father had taken the entire family to the south for a holiday. And there, for the first time she saw the sea. She had been enraptured and she never forgot it.

"Girasole has a new nickname now—'little fish,' " her father had joked at the time. "She's been in the water all day. She's turning into a blue little fish right before our eyes!"

Now, as the wind whipped at her legs, her skirt, her hair, she remembered again. Ah, such tempestuous sea wind. But nothing compared to the sea itself! There, down below perhaps thirty feet, the deep green and black waves exploded into foam at the shoreline. Then waves of salty, sandy sea air rose up to mist her face, her bare arms, her legs under her skirt. It was so thrilling, she shivered.

"Are you cold?" He had been watching her every move. He seemed poised to obey her every command. "Would you like me to get you a sweater?"

Shivering again, she relented. "Thank you, yes. In my bag there is one, uh, the color of *crema.*"

"*Crema,*" he repeated, smiling as if he thought cream a lovely color for her. Or perhaps he just liked saying a word that she had just said. *Crema.*

The sweater was a mistake because as he helped her on with it, he touched her skin. His tan, powerful hands touched her arm, her shoulder by accident ... and then touched her neck, her ear, her cheek on purpose. The movements of his hands, from accidental to purposeful, were so smooth and natural that it was only after he had brushed her neck, then brushed the hair behind her ear, that his touch actually registered. And by then he was touching her cheek, stroking it, and she was drowning thirty feet above the sea.

"You belong here. Your skin is as cool as the sea." He pressed his nose to her cheek. "It even smells like the sea. You were born to be here, born to stay here."

But at that, she pulled away. She thought of her daughters at home, of her business and responsibilities and obligations. *Born to stay here? With him? Is that what he meant? No! Never!*

"What do you know of why I was born? Nothing, nothing!"

Nonplussed, he stared at her helplessly.

"Please, never speak of it again. I am here to speak only of business. Business! And that is all."

He nodded and gestured to the lodge. "Maybe this would be a good time to see the interior?"

She gestured for him to lead the way, grateful for the delay while he worked over the rusty lock with a set of jingling keys.

Why had she gotten so upset? What, really, had he said that was so terrible? she asked herself, shaken and not a little guilty. But there was no time for an answer; the key had finally turned and the door was open.

In single file they entered, their backs in blazing sunlight, their fronts facing the musty darkness and silent gloom of the boarded-up lodge. The old door creaked on its hinges, the old air made her sneeze. But as Gregory Wolf unlocked shutter after shutter, sending in ray after ray of light, Silvana's breath began to quicken. She clamped a hand to her mouth to hide her mounting enthusiasm, but of course Silvana's passions were not easily reined in—even by herself.

Finally, when he had pulled open all the shutters and the place was flooded in light, he turned to her to see her reaction. He found her standing in the middle of the main room, head thrown back, staring up at the beams and rafters of the pitched, slatted ceiling.

Then all at once, two small, dark, forked-wing birds took flight, screeching and diving excitedly over their heads.

"What are they?"

She opened a window and the two birds flew right out, cheeping and squawking madly as they exited. "Swallows," she told him with a bemused smile. And suddenly she was back again in Rome, back in her room on the old ghetto street of her youth, awaking to the shrieking symphony put on every spring and summer morning by the swallows.

"Strange," he remarked, joining her at the window to watch them fly away. "We have a lot of birds out here—red-winged blackbirds and blue jays and even herons and finches—and I thought I knew them all. But I've never seen swallows before. Are you sure—?"

"Oh, yes. They were most certainly swallows. I know because I used to have them outside my window in Rome as a girl." He was standing very close to her but neither of them had realized it. Which was why she turned to him before she spoke again—she thought he was many feet away. "But I never thought I would have to come here, to Montauk Point, the very end of the world, to see them again!"

When she laughed, he laughed, yet he hardly knew what she had said because the deafening roar of his own heartbeat, his own breath, even his own digestion echoed in his ears. It was as if he were turning inside out—suddenly he could hear everything going on inside of his body. And he had become deaf to everything outside it. It was disorienting, to say the least— but she was the cause.

All his life, he had gotten every girl he'd ever wanted. Some, even, that he hadn't particularly wanted. Tall girls, short girls, big-chested girls, flat girls. The gigglers and the serious ones. All of them found him dreamy, mysterious, irresistible. It was they who followed *him* home from school, they who called *him* on the telephone.

It got so that every time the phone rang, his mother gave him an ugly look of disapproval. Even though she knew *they* called *him*, she warned him incessantly, "You better behave yourself, young man, or do you want people to call you a skirtchaser, just like your father?"

But it had always been this way; the girls had always chased him—even as a kindergartner—and his mother had never liked it. Never really liked him.

Perhaps that was one reason he had loved Montauk so much. When his father got sick and the family moved out here, the first thing Gregory Wolf discovered was that out here there was simply more space—and less girls. But then his father died and his mother and sister moved back to New York and he became a restaurant owner—and the women began chasing him again.

Silvana was the first woman in his entire life who he had ever gone after. And he could not say why. Yes, she was beautiful, but she was also considerably older than he was. Perhaps even more important, she was the only woman who had ever rejected his advances. He had no experience whatsoever with the feeling of rejection. The only woman who had ever said no to him for anything had been his mother.

So this obsession with Silvana was even a little baffling to Gregory Wolf himself. Yet that was, in fact, what it had become—an obsession. He was obsessed with winning the one woman in the entire world who did not seem to want him, who could look into his polished silver eyes and say no.

And who could yawn in his face.

"You're so—refreshing!" he told her, moving even closer to her at the window. Immediately she began pulling back, moving away. But although she could not know it, by recoiling she was actually inflaming him.

She hurried through the swinging doors to the large, old kitchen. Perhaps instinctively she was drawn to the one room in any house that had always offered comfort and refuge, the one room where she always felt most at home. This one in the lodge seemed to promise no less.

A huge walk-in stone fireplace dominated the cooking area, despite the fairly modern stove and oven opposite it. In this room, the focus was on the fireplace, not the modern equipment. All of the counter space was built in a C-shape so that a cook could chop, slice, mix, and stir and still have a view of the fireplace at all times. Reminiscent of an old Italian taverna, wood beams crossed the ceiling and ceramic tiles lined the floor. If it were not for the floor-to-ceiling wood cabinets, which were painted the green of an overripe artichoke, she would have stamped the kitchen perfect.

I'll have them painted off-white, Silvana dreamed to herself, *but I'll change nothing else. A trattoria in Montauk!* Flooded with memories, filled with nostalgia, she tearily fantasized owning this extraordinary structure sitting on the most scenic spot she had seen in all of New York.

It was then that she heard the doors swing and found Gregory Wolf beside her again, her reverie shattered.

"Why don't you want me? What makes you so special? I know what you really want, so let's stop pretending," he said, and suddenly she went from feeling tearily hopeful to feeling faintly afraid. Gregory Wolf was pushing too hard and she no longer found him appealing. Even if she had known that her own rejection of him had sparked this new outburst of swaggering arrogance, she would not have behaved differently. For he had chilled whatever erotic heat there had been, and all she wanted was to get out of there quickly now.

"I think I'll have one more look at the ocean and then I'd like you to take me to a motel." As she spoke, she moved swiftly toward the front door. Gliding past him, she felt a momentary exhilaration that she was free, that everything would be all right. Then, suddenly, his hand was on her shoulder, stopping her.

"I said that I know you want me." He spun her around. "Now you say it." This was not a request. This was a threat. "They all do. You're no different than any of them. Why play games?"

Once again their eyes met but this time she felt no magnetic pull. This time she felt fear. "I do not like how you hold me, how you talk to me. I want you to let me go."

Instead of freeing her, his arms squeezed her against him. Pinning her arms behind her, he forced his face into hers, trying to catch her mouth in a kiss. But she knew what he wanted and she would not let him have it. Not this way. Not when he had ruined it all by trying to take it from her by force. From side to side she swung her head, looking right, left, right, left, dropping her head in an arc to evade his lips.

"Kiss me like you want me!" he commanded. When she would not, he shook her roughly by the shoulders. And that stilled her. Momentarily. As his mouth sunk down onto hers, however, she broke free of his hold and in one huge lunge pushed him off her. Then she was out the door.

But he was almost immediately behind her. Driven by an anger that surpassed fear, she stomped straight ahead, her shoes sinking into the soft sand. And then she was falling to the ground, facedown, at the edge of the high dune, and he had her by the leg.

Twisting herself onto her knees, doggie style, she kicked her free leg back into his middle and then dove, head first, into a rolling fall down the sandy dune.

Again, he was right behind her, following in a cloud of gritty sand that momentarily blinded her. To brush the sand from her face wasted precious seconds, however. And a search for her shoes, which flew off in her fall, wasted another minute. By then he was on his feet, standing over her.

Before she saw it, she heard it—the metallic click of his belt buckle. A part of her felt almost giddy to be in this ridiculous situation with this mere ... boy! And another part of her felt what could only be described as terror.

"No, Gregory!" she yelled uselessly into the wind and the roar of the waves. Even he, standing directly above her, could hardly hear her. But he could see her terrified eyes and her mouth calling, beseeching, begging.

Finally, she's begging. Always saying no, always rejecting. Now, finally, she's begging. It's about time. She wants me. I knew it all along.

He fell on top of her and immediately buried his face into the soft pillow of her breast. Meanwhile, his hands pulled at the front of her blouse, popping off buttons, ripping the fabric. She clawed at his face, pulled his hair but nothing, it seemed to him, could stop him now.

She wants me! I knew it.

"And you're gonna love it. You're gonna be sorry you ever said no!" he shouted in her ear.

Then his mouth was on her neck, his teeth were nipping at her skin. With one hand he had pinioned her arms to one side. With the other hand, he was pulling off her panties.

Once before in her life she had felt desire for a dangerous man and had lived to regret it. Once before, she had been talked into passion and had been abandoned in shame.

Am I to live that nightmare all over again? she wondered desperately, glancing up at the clear blue, tranquil sky that gave no hint of this storm below. *Is there no one again—no one at all to save me?*

She was panting, twisting, resisting, but it was futile. His hand was deep inside her, and she knew what was coming next.

"You're wet inside. You want me. Say it!" His eyes were closed. She had to do something, say something to open his eyes.

"Your father is crying! Gregory! Your father! I can see him and he's dead and he's crying. He's sobbing. Your father is sobbing!"

"Wh-what?"

She screamed in his ear, "He says he was wrong. He wants you to forgive him."

Gregory opened his eyes. "He wants *me* to forgive *him?*"

"For leaving you. For dying. For leaving you with her. With your sister . . . and with her."

He stopped pulsing, he stopped writhing. He let go of her arms. He did not even look at her. He looked at something above her, in the sky.

"For leaving me with Ma?"

"Yes." She nodded, sliding out from under him. "With Ma. He's so sorry he isn't there to—" she fumbled, not sure what to say, but he provided the answer.

"To protect me from her viper's tongue. From her hate. Dad always knew she hated me."

Right before her eyes, Gregory Wolf suddenly seemed to shrink, to become a little boy again. A very hurt and very lost little boy. Two minutes ago he had been a crazed and violent man. Two minutes ago he had been about to rape her. And the danger, she knew, was not yet over. But Gregory Wolf had suddenly transformed from a menacing threat to a seriously disturbed and confused young man.

"Yes, he knew," Silvana agreed, not only to calm him. Unwittingly, she had reached him by uncovering a hidden and painful truth. She was almost as surprised as he was.

"And before he died, he tried to get Ma to love me. But you can't make someone love you, can you?"

Stunned by his own words, he became very still. *You can't make someone love you.* The words repeated over and over inside his head, like an echo in a dark cave. He lay in the sand on his side, in a classic fetal position, and he was so quiet that he might have been napping, except for his metallic gray eyes—which remained wide open, but fogged with sadness and confusion.

Carefully Silvana sat up. She was afraid to stand, however, afraid to attract his attention. And so, for some time, they both remained there on the beach, listening to the surf, listening to their heartbeats return to almost normal. She did not know exactly when she caught him looking at her with a clear gaze, but it was probably at least fifteen minutes later. The fog, she noticed, had cleared from his eyes.

"You didn't see my father," he said, sitting up. "You didn't see him crying."

"I did—" she began to protest but he stopped her with a reassuring look. It was as if he were telling her not to worry, that he understood why she had lied.

"But you made a sharp guess," he admitted and almost smiled. A very small, a very sad smile. "So sharp, you got to me. Stopped me. Stopped me cold."

She wasn't sure. Was he blaming her or thanking her? She realized that she was still in shock, still afraid, and she pulled her sweater tightly over her ripped blouse. She knew she no longer was his prisoner but she did not feel entirely free yet, either. She was confused, terribly confused, as everything seemed to be getting more and more complicated.

His mind, however, was becoming clear. But as the events of the past half hour began to come back to him in vivid detail, a look of horror contorted his face. He rubbed his eyes as if he could erase the pictures he saw before him . . . but of course, he could erase nothing. Everything he saw had really happened. And it filled him with shame.

"My God!" he cried. "How could I do that to you? My God, I'm a monster!" His voice broke with emotion. "I must be crazy! I must be out of my mind because I never, ever could have done anything like that before."

She waited, not willing to trust anything he said. Hardly willing even to listen. Yet, she knew that what he spoke this time was the truth. She just didn't know how to feel about it. Should she feel sorry for him? Sympathetic? Or should she spit on him and his self-mortification? After all, wasn't it she—and she alone—who deserved the sympathy here? And he who deserved the punishment? Didn't she blame him for what he had done to her? Yet if she did, why did she also feel regret? And why did she feel this enormous cloudburst of sorrow? Was it only for herself . . . or was it also for him?

Not for the first time he seemed to read her thoughts and said, "I'm not going to ask you for forgiveness. I wouldn't expect you to forgive what I did to you." He looked at her hesitantly and she nodded, permitting him to continue. But he had to take another minute to compose himself again before he went on and said, "I—I don't even know exactly why it happened. But what you said about my father was what pulled me back. I was really over the edge. Horribly over the edge. I know you were trying to save yourself. But what you said . . . well, it also saved me."

Again, Silvana nodded. She was too flooded with conflicting emotions to speak. But she heard him. She heard every word.

"Are you going to call the police?"

The question jarred her. Suddenly she needed to stand up, walk. She needed to test whether he would really let her go, whether she was indeed free. "I don't know," she said and began walking down the beach. The sand was cool and smooth but she hardly noticed. All she was aware of, turning back to look, was that he was still sitting where she had left him.

For some time she wandered down the beach, but she saw no people and no houses. Of course, she could have scaled the dune and flagged down a car on the road, but her blouse was ripped and she felt vulnerable to the stares of strangers. She returned to where Gregory still sat in the sand, and where her shoes lay, half buried.

"Are you able to drive?"

Sadly, he nodded yes.

"Will you drive me to the train station?"

"There won't be a train for"—and he looked at his watch—"another hour and a half."

"I'll wait."

For a second their eyes met and held. Then he nodded and got to his feet. Separately, they made their way up the dune. When he saw her struggle against the sliding sand, he almost impulsively reached out and offered his hand, but then he thought the better of it. She would not want any part of his hand. He

decided, too, against saying anything to her in the car.
They drove to the train in utter silence.

Even at the station, as she pulled on a suede jacket
that she found in her bag, he could only stand by and
watch, neither helping nor touching nor speaking.

But suddenly, as he was about to turn and go, it
was she who spoke, she who broke the silence.
"Why?" she wanted to know. Just, "Why?"

To answer her, to answer her with honesty, with
clarity and with apology—that was how he wanted to
say good-bye to her before she rode out of his life. It
was not enough. Someday, he knew, he would think
of a way to make this up to her. For now, however,
he would be satisfied just to answer her wisely. But
forming such wise thoughts, such wise words, called
for a depth of philosophy and eloquence he knew he
did not possess. Therefore, he spoke plainly, but in
the end, he surmised, perhaps it was preferable.

"I did a terrible thing to you today. I know you'll
never forget it—and neither will I. But it is difficult
for me to understand exactly why it happened. All I
know is that my mother could never love me. Maybe
it was because my father began straying after I was
born and she blamed me. Anyway, my father became
the buffer between my mother and me. After he died,
she let out all her hate."

The sun was fading and she was extremely hungry
but she knew she wanted only to hear this and then
have him go. To watch him climb into his car and
drive away. To leave her alone.

"Anyway, for some reason winning your love became very important to me."

"Did I remind you of your mother?" she could not
help asking.

"I don't know. Certainly, you look nothing like her.
But she was the only woman who ever rejected me—
until you. And when you did, it just drove me crazy."

"You need a doctor, Gregory."

"I know."

"A doctor for your head. A psychiatrist."

She was right and he promised her, "I will ask my

doctor for a referral tomorrow." Then there did not seem to be anything more to say.

No, he would not tell her again how sorry he was. Only because he knew she did not want to hear it. And he would not tell her that he intended to try to make it up to her. He knew she did not want anything more from him, particularly not to hear his future intentions. But already an idea was forming, a way he could do something for her. It was a gift that would require certain legal procedures to execute, but by the new year—1970—he hoped it could be hers.

The train started up and sounded its whistle. From where he sat in his parked car, he could no longer see Silvana, who by now had boarded, but he could see the train as it slowly pulled out of the open-air station. Imperceptibly picking up speed, it rushed westward, passing him and finally speeding out of view.

It was then that he said his good-byes, silent and alone. But Silvana was there in his thoughts and always would be—the woman who would not love him. Always, he would remember her fondly and with sorrow, as the only one he had ever really wanted ... until he wanted her much too much.

Chapter Twenty

On an extremely crisp, sunny morning in April, Elena skipped lightly down the granite courthouse steps on Centre Street, a free woman. But to whoop and to cheer would have been excessive, even now, even though she was on the outside of that very sedate courtroom, because she still felt its restraint. Nevertheless, the entire final divorce proceeding had been so exceedingly brief and uneventful that she felt somehow let down, somewhat cheated.

"There should be balloons and horns and paper streamers. Instead there was just that old judge reading in a cracked voice that my divorce was granted and final. It was anticlimactic."

"You want to celebrate? Okay, let's celebrate," Anna Michela agreed amiably, making a happy clown face, twirling her hands in the air and at the same time mooing like a cow. Now that she had been allowed to cut school for the day in order to accompany Elena to the courthouse, Anna Michela was willing to do anything to put a smile on her half sister's face.

Elena, after all, was like a second mother to Anna Michela, yet still young enough to be a friend as well. However, Elena had one failing: she did not giggle. Ever. In fact, getting her to smile at all was almost always a hopeless task, which was why Anna Michela so often volunteered to try. The rare success—a smile that opened with warmth and light like the dawn itself—was worth a hundred failed attempts. This was particularly true since Elena's perpetual sorrow placed Anna Michela in such an exalted position within the family hierarchy; as the only one able to get Elena to smile, she was seen and accepted by all as the "favorite."

Alternately over the years, Silvana and Elena had raised Anna Michela. In the early days, Silvana could be seen cradling Anna Michela in her arms, singing to her the same Italian folk songs she'd sung to Elena, and that she would soon also croon to Debora. Then, when Silvana had to go off to work and Elena's homework was done, Elena would take over from Lena Milgrim and feed and diaper her baby sister. And perhaps just because Anna Michela had in Elena a loving second mother to care for her, Anna Michela never cried when Silvana was not there; Elena always was.

Instead of widening, the age gap between them only seemed to get narrower as Anna Michela and Elena got older. By now, it was to Elena that Anna Michela turned with all her adolescent thoughts and secrets. And more times than Elena would have liked to admit, she did the same with Anna Michela. The age gap, however, did exist, which was why Elena, almost thirty-one, was embarrassed to admit she confided all her secrets to her half sister who was not yet fifteen.

There was only one secret she had not yet told Anna Michela. Until today no one knew; no one at all except Elena and her obstetrician. Today she would have to tell her sister. But not until later. First, they would celebrate.

"Let's go to a really fun double-feature movie and eat popcorn and chocolate cherries and laugh until we get a bellyache," Anna Michela suggested. Her idea of a good time was to have a good laugh and a junk food snack. Not Italian food. Not Jewish food. American. No Sabbath roast chicken, no chopped chicken livers with sage, and definitely no tomato sauce or pasta. Nothing Italian at all. She made no secret of the fact that to her eating spaghetti was a boring chore.

"Give me a burger and fries and I'll be your slave for the rest of my life! But give me another bowl of linguine and I'll scream, I swear!" she only half joked.

Anna Michela was thoroughly American. So American that the ritual of a Sabbath meal, for which

Silvana sped home from work each Friday night, had become an annoyance that cramped Anna Michela's social life. Of the hour that the family gathered around the table, lighting the candles and saying a *barucha* before eating, she felt only impatience.

And little Debora was following Anna Michela closely in everything. She was just as American, just as fun-loving. And just as tall. Oddly, even though Debora was five years younger, she was almost as tall and dark as Anna Michela, with Warren Nachman's same angular features. They might have been twins. They differed in only one respect: Elena adored Anna Michela; she could not stand Debora.

Today, of course, Debora was not permitted to trail behind Anna Michela. While the two half sisters—one short, one tall—went off to court, Debora went off to school. Nor would she be part of the celebration afterward. As it was, Elena felt thoroughly humiliated at depending on her not-quite-fifteen-year-old sister for companionship. Having ten-year-old Debora along would have been the final straw.

What has *happened to all my friends?* she wondered. And then the last five years came flooding back to Elena, and she knew exactly where her friends had gone—into graduate school, careers, and happy marriages. Or so it seemed. While she had withdrawn into a twilight zone, neither light nor dark, filled with endless fear and shame and pain.

"I will not give him up, do you hear me!" she shouted at her mother two days after Silvana had told Gino off. Elena felt she had to defend him; if she did not defend him, she would lose him. And although a part of her wanted to be rid of him, rid of the fear and the pain he had caused, she was still secretly in love with him. Ashamed of this love she still felt for him, and ashamed that he cared so little for her in return, she turned on herself, grew furious with herself—even blamed herself for his abuse.

Your fault! It's all your fault! she hissed at herself. If it was all her fault, then he was innocent, and she did not have to leave him. But to make him innocent, she had to make up a rather elaborate fantasy. And she had to make herself believe it.

"He loves me," she told her mother. "I'm his life. So don't you ever threaten him again."

"If he ever hurts you again, I will. I'm your mother."

"He doesn't hurt me. I'm the one who hurts him."

"I don't believe you. And I hope *you* don't believe your own lies, because that's what they are, my poor darling."

"You call me a liar? In that case, I quit!" she announced and marched out of the restaurant Silvana had named in her honor. She was back at work the next day, but the residue of strained silences and stormy scenes remained.

Almost six wretched years followed while Elena, resisting all her mother's tearful entreaties, endured the abusive rages of her husband.

"Why?" Silvana would beg her to answer. "Why do you stay? And if he loves you the way you say he does, why does he treat you so poorly?"

Elena knew why; she just could not tell her mother. How could she admit that she'd tricked Gino into marrying her—pushed him, cajoled him, fast-talked him? How could she admit that although she knew he no longer loved her, she went ahead and pushed him into marriage anyway? Swallowing her pride, her dignity, her integrity, she railroaded him to the altar. And for that treachery Gino had a right to rage and storm, even give her a few black and blue marks, she reasoned sheepishly. Because it was her fault, all her fault.

The minute he hit her that first time, she had thought, *What did I do wrong? I must have done something—something very bad to deserve a punishment like this. What did I do? What?*

The minute he hit her, mistakes, errors, blunders paraded before her; she examined them all. The first undercooked marital dinner when she had insisted to Gino, "Tonight *I* will be chef," and was so nervous, she removed the casserole still raw from the oven. The

cheap satin sheets she bought for the bed that made
a snaky, slithery sound with their every movement and
that irritated Gino so much that he could not sleep.
Mistakes. Blunders. She examined every item she had
bought, every word she had said, and found more than
enough to regret ... but not the cause. The cause of
this punishment would become clear and then elude
her again.

And then it became utterly transparent. It came as
she opened her eyes one morning, arriving like a clear
glass of water on a tray. The thought was so clear and
so cold that she shivered, and as she shivered, she
knew it to be true.

*It was my fault because I outwitted him into mar-
rying me,* she told herself while Gino still slept beside
her. *It was my fault. I never should have. I could see
he didn't want to. So I made him. And now I must pay
for my sin.*

In a way, she had become a saint after all—a mar-
tyred Saint Theresa. Like a true martyr, she was paying for her sin without complaint. Except that she did
not think the punishment would go on so long. She
thought it would be over that bloody, brutal day
when they had been married less then six months.
Then she thought it would be over in another week.
She never thought that after five more years, it still
would not be over. But by then, even she had had
enough. By then, she was no longer a saint; she
wanted out of the marriage to save herself. By then
she had even told Anna Michela.

Still, though the judge had declared her union severed and she had a paper to prove it, she knew she
was not yet free of Gino. Hadn't she let him into her
new apartment just six weeks ago, after begging and
banging and breaking her heart all over again until
she unlocked her door and allowed him in? Hadn't
she stood there in her nightgown, secretly as pleased
as she was frightened, while he dropped to his knees
and pressed his face into her belly? *He still wants me!*
And for a couple of seconds hadn't she actually felt

desired and lucky, forgetting for the moment the horror of the last five years?

His nose pushed against her pelvic bone and the room was so quiet she could hear his breath as it blew haltingly out of his open mouth. Then he lifted her skirt and jammed his fist up her vagina, yelling, "You think you can leave me, you bitch-devil? You think you can divorce me?"

"No, don't!" she managed to say, but he liked it when she resisted.

"Fight me. Go on, fight me off," he had often encouraged her. When she did—and often it was for real—it only inflamed him.

She knew he liked to watch her squirm, she knew he liked it when she cried and begged, but she did all of those things anyway. Not because he liked it but because he was hurting her and she was no longer a stoic.

And perhaps in the end that saved her because her tears of pain got him so excited, he stopped torturing her and just raped her. In less than two minutes it was over. He stood above her and warned her, "You're still mine. You're just no angel anymore, are you? Now you're the goddamned devil." Then he was gone. But he left his seed inside her.

Now she wanted to forget all that for a few hours, and just celebrate her freedom. But Anne Michela's idea of a good time was not hers. What was hers, however?

"Actually, I have no idea what would make me happy," she admitted to Anna Michela, and began to cry.

"This is such a happy day. Don't cry, Elena. You're rid of Gino. He hit you, he hurt you, and now you're rid of him. So what do you want now? Think. What do you want?"

By now Elena was hiding her face in her hands while she shook with gasping sobs. She did not feel like celebrating anymore; she did not even feel free. At the moment she felt like a lost, hurt little girl, without direction or love, who had a new, secret life growing inside her—and no husband to share it.

"I want my mother, that's what I want!" she bawled.

"Your mother? You mean Mama? You want Mama?" Anna Michela repeated, dumbfounded. To her, Elena had always been older, wiser, out on her own—independent. Elena had her own restaurant named after her where she worked every day. Elena had her own apartment; Elena bought her own clothes. Elena was an adult. Always.

For Anna Michela to see Elena bawling out of control in public, whining that she wanted her mother, was a picture so strange, so confusing, that she ran away. Ostensibly, she ran to get Elena some water or a soda, but she really just fled.

"I'll be back in a minute!" she called, and ran fast, as if distance and speed could somehow obliterate the demoralizing image of her big sister Elena crying for her mommy that Anna Michela would remember, she was sure, for the rest of her life.

But by the time she returned, carrying a bottle of Coca-Cola, she found Elena composed and serene.

"Sorry about breaking down like that," Elena apologized and actually gave a small smile. Greedily, she accepted the soda and sipped without stopping until it was finished. Then, just as suddenly as before, tears began rolling down Elena's cheeks again. She handed the soda bottle to Anna Michela and held out her arms as if to say, "What can I do? I just can't stop crying."

"C'mon," said Anna Michela in an older, huskier voice than usual. She took her big sister's hand. "Let's go to Mama's."

Elena and Anna Michela were both awake, both there, waiting for Silvana when she dragged herself home from work, but once Silvana saw Elena standing in the doorway, she saw no one else. Elena, home at last!

"No! Is that really you? Is that really my Elena?"

Like a blind woman trying to "see" with her hands, Silvana reached out and patted Elena's cheeks, ran her fingers down Elena's nose, smoothed the worry lines from her forehead. She pressed her hands against Elena's head, she traced Elena's unsmiling lips, she kneaded Elena's shoulders. Only by touching Elena's flesh could Silvana convince herself that, yes, Elena was real, Elena was here, Elena had come home again! *And in one piece, thanks be to the Signore!*

"My baby," she whispered tearily, and then laughed when she saw the incredulous face her two daughters made. "*Sì, sì,* my baby! To me she will always be my first baby." To prove it, she embraced Elena tenderly and kissed her.

Silvana, who an hour before had felt almost faint with exhaustion, who had yawned blearily all the way home in the cab, now threw off her coat, took each girl under her arm, and marched them automatically to the kitchen. Pushing up her sleeves, chucking Elena under the chin, she asked, "How about some pasta, eh?"

Anna Michela rolled her eyes as usual, but Elena actually grinned. This was what she had been hoping for—to come home, to *really* come home. To find Mama again. To be petted and cared for and made a fuss over. To eat a late-night snack of her mother's hot, fresh pasta—which to her was always more warming, more comforting, than a cup of hot tea, a mug of hot milk, or a hot-water bottle.

Home. For too long she had kept away, angry and hurt at her mother's treatment of Gino. Ashamed, too. Ashamed that her mother knew. Not just that Gino was a brute, but that she, Elena, was so unloved. Ashamed that her mother knew the abuse she had been willing to endure in order to try to hold onto a husband who did not love her. The shame was what had really kept her away.

Silvana said little as she put the spaghetti water up to boil. It was a delight merely to hum along as little Debora slept soundly next to Mrs. Milgrim's room and her two big daughters harmonized to an English rock

song. While they sat at one end of the long, wooden
table, she stood at the other end, chopping garlic,
mushrooms, onions, leftover eggplant, and cold
chicken for an impromptu sauce.

Quickly, in hot olive oil, she sautéed the garlic and
onions and bent over the pan to breathe in the aromatic vapors. How many hundreds—thousands—of
times had she sautéed garlic and onions? Always, it
was the same. Always the aroma filled her with pride
and pleasure and promise of good tastes to come. Oh,
it was grand to be cooking again—and grand to have
children at home to cook for!

At her restaurants, it was different. With professional chefs to do most of the on-line cooking, she
was growing used to letting others do the sautéing and
simmering and chopping and stirring for her. Still,
there was so much work to be done! *I wear pretty
dresses,* she said to herself, *and my fingers no longer
smell from garlic all day long, but I work just as hard.*

Adding one cup of white wine and a tablespoon of
minced sage (grown on her windowsill) to the hot pan,
she stepped back as a momentary cloud of steam rose
up like the clouds of herbal steam her mother had
made her bend over, a towel draped over her head,
whenever she was sick with a cold. How she had loved
infusing hot spurts of steam scented with rosemary
and peppermint and chamomile under the secret universe of the terry-cloth tent. If she bent too close, the
tip of her nose was singed, but if she backed too far
away, her nasal passages did not clear and she could
not sleep. She learned the trick was to lean in close
as she exhaled, back off as she inhaled. And she had
taught the trick to all three of her daughters.

The mixture in the pan died down to a rolling bub-
ble. Then, almost magically just a few short minutes
later, as she shook the pan over high heat, the liquid
reduced to a mere tablespoon. At that point she added
a minced, ripe tomato, the leftover eggplant and
chicken, and one cup of chicken broth and allowed
the mixture to reduce again for several minutes. This,
she realized, was the way her mother had cooked—

using up whatever was leftover, mixed with whatever was fresh and new. But of Silvana's dishes her mother had said, "When you put two ingredients together, *presto!* It becomes a masterpiece. If you were a painter like Donatello, or Caravaggio, your suppers would be worth millions!"

Oh, Mama! she prayed, not for the first time. *Let me return to you. Let me in. Your little girl has been wandering in the desert too long!*

It was time to fold in the cooked pasta. Along with it she added some chopped mozzarella cheese, Parmesan cheese, and chopped parsley, and allowed it all to heat together for a minute or two before serving.

This was not a recipe that anyone had taught her, nor had anyone, as far as she knew, ever prepared it before. It was solely her creation, inspired by Elena's homecoming, improvised, using leftovers, in exactly thirty-one minutes. Here at home, she enjoyed improvising rather than adhering to the historically accurate recipes she offered at her restaurants. And sniffing the aroma in the pan, she could tell that the result of this improvisation was going to be a tasty delight.

But as she set a place for Anna Michela, her middle daughter shook her dark, silky head no. "I'm not hungry."

Knowing Anna Michela's *Americana* tastes, Silvana offered, "I can make a *frittata* or—"

"Omelet, Mama," said Anna Michela impatiently, rolling her eyes as Elena used to do.

"*Sì, sì,* in your America, it is called an omelet. I forget sometimes."

"Mama, this is your America, too," Elena reminded her, not for the first time. But she softened her words by wrapping an arm around her mother's shoulders as she bent over the pan. "It smells delicious."

However, Anna Michela insisted, "I've been eating all day and now I'm just so sleepy. Elena and I have been sitting here for hours, watching television and talking. It's so strange to have her home with us again, isn't it, Mama?"

Silvana caught Elena's eyes. "*Sì,* it is strange ... and wonderful."

There was no smile from Elena, of course, but she did sigh and caress her mother's hand.

So much affection from Elena in one night! Silvana had to hold herself back from whooping with delight ... or breaking down in tears.

She also had to hold herself back from falling to her knees and thanking the Signore for bringing her and Elena back together again. As she set only two places at the table (Anna Michela went off to finish her homework and go to sleep), she silently remembered how strained and worried she had been about Elena these last few years. Oh, how she had feared that history would repeat itself! That the ties between her and Elena would be irreparably severed—just as they were between Silvana and her own mother long ago.

"I quit!" Elena was always saying and worked at the restaurant only intermittently—quitting, returning, quitting, and finally returning again. Yet even when she was there, working in her tailored suits and French-cuffed shirts, there was hardly ever an intimate or tender moment between them.

Business discussions were plentiful, of course. There were always myriad business matters to discuss—not only staff problems and the unavailability of certain ingredients but the rising costs of newly imported food and wine and the growing pressure to develop new recipes.

New *serio* Italian restaurants were opening down the street—in fact, all around the city—and a new interest was growing in *cucina Italiana.* Despite all the talented new chefs, new tastes, new excitement, however, Silvana remained queen of *cucina Italiana* ... for now.

"But I know that in your America, no one believes in royalty. I may be queen today, but I can be voted out tomorrow."

"That's why I think you should write a cookbook,

Mama," Elena suggested, not for the first time. "To protect your crown ... and your dynasty."

"I know. But all my recipes are in my head ... in Italian."

"Dictate them to me and I'll translate them for you."

"Thank you, *mia dolcezza.*"

During those years Elena's sudden sweetness and offers of cooperation always caught Silvana off guard, stunning her into momentary silence while Elena made excellent suggestions.

"Today, Mama, you must advertise. You need a promotion campaign. It is not enough that everyone in New York now knows your name. Everyone in the world must recognize it, too!"

Then mother and daughter would set to work coordinating the dates of Silvana's radio and TV guest appearances and the growing pile of invitations to lecture at cooking schools and restaurant business conventions. They would work tirelessly, agreeably. But there was no warmth or contact and mother and daughter would carefully avoid physically—or emotionally—touching each other again.

"If you want me to work here, you have to respect my rule," Elena had warned her early on.

"And what is this rule?" Silvana had asked, smiling wryly, unprepared for Elena's emotional asceticism then.

"Hands off. No kissing, no hugging, no touching, period. And no personal questions. In short, hands off. That's my rule."

Even then, Silvana had noticed what an odd choice of words Elena had used: *Hands off.* As if Gino's hands, given too free a rein, made all other hands entirely forbidden, even a mother's caress.

Over the years, Silvana had attempted to bend Elena's rule, to pretend to forget and just reach out and try to touch Elena's cheek or give her an impromptu hug. But Elena would arch stiffly at any sign of affection—even when she was caught off guard—

and Silvana learned to abide by her daughter's rule.
It was either that—or risk losing Elena altogether.

During this time Silvana suspected that Gino had
continued to hurt Elena, but he was clever—he never
hit her on the face again. Whenever Elena phoned her
at the restaurant to announce yet again, "I quit!"
Silvana knew the unhappy couple had probably had
another fight.

"You'll see," Lena Milgrim assured her. "Elena's
good sense will prevail. One day she will get rid of
that no-goodnik. And on that day she will come back
to you. You'll see."

Although Silvana loved to hear these words, which
she found as soothing—and as temporary—as the heat
of a warm, quiet bath, Silvana did not really believe
them. What she really believed was that she would
lose her daughter and history would tragically repeat
itself once more.

Thus, at Elena's tender pat of her hand, Silvana
almost marched right into Mrs. Milgrim's room, awakened her, and announced, "You were right! I do see!
It happened just as you said—she has come back to
me!" But in deference to the aging lady, Silvana decided to wait until morning.

Meanwhile, she brought two steaming bowls of
pasta to the table and finally, after more than six continuous hours of standing, sat down.

Elena ate eagerly, even greedily, inhaling each bite,
comforted by each taste. Once seated beside Elena,
however, Silvana left her own food untouched. She
simply could not stop staring at her daughter, finding
endless excuses to reach over and brush a hair from
Elena's cheek, smooth the shoulder of her blouse,
squeeze her small, dear hand. It was enough simply
to watch Elena eating.

For some minutes only the ticking of the clock,
above the sideboard that held the unlit Sabbath candles and a silver Hanukkah menorah, was the loudest
sound. Then Elena pushed her empty plate away and
regretfully broke the contented silence.

"Mama, I have something to tell you and I don't

want you to get upset because I—I'm going to need you now—need you more than ever before."

Silvana peered at her daughter, trying to guess what Elena was about to tell her. She wondered, *Is she going to quit again? Or has she some complaint to make—probably about me, as usual? Does she want to talk about the divorce? She can't be sorry she divorced him, can she?*

But nothing she imagined could prepare her for what Elena was about to tell her.

"Mama, I'm pregnant."

Silvana blinked, uncomprehending. She blinked again.

"Do you understand what I'm saying, Mama?" Elena watched her mother blinking rapidly, unsure Silvana was absorbing her words. Quietly she repeated them. "I'm pregnant. I'm carrying Gino's child."

But Silvana had heard every word. Instinctively, her hand shot across the table and found Elena's. Wordlessly, she threaded her fingers in between Elena's and there they sat, their hands tightly joined, as the tears began to fall from their eyes.

After some minutes Silvana managed to ask, "How far along are you?"

Elena was not exactly sure. "Almost two months, I think."

"So you knew—and you divorced him anyway."

Elena nodded.

"I'm proud of you, my poor darling. You have your father's courage. And now you can take with you the one beautiful thing that came from this marriage, the one good thing that Gino gave you."

"Oh, Mama!" Elena sobbed. "I'm so sorry! For everything."

Both mother and daughter now could not seem to stop talking. There was so much to catch up on, and endless new plans to be made. But finally, as midnight melted into one o'clock, even their renewed closeness could no longer enliven them. A leaden exhaustion at last quieted them.

"May I stay the night, Mama? It's too late to go home to my apartment."

"*Benvenuta*, my darling. Welcome," Silvana whispered and walked Elena to her old room—still as crisply white and yellow as when Silvana first spied it those many years ago. "And *buona notte*. You must get rest and strength for your baby. Sleep well."

But at the door, Elena suddenly stopped and about-faced. "Oh, Mama, I almost forgot. You received a letter—a large envelope. Someone delivered it while Anna Michela and I were here." She hurried off to the foyer to retrieve it.

As soon as Silvana saw the return address on the envelope—Montauk—she paled. For a moment she thought of the tanned, good-looking man in the fish market—Sloane Harding. He had come from Montauk. But another look at the envelope, and she knew who it was from. *Ten months!* After ten months, she had almost forgotten him, almost forgotten what he had tried to do to her on the beach. Now it all came back to her and she realized she had not forgotten at all. She had just pushed it out of the way.

"Did you see the person who delivered this?" Silvana held the large envelope gingerly, as if even a mere letter from Gregory Wolf could somehow go berserk and attack her ... or arouse unsafe, inappropriate passions.

"Yes. He was old and skinny and he wore a gray uniform. Why?" Elena asked as she moved toward the bed and kicked off her shoes.

Silvana sighed with relief. At least Gregory Wolf had not come to her door to deliver this letter. She did not want him near her girls. The thought of it made her shudder. She did not want to remember Gregory Wolf at all, but holding his letter in her hand, his face flashed before her. And then, suddenly, another face flashed before her—the face of another man she did not want to remember—Benno Levi.

Benno. Would she ever forget him? Benno, more dangerous, more lethal than a hundred Gregory Wolfs. Benno, who had robbed her of her youth, robbed her of her innocence, robbed her of her mother.

Benno. She had never spoken of him and of what he had done to her, but she had never forgotten. She just prayed that she would never have to mention his name. Because at the sound of his name, all she felt and remembered was the shame, the unbearable burden of shame.

Now, climbing between the cool, smooth sheets of the huge old bed, her eyelids, so heavy several minutes ago, flashed open and fluttered as lightly as butterfly wings. Gregory Wolf's letter!

With a mixture of both curiosity and mild dread, she tore open the envelope, thinking of that night at the restaurant when she had first felt his eyes upon her, thinking of how she had almost melted. Once, too young and too innocent, she was ruined by a man who knew better, but who did not care. Now it was she who knew better and this time she had the maturity and the will to resist. And by resisting, that terrible day with Gregory Wolf in Montauk became the day she stopped history from repeating itself.

Then why did she not feel safe and free? Why did dread still stalk her, warning her that it was not yet over . . . that sin and betrayal were still in the blood?

She stared at the legal document on her lap and although she could see that it was a deed, she could not quite believe it. Yet she did not read the accompanying explanatory letter right away. She was still thinking of Benno Levi and Gregory Wolf and Gino Bracca, men who did bad things to women.

When, she wondered, would she ever meet a man again who was good for her, right for her? Or was it all over? Was it too late for her ever to know passion and love and ecstasy again? Was she, in fact, too old?

At last she read Gregory Wolf's letter.

Dear Silvana,
    I know I can never make up for the pain and anguish I have caused you, but I hope you will accept this gift as a gesture of my wish to try.
    It was clear to me from the first instant that you

loved the lodge—loved it, in fact, more than I do. For
five years it has sat idle because I have not had the
energy or the interest to do the work to convert it. I
know you possess all that it takes . . . and more.

Please accept this deed to the lodge, for you will
make it flower. I, on the other hand, know I never
will. In fact, Montauk and I are about to part ways. I
have sold my restaurant and am moving. Please—also
know that after you sign and return these papers to
me, I will never try to contact you again. The property
is yours, free and clear.

> Most sincerely yours,
> Gregory Wolf

Afterward, Silvana lay with the letter and the deed
on her lap, moved by the sincerity of the gesture and
the enormity of the gift. It was, however, much too
enormous a gift. For if Silvana had learned one thing
in her long and difficult life, it was that she must not
depend on the "free" gifts men offered her.

Oh, she wanted the lodge; she wanted it badly. But
she would instruct her lawyers to make a reasonable
offer of payment. And if they expressed surprise, she
would explain, "Because the most expensive things in
the world are those that you get for free."

But she would save this letter from Gregory Wolf,
save it always. Because contained in its short message
was the proof that you can indeed heal from the
wounds of your past. He was healing . . . and so at
last was she.

Chapter Twenty-one

Is it too late? Two years later, the question had become a silent, secret ache inside her that until recently she had been able to ignore. Unlike many beautiful women, the admiring attention Silvana consistently got throughout her life never turned her appearance into an obsession. Quite the contrary. Though she loved well-designed clothes and wore them with polish and style, she maintained an objectivity bordering on disinterest that liberated her from the tyranny to which so many women succumb—perpetual anxiety about their looks. Lately, however, she had become curious. It was time for Silvana to examine herself in the mirror.

For too many years Silvana had been able to ignore that ache, to avoid seeing, to avoid knowing, but now it was 1976 and she was almost fifty-two years old and she needed to know the answer to the question that had lately been haunting her ceaselessly: *Am I too old for love?*

Certainly, her body did not feel too old inside. Nor did her mind. But did she look too old to search for love ... and passion? And if she were lucky enough to find it, should she hide herself, keeping her wrinkles and sags hidden from her beloved?

She had a special reason for finally paying attention to the question that had become like an ache inside her. But to answer it, she had to do something she had avoided for over thirty years—scrutinize herself, naked, in front of a full-length mirror. The habit of avoiding looking at herself began when she was young and entirely ignorant of her own beauty. Now she knew with certainty that she had possessed a rare kind of melting allure ... then. What she did not know is whether she had lost all of it by now. Tonight it had become desperately important to find out.

With trepidation bordering on terror she approached the mirror-lined closet door in the motel bedroom. Before tonight, she had never more than glanced at herself in the mirrors in her home. Tonight, however, far from home, alone on a chilly early summer night in Montauk once more, she stood before the tall door mirror, a lamp lit behind her on the desk, and untied the belt to her terry robe. Then she stopped.

It was time to really look at the woman staring back at her in the mirror.

Dropping the robe off one shoulder, she peered at the reflection of her neck, her clavicle, her shoulder, and her arm, tightening her deltoids and then her biceps. Hers were not the muscles of a bodybuilder, but they did have the subtle definition and tone that comes from years of lifting heavy pots to the stove, lowering heavy roasts into the oven, and from the endless whisking, beating, chopping, and pounding of a professional chef. The critical tests were yet to come, however: were her breasts sagging, her belly soft as mush, her thighs bulging and puckery?

Not yet ready for the complete answer, she slid her other arm out of its sleeve, caught the robe before it dropped to the floor, and retied it at her waist. She stared in satisfied surprise.

"Mama, thank you for these!" she sighed, running her hands over her voluptuous breasts, noting their swollen tautness and their elasticity when she pressed them. Then she covered each breast with her hands and pressed them together, squeezing until she sighed again.

A certain man still might be able to admire these. And want to touch them like this ...

She finally allowed the robe to slip entirely off her.

"Oh, please!" she cried out loud when she took in the full sight of her *bella figura*. "Won't somebody

love me? Please, let *him* look at me and see—I am
still ripe for love!"

He was perhaps the only man who having seen
Silvana up close did not remember her. But then,
these days he was rather distracted. His wife, he now
knew, was dying.

He was gray at the sideburns and his voice was
husky from too many years of cigarettes before he'd
finally given them up, but he was as robust and vigorous as men at least fifteen years his junior, men no
more than forty. From years of being out on the open
sea, his skin had developed the permanent color of
teak, like the honey-and-cinnamon-colored wood that
lined the walls and doors of his sloop moored at
Sloane's Dock, the marina named for him. These days
he was so busy on land that the only way he got to
see the water was by looking out his office window,
which overlooked his marina on Montauk Harbor.
The teak color of his skin remained, however, emblem
of the early years he had put in as a sailor on the
open seas.

"Sloane, look at you now, a landlubber with an office building and a boat that never leaves the dock,"
everyone teased when he bought the three-masted
sailer and the three-story brick building overlooking
his marina eight years ago. "When we see you in a
suit and tie, we'll know you've traded in your sails
for good!"

They all knew him—the lobstermen, the scallopers,
the deep-sea fishermen, the boatmen, the dockwork-
ers, the truckers, the fish store owners and workers.
All men. Out here, the sea had always been a man's
world. And all of the men out here knew him and
liked him. He was one of them, just as his father, a
scalloper, had always been one of them. He was a
Bonacker, one of them ... even if he had made
good—made phenomenally good—and owned a lavish
house, owned a marina and sailboat, and owned the
fish wholesaling and distribution business for which

many of them worked. For all his success, Sloane Harding hadn't "turned."

"Still wears his cap low on his forehead and his jeans high on his hips," they said.

"Still smells like an old salt, too," they agreed.

"He didn't forget us, neither. Didn't forget we deserve to be a paid a decent wage."

"And didn't forget how to play poker, that's for goddamned sure. I still can't beat the rich son of a bitch. You'd think by now he'd let up, even lose once in a while."

"God knows he can afford to."

"Sloane can't afford to let up, don't you know that?" said Terry Wade, Sloane Harding's best friend. "He can't lose ... at anything."

"He's losing the battle to save Helen, that's clear, even with all that money and all those fancy doctors."

"That's true," Terry Wade agreed, "but he doesn't admit he's losing that battle. Doesn't ever admit it, not to me, not to anyone."

"Helen's just skin and bones these days. Anyone can see—"

"Don't even say it to me," Terry Wade protested. "I can't bear to hear it either, to tell you the truth, knowing what it's doing to him."

Everyone understood. Not because they were so sorry for Sloane Harding's dying wife, Helen; they weren't. It was Sloane, their boss, their friend, for whom they felt the sympathy. Sloane because, though no one could love his selfish and surly and insatiably greedy wife—not even him—he was wracked by sorrow and guilt that he could neither love her nor save her.

For Helen Harding herself, however, the men had only contempt—contempt in the exact same measure that she had meted out to them over the years. And not only to them. To their wives as well.

"Are you coming to my 'Dressed in Your Designer Best' party?" Helen Harding would ask innocently, knowing that fisherwomen did not own designer clothes. And then smile a knowing smirk when the women, forced to decline, all stammered similar lame and obvious excuses.

"Who did your hair, Sally?" she was always asking, knowing full well that there were only two hairstylists in town—a cheap one and an expensive one—and that Sally (and Edie and Megan and Felicia, for that matter) had never been inside the expensive shop in her life. And she would ask, "Where did you get that bag?" when there was only one store in which to buy handbags and she knew the price of every article sold there.

She did it, of course, to embarrass the women and assert her superiority while appearing chatty and friendly. And of course, none of the women was taken in. They hated her, but they felt almost sorry for her, too. The men just hated her.

Mixed with the hate, the men felt a violence toward Helen Harding that had she not become so ill, they might have yielded to. At least, they fantasized often enough about what they would do to her.

"One of these days I'm going to see her crossing the street and the brakes on my car are going to slip and I'm going to plow right into her and splatter her Chanel suit and her two-tone Chanel heels right into a barrel of sweet-smelling, five-day-old fish!"

"Well, I'm gonna twist one of those long designer scarves of hers into a noose and then hang her from her designer neck."

"Cars and hangings are too fast. She has to die slow. Very slow."

"How slow do you have in mind?"

"A half teaspoon—a pure silver spoon, by the way—of poison a day. Just enough to make her writhe on her designer sheets for a while."

"For quite a while, you mean. For, like, five years of continuous writhing. Until every last designer sheet of hers wears out."

"Oh, no! What will she writhe on then?"

"She won't. Without designer sheets, she'll just give up and die."

They stopped laughing, however, when Dr.

Starkman's nurse, married to a fish trucker, told them
what Helen Harding had. Suddenly their fantasies had
come true—Helen Harding would indeed be writhing
in pain on her designer sheets—and they would never
know for sure if their curses had been powerful
enough to actually change the course of her life and
death. The possibility, however, was sobering.

Even more sobering was the effect all this was having on Sloane Harding. They knew for sure that he
was in some kind of private hell when the beautiful
woman with the sexy Italian accent failed to make any
impression at all on him. They certainly remembered
her, however. Every one of them did. They stared at
her with longing when she came to the marina unan-
nounced and asked some of the men on the dock
where she could find the boss. She said she needed to
discuss some "business" with him.

"There he is right now, coming out of that
building."

They pointed to a man in jeans and a navy cashmere
sport jacket hurrying over to an expensive, imported,
canary-yellow sports car. She noticed that the man
and the car did not go. The car was flashy; the man
was subtle.

"Oh, signore!" she called, and it was then that she
recognized him. She waved to him in slow motion, as
if in a dream. "I need to speak to you. Please wait.
Hello again . . . Mr. Harding."

Stopping, he waited for her to cross toward him but
even when she had caught up with him, she could see
he was not really looking at her. He was in a hurry
to leave. A big hurry. Nevertheless, it was unusual for
a man to look right through her like that, not to see
her at all. Especially such a handsome, virile-looking
man. Men in their prime usually took special note of
her. That this one did not shook her more than she
realized. It was then that she began forming the question, *Am I too old for love?*

"I'm sorry, miss. I'm late. I've got to get to East
Montauk Hospital in ten minutes." He looked at his

watch and then simply pulled his car door open. He did not remember her at all.

She would not allow her disappointment to show. What had she expected? Clearly, he was a busy man and she had approached him without an appointment. On impulse, she had decided to take a chance, just as, on impulse, she had decided to come out to Montauk and look over the lodge after staring at the deed for a year.

Once here, she had been busy. She had met with an architect and made some promising calculations about costs. Gregory Wolf's thought of turning the lodge into an Italian seafood restaurant was not a bad idea. She already had a name for it—Anna Michela's by the Sea. What she did not yet have was a good wholesale supplier of fresh fish who would give her preferential prices on orders of perhaps five hundred pounds or more a week.

She had come to see Sloane Harding about fish for her new restaurant. Until now, the name had been only a faded memory. Or perhaps she would not let herself believe more. It was when she saw him that the man and the name became real again. Sloane Harding, the brash man in the New York fish market who made her feel desired on a day so many years ago when she had almost forgotten she was a woman.

They had spent an hour together, a mere moment in time. She had been pregnant then, and her hair had been longer. It was no wonder he did not recognize her, she reasoned. After all, she had been much younger then.

Bene, she told herself. *Fine.* But just because he did not remember her did not mean they could not do business. She would wait in his office for him to come back. She did not have much time and he was the key to her venture. Everything depended on what he would charge her for the fish. She waited over two hours.

"Fish?" he repeated when his secretary finally led Silvana into his office. "You want to see me about fish?" Rarely did he ever deal with women in his business and the sight of Silvana was a surprise. Particularly since this was the first time he was really seeing her. He stared at her with the strange feeling that she was familiar to him. It felt as if he had known her forever. Yet he knew he had never seen her before in his life. Or had he?

"Yes, fish. Remember I stopped you outside and told you I'd wait for you here?"

Then it came to him: the short conversation beside his car with this woman with the throaty accent who said she now owned the old Wolf's Fishing Lodge. And it also came to him now what his friend Terry had meant when, returning to his office building, he'd met Terry Wade downstairs.

"She's waiting for you upstairs, Sloane. She says she'll wait for you forever," Terry had teased.

"Who?"

"Who?" Terry had repeated, unbelieving. "Why, that gorgeous woman with the accent. 'Oh, signore...'"

But Sloane Harding just stared at Terry without recall. His mind was a blank. And no wonder. He had just been to the hospital to meet with Dr. Starkman. The doctor wanted to tell him in person the dreadful results of the latest tests done on the deadly spread of Helen's disease.

"Three months," the doctor said. "That's what the doctors in New York gave her. Now I've looked at the tests and examined her and that's what I say, too. Three months ... maximum. I'm sorry."

Three months. Nine doctors had now said the same thing. He hadn't believed eight of them, but Dr. Starkman pierced the wall he had erected against his fears about Helen. Dr. Starkman had gotten through. Now Sloane Harding knew not only that his wife was going to die ... but exactly when. And it would be terribly soon.

So no wonder he had no memory of this long-legged woman with hair that poured like liquid sunlight down her back. No wonder he had not noticed her wide, moist mouth and her way of talking with her strong, graceful hands. He had not seen the almond shape of her extraordinary eyes or the assertive line of her prominent nose ... but he saw them now. He saw all of her now. *Silvana?* The name echoed eerily inside him.

And then he promptly made himself forget what he had just half remembered. He made himself wipe Silvana out of his mind. Three months. That was the only thought his mind really allowed in right now. *Three months ... maximum.*

"How much fish, exactly, do you need?" He went through the motions while his heart thumped with life and his mind thought only of death.

"I'll be needing at least five hundred pounds. More in lobster season. Probably close to a thousand."

Sloane Harding whistled. "That's a mighty big restaurant you're planning. You sure you know what you're doing?"

She did not answer him exactly; she smiled. But her smile was so knowing, so confident ... yet so utterly sweet that he could not help smiling back. *Yes,* he thought, *this one knows what she is doing. She knows her business and she's probably damn good at it, too. If I do business with this one, we'll both make money. I can tell.*

It was the smile that told him. It was the kind of smile he himself might give. It was a smile he had somehow seen somewhere before.

Their deal was struck in ten minutes, but though Silvana walked out of Sloane Harding's office with exactly the agreement terms she had hoped for, she felt a vague tug of anxiety. When they shook hands and said good-bye, he had looked through her again, just as he had at the car. Already, she was forgotten again. Forgotten ... and unwanted.

But he was not forgotten. She could not get him out of her mind. The deep, warm tones of his skin. The squint lines of anguish at the corners of his narrow, pale blue eyes. The charming lopsidedness of his smile. The deep, slightly hoarse quality to his baritone voice that hinted at a heart full of unexpressed emo-

tion. And his size. At six feet three inches, there was
impressive strength in his very presence.

All this she had noticed and remembered. While
he had neither noticed—nor remembered—anything
about her. To be less than a memory, in her present
mood, confirmed her deepest fear: *It is indeed too late
for love.*

Probably Silvana would have been proven correct if
she had taken the train back to New York late that
afternoon. Chances are that if she had not delayed her
return until the next day, and had not encountered
him in town, he would not have remembered her. Or
rather, he would not have allowed himself to. Because
he had no room for her in his mind and in his heart.
Not now. He had no choice but to forget her. So if
he could just rid her from his mind, he reasoned, then
perhaps he could rid her from his heart.

But when she wandered into the town diner for
breakfast early the next morning, carrying her suitcase
in one hand and her business briefcase in the other,
there he was, sitting in a booth all by himself, staring
straight at her. And for a second, even then, even with
their eyes staring straight at each other, he thought of
looking away, of ignoring her. If he could have pretended he had not seen her, he might have tried out
that ploy. Not because he did not notice her, however.

Because he did.

And because he did not like what noticing her
was doing to him. It was making him feel disloyal.
And disloyalty, to Sloane Harding, was simply unac-
ceptable.

When he and Helen married twenty years ago, he
promised himself that he would never be disloyal to
his wife . . . for all the right reasons. Reasons having
to do with love and honor and respect. Reasons that
made his vow easy to abide by . . . then.

But less than one year later, Sloane Harding made
a startling realization about himself. What he had felt
for Helen had not been love at all—not nearly anything so enduring and deep as love. That, at thirty-

five, he was old enough to have known better did not
stop him from making a fool of himself anyway.

"Chalk it up to loneliness and sexual hunger," he
once told Terry Wade with uncommon honesty. "Yes,
I'd been involved with women, but I'd never really
been in love and for almost two years after my affair
with Susan ended, there had been no one in my life.
So when Helen came along, I became very infatuated.
The problem was, I confused infatuation with love."

Helen was attractive and energetic and Sloane felt
an immediate sexual intoxication that, like liquor, produced a thundering headache afterward. But by
then—by the time his head began pounding—it was
too late; he had married her.

Helen sensed that something was wrong almost immediately. "Tell me. Did I do something? Say something? Tell me so I can change and please you the
way I did in the beginning!"

But the more he got to know her, the less she ap-
pealed to him; to please him the way she did in the
beginning, she would have had to change and improve
everything. Of course he could not ask her to do such
a thing, yet he knew it was his dislike that was ruining
her. He was a man with a powerful conscience and it
tore him apart to watch helplessly as she turned surly
and sour and sunken. All because she still loved him
and did not want to let him go.

Later, when he became more prosperous, she briefly
seemed more lively, more animated, and he thought,
*Good, now that she is on her feet, I can leave her free
of guilt.* But then he saw that she had really only become more acquisitive, not happier. She came to life
only when she went shopping or went on a vacation.
So he stayed with her. Though she turned selfish and
greedy, he stayed. Because it was his fault. He made
her fall in love with him, and when she did, he withdrew, leaving her life empty. He was really all she
had, and when she lost any hope of his love, there
appeared a permanent stricken look in her eyes.

Publicly, Sloane Harding was a successful, appealing, generous, virile man. Privately, however, he was

filled with secret guilt and regret. His was a life empty
of family, joy, or love ... but then, so was Helen's.
And he was the cause of it all. And now that she was
dying, he was sure that he had caused that, too. So
he stayed. At least she knew she would always have
him there, even if she would never have his heart.

Now this tall, stunning woman whose hair had all
the golden yellows of the kitchen in it—streaks of iced
tea, honey, butter, maple syrup, and egg yolk—was
gliding toward him, standing over his table, waiting
for him to invite her to sit down ... and he froze.

Was this infatuation all over again ... or the real
thing? How do you tell? he wanted to know, but she
was not the one to ask. Perhaps he did not really want
to find out at all. For what if he made a mistake again?
What if he repeated the horror of his life once more—
with her?

"Are we always going to have breakfast together
... every seventeen years?" She had that knowing
smile again.

Breakfast! Yes, that was it! The New York fish market. She was pregnant. They both were recently married. Yet they had had breakfast together—the best
breakfast of his life. He had vowed he would never
forget ... but he had.

What could he say? he wondered. Too embarrassed
to speak, he shrugged his shoulders as if to say, "I'm
hopeless." Then he motioned for her to sit down. She
slid into the seat opposite him and they fell into a
silence rich in reminiscence. He recalled it all now,
every moment of their hour together. The memory of
it made him smile, not speak. Finally, however, she
did.

"Are you the kind of man who doesn't like to talk
to anyone until he has had two cups of coffee?"

How did she know? How did she understand? How
did she look so beautiful before nine o'clock?

"Usually." He nodded, melting. "But on rare occasions I've been known to make an exception. This is
one of them."

She could see that he remembered everything now

and she laughed as he signaled for Judy, the waitress. "Judy," he said with mock impatience, glaring at his watch, "we've been waiting for seventeen years. Do you think we could have some breakfast?"

Judy looked confused but after they had laughed at their own private little joke, Silvana reassured her that the service had not really been tardy.

"I would like *frutta fresca*—a fresh orange or *melone,*" she said with the waitress, feeling him watching her, smiling, making her smile, too.

Judy nodded and wrote it down. "Will that be all?"

"No," said Silvana. "Then I would like two poached eggs and toast with *marmellata*—jam—and potatoes— how do you call them—house fries? Home fries? And coffee. With *crema.*"

Sloane Harding had to laugh again. When had he last seen a woman eat breakfast . . . and such a hearty one, at that? *Exactly seventeen years ago,* he answered his own question.

Certainly, Helen never indulged in more than juice and coffee. She was always starting a new diet in the morning—that is, on the rare occasions when she was awake before noon . . . and before she had become sick. Even his secretary never touched anything but black coffee all morning long. So it was refreshing to see a woman order so much food so early . . . and with so much relish.

"This sea air gives me the appetite of a *cavallo,* a horse." She laughed as she bit into her second slice of toast. "Do you think I am destined to grow fat out here in your Montauk?"

Your Montauk, she had said. This was crazy, he knew, but he suddenly wanted her to think of it as *our Montauk.* Then he said something to her almost as crazy.

"You'll never grow fat. But even if you do . . . even if your hair falls out and your teeth fall out and your face wrinkles up like a prune, I'll always see you the way you look right now. It reminds me of the way your face looked then—the first time. I'll always see the sun coming in through that window, highlighting

the millions of different tones of yellow in your hair.
And warming the apricot of your skin. And bouncing
off the tip of your nose. I'll always see you walking
through that door, so lithe and springy—and—"

A flush of embarrassment suddenly stopped him
midsentence. This really was crazy. What was he
saying?

But she reassured him by squeezing his hand and
telling him truthfully, "You'll never know how much
your words mean to me, particularly now. Last night,
I was asking myself if I am too old for—all this. I
studied myself in the motel mirror and—"

Suddenly she, too, felt flushed with embarrassment
and could not continue. For she remembered how she
had stood stark naked before that mirror, praying that
he—Sloane Harding—might find her young enough,
beautiful enough to love! He was the reason for her
prayers!

Their hands clasped across the table, their eyes
gazed, unblinking, and their breakfast grew cold.

"Check, please, Judy!" he called without turning
from her. When the check was paid, he led her out of
the diner.

"I want to show you something," he said and although a part of her wanted to follow him anywhere,
wanted to close her eyes and just let this solid yet
thrilling man lead her wherever he wanted, she could
not help peeking at her watch.

"This won't take long," he told her "I'll have you at
the station in plenty of time for the ten o'clock train."

How did he know? How did he understand? And
how did he manage to look so vigorous, so sensual,
before nine in the morning? she wondered, not realizing that earlier he had had the same kind of thoughts
about her.

They drove to a hill not unlike the one leading to
the Wolf Lodge, except that this one led not to the
ocean but to an open view of the bay.

"See that large sailboat down there?" He had kept
the car engine running while he stood outside the
sports car with her, looking down at the bay.

"You mean that very, very, very big sailboat?"

He laughed again and realized he had laughed more this morning than he had in a month. It was this woman, this Silvana. She had entered his life at the darkest possible moment, but immediately she had let in bright daylight, like a window shade suddenly rolling up.

Below them the bay shimmered in the morning sunlight. Always before, Silvana had thought that only the ocean—the sound of it, the smell of it—could transport and soothe her this completely. Now she saw that the wide mouth of this expansive bay gave her the same feeling. She loved it all—she loved the endless, pounding enormity of the ocean and she loved the busy yet picturesque tranquillity of this bay. Montauk! She had truly found a new home.

He saw it in her eyes—her genuine appreciation of this special place. She had originally come from Rome, she had told him, but anyone could see that she belonged here ... with him ...

No! He would not allow himself these thoughts now. None of them! Just as he would not tell her that the very, very, very big white boat was his after all. Yes, he had brought her here to impress her, to let her look upon all his holdings down below—his marina and the building that housed his company and his boat. To pull her closer to him. In the distance, even his house, directly on the bay, was visible. But now he knew he would not point that out to her either.

And he would not kiss her, although he had brought her here to do that, too. He would wait to kiss her until he owned her mouth and knew every inch of her body. Then he would kiss her until there was no more darkness at all, only light, only her warm, heavenly light.

This was not the time for passion. And this was not the time for love. At East Montauk Hospital Helen was dying. This was a time of darkness and pain. This was not a time for betrayal.

Soon Silvana would be returning here to Montauk to complete the restoration of the lodge and to open her restaurant. He would see her again. Perhaps they could even become friends. Already they were business associates. Already she had won his heart . . .

Let it be, he told himself, obeying his mind, obeying his vow. *The time for this passion is not now. If passion is all it is, it will fade like an infatuation. And if it is more, it will grow.*

He took Silvana into his arms and hugged her. Then he let her go. He did not tell her that he would yearn for her and he did not tell her why he could not tell her.

But somehow, she knew. One look at him, at the heartbreak in his eyes, and she understood. She could not have him now. Once again, she would not be able to have him. She understood.

Allora. Well then. *Okay,* she told herself as they drove to the train station, *I will wait. I will wait for him because the way he looks at me makes me feel that I am still young, still beautiful . . . still loved. For that, I will wait for him forever . . . if only he gives me some sign, some shred of hope that I will not wait in vain.*

"Good-bye, Sloane. I hope next time we have breakfast, it will not be another seventeen years." She waited and then she climbed up onto the train. *Sloane, give me a sign!*

"Have a good trip."

"Thank you." She nodded miserably.

"Come back soon."

"Yes, I will."

"Very soon," he added.

Her heart began to hammer, but she said nothing.

"But not to *my* Montauk."

"No?"

"No." He shook his head earnestly. "To *our* Montauk. Yours and mine. It always will be ours from now on."

"Ours," she said, satisfied. *"Si."*

Chapter Twenty-two

"I sold it! I can't believe it. Can you believe it?" Eduardo held a business letter in his hands and displayed it for his robustly pregnant wife, Mary Catherine. But he was so excited that he threw the letter into the air before he had given her a chance to read it. Then he clutched her by her slim shoulders and gently shook her, as if it were she who was dazed, she whose feet were floating several inches above the ground.

Even as he was shaking her shoulders, Mary Catherine still managed to shrug them nonchalantly. "Of course I believe it. I predicted it, didn't I?"

It was true. She had predicted his novel would be published—and Mary Catherine's predictions had invariably proven to be correct—but after so many years and so many rejections, it was difficult to believe anyone—even his beautiful, redheaded soothsayer of a wife.

"What does it say?" she asked as she carefully lowered herself into the one chair at the modern teak table that was not piled with toys. Their three-year-old son Marco was rapidly transforming the dining room into his private playroom.

"But who can blame him?" Eduardo always said with the ready forgiveness of a proud and indulgent father. "Marco needs room for his trains and trucks to speed down the U.S. highways and for his horses to gallop across the empty western plains." Marco, Eduardo liked to boast, was a genuine American boy born on genuine American soil. Even his name had been given an American spelling—Mark; they called him Marco only as a nickname. "Being American, he naturally needs to spread out."

"Yes, but there's no room to eat dinner. He's taken over the whole apartment!" Mary Catherine, who attempted daily to re-create order amid the chaos of their cramped quarters, was beginning to despair of ever finding an uncluttered corner. Once this had been Eduardo's spacious bachelor apartment; then it became their lovers' lair. Once they had grilled steaks here and made love on virtually every available surface; then they married and it was here that they learned how to live together.

From this, their home, they went off to work at Club Midnight together each afternoon; together they returned here late each night. Eduardo had finished his novel here, and Mary Catherine had sat at his desk the entire weekend, reading it. Here there had always been room enough for all her clothes and plants, her sewing machine and her fitting mannequin, her jewelry box with her gold cross and chain still coiled on the bottom, and her Mark Kroll wedding gown, wrapped in tissue and plastic.

But as soon as Marco was born, the apartment seemed to shrink—almost overnight. Baby furniture crowded every empty square foot of space. Later, Marco's toys did the same. Like one of the magical children's tales they read to their son, the bigger Marco grew, the smaller their beloved abode became. Finally it was no longer beloved, no longer even habitable. To Mary Catherine it was now merely a small indoor playground, nothing more. But they could never afford to move ... not until today. Not until Eduardo had received this letter.

"What does it say?" she asked again. "I want to know every word."

Scooping up the letter from the floor, he read it out loud:

April 16, 1976
Dear Mr. Levi:
    This is to confirm our happy telephone conversation of two days ago.
    We are most pleased to be able to publish your novel *A Jewish Family in Rome*. Although it is a novel

(and its story is certainly gripping), it almost seems like an actual account of a real family in a real Italian/Jewish community. Every character lives and breathes and we care about all of them. A fine job, Eduardo. Congratulations!

Enclosed is a contract outlining the terms of our agreement. Please read it carefully before you sign. After you return one copy to me, a check for an advance against royalties of thirty thousand dollars will be shortly forwarded to you.

Again, Eduardo, congratulations and best wishes.

Sincerely,

Simon Gray, Publisher

"Thirty thousand? Is that what it really says—thirty thousand?" Limp with surprise and delight, Mary Catherine let her mouth hang open while she waited for her husband to tell her that no, she was just dreaming.

Instead he said, "That's what they offered three days ago on the phone. If I hadn't been so stunned and so starved, I might have gotten them up a few thousand. But that didn't occur to me until I'd already hung up."

"Thirty thousand. Thirty thousand." She found she simply liked saying it. "Why didn't you tell me three days ago?" If she'd known, she might have found a house for them by now. Oh, what she could have done in three days with thirty thousand!

"In case I was only dreaming."

"Oh," she said, nodding. That she most certainly understood, and to prove it, she pinched herself ... and grinned.

He held out his hand to her. "So let's go."

"Where?"

"House hunting."

Immediately she rose and tried to curl into his arms but her belly got in the way. "If I get much bigger, we won't need a house; we'll need a thirty-acre estate."

"Not till I sell the next book."

As she began walking to the door she felt something trickling down her legs. *My water!* she thought, and at that exact moment, it broke, soaking her panties, streaming down inside her thighs to her shoes, and creating a small puddle on the floor.

"Hurry up. Start writing," she told him, managing a wry joke before the pains began. "You're about to have another mouth to feed and we'll be needing that estate after all!"

He saw the puddle and suddenly he was no longer in a daze. Swiftly he lifted Marco into his arms. Here in America in 1976 a man over fifty was considered old to be starting a family, Eduardo supposed, but he had the energy of a man half his age. The war had held him back, cheating him of important years, delaying his start. Now he was determined to make up for that. Already he had come to terms with his past. He had written a book based on his family's experiences and bravery and loss and he believed it honored his family's memory. He was proud of this book. Mary Catherine was proud, too. About the only person who wasn't was Silvana. She had refused to read it. Someday, she would have to come to terms with her past—just as he had. The book, he knew, could help. He would send her an autographed copy when it was published. Meanwhile, his baby was waiting to be born.

He took Mary Catherine and his son by the hand and led them all downstairs to the car.

"Yay!" Marco cheered. "Here we go to buy a big, big house! Right, Daddy?"

Eduardo hesitated. "Well, we have to do something first, Marco."

"What, Daddy?"

Reluctant to disappoint his son but at the same time thrilled to be the one to break out the news, Eduardo milked it just a bit longer.

"Something really important."

"What?" Marco was becoming exasperated.

"Take Mommy to the hospital."

Silvana had not yet seen her new baby nephew—Eduardo and Mary Catherine's second son—but she had seen her beautiful granddaughter, Grazia, born to

Elena on her birthday, May seventh. If only she could make the trip into New York and visit her newborn nephew. If only she could bring Elena and her granddaughter out here so she could see Grazia every day! But there they were in New York and here she was in Montauk, and although it was now only a three and a half hour direct train ride, she kept putting off her return to New York City. Out here, there was just too much to be done. Her ambitious new restaurant, Anna Michela's by the Sea, was taking up most of her time and the magical Montauk house that she had just bought took up every extra energetic minute. Thank goodness that Elena was back at work managing Mia Elena and keeping an eye on Per Sempre Silvana. Otherwise, Silvana would probably run back and forth more often. On the other hand, perhaps she would not. Out here, she had come alive again.

The new restaurant, a thrilling enterprise, had certainly played a part in reviving her. For a year it had absorbed her time and her creative energies almost exclusively. In the beginning, Mark Kroll would come out and give her ideas. But he had his hands full with his hat designs and his burgeoning wedding planning business.

"Get yourself a local architect," he advised her. "Someone who knows local building codes and local contractors. Even if I could keep running out here, you'd still need an architect. Now, if you get remarried, however, Fabian and I will move out here for a month just to plan your wedding!"

Heeding his advice, Silvana hired Noel Jourdan, a local architect with a quiet manner and a competent portfolio, and together they fashioned a renovation that managed to preserve the original character of the lodge despite a complete overhauling and modernizing of all the systems and kitchen equipment. The result was so stunning that Silvana was determined to force the usually taciturn Noel Jourdan to admit that he was pleased, too.

"It is pretty, no?"

"It is pretty, *yes,*" Noel Jourdan agreed with unexpected ease, and together they toured the brightly lit, just completed Italian seafood trattoria that would be officially opened for business in exactly one hour.

"I am familiar with this time of rapid heartbeats. I have been through this before," Silvana sighed as they surveyed the large main dining room with its sea-blue cloths and napery, its antique ship lanterns, its newly repaired floor-to-ceiling stone fireplace and old wood ceiling beams. The wide picture windows looked out over the dune and the mammoth ocean beyond. Soon the sun would set and the ocean would turn inky black, but for now, the view was of crashing, foaming waves and endless deep water the color of spinach and sapphires.

"You mean renovations?"

"*Sì,* but even more, restaurant openings. This is the third time and you would think it would get easier."

The architect, silver-haired and slightly stooped, said knowingly, "But it never does, does it? You're always just as nervous on opening night, even if you've starred in a hundred productions before, isn't that true?"

"Opening night. *Esattamente!* Exactly."

She had hired Noel Jourdan as soon as she met with him almost a year ago. She had liked his quiet manner and by now he had become a trusted friend. Not only had he superbly renovated the lodge for her, but he had steered her to a striking house that was up for sale. It sat on a finger of land that pointed out into the bay and, from its soaring windows, offered views of the water from all sides. She of course bought the house and promptly called Mark and Fabian to help her decorate it. They arrived for the weekend, looked the property over, and pronounced themselves the wrong team for the job.

"There should be no fussy furniture in this house. Everything should be sleek and built-in," they suggested, "so nothing competes with the view. Silvana, you know that's not what we do. What you need is an architect."

She suspected that they were right; she even knew

the man for the job—Noel Jourdan. But she was not entirely convinced until she saw the completed series of dark oak banquettes Noel Jourdan designed for her. The banquettes lined the two walls of windows and he topped them with marine-blue cushions and piles of blue and white striped pillows.

"Paradiso!" she exclaimed.

Anna Michela and Debora, however, liked to throw the pillows down on the furry white rug and stare at the view from the floor.

"It is good we did not buy much furniture," Silvana mused. "My girls would never sit in it, anyway! They sit only on the floor."

Knowing this, Noel designed a room for them with beds so low to the floor that the two sisters felt as if they were sleeping underground. Instantly they pronounced the bedroom "groovy"—their highest accolade.

To start a new restaurant, there were many other people Silvana had to work with that year, too—bankers and mortgage brokers and town officials at first, and later carpenters, plumbers, painters, people to staff the restaurant kitchen and dining room, and people to build a dock for her new house. But of all the people she met and came to know, there was one she avoided: Sloane Harding.

"When I want to order more fish, I want you to call our wholesaler, Sloane Harding, for me," she told her assistant, Charlie Crowley, who had worked as assistant manager at Mia Elena and had moved out here to help her start up her Montauk operation. She had brought Charlie Crowley out here because she could trust him—but not enough to tell him about Sloane Harding. She could hardly bear to utter his name to herself. *Sloane, oh, Sloane!*

Sitting at her antique rolltop desk in one of the old lodge bedrooms newly converted to an office, she glared at her assistant as if it were he she wanted to avoid, as if it were his name—and not Sloane Harding's—that she could barely speak.

Nervously, Charlie Crowley nodded. "Sure, Mrs. Levi. I mean, Mrs. Nachman."

"What's the matter with you, Charlie? Just call me Silvana, the way you always have. Now, if *he* calls and says he wants to speak to me, tell him that you are in charge of all the ordering," she directed, adding, "and under no circumstances allow him to speak to me. I don't ever want to speak to Sloane Harding. Ever! Do you understand?"

Charlie Crowley understood, all right, but it was clear to him that this arrangement meant trouble. In all the years he had known her, the only time he had ever heard his boss speak with such icy tightness was when she said she wanted nothing to do with this man, Sloane Harding. But she kept saying it—sometimes three or four times a day. That, to Charlie, was the tip-off.

To one of the new waitresses, he confided, "She says she doesn't want to speak to Sloane Harding, doesn't want to have anything to do with him, but she's the one who keeps bringing up his name. I think he's unfinished business. I think she's carrying a torch for him."

Silvana was fascinating to them all. The waitress, dressed in a sea-blue uniform to match the table linens, and a white half apron tied at the waist, had her own thoughts on the subject of Silvana: "Probably, it would be better if she saw the guy one more time instead of denying her feelings. Once she saw him, she'd know if she was still carrying a torch. She'd know it instantly."

But Silvana already knew she was "carrying a torch" for Sloane Harding. That was not why she was avoiding him. It was because she was sure that he was not carrying a torch for her.

After all, the death of Helen Harding had been reported in the New York as well as the local papers six months ago. And after reading the obituary of Sloane Harding's wife, which reported that Helen hung on for six months, although the doctors had given her only three, Silvana felt she now understood Sloane.

She understood what he was going through those first six months and why he had made a decision to avoid kissing her that day on the hill overlooking the bay a year ago today. His loyalties were still with his sick wife then. She not only understood that now, she would not have wanted him to be any other way.

"But it has been many endless months since then," she complained miserably to her old friend Lena Milgrim on the phone. "He does business with my restaurant, so he knows I'm here, yet he never once called to speak to me, never once came to visit."

"And to what conclusion have you come?" old Mrs. Milgrim asked, her tone ever so slightly sardonic because she knew very well what Silvana was thinking.

"It's simple. He loved his wife. Now she is dead and he does not want anyone else. If he knew my feelings for him, it would be an embarrassment, that is all."

"How can someone who creates such complex sauces be so simplistic when it comes to men!"

"Lena, don't try to give me false hope. That is what he did. He told me to come back to 'our Montauk.' But when I did, he ignored me. He does not want me and I must make myself forget him."

"That is a possibility—but it is not the most likely possibility. In life, things are never that simple. And I suspect his feelings for you are anything but simple. It is time for you to find out."

"No! I couldn't bear it! To see his eyes no longer warm. No! I prefer to hide from him than to see he does not care."

Hiding from Sloane Harding had become as automatic as driving a car—something she had learned to do out here. She simply avoided going near the marina . . . no matter what.

"Why won't you ever go with us to Sloane's Marina, Mama?" Now that Anna Michela and Debora had moved out here for the year, they had discovered the picturesque marina, crowded with lobster traps, ice barrels, fish nets, fishing boats, and men cleaning huge bluefish and mako in the open air. Gulls hovered hungrily above the fish guts and fish blood and fish smell.

"Eeeyuw!" the girls always groaned but they returned to the marina almost every day after school. Something raw yet thrilling drew them to the place although neither girl could give it a name.

"It's great down there, that's all," they told Silvana. "Promise you'll come?"

Silvana made the only promise to her girls that she knew she would break. She was that determined to avoid Sloane Harding and that was the way she remained for the entire year. And perhaps she would never have seen him again—not to this day—if her car had not broken down one afternoon on her way to meet Noel Jourdan at an antiques shop in the next town. The car simply died on the road near a turnoff for the marina, blocking the exit. Soon someone was beeping his car horn behind her.

"Lady, would you mind moving your car?" the driver demanded with suppressed annoyance, pulling up beside her but unable to pass her.

"Oh, signore, I am sorry but I—"

It was then that she saw him and that he saw her, each through the open windows of their cars, and although the early summer's day was sunny and bright, it was as if a thunderclap had pierced the silence, as if lightning had sliced across the sky.

"No! It can't be. No! Is it really you, Sloane?" And then, before he could answer, she covered her face with her hands, embarrassed by her emotions.

He was out of the car and at the side of hers in seconds, but it felt as if it had taken him hours, years to reach her. Oh, why had he waited so long? One look at her and he no longer understood what had held him back all these months, though it had seemed so clear then. Now it all seemed like such a huge waste of time . . . and of happiness. Because seeing her again made him happy, as nothing else in his life ever had. Just as happy as the first time he saw her. Between those two ecstatic moments, however, there had been only fear and despair. But he'd had enough. He knew that now. Seeing her again, he knew it with absolute certainty. Nothing had ever felt quite so important as this moment here with her and her broken-down car. The only thing he did not know was whether or not she felt the same.

"May I?" he said to her through the open window, and clicked open her door. Then he leaned in and pried her hands from her face. "Come out here where I can see you." Holding her under her arm, he coaxed her out, and did not entirely let her go. One hand still gripped her upper arm.

His hand on her arm reminded her of Gregory Wolf, who had gripped her hand to get her attention. This felt different, however. Sloane Harding's touch was sure but gentle. She did not feel imprisoned; she felt caressed.

For several moments they simply gazed at each other, at their real faces, instead of the images they had been carrying around inside their heads. Surprisingly, the real and the imagined almost matched, perhaps because they had so wanted to remember each other just as they really were. Or perhaps they knew that their memories of each other had to be as crisp and clear as photographs because they would not see each other for a while. However, neither had thought it would be this long.

"Not a day, not an hour older," he said, moving closer. The need to make up for lost time drove him closer, closer, though he was also uneasy because he did not yet know if she felt the same way. "Still utterly beautiful." She was wearing a tangerine cotton dress with white high heels that he appreciated as chic yet summery. Smiling, he looked her up and down. "Maybe even more so."

"I am a year older than I was when you saw me, and at my age, it shows. These days, each time I look in the mirror—and I look quite often now—I see a new wrinkle." Instead of telling him how much she had missed him, she tried to scoff at his romanticism. To protect herself just in case she was misreading the message in his eyes. And to warn him not to idealize her beauty, for she was young no longer.

Tell her now! A stern voice inside him warned him not to waste another moment. *Explain to her why you haven't called. You owe her that.* And he agreed.

But suddenly a car pulled up behind them. Wishing to pass, the driver beeped his horn.

"Let me push your car over to the side of the road and then I'll drive you to a garage," he suggested, unwilling to leave her for even an instant now that he had found her again ... and found his own heart there beside her.

But when he pulled into the garage near town, he suddenly panicked. *What if she reports her disabled car and goes with them to tow it and I never see her again?* Once she had left his car, left his side, he was afraid she might never return.

"Remember last time I showed you something special to me? That vista of the bay?" Though he could hear the desperation in his own voice, he did not care. He would not lose her again. That was final.

Silvana nodded, and though he could not see the beating of her heart, she placed her hand on her chest to hide it anyway.

"Well, now I have something else I'd like to show you. Something to tell you, too. After we finish here, will you come with me for a short while?"

"Don't you have to go to work?" Hiding her uneasiness was impossible. She had been hurt too many times in her life, by too many men. Then, perhaps most disappointing of all, just when she had thought she had found a man both caring and yet careful, he hurt her, too. Why was he suddenly so friendly after a year without a word? No, she was not ready to trust him. She was not eager to be hurt again.

"I've just given myself the day off. I'm the boss," he joked, "remember?"

"Okay," she agreed warily and phoned Noel Jourdan to reschedule her antiquing date with him. Then she gave the tow-truck driver her car keys and directions to locate the car. But when she slid back in beside Sloane Harding again, her hands were trembling. All of her, in fact, was trembling. She recognized, just as he did, that this was the deciding encounter between them. From this moment, either love would begin to flower ... or they would go their separate ways.

"*Allora.* I am all yours," she said, realizing as soon as she had spoken that what she had really meant to say was "I'm ready."

He, too, realized the double meaning of her words and might even have pounced on them—pounced on her—by saying something obvious and suggestive, but she burst out laughing.

Mocking herself, she spread her arms out wide, as if she *had* really meant to say, "I am all yours. Take me!" but still laughing too hard to speak. Finally, she managed to sputter, "My crazy, broken English still gives me many fat problems!" And that simply broke him up. He roared with laughter until he had to pound the steering wheel, breathless and gasping.

The laughter united them, freed them. Like a summer rainstorm, it left the air cleaner, cooler. Now, as he began to drive, she sat close to him, unafraid. A song came on the radio that they both knew, and they joined in. Tittering with embarrassment when she forgot some of the words, she might have stopped singing altogether, but Sloane, in his deep, rich baritone, coached her by singing the lyrics in double time before each line. As she sang she caught his eye and thanked him without saying a word.

He could see a few heads turn at the pier when he drove up, but he didn't care who saw him. At last he was going to live his life. At last he was going to live it with joy. He was through with guilt and fear.

"Ah, so now I understand why you showed me the very, very, very long, tall sailboat that day." Her smile was knowing as he led her onto his sleek, eighty-six-foot sloop. "It is yours, isn't it?"

He nodded and led her to the stern, where he seated her at a U-shaped set of comfortable banquettes with red and white striped cushions. "I'm just going below to get us some drinks."

To his surprise, she followed him.

"I thought I might help," she explained, but her cheeks were the color of her dress.

For a moment he thought of Helen. Whenever they had gone out on the boat together, she would sit on those red and white striped cushions and expect to be served. "What's taking so long?" she would often call down to him without it ever occurring to her to come below and help. Now here was this golden creature, this sylph of his dreams, and she was right down here with him, not up on deck like Helen, and her eyes were taking in all the richness and refinement of the teak-paneled interiors ... while his eyes were taking in all of her.

Oh, she was such a beauty that he longed to cover every inch of her with his mouth, his tongue, his teeth. He could hardly hold himself back, but he knew he must not rush her. There was time—a lifetime, in fact—if he could only make her understand and forgive him. To do that, however, he could not look at her, for to look at her was to be overwhelmed by desire for her.

"Helen—my wife—never liked this boat," he began, while setting a bottle of champagne into an ice bucket. "There really wasn't much she did like. But I blame myself for that—because she knew I didn't love her. The truth is, I've never been in love."

"Not ever?" Silvana was surprised. Such a rich, handsome, powerful man ... yet his life had been essentially spiritually empty. She found two champagne glasses and a package of napkins and placed them on a tray. Then she could not help adding, "Not with your wife ... or any other woman?"

Suddenly everything stopped. He stopped twisting the cork. He stopped still. He did not answer her question; he just stared as if he had just seen something remarkable. And she stopped, too. She had found a package of crackers and a slab of cheese in the tiny refrigerator and was about to arrange them on a platter when she felt his eyes upon her, and froze, a cracker still in her hand. Between them was a throbbing silence ... and the unanswered question.

"Yes," he finally responded. "Once. Now. Right now."

He could see that she was moved by his words but still unsure if she should trust him. He understood.

"I hurt you when I didn't call you this entire year, I know that."

"Yes, very much," she agreed, admitting it at last.

"But I couldn't call, Silvana. At first, it was because I wasn't free. The doctors gave Helen three months but she hung on for almost six. Then after she died, I found I still wasn't free. I became afraid to call you, afraid that I didn't know how to love and might do to you what I had done to Helen. This time—with you—I wanted to be sure."

"And ... are you sure?"

At last, Sloane exhaled. He felt as if he had been holding his breath for the entire year. Each word of his apology had been difficult, had been pure agony. But now all he breathed was relief. Are you sure? she had asked. And he had exhaled with relief. With delight, really. Because, yes, he was sure and he knew he was sure. He felt it, he breathed it. Now it was only left for him to live it.

"I am sure!" he shouted. "One hundred percent sure. You are the one—the only one. Silvana, I want you to be mine!"

It was not necessary to wait for her answer—all he had to do was see her glistening, limpid eyes to know that she shared his feelings, that she actually cared for him. Nor could he wait. Not when his mouth needed to crush against hers, not when his hands needed to caress every inch of her flesh.

But when their lips were meshed and their bodies began to press together as closely as their mouths, he pulled back in order to tell her something he had just discovered: "Even a kiss is different when you're in love."

Again he did not wait for her response. Instead, he

mashed his mouth against hers again, and this time, he did not pull away. This time, he breathed her breath, tasted her saliva, felt the nip of her teeth. This time, the kiss was like making love to her mouth with his tongue. Stiffly, sinuously, he drove it in and out between her lips until he at last heard her moan. And then he still did not pull away. He felt as if he could stay right there in her mouth forever. Except that there was so much more of her he wanted to explore and there was one part of her he had to have before too much longer.

Yes! This was it. This was love. He could tell the difference. Sloane Harding was in love. He was wildly, passionately, deeply in love. And although he had not known it, he had been in love this entire long year.

For Silvana, there had been Michele, and love and lovely kisses before this, so she was perhaps even more unprepared for the intensity of her feelings than Sloane, who had never known love at all. And until now, no love, she had thought, could ever quite match—much less surpass—the love she had known with Michele.

Yet here she was, lost in Sloane's arms, so thrilled to learn that he loved her that there was nothing she would not have done for him. She was breathless, overjoyed . . . and yes, young again! For that gift alone, she wished to repay him. Yet it was he who was showering her with more "gifts" . . . and more— bringing her to a height of unrestrained passion. His hands were everywhere—on her, in her—making her feel desired, loved, adored, making her actually vibrate. At Sloane's every touch, she wanted to scream, to laugh, to groan, to tell him, "More. Yes! More!"

The vibrating increased. Her legs became wobbly, rubbery; finally, they could no longer support her. Falling against him, her arms locked around his neck, she begged with her eyes two pools of passion, "Don't stop, but hold me. Hold me up."

"Oh, Silvana, I'm going to hold you, don't you worry," he promised and bent down and lifted her into his strong, muscular arms.

With his foot he pushed open the door to the next cabin and carried her—not to the bed—but to a tailored, upholstered chaise in the corner. Setting her down, he draped her along its cushiony length, spreading out her beautiful golden hair, her long, graceful arms, and her still dazzling legs. Then he brought back two glasses of champagne, and sat down beside her.

"*A la dolce vita,*" she toasted, clinking her glass with his. "To the good, sweet life."

"To *our* sweet life," he corrected. "To our good life from this moment on."

Although champagne was meant to be sipped, they drained their glasses quickly and set them on the side table; they were in too much of a rush for refinement and delays.

Sloane stretched out beside Silvana and took her into his arms, but the chaise, designed for only one person, was a rather tight fit.

"Mmm, it feels as if every part of your body is touching every part of my body."

"Not every part!" she exclaimed breathily, pulling at the buttons of his shirt.

"Hmm, you may have something there," he agreed and found the zipper located on the back of her dress.

But when the tangerine dress had been flung to the floor, and her bra and panties had been slipped off, Silvana suddenly felt a spasm of shyness. It had been so terribly long since she had let a man look at her unclothed body ... and she was so much older now. Fear overwhelmed her, fear that he would not find her pleasing. Not wanting to see his face when he looked at her for the first time, she squeezed her eyes tightly shut.

"Am I—am I—acceptable?" she could not help asking in a small voice.

"Acceptable?" He laughed. And then again: "Acceptable? You are definitely not acceptable. You are exceptional. You are divine. Oh, Silvana, I've never seen a body as beautiful as yours."

Perhaps he was lying. Perhaps he was exaggerating. Perhaps he was even telling the truth. It no longer mattered because she wanted to believe him. Because he made her happy.

In one swift move she raised her leg over his hip and found him with her hand. Then firmly, surely, she guided him into her.

"Oh, God, Silvana. We fit like we were made for each other!"

It was true. Even their undulations synchronized instantly, so that with each grinding roll, their bodies joined more tightly, more deeply than the moment before.

Silvana wanted to tell him she knew what he meant, that she felt it, too, the perfection of their fit, the perfect pleasure of it. But suddenly she had forgotten what she had wanted to say. A new thought, instead, was forming. It rose from deep within her, and was traveling rapidly from her pelvis up to her heart and then to her throat. She had no choice. She had to tell him. She had to shout it out.

"Oh, Sloane! Oh, Sloane! Yes! I *am* all yours. I am!"

His teeth were clenched, and for him, words were now impossible. He had wanted to bring her to orgasm again—and again—but he could not wait. Not this time. Not this first unbelievable, overwhelming time ... after having waited so long. But for them, there would always be this moment ... and a million more moments of ecstasy in their future together. All he would ever have to do, he knew, was look at her body, as he had done today, and he would want to make love to her again ... and again.

But not now. For this one time, this first time, he would not hold himself back. He would simply explode.

"And now me!" he groaned and followed her. "Now me, my darling. I've found you, Silvana! Oh, God, I've finally found it. Yes! Love! Love!"

PART FOUR

Prologue

1995

Eighteen years. I would have thought that eighteen years, containing all those hours and days and weeks and months, would go on endlessly, almost like a lifetime, but they are over in a heartbeat. Time contracts as I get older; it shrinks. The years shrivel up just like a large head of escarole in a pan of hot oil—all the juice squeezes out. A year becomes just two or three sharp memories. Eighteen years is not much more than that. At my late age I have only just learned this.

These days, everyone says they recognize me from seeing me on TV or in magazines. They call me a celebrity even though I have retired from professional cooking—except for the occasional gala dinner. There is one of those next Saturday—the Outstanding Restaurant Chef Awards Dinner—but at this even I will not be cooking, for it is in my honor. I hear they have created a new award, called the Silvana Lifetime Achievement Medal, that they will pin on me. So I will wear a new black velvet gown and I will not wear a chef's apron all night.

But I still make the rounds of my five restaurants, of course—yes, there are a total of five now! In addition to the first two, there is Anna Michela's by the Sea, which I opened in Montauk. It is still thriving, though we come out only for the long summer season to help Anna Michela run it. Since Sloane has retired, too, we spend the winter in New York, keeping an eye on the other four restaurants.

The fourth enterprise was started when I began to long for an espresso and pastry shop like I remembered in Italy. So I opened Debora's Dolci, a dessert café on the ground floor of a former glove factory in Greenwich Village, where the aroma of espresso hangs like a coca cloud of perfume over the tables. Sloane and I do not make a lot of money from this one, but it is so charming that there is talk of making it a city landmark.

Sloane Harding and I have been together ever since that day he took me to his very, very big sailboat and told me he was in love. With me! I wasn't wrong to believe him. This time, I was not wrong.

And oh, the wedding Mark and Fabian made for me! On the beach, barefoot! Clams, lobsters, mussels, corn, and seaweed steaming in cauldrons over fire pits, giant prawns, baby chickens, and local potatoes roasting over braziers. And flowers everywhere. Mark even braided my hair with flowers and dressed me in flowered yellow chiffon as transparent as a nightgown. Sloane said I looked like a little girl about to say my prayers. But I have only one prayer, and it is always, always the same. *Mama, forgive me, please!*

It is still unbelievable to me that I have such a good husband at last—so caring and so *robusto*. Although lately, everyone—except me—seems to notice that Sloane is finally slowing down. But then, I get to see him in bed, where he is still almost as randy and eager as ever, and where he still makes me feel young and beautiful and unfailingly desirable. May I speak frankly and say that, yes, sexual passion is still present between us, even now, in our seventies? It is less frequent, perhaps, but each time it occurs it feels like a wondrous blessing.

Sloane did not want me to open this fifth and final *ristorante,* Casa di Grazia, even if it was named for my granddaughter Grace.

"Between us we have more than enough restaurants, houses, boats, marinas, and businesses. The last thing we need is one more. Now is the time to start scaling down," he argued.

And he was right, of course. But I wanted to provide fortune for all of my girls through this dynasty I

had created—believing that if they were financially secure, they all would be safe. I forgot that disaster can
strike even when your pockets are full, when you are
feeling most sanguine, and, most of all, when you
begin to believe you are invulnerable.

It was through Grazia that I had to learn it all
over again.

I remember my first sight of Grazia, Elena's girl.
For the birth of my beautiful granddaughter I had
more tears than for my own little ones. Tears of joy
that were as much for Elena—such a happy mother!—
as for Grazia. I did not know then that Grazia would
still be bringing me to tears eighteen years later.

But then, how could I know that Elena would get
married to Freddo, that snake with a ponytail? All
night he sits at the bar of Casa di Grazia, staring at
his beautiful stepdaughter Grace. Stares and stares.
His lust makes her smile and toss her blond mane and
turn the color of a *melagrana,* a pomegranate.

Am I the only one who sees what is going on between them? Certainly, I seem to be the only one who
now realizes that Grace was always doomed to inherit
my irresistible innocence ... and my hidden, tortured history.

No one else but I, however, could ever hope to stop
them. For it is I who knows what Grazia is thinking
and feeling. Therefore, only I can reroute this deadly
train before disaster repeats itself and the Levi blood
is doomed forever.

Not only my granddaughter must be saved, how-
ever. In truth, the entire family, *la tutta famiglia,* is at
risk. If we do not hold together, we will be torn apart.
Thus, at all costs, I must save us all ... for we are the
last of the Levis.

Chapter Twenty-three

Saturday, April 3, 1995

For all who were intimately connected to Silvana Levi Bassani Nachman Harding, this promised to be a memorable day. Each of them awakened early, eager to begin their own preparations for the gala awards dinner that evening. None had awakened earlier than Eduardo, however; he had been up since five.

Beside him on his "reading" chair was a copy of his first published book, *A Jewish Family in Rome.* If it had not been for Silvana, that first book would have been almost forgotten by now, for since its publication eighteen years ago, there had been three more. Even now, at almost seventy-seven, he was at work on another book—although this one, he was sure, would be his last.

But today he would not be working on the new book. Today he would finish writing the speech he would deliver tonight at the dinner in Silvana's honor. Except that now so much of it needed to be changed. Because of yesterday. Because of what Silvana had said.

Yesterday she had rung the front doorbell to his house, surprising them all. His sons Marco and Umberto (named for Eduardo's father) had just arrived home from college so that they could attend the gala the following night.

"Auntie Silvana!" they shouted at the open door. "Ma! It's Auntie Silvana!" Umberto, with hair as red as his mother Mary Catherine's, escorted Silvana into the living room. Marco ran to the kitchen to tell his mother to make another cup of espresso. Eduardo rose stiffly and offered her the seat beside him on the sofa. Then they all gathered round her.

"Why didn't you tell us you were coming?" Mary Catherine asked, a tray of afternoon coffee in her hands.

"Mama! What a surprise!" Debora echoed, following with a plate of her *dolci,* an assortment of sweets—slices of kosher fruit pie, hard Jewish cookies, and *savoiardi* (Italian lady fingers), brought from her café. Debora, who had become an Italian language teacher, had also developed into an estimable baker, truly earning title to her dessert and coffee bar. On the rare occasions—like this particular afternoon—when she was not teaching or baking or serving, she enjoyed visiting her Uncle Eduardo and Aunt Mary Catherine at their huge town house.

Unlike her sister Anna Michela, Debora loved the city. And perhaps because Anna Michela now lived in Montauk year round, Debora and her half sister Elena had grown closer. Today, Elena, too, would be stopping by with Grazia before work. That is, if mother and daughter were still speaking; Elena and Grazia were always at war about something. Always.

"I have come here today—" Silvana began, patting a flat package on her lap when the doorbell rang again.

Elena and Grazia arrived, but it was clear that they were at war again, for they took seats at opposite ends of the room. Grazia chose the large, upholstered chair beside Eduardo, folding her legs, long and lean as a colt's, under her, and left Elena, her mother, to sit on a small stool. "May I have some coffee?" she asked in an angel's voice, and waited to be served.

"Demanding. That's her middle name," Elena often complained. "She is so beautiful—even though she thinks she's ugly—that she has always gotten whatever she wanted. Now she expects it—no, she demands it! And if we don't give it to her, she finds a way to make us bend to her will. She wouldn't eat for a week until I finally gave in and bought her a pair of shoes that were too expensive. I really can't do anything with her!"

Silvana, of course, knew all this, but to her Grazia would always be her adored granddaughter, Elena's beautiful child. Now, on the day before her awards dinner, Silvana had expected to have a private talk with her brother Eduardo. Instead, with most of her family gathered round—only Anna Michela and Sloane were missing—this would have to be a public discussion.

So be it, Silvana said to herself. *Let them all hear. Let them all know.*

"I came here today," she began again, "to tell my brother that after so many years, I have at least read his book. I want you all to know that I have always considered it a terrible thing that I could not even open it, though it has lain on my bedside table since he gave me one of the first published copies."

As she spoke, she unwrapped the package on her lap. No one was surprised to see that it was her copy of *A Jewish Family in Rome.* But when she pressed it to her breast, and then kissed it as if it were a sacred text, tears filled Eduardo's eyes.

"Forgive me for taking so long, for not being able to tell you sooner," she beseeched him.

"Tell him what, Grandma?" Grazia asked innocently.

Silvana turned to her granddaughter. Perhaps Grazia could learn a lesson from this today; perhaps not. But Silvana was certainly not going to give up trying to reach her errant granddaughter.

"To tell him thank you. Thank you for creating something so beautiful and so important. Have you read this, Grazia?" She held the book up.

Grazia nodded.

"Then you know the full story of your ancestors and the struggles they endured."

Again she nodded. Over the years, Grazia had thumbed through parts of the book, reading the exciting sections about the war and the Fascists and the German concentration camps, but she never really understood what all the fuss was about. Though her family said the book was a "masterpiece," she could not say why.

As if reading her thoughts, Silvana spoke directly to her. "Do you know why this book is so important? Because on every page, between every line, there is respect."

Eduardo sighed and allowed a tear to run down his cheek. He had given up hope that his sister would ever read his books, especially this first one. That she had finally done so, at this exceptionally late date, made it that much more moving to him. He composed a line in his head for his speech that he would write tomorrow morning: *My sister is testament to the magnificent ability we all possess—the ability to grow ... to grow wiser, greater, braver every day of our lives, right up to the minute that we die!*

"Respect," Silvana repeated. "Respect for life, for history, and decency, and family." She turned to Eduardo and saw his tears and smiled tenderly. Then she returned to Grazia. "And most of all, respect for the mothers who bring us into this world."

To Silvana, the most stirring character in the book was the mother, so like Anna Levi that it seemed as if Silvana's mother had been brought back to life. "Mama! A miracle!" she had sobbed.

To Grazia, however, it was the most boring part. She stifled a yawn. Although she would be the first to say that her Nonna Silvana was a darling, lately, however, she was always making boring speeches. Mostly about what a wonderful mother Elena was. *Does she know?* Grazia wondered with alarm. Nonna Silvana was an old woman, but her eyes saw everything. Which made Grazia wonder why only now Nonna Silvana was making speeches about mothers—about *her* mother. Then she told herself, *So what if she knows. I don't care. I want the whole world to know I'm in love. Even Mama. Then she'll know at least one person thinks I'm beautiful. At least one man really loves me.*

"So thank you, Eduardo," Silvana was saying.

"Thank you for making me look at the past as you do—with respect. For so long I have been afraid to look, afraid what I might see. Oh, yes, I know your book is fiction. But it is based on the past—our shared past. And you have given it the dignity I could not."

Again the doorbell rang and Silvana immediately recognized Sloane Harding's voice as he was escorted into the busy room. But he had eyes only for his Silvana. "Aha! I thought I might find you here!"

"Caro mio," Silvana murmured, secretly delighted. With the room so full of her loved ones, she missed her husband's presence. "I will be gone only an hour," she had told him evasively, but he had guessed where she was and had come to fetch her.

"I'm hungry, you see." He shrugged helplessly.

Silvana laughed and crossed the room to his side. "He's impossible. I promised to come home early and make his favorite dish—stuffed breast of veal with pistachios. It comes from a little town in Italy where it was called *chazirello,* piglet, because it was like the *porchetta* that we Jews could not eat. It takes hours to make."

Sloane covered his heart with his hand. "You know I live for your cooking."

"Sì, I know," Silvana agreed, patting his hand, and began saying her good-byes. Kissing her two daughters Elena and Debora, she automatically felt the absence of her third, Anna Michela. "Too bad she could not be with us today."

"Oh, I forgot." Reminded, Elena comforted her mother with the news: "She called me before to say she'll drive in from Montauk and meet us at the gala tomorrow."

Silvana sighed, pleased, as Sloane poked her gently. "Let's get going. We still have to stop at the store and get the pistachios."

Only Grazia had not yet been kissed. Silvana held open her arms to her. "Be good, my child," she whispered in her granddaughter's delicate pink ear. "You will be good, my *bella* Grazia, yes? I love you so."

Chapter Twenty-four

Saturday, April 3, 1995

In the apartment of Sloane Harding and Silvana Levi, high above the noise and dirt of the city streets, dawn painted their enormous, glass-walled bedroom in pale, smoky light. Though this New York dawn was particularly gray and unspectacular, it nevertheless was bright enough to awaken the peaceful couple who slept rather lightly now that they had entered old age.

This was a morning to be up early anyway. Before the gala awards dinner at seven-thirty tonight, they both had to attend to numerous chores ... and their racing days were definitely over.

Sloane Harding opened his eyes first and immediately checked Silvana. Since her eyes were still closed, he did not touch her or try to awaken her. She slept little enough as it was.

Instead, he gazed at the pastel penthouse bedroom that Silvana had made into such a striking skytop aerie. Filmy, silky cloth—the kind used to make parachutes—was neatly strung with cord and folded into Roman shades that, on extremely sunny days, were lowered over the skylights and the huge windows and French doors leading out to the planted terrace. The billowy, cloudlike quality of the lowered shades were to Sloane like loose sails at half-mast. And when the shades were rolled up and pure light streamed in through the bare windows, they were the furled sails on an undocked boat before setting out to sea.

From the skylights, Sloane's gaze traveled out to the apartment's terrace, from which he could view the

Hudson River—sometimes for miles. Silvana knew him so well, knew what he loved, and had given it all to him here in this room—a mariner's dream in the sky.

The truth was, Silvana had given to him all the qualities he most loved in his life. With her he now had enduring affection, companionship, laughter, and passion, not to mention a savvy business partner, a built-in and extremely lively family ... and the best dinners he had ever tasted. Often, he would tease her in the kitchen as she prepared a meal, claiming, "This is why I married you. For your cooking," knowing that the joke was only half untrue.

But it was not only the superb meals; it was the spiritual Jewish rituals that Silvana had introduced to him, as well. Now he enjoyed Passover seders where he, too, read from the Haggadah—the Passover text—listened to the youngest of the family ask the four questions, and ate *matza* pancakes, roast lamb, and spinach with garlic. Even the holiest holiday, Yom Kippur—the Day of Atonement and Forgiveness—that began by fasting and saying prayers, ended with a loud and lively family meal at sundown to break the fast.

Jews, Sloane had discovered, found almost any excuse to celebrate with a meal. There were minor holidays and high holy days, and most of them involved a ritual meal. "So I'm lucky you're Jewish," he often told Silvana, "because I get to celebrate all your holidays and all your special dishes."

But the dish she had made for him last night, stuffed breast of veal, was his favorite of all. Though Silvana had first served it at a Rosh Hashanah dinner celebrating the Jewish New Year, now she prepared it year round, whenever he begged loudly enough.

Now, smiling at her beside him, he comforted himself that at least tonight she would not have to cook. Tonight all she would have to do is look beautiful, which for her was still easy.

He turned to her and she opened her eyes. Immediately she was wide awake.

"Good morning, my darling." Her smile was like an unfurled ketch heeling in the crisp wind on the deep blue of the sea. *She* was his mariner's dream. He told her so.

"Don't you miss it, sometimes, Sloane?" she asked him.

"Miss what?" he said evasively although he knew exactly what she meant.

"The men, the dock, the smell of fish, the tons of ice, and the business you built up and sold? All the sailing you once did? The salty air? Your life before . . . me?" Silvana knew how to hit a nail on the head. She did not often question him, but when she did, she was always sharp and specific, forcing him to answer her when she knew he would have preferred to be silent.

"I have learned that sometimes it is better to speak of difficult things than to keep them hidden inside," she added, reminding him of several revelations they had shared over the last eighteen years—most recently, the discovery that she could face the pain of the tragedies in her past and read Eduardo's book at last. And yet, although what she had said to him she devoutly believed, there was one subject secretly smoldering inside her under a lid still too hot to lift. Of this she had said nothing.

Soon, she promised herself. *Soon I will tell him. I will confide my only remaining secret and bare to him the deepest, most hidden part of my soul. Just as he has done with me.*

"Okay, sometimes. Sure I miss it. But only sometimes," he was finally forced to admit. "You don't spend a lifetime building up a business—two businesses, really, because there was the marina and its dockage fees and then there was the fish wholesaling business. Anyway, you don't build them up and then sell them off—even at a big profit—without missing it all sometimes."

"*Sí.* I know. And I understand, Sloane." And she did understand. This was not a first marriage for either of them. Each had had separate lives before they

joined together. She felt the need to reassure him that
even now, parts of those former lives would be missed
sometimes. "It is—how do you say—*normale.*"

"*Normale,*" he agreed. Then he felt the need to
reassure her.

"Still, I wouldn't trade one minute—one millisec-
ond—of any of this." His arms embraced apricot satin
and for a moment he could not tell if he was caressing
her nightgown or her actual skin. Then he told himself
what he always told himself—next to her skin, even
silk satin felt like sandpaper. To prove it, he commenced a kissing journey along the wrinkled but still
velvety skin of her body, pressing his lips into the
palm of her hand, then traveling up the inside of her
arm and down the backside of her thighs. His mouth
left a wet, sensuous trail that resonated below her
skin's surface layers, that resonated deep into the core
of her.

"Oh, Sloane," she groaned softly. "You make me
feel young . . . and, yes—I'm not embarrassed to say
it—sexy. I want you, Sloane. I want you this morning,
I want you this minute!"

"Take this off," he commanded huskily, pulling at
her nightgown. "I need to see all of you, to feel all
of you."

"But it's morning and it's so light in here," she
softly protested, modest suddenly despite her years . . .
or perhaps precisely because of them.

"It's all right," he reassured her. "You know I don't
see the wrinkles; I just see your body. Oh, God, just
the thought of seeing it makes me forget everything
else. Your body is what I need."

Sighing, she teasingly pulled the satin nightgown
over her head, exposing her naked body to him inch
by inch. After several inches, he exhaled with deep
pleasure. As always, his arousal was doubly welcome
because it not only pleased her, it freed her. Now she
could enjoy herself with uninhibited abandon.

"Here is something else you need," she said, facing
him as her eyes narrowed to slits.

"This is going to be good. Oh, God, I just know

it," he sighed with anticipation. He loved it when she invented these lovely sexual surprises for him.

She smiled in agreement and slid her leg over his hip. Then she searched for him with her hand, between their braided thighs. When she found him, she massaged him until she could hardly hold him back. Still, she would not let him go, for feeling him grow at her touch excited her just as much as it did him.

So this time, she did not quickly guide him in—the way she had done that first time eighteen years ago. This time, she knew they were in no hurry. The intervening years had taught her all about ecstasy, and just how to find it. She continued to hold on to him, pressing up against him—but not letting him in.

"Oh, God, you teasing vixen, you!" he groaned. She had learned how to tease him and how to pleasure herself in the process. He groaned, but she knew he was as aroused and as happy as she. By now, she was a pleasure expert.

But however much she had learned, he had learned equally as much. They had become informed together. And by now, they both knew the secret to great sex at last. They both knew that getting there was more than half the fun.

Grazia, too, arose early—early, that is, for her. Like most restaurant people, Grazia worked late hours and mornings rarely began before nine or ten. Not that she minded—she was born, she always said, to the restaurant life. That was why she had convinced everyone that she should put college off for a year and work in the restaurant Silvana had named for her, Casa di Grazia. And now that Nonna Silvana was actually allowing her to cook sometimes, she knew she would never go away to school. This was where she wanted to be.

Every afternoon she spent an hour dressing before going off to work. She dressed in ever new clothes that she was constantly begging her mother Elena to buy for her. "On my salary, I can't afford anything—

and you know I have to make a good appearance as a hostess."

It was not just for work that she so meticulously matched her outfits to her shoes and to her carefully applied eye shadow. It was not just for work that she dabbed expensive perfume in every crease and fold of her body. It was for her stepfather, Freddo. Mostly, it was for him.

Ever since her mother had married Freddo Toscano five years ago, she had felt strangely alive in his presence.

"He's really cool-looking," she had told her friends then, "too cool for my mother. I swear, he looks like he could be a rock star." But for five years, her good-looking stepfather had been a remote figure in the household, rarely engaged in family activities that involved her. Sometimes it seemed to her that he purposely avoided her, and that when he could not, his eyes burned right through her with a kind of fiery longing. But then he would become remote again, and she would forget the look in his eyes, daydreaming not of him, but of the boys in her high school.

It was only when she began work as a hostess at Casa di Grazia that everything changed. The restaurant had been Freddo's hangout, but now he had a new reason to spend time there. And now his eyes did not leave her for a moment, and if she were not so busy at work, she would probably just melt down from the fire in his stare. The work, in a way, was a blessing. The hostessing kept her moving but the cooking—preparing the special orders—kept her from thinking. When she cooked, she did not think of Freddo Toscano. When she cooked, she was in love with only one thing: cooking.

Everyone in the family knew that Grazia was destined to become a great chef like her grandmother. It was Silvana who Grazia most took after, they all agreed, not only in looks—the golden, gleaming hair, the prominent nose, the long, lean limbs—but in talent. Grazia had inherited her grandmother's extraordinary culinary talent.

"It came from Silvana."

"Grazia has Silvana's genes."

"Grazia has more of her genes than Silvana's own daughters," they said emphatically and in complete concurrence.

No one ever mentioned that Grazia's father Gino was a great chef, too. No one ever mentioned him at all.

Not that Grazia's stepfather Freddo was a prize. But he was Elena's husband and everyone had seen how hard she had tried to make this second marriage a success.

Many were sympathetic. "It is not Elena's fault. She tries to be a good wife. Her home is beautiful."

"Yes, but that's because she's never home to dirty it. She works so hard, running from one restaurant to the other, poor thing. No wonder Freddo gets lonely," others argued.

"So what if he gets lonely. He's married, isn't he?"

"Marriage doesn't stop some men."

"Maybe. But incest should stop them for sure. Stop them cold."

"Where's the incest? There's no blood between Freddo and Grazia," some observed. "And Grazia is no longer a child. Just turned eighteen, didn't she?"

"Incest? There's not anything between Freddo and Grazia. She may be eighteen but she's still a baby, for crying out loud!"

"But *if* there were something between them? Would that be incest ... or not?"

Some said not. Some, however, said yes.

Despite all the stares and compliments she had received throughout her life, Grazia Levi-Bracca was not sure what she really looked like. She would ask herself, *Am I ordinary ... or really memorable?* There were times when she glanced at herself in the mirror and saw what others saw—a long-legged, golden-haired, sharp-nosed beauty. At those moments, so rare and so brief, she felt warm and complete and even her mother seemed dear to her. But most of the time she thought herself a tall, lanky girl whose nose was too big and whose eyes were entirely too close together. From magazine articles she knew that she could never become a photographic model, her highest standard of beauty. For one thing, her breasts were too large. And her nose. Plus, she had closely set eyes. All models had eyes widely set apart. With eyes like hers, she concluded, how could she be beautiful?

"Believe me, you're beautiful," Freddo told her over and over.

And she did believe him. Whenever her stepfather's eyes were upon her, or when the "eye" of his camera was blinking at her, and he said, "Oh, Grazia, you are so incredibly beautiful," she believed him. He had the ability to convince her of anything.

Freddo, a food stylist and photographer, knew how to photograph anything and make it look better. A restaurant's signature dish, photographed by Freddo, would make the food look so luscious, so succulent, so mouthwatering that a minimum of twenty new customers was almost guaranteed. Needless to say, his services were in great demand by New York restaurants. In fact, that was how he and her mother, Elena, had met. Assigned by a leading gourmet magazine, Freddo photographed several dishes prepared at Mia Elena Ristorante, and later showed the developed pictures to Elena. Instantly she fell in love with his pictures ... and with him. Five years ago they were married.

But immediately after Grazia began working at Casa di Grazia, she became aware of her stepfather's penetrating stares again. And not just at work; life at home became uncomfortable, too. Whenever her mother was not there, Grazia felt unsafe in the house alone with her stepfather. Unsafe, and yet so highly charged that she felt electric shocks when she was near him. It was unendurable.

"I'm moving out," she announced to her mother. "My friend Joan needs a roommate and I need some privacy. It's really like being away at college, no big deal. We'll talk on the phone and I'll come home holidays." To her surprise, Elena quickly relented and even offered to help her with the rent. *Does she know?* Grazia wondered momentarily. But then gave a bitter laugh. *Mama just wants to be rid of me so she can be with him.*

Moving into her own apartment, Grazia had thought, would end it, but it did not. Freddo spent all his free time at her restaurant now and never took his eyes off her.

Confronting him one day, she demanded, "Why are you always staring at me? Can't you see it makes me uncomfortable?" But by then she was already secretly dressing just for him.

He did not answer. He just continued to stare. And although it made her uncomfortable, she could not help wondering, *What does he see when he looks at me? Someone ordinary . . . or memorable?*

Again she confronted him, wearing a skirt so short that she unconsciously kept tugging at the hem. And this time Freddo told her, with a grin that said otherwise, "I would never want to make you uncomfortable."

"Then why do you do it?" she persisted, sliding onto a bar stool beside him. And that was when he caressed her cheek with his hand, making her face feel sunburned. Then he blew his warm breath into her ear and she trembled. That was the day she stopped running from him . . . and running from herself.

He saw he had her and he told her what she most wanted to hear. "I want to photograph you."

"Really?" she asked, embarrassed, delighted, and could not entirely stifle a girlish giggle. "Why?"

"Because you're like a tight, unopened—" He stopped, searching for an image. "Like an unopened endive, or like a cabbage. Yeah, a cabbage," he repeated, making her laugh.

"Oh, great. A cabbage." She pretended she was disappointed but she did not run from him. And she did not push his hand away.

"Tight." He made a fist to show her what he meant. "I want to open you and photograph you. Would you like that?"

"I don't know."

He persisted. "Would you like me to photograph you as you have never been photographed before?"

She did not answer him that time, and the next. But his eyes were always upon her, heating her, and his hands were always finding an excuse to touch her, to stroke her, to pull her closer.

"Come see my studio," he was always urging. "Come see my work."

"I can't. I've got to work," she'd say.

"I can't," she'd say. "I've got to meet my mother. We're going shopping."

But nothing deterred him, not even when she invoked her mother's name. And she was curious. She had never seen a photographer's studio before. In the past, he had always said, "No one is ever allowed in my studio. No one." Now she was to be the privileged exception. She liked the feeling. He was the only man who ever made her feel privileged, exceptional. It was the way she felt when Nonna Silvana let her cook at the restaurant.

She finally agreed to meet him at the studio. She wore a short skirt. She told herself she knew what would happen. She told herself she wanted it to happen. She had to have him. And yet, afterward she cried.

"Are you sorry?" he asked, wiping away her tears.

She told herself she was glad. For there she was in his studio. "No," she told him. "Even Mama has never been here!" After that, there were no more tears.

Now she was there almost every day. Neither one of them could get enough of the other. But today she was going to make him choose. Either he moved in with her ... or it was over. If he loved her, as he said he did, he would have to prove it and choose her openly. No longer would she sneak and hide. Hadn't he convinced her that their love was blessed? Yes, blessed!

"I am proud of our love. You should be, too." He had convinced her of everything, even this. He had turned her tears of guilt into cries of passion. He had opened her, just as he said he would, and he had filled her with all of him, even his thoughts. He said she should be proud; now she was.

And that was why, it seemed to her, they should proudly announce their love to the world—and to the family—and be accepted. Today, she would tell him. "Choose." *Choose me!* Today, she would have her answer.

But first she had to collect her dress from Tomasso, the tailor. He had promised to complete the alterations today on her new, ballerina-length, powder pink silk chiffon dress so that she could wear it tonight. Not really wear it—float in it—for it was as light and as delicate as a rosebud petal.

So many chores, really. To go with her dress, she needed a lipstick in the very palest of pinks. Her Aunt Debora said the shop on Sixty-sixth Street carried the lipstick she wanted. "I'll try them," Grazia told her aunt, not mentioning that the shop was conveniently near to Freddo's studio.

And then there was the florist, where she would also have to make a stop, she reminded herself as she slid into a pair of tight, straight jeans. She was going to buy Nonna Silvana a corsage to wear with her new black velvet gown.

Tonight, Grazia knew, was enormously important to her grandmother. Everyone was coming; not only the entire family, but celebrities, the press and television cameras, and all the top chefs in today's restaurants from around the world. It was going to be a night to remember. She had no idea, however, how truly unforgettable this night would turn out to be.

She hurried out the door of her small, dark apartment and stopped as she was about to lock it. Remembering that she had not checked herself in the mirror one last time, she returned. But the young woman reflected in the bedroom mirror did not look beautiful, did not feel beautiful. Only Freddo was able to do that, to transform her with his lens into someone even she found appealing. Now, however, she had to stare at the mirror alone. Self-doubt turned to self-hate. Guilt crawled up her arms and she itched with disgust at herself. "You should be proud," he had told her, but suddenly she felt only shame. If only she had the pictures he had taken of her last week to cheer her up. But now she would have to wait until tonight to see them.

"I put them in an envelope in the back of my cuff link drawer at home. That way, I won't forget to slip them into my tuxedo pocket when I get dressed tonight," he had told her on the phone this morning.

"But I'm coming to see you at the studio this afternoon," she reminded him. "You could have given the photos to me then."

"I forgot! So make sure your purse is big enough tonight. I'll slip the pictures in when no one's looking."

"Are they—do I—look all right?"

"All right? Grazia, wait till you see them! You're gorgeous. Every inch of you, baby. Every inch."

While he was on the phone with her, he had made her feel beautiful. But now she was alone again and her doubts had returned. The truth was, no matter how much reassurance she got, it was never enough. Alone with herself, she would wonder and worry, *Why can't I be beautiful? Why can't I be good? Oh, Mama, don't hate me!*

If only she were really beautiful, she would be happy forever. If she were really pretty, she would feel like a good girl at last and her father would come back to them and her mother would see that she was really a good girl and never be tired or angry at her again. Why did her father leave? Why did her mother divorce him? No one would tell her; Mama just said, "It's best this way, believe me." But if it was for the best, then why did she feel like she'd done something terribly, horribly wrong? And why did she feel that way today?

But soon she would see Freddo and he would make

everything all right. He would make her his one and only love and then she would never feel this gnawing, grinding guilt again. She would feel beautiful ... and loved. And she would never have to spend another minute alone with her thoughts again.

"Do you love my breasts? Do you love these?" she asked the lens, lying on a white sheet of photographic paper.

Overhead, a white professional umbrella softened the intensity of the hot, bright lights and deflected the shadows away from her face. Several feet away, Freddo stared into his camera. When he answered her, he spoke to her through the camera.

"Yes, baby, oh. That's right. Squeeze them with your hands. Show me what you've got. Push them together and squeeze!"

"And do you like this?" she continued, facing the camera as she massaged her pudendum, inserting one finger into her slit.

"Oh, baby, I love it! You're so gorgeous. You're so hot. Oh, God, I don't believe your skin, your thighs, your tits."

"And this?"

"That, too. Definitely." He snapped his camera and it made a zizzing noise. He snapped it again. And again. "I get so hot taking these photos of you, Grazia. They're going to be the best ever, I can tell!"

She turned over onto her stomach. "Don't forget to give me the other photos tonight."

"I've got something I want to give you right now." He snapped off the overhead lights and pulled off his shoes. Then he crawled on all fours toward her on the clean, white paper.

She, too, was on her knees. "Meeow," she purred, arching her back.

"I've got something for kitty, something for kitty to lick right up with her pretty red tongue."

Out came Grazia's tongue to taunt him as she backed away, sliding on her bare knees.

"Here, kitty, kitty!" He held out a hand to her.

"Meeow!" she purred again, and leapt to her feet. "Kitty is tired." She gave a mock yawn and sauntered to the bed that he kept hidden behind a three-panel screen.

Smiling, he followed her. "Well, we'll just have to put kitty to sleep then, won't we?"

"Sometimes kitty can't fall asleep until she's completely relaxed."

His hands found her under the blanket, and the minute he began stroking her body, he could tell she was ready. She was the hottest little cabbage he'd ever had. Often it was she who got so impatient for him that she'd whimper, "Now, Freddo, oh, please, now," and spread herself open the way he had taught her and writhe and whimper until he rammed himself into her.

"Poor little kitty," he whispered huskily. "But here's something that will relax her and put her right to sleep. Here's something to make her purr."

"Oh, meeow. Oh, Freddo, meeow!"

The ringing phone awakened them with a start. He reached across Grazia's naked, motionless body and grabbed the receiver on the fourth ring.

"Yes?" He tried to hide the sleep in his voice. Then, as he listened to the caller, he sighed with irritation and rolled his eyes.

"Elena, I have no idea where your goddamned gold cuff links are and I have no idea why you'd interrupt me in the middle of work to ask me something stupid like that."

He listened some more and nodded. "Okay, okay, I'll be home in"—he looked at his watch, surprised at the late afternoon hour—"at seven. That'll give me just enough time to put on my tuxedo and get to the hotel. No, don't wait for me. I know you have a lot to do. I'll meet you at the grand ballroom."

When he hung up, he turned to Grazia and found her sulking. Lifting herself up on her elbows, she stared straight ahead and wondered out loud, "What would you do if my mother ever found out about us?"

Quietly, slowly, meticulously, he answered her, his entire body in rigid control except for his eyes. His eyes were wild with alarm. But she was not looking at his eyes.

"Grazia, you know that must not happen. You know she must not find out. And you know why."

"No, I don't know why," she argued petulantly.

"Grazia, we have gone over this and I thought by now it was understood. Your mother can't know. Period."

"You don't love her. Anyone listening to you two on the phone just now would know it in a second."

"No, I don't love her the way I love you."

"And it's not as if you've been my father. I've only known you a few years."

"That's true," Freddo conceded warily. Although he had told her all these same things, he sensed something dangerous in the way she was throwing them back at him today.

"And it's also true, isn't it, that you're the one who convinced me we have nothing to be ashamed of," she proceeded stealthily, like a lawyer developing a cross-examination. Then, suddenly, she looked straight at him. "Do we, Freddo? Do we have anything to be ashamed of?"

"Not between us. Between us there is no shame," he said smoothly. He had told her this many times before; indeed it was the argument that broke down her resistance and finally won her over. She loved hearing that they were a special couple, unique, one of a kind. And that his love for her was like no other in this world. "Between us there is only our love and the exquisite beauty and freedom of our love." To underline his words he tried to kiss her, but when he reached for her, she shook him off. So he added, carefully, "But others might not understand."

"No?" she taunted.

"No. Your mother wouldn't. That is why it's so important that she never find out."

Grazia stood up and began pacing, entirely unconscious of her nudity. "You told me that we can't help it if we fell in love. It happened. No one's to blame."

Again he cautiously agreed.

"Well, if we've done nothing wrong, why do we have to hide?"

"Because I told you that your mother—"

"I know! I know!" she shouted. "My mother! She won't understand. Okay, neither do I. You took me, you taught me to love you. So why are you only worried about her feelings? One of us has to get hurt. I'm prepared for that. Are you?"

"What are you saying, Grazia?"

"Choose! I'm saying, choose. Choose one; lose one. You can't have us both."

It was time to end this, Freddo knew, but he was afraid she was not going to relent unless—

He ran to her, threw his arms around her cool, bare skin, and pressed his mouth hard against hers. Then he held her face in both his hands and spoke to her as if his heart were not hammering wildly in his chest.

"I love you, you gorgeous animal, you. But if you don't run home and change right now, you'll be late. You know how long it takes you to dress."

It was true. Dressing sometimes took hours. And already the studio was growing dark. But she wasn't finished with this discussion. She wanted an answer— if not now, then soon. And she told him so.

"I promise, baby, next Friday, after I finish this project I have in the darkroom, we'll talk. Next Friday we'll work it all out."

He kept his mouth on her breast, her neck, her mouth as she dressed, and embraced her lustily as he walked her to the door. But as soon as she was gone, he sighed heavily. Then he caught sight of himself in the hall mirror and smiled.

"Well, you just bought yourself six more hot little days. Not bad," he commended himself. "Not bad at all."

Chapter Twenty-five

Same Day

Elena had already bathed and was half dressed when she had phoned Freddo at the studio to ask him about her favorite gold cuff links. It was really quite baffling. She had seen them in her jewelry drawer last week. Now they were gone. But though she wanted to wear them on this most special of nights, she could not afford another minute to look for them. At this very moment she was supposed to be meeting Sloane Harding at the grand ballroom, where they had volunteered to check on all the last-minute arrangements. And so, with cuffs flapping, she applied the last of her makeup, wondering frantically about changing her outfit, when the phone rang.

"Mama! I'm so glad you called," she gushed to Silvana in a rush of relief, holding the phone with one hand while struggling into her silk raincoat with the other. "I hate to ask on this of all days—but would you do me a big favor?"

Just as Elena had hoped, Silvana reassured her that the cuff links would be found. "I'll come to your apartment on my way to the hotel. You're only three blocks from me. I'll tell my driver to wait."

"They're somewhere in my bureau, I'm almost sure. But as usual, I'm late. And after I finish at the hotel, I so wanted to surprise Grazia at her apartment and escort her to the gala. With your help, now I will have just enough time."

"Good. Now say good-bye because I have just

enough time, too—for a nice, long bath before I dress."

"Thank you, Mama," Elena told her and then added, "thank you for everything. *Tutto,* Mama. *Tutto.*"

By late afternoon Silvana was glad to turn off the phone, do up Sloane's tuxedo studs, kiss him on his cheek, and send him on his way. She needed time to be alone, to compose herself, to soak in the bath. Sloane was in the way now. It was good that he had arranged to meet Elena at the hotel so early. There were still myriad last-minute decisions to be made and she wanted no part of them. She had other things on her mind. One thing, really.

Freddo.

Freddo had been on her mind for the last three nights. All her dreams were of him, and they were all nightmares. Because she knew this one, this Freddo. She knew him and she knew that he was dangerous. Once before in her life she had known one just like him; so she knew who Freddo Toscano was and the damage he could cause.

How Elena could have married him, Silvana had never understood. But then, Elena never had great taste in men. Yet it was a weakness for which Silvana could not fault her daughter because her Elena had grown up fatherless. Just as fatherless as Elena's daughter, Grazia, was now.

"Grazia, my poor darling!" Silvana sighed. "My poor, foolish darling."

Silvana was not sure what that snake was doing to her granddaughter. But two nights ago she had seen him at her restaurant, touching her Grazia as if he owned her, and what for months had been a vaporous worry suddenly became solid, as solid and red-hot as a fire's last ember. And it was burning right through her chest.

Oh, yes, she knew this one well. She knew how he could ruin her Grazia. And how he could being shame and ruin not only to Grazia, but to the entire family.

Had it already begun? She did not know. She only
knew that she had to stop him.

And suddenly she knew exactly how.

The bathwater grew cold and she sat on, shivering
and glowering ... and plotting. How odd, she mused,
that she sat shivering while her thoughts burned like
fire inside her. Like embers in a pot flaming to life
again now that she had lifted the lid. Now that she
had lifted the lid at last ...

At precisely six o'clock, with more than enough
time for this detour, Silvana told her driver to wait,
and swept elegantly through the lobby of the building
where Elena and Freddo lived. Letting herself into the
apartment with her own key, she untied her hooded
velvet cape and laid it beside her evening bag, bulging
with its ominous contents.

As she entered her daughter's bedroom, she could
detect the smell of the snake her daughter had married, and almost fled. But she had promised Elena to
find her cuff links and would not disappoint her now.
Certainly, there was plenty of time. Later, after the
festivities, she would deal with the snake. That was
the plan she had formed in her bath and had carried
in her head. Because somehow, after all these years,
she still expected life to follow a plan. Yet somehow—
even she would be the first to admit—it never, ever,
did.

And so, despite the scent of a snake in her nostrils
and a distinct sense of dread in her heart, she would
search for the gold cuff links that her daughter always
wore on momentous occasions.

Drawer by drawer, she scrupulously lifted and replaced the contents of Elena's antique English high-
boy. When she could not find the cuff links, she
proceeded to Freddo's bureau, and began pulling open
his drawers. Then, suddenly, she stopped. The right
glossy corner of a photo sliding out of a yellow manila
envelope stopped her. Stopped her and paralyzed her
so that she could not move her hand toward the half-
hidden picture for many seconds.

When she was finally able to, she reached for it
quickly, because she had a dark sense, a premonition
of who would be in the photo. It put a name to the
dread she had been carrying inside her all day.

Looking at the long, nude limbs of her granddaughter in an obscenely lewd pose, she was not surprised.
Somehow, she was not surprised at all. Suddenly she
understood why she had been feeling such a heavy
weight in her heart.

Here in her hand was the reason.

One by one she looked at all the photos that Elena's
husband Freddo had taken of her beloved granddaughter, Grazia, and by the time she had viewed
them all, she knew that what she had planned to do
later, she would do instead now, right now.

Oddly, as she swept her cape back over her shoulders again, and tucked the envelope of photographs
under her arm, she discovered Elena's cuff links in a
small, crystal ashtray on the table beside her bag.

Concentrate on these, she told herself when she was
seated again in the limousine and the cuff links rested
in the palm of her hand. *Concentrate on the mellow
gold and the smooth finish. Don't think of this envelope
and the filth it contains. And don't think of him. Soon
enough you will have to look into the eyes of the snake.
Soon enough.*

"You are surprised, no, to see your mother-in-law
here on this, of all nights?" Silvana asked Freddo with
a sardonic smile as he held the studio door open for
her.

"No, no!" he insisted, but he continued to stand at
the door, too surprised to remember to ask her in.
She had to suggest it herself.

Once inside, however, he appeared to have recovered his composure. And even though he worried anxiously and secretly about what could have possibly
brought her here, a compliment rolled off his lips with
facile ease.

"I have never seen you look more beautiful,
Silvana. Elena is also wearing a black gown, but hers

has white satin cuffs. Don't tell her, but I think your dress is smarter," he joked.

When Silvana did not even smile, he tried again. With one arm, he swept the room. "Well, now you've seen it—a photographer's studio. Please, Silvana, do sit here." He motioned to an upholstered chair. "It's the only one that's worthy of such beauty."

She continued to stand. She did not tell him that she was not here for comfort. She had only one thing, really, to tell him. Only one purpose, really, to achieve here. To stop him. Once it was done, she could go. But she would not leave before she had stopped him. Nor would he. Until this was finished here, he would not leave either ... because she would not let him. She was going to stop him ... one way ... or the other.

"Freddo!" she said with an angry bark in her voice and tapped her purse. "Now I make you a proposal, *sì?*"

Snap!

Freddo warily kept silent and waited.

With a snap, her purse clasp clapped open and she quickly found her checkbook and her antique fountain pen. To write out the check, however, she had to sit down, but as she lowered herself into the chair, she looked up at him and said, "We can finish this in a minute. The fewer the words, the better. You tell me how much; I write you a check."

Astonished, nonplussed, and extremely nervous, Freddo opened his eyes wide in a look of injured innocence.

"If I did not know you better, Silvana, I'd think you're trying to buy me off for something."

"You don't know me, Freddo. You don't know me at all, but I know you. Oh, yes, I do, and this *is* a buy-off. If you're smart, you'll name your price and go." Slowly, she pulled the manila envelope out from under her cape and placed it menacingly on the table. "Are you going to be smart, Freddo?"

"Silvana, what in the world are you talking—"

"I am talking about these, you filthy snake."

"I have no idea what you have in that env—"

"I could have you arrested this minute for what I have in here. Or worse, Freddo, I warn you." She stopped to pat the bulge in her bag. "Or worse. Instead, I am offering you—how do you call it?—a deal. I want to buy back my granddaughter's stolen innocence. I want to buy my daughter Elena's continued ignorance. Do you understand now? For Grazia and for Elena I will pay any price. I will even let you go. But you must shut up and go away this minute. Now, no more. *Basta!* Just yes or no. Which one will it be, Freddo, eh?"

Still, he prevaricated. Still, he continued to deny, deny, deny. "I've done nothing, Silvana. Nothing," he insisted, staring not at her, but at the manila envelope.

But Silvana had no more time, no more patience ... and no more secrets. She came to a crouching stand before him, a black panther before a squealing, cornered prey. Even as he continued to filibuster he could see that she was ready to pounce.

"Really, I've done nothing. I'm innocent—"

"I know you," Silvana interrupted in a low growl. Her hand pawed the bottom of her bag and pulled out Michele's old gun. All these years it had always sat, wrapped in his old sweater, in an old trunk that went with her everywhere. Today, for the first time, she had unwrapped the sweater and loaded the gun. Today, for the first time, she was ready to fire it. She was going to stop him one way ... or the other. She aimed the gun at Freddo.

But holding the gun, she was taken back, back where she had never again wanted to go. The gun brought it all back.

"Oh, I know you. I've known you since I was fourteen," she told him, "when a man just like you married my mother—to get at me. And when I was only fifteen, he did. Oh, yes, he did! He raped me. And when he did that—when he raped me—he told me that it was beautiful, that it was love. So I let him. After that, I let him. So you see, I've known you my whole life."

"Your whole life?" Freddo gasped, but she contin-

ued, staring not at him but straight through him, to
his shrunken, duplicitous soul.

"How he insisted, whispering silky words, touching
me with silky hands, until I was as useless and as
mindless as a zombie! Gone!"

"Gone?" Freddo asked blankly. The gun stared
blankly back at him.

"Gone was my own sense of right and wrong. He
twisted my heart and my mind into believing our love
made us exempt from the ordinary rules, that our love
permitted everything—even sin and betrayal."

Freddo observed Silvana carefully. Somehow she
seemed aware of everything that had been going on
between him and Grazia. She had described it with
painful accuracy. Yet on the other hand, she was
speaking not only about him, but of someone else,
someone from her past. *Did Silvana have a stepfather, too?*

" 'Why?' my mother screamed at me, shaking me
like a dusty rug. 'How could you?'

" 'He made me, Mama!' I told her. I tried to explain
how he was always waiting for me after school, taking
me home alone. How he was always staring at me,
touching me, whispering words of love. How he made
me feel so . . . so . . . pretty, so desired.

" 'But he is my husband . . . your stepfather!'
Mama said.

"She could not seem to picture the way he forced
me, making me cry with pain and shame. The way he
just took me! And afterward, how he kept on, week
after week, year after year. And always telling me his
love for me was special.

" 'You have brought shame to this house, shame to
me,' Mama said.

"She could not imagine how he twisted everything.
How he told me I was already a woman, not really a
little girl—even though I *was* a little girl! A little girl
scared he'd be angry with me if I didn't let him. So
confused, so torn.

"How I begged her to forgive me. How I cried. 'He

took me, Mama!' I told her. "I was just a little girl
. . . and he took me!'

"But Mama said, 'Look how I caught you! You
weren't fighting him off an hour ago when I caught
you.'

"And so I admitted that once it began, I learned to
like it. You taught Grazia to like it, too, didn't you,
Freddo? You taught her to believe everything you
said—just as he did. That your love is special. I actually told Mama, 'Benno says our love makes anything
we do all right.'

" 'He told you that?' Mama said. 'He told you it
was all right to sin against your mother, all right to
betray her?'

" '*Si*, Mama. He told me that in this case, it wasn't
a sin. Because, Mama, he wants to marry me. So give
us your blessing, Mama. Please.'

" 'You fool,' said Mama. 'Get out.' "

Freddo shuddered. *Was this her past . . . or his
future?*

"Oh, how I begged her not to be angry! How I
begged her to try to be happy for her Girasole. Because he was going to make it up to me for doing
such bad things to me. By marrying me now that I
had turned eighteen. He was going to marry me to
make me a good girl again.

"But Mama said, '*Stupida!* He is gone. Gone.'

"She had kicked him out as soon as she caught the
two of us. While I hid in the bathroom, sobbing. But
I didn't believe he'd run away and leave me. I insisted
that he loved me, that I had to look for him and
find him.

" 'You foolish, foolish girl,' Mama said. 'He loves
only himself, don't you see that yet? No? All right
then, go. Get out, too. But if you run after him now,
you are dead to me. You are no longer my daughter!'

"How I cried. 'Mama, I must,' I told her. 'I must
find him.'

" 'Then you are dead to me, my daughter. You are
dead, my Girasole. And every year I will light a *Yortzeit* candle in your memory, for I have a daughter

no more,' she said to me that dark and terrible day. '*Arrivederci, Silvana. Finito.*'

"How I looked for him! Desperately, wildly, stupidly. But I could not find him in all of Rome. He, who said he loved me. He, who ruined me and sent me from my mother. He, who did not marry me, but ran away instead! He, my father . . . my love . . ."

Woodenly, Silvana raised her right arm shoulder high, aiming the gun directly at Freddo. But her eyes were as opaque as milk glass. And it was not Freddo she saw before her.

"That dark day when he abandoned his little Milano, I died. I saw it all on my mother's face, that I had killed her daughter right before her eyes. To her, I was forever after dead. Then she was taken away—deported—and I was not there to protect her, to save her. Not even to kiss her good-bye. She was gone. Gone from me forever."

Silvana cocked the gun. "Now, it is your turn. Finally, it is time to do the same to you."

Freddo raised his arms and shouted, "No, don't, Silvana! Don't shoot! Look. It's me, Freddo. Don't shoot me, please, I beg you! It's me. It's Freddo."

"Freddo," Silvana repeated, and suddenly her raised arm began to shake violently. It was as if her arm were palsied. It shook uncontrollably until the gun was thrust from her shaking hand onto the floor. She stared at the dull black revolver there on the floor until the shaking subsided. When she looked up, her eyes were clear.

Freddo, nevertheless, continued to tremble. He did not seem to realize that the crisis had passed, that he would not be shot. He did not see that Silvana had decided that neither this stepfather—nor the other one—was worth it. Now that she had killed the memory at last, there was nothing more to kill.

Rather, there was still Grazia to be saved.

"You will do as I say or you will be put in jail today."

Freddo nodded obsequiously even though Silvana no longer had the gun.

"From this moment on, you will simply disappear. No good-byes. *Niente,*" she warned with icy finality. Her mind was now clear and cold; she knew exactly to whom she was speaking. "We do not want to see your face again. Ever! None of us, Freddo. I speak for my entire family."

Then she retrieved the gun from the floor, unloaded it, and replaced it in her purse. "Or next time, I will pull the trigger."

She slammed the door behind her.

Elena, meanwhile, had to pound on Grazia's door with her satin-cuffed hand because Grazia was taking a shower and could not hear the bell. Finally, clad only in a towel, Grazia opened the door and made a sour face.

"Oh, it's only you, Mama." Her disappointment was palpable.

And perhaps it was the sour face that unhinged her mother. Or perhaps it was the irritating wait at the door. Or the words, "Oh, it's *only* you, Mama." But now everything was ruined—her surprise had boomeranged; her daughter was ungrateful. Elena burst into tears.

"How could you? Don't you have any love for me at all? Me! The mother who brought you into the world?"

Mama knows! Grazia thought breathily, her pulse pounding wildly against her temples. And although she had told Freddo this was what she wanted, now all she felt was fear and shame. It was the look on her mother's face that reached her deep inside, changing everything. Then, mistaking her mother's tears of frustration for the ultimate sorrow, she followed Elena into the apartment begging, in a little girl's voice, "I'm sorry, Mama. Please forgive me. Oh, Mama, I'm so sorry."

Her mother's tears, emblem of the pain Grazia had caused, were unbearable. Now that she thought Elena knew everything. But just as Grazia began to sob, too, someone else began knocking on the door outside. It was Silvana, of course, come to complete what she had started. "Grazia? Elena? Are you in there? Hurry, let me in!" she called. "It's Nonna Silvana."

One look at the sobbing daughter and granddaughter, and Silvana, too, mistakenly assumed what had transpired here. *Elena knows!* she concluded, just as her granddaughter had. And how eerily familiar it all seemed. *Yet it is the outcome that must be different this time,* Silvana resolved. *Entirely different.*

"Sit down," she commanded, sweeping into the crowded room and flinging her velvet cape over a chair. "Sit down, both of you. Before we leave for the hotel I have a story to tell you. A story about me when I was a girl and my mother married a man named Benno."

Elena gasped out loud. Benno! Her mother never allowed anyone to speak his name. Now her mother was saying it openly, speaking his name out loud!

As if anticipating her thoughts, Silvana said to her, "Elena, I am your mother, but you do not really know me. Today I will show you the part of me I have always hidden, even from you. If you have ever feared for your Grazia, perhaps my confession will help you save your daughter. And if you do that, you will save us all . . ."

The two tearful women did not want to listen, for different reasons. Grazia's present misery consumed her and she thought she could concentrate on no more sad stories of the past. And although Elena had been curious all her life about this secret, she now had a certain vague foreboding. *Why now? Why is she telling us now? And from what does she mean I should save Grazia?* she wondered. *From whom?* But with Silvana's first words, she drew them in:

"When I was a girl, I was seduced by my stepfather in the name of love."

Despite the identical nature of the story, it was not Grazia whose mouth fell open and whose eyes suddenly squeezed shut; it was Elena. *Oh, no! Freddo!* she groaned inwardly, immediately making the connection

between her mother's story . . . and her daughter's.
Freddo, you didn't. You wouldn't dare!

As if in search of a repudiation of her shocking
thoughts, she turned to her daughter Grazia. But
there, on her daughter's face, was a look of such re-
morse and shame that Elena groaned again and
clamped her hands over her mouth for fear of screaming out loud.

"I felt pretty and desired . . . and exempt from the
label of sinner," Silvana was explaining, bringing a
note of understanding and sanity to this double drama.
But it took all of Elena's will to listen. Inside, she was
sobbing, *Oh, Mama, I can't believe this. I can't believe
this has happened to you. And I can't believe this has
happened again to my baby! Oh, my poor, foolish,
beautiful Grazia!*

"I, too, stood on the brink of disaster," Silvana told
them, alert to the level of emotion in the room. But
when she saw Grazia kneel before her mother and
take her in her arms, Silvana spoke directly to her
young and broken granddaughter:

"However, until now, I thought I could not save
you, Grazia, because I thought you had my genes,
because I thought you had inherited my blood. But
now I know I must save you. Not only for you, *mia
dolcezza,* but for all of us, for *la famiglia.*"

The sobs erupted again and mother and daughter
wept piteously while Silvana looked on helplessly.

Elena never had to ask, "Did you? Did he? How
could he? How could you?" The answers were all
there, in the sorrow of her daughter's beseeching eyes.

"My baby," she finally sighed and searched for
Grazia's hand . . . and when she found it, she clasped
it as if she never, ever meant to let go of it again.

Observing the pained reunion of mother and daughter, Silvana remained seated stiffly in her chair, for
she knew that her task was not yet done. Until then,
she could not let go. Until she made her last plea—

"I must stop you, Grazia, save you, but even I know
that I can't do it alone."

Elena met her mother's eyes and nodded. Grazia

reached over to her grandmother's lap, and clasped Silvana's hand. It was all the encouragement Silvana needed.

"If we three women, we three generations, formed a chain, an unbreakable chain of strength, we could do it."

Elena raised her enclasped hands and Grazia whispered, "Look! A chain!"

"A chain!" Elena agreed. "More united than ever before. An unbreakable chain this time ... and forever more."

Now Silvana could begin. Now it was time to tell them her entire story, the one that had burned a hole in her heart for more than half a century, for almost all of her life.

Chapter Twenty-six

The massive, French-paneled room had a capacity of one thousand people, and it seemed as if all of them were crowding at the door, now that they had heard Silvana was finally arriving. Even the band had been alerted and was playing a stately march as the opulently dressed onlookers clapped in time to the beat.

"Make way, make way!" someone called, and like a story from the Bible, the sea of people parted, leaving a pathway for the arriving party.

At the front of the line stood Sloane Harding, waiting for his beloved. (Elena had phoned him at the hotel a half hour before to say that she and Grazia were having a "heart-to-heart talk" with Silvana and that they would escort her soon.) Beside him stood Anna Michela and Debora, with their husbands, and Eduardo, Mary Catherine, and their two sons. Mark Kroll, Fabian, and the now elderly and frail Noel Jourdan stood together, and behind them, making a vast line, were all the chefs, managers, maître d's, waitpersons, and kitchen help who had ever worked for Silvana.

The only person missing was Lena Milgrim—second mother to all Silvana's girls and best friend to Silvana herself—who had died ten years before.

But after the "intimates," the line stretched on and on, with famous and nonfamous well-wishers, all opulently dressed for the biggest event of the season. And when someone called, "Here she comes!" they all made a deafening roar of shouts and cheers and began applauding even before they could see her.

Then, finally, Silvana was there, sweeping by in her long-sleeved, black velvet gown, Sloane Harding now at her side. These days, she sometimes stooped stiffly when she walked ... but not tonight. Tonight she walked proudly, head high, nose prominent, face gleaming.

"Brava, Silvana! Brava!" the crowd cheered as she made her way down the people-lined aisle.

Every two or three steps, she stopped to accept an embrace or a squeeze of her hand, clearly touched by this impromptu outpouring of affection.

"Grazie! Molto grazie!" She blew kisses to everyone.

"No, Silvana, it is we who should thank you!" the new pastry chef at Per Sempre Silvana said, reaching over to kiss Silvana's cheek. Then she directed the crowd to do just that, calling out, "Tell her. Thank her!"

"You gave me my first job!" someone shouted.

"Me, too! God bless you, Silvana!"

Applause rang out.

"You made me love food." It was the chef of the Mi Elena Ristorante.

"Thank you. *Grazie,*" Silvana told them, beaming. "And you have made *me* love all of you!"

But more still pressed closer; more still wanted to be heard. They would not let her proceed. Throngs jammed the aisle.

"Silvana, I remember the Italian restaurants in New York before you opened Per Sempre Silvana. Meatballs and spaghetti, that was it. Thank God for your courage!"

"Thank God for your vision!"

"And what a pleasure to work for you. I'm a waitress at Casa di Grazia," a young woman called out, turning to the crowd, "and she's the best boss I ever had. I love her!"

"Thank you, Emily," Silvana said, recognizing her. "Thank you all ... *molto.*" Her huge almond eyes, heavy-lidded now and wrinkled, blinked wetly and gratefully.

Now Sloane took her arm and led her, gently pushing through the crowd, to the podium. But she was much too overwhelmed to make the long speech she had planned. She did not even bother to remove the handwritten notes from her bag or to remove her reading glasses from its case. When Sloane made a move to help her retrieve her speech, she shook her head no.

"Non è possible," she whispered. "It's not possible." Then she turned and directed her faded eyes out at the audience.

"I will speak to you not from words on a paper but from feelings deep in my heart."

Everyone cheered. When it was quiet gain, she continued. "I see faces here that I have not glimpsed in twenty years. And I see other faces that I know as well as my own—though none, I admit, with quite so many wrinkles!"

As the crowd chuckled, she sipped from a glass of water, her mouth as dry as old bread. "So many faces—and on each face, so much love! Do you know how that makes me feel?

"Let me tell you. Let me tell you what I know about love.

"This love that I feel from you tonight—it is the most valuable kind of love. Because love that is earned can make you feel truly rich—in a way that money in the bank does not. Tonight all of you— my family, my friends, and colleagues in the food and restaurant industries—have given me a priceless gift— your love and respect. Tonight I am a millionaire! *Molto grazie!"*

As the crowd roared its appreciation, Sloane took the microphone from her hand. In its place he offered her a martini. Then he raised his glass to her and motioned for everyone in the room to do the same.

"Grazie, bella Silvana!" he said, and kissed her hand.

The crowd echoed the toast as one voice, *"Grazie, bella* Silvana!" They repeated it again as Elena, Grazia, Debora, and Anna Michela came to Silvana's side and locked hands with her. Elena and Grazia were sobbing, but then, so were many in the house.

The dinner menu, prepared in Silvana's honor, included some of her favorite dishes. After a colorful cold Roman antipasto of capers and roasted red, green, and yellow peppers salad, waiters carried out huge silver tureens of *Brodo con Tortellini di Zucca,* Broth with Squash-Stuffed Tortellini.

Then the speeches and the awards ceremonies were started, beginning with Best New Chef and Best New Restaurant.

"How young they seem!" Silvana mused to Sloane as the newest stars in the restaurant galaxy received their peers' recognition.

"You were young when you started out, too," Sloane reminded her. "I didn't know you then, of course—but I wish I had. You must've been something!"

"I admit," she agreed, whispering in his ear, "I was quite something!"

Now an endless stream of waiters carried the next course into the room on sizzling platters raised high over their heads.

"Ah! *Quaglie con Uva!*" Silvana could recognize it by the aroma.

"*Quaglie*—what?"

"Quail with Grapes. It's a Tuscan dish prepared with pale grapes, cognac, and herbs," Silvana explained. Then she patted Elena's hand across the table.

"You did a good job planning the menu."

"Thank you, Mama," Elena responded, surprised.

"I don't tell you enough, but you always do a good job, Elena dear. Always."

Now there were new tears, fresh tears between mother and daughter. Between mother and daughters, actually, for Debora and Anna Michela joined in. But it was Grazia who made them sob by joining their hands in an unbreakable chain.

"Now we are truly one. *Viva la famiglia!*"

*   *   *

By the time Silvana was called to the stage to accept her heavy gold medal, she had begun to tire and was eager to go home, where she could remember this evening in comfort. Again she cut her speech short and simply thanked everyone from the bottom of her heart and vowed sincerely that she would never forget one moment of this extraordinary night. Then, as the applause and the music blared, her family walked her out.

The night air, as she emerged from the hotel entrance and stood under the canopy, was as bracing as the martini and the wine she had sipped during the evening. Both the alcohol and the night air made her shiver delightedly. Then she saw him and all delight drained from her face.

"I told you. You're not welcome here."

But Freddo weaved drunkenly, his long hair matted and unkempt, and ignored Silvana altogether. Grazia was who he was there for; Grazia was who he wanted. And no one was going to stop him or send him away. With shocking suddenness he lunged for her, making Grazia scream out in fear . . . and disgust.

"Call the cops!" Elena yelled, yanking Freddo back by his coat sleeves with all her might. "This man is assaulting my daughter! This vile . . . this vile *stranger!*"

"Yes, arrest him!" Grazia cried, surprising even herself. She was free, she realized, free of his hold at last.

Shock registered on Freddo's face. Long ago he had lost his wife; tonight she looked at him with hatred. Now Grazia looked at him with disgust and he knew he had lost her, too.

But just to be sure, the women, without a word, formed a phalanx around Grazia, an unbroken chain of protection. Then just to be absolutely sure, they snarled at him, snapping angrily with their teeth, like mares protecting their young.

"You're not going to get away with this!"

"You'll pay!"

"That's it! Hold him."

"We have you now and you're going where you belong."

"Jail."

This time, they were taking no chances. This time, the cycle would be broken.

Epilogue

1996

From my new, first-floor apartment window, where I now like to sit in the afternoons with a tiny cup of espresso, I can see the life of the city rush by. I myself no longer rush anywhere, but I do love watching the throbbing life of this city. I admit, I love New York. I love this entire country now; it has been good to me ... and I like to think that in my small way, I have contributed something back.

Last year, after my beloved Sloane died, my family took me back to Italy, to the land of my birth. I had never thought I would walk the narrow streets of Rome again, or see the old Jewish quarter where I had lived—and lost my innocence. I cannot say it was easy. It brought me to my knees; it made me sob. But perhaps it was necessary. For now I have a sense of completion—as if all the missing parts in the puzzle that has been my life have at last been found and fitted into their proper places. The puzzle is now completed.

My family has given me that—my lively, robust family, who have formed an unbroken chain of enduring love around me. If it were not for them, I would join my poor Sloane, for I miss him so! But for them, I cook the weekly Sabbath meal, I light a *Yortzeit* candle and say a *barucha* for Sloane and for all the others I have loved and lost. Then we gather here to eat good food and share our news.

Food, even now, brings us together. We eat red snapper that I roast with fresh herbs and set aflame with grappa at the table. We eat pomegranates marinated in orange liqueur and the almond *biscotti* that I still bake in large batches. Food, always food. It was there at the beginning; it is here at the end.

With the end so very near, I hear you asking: Am I happy now? Am I happy at last? And all I can say is this:

My life has been filled with a million moments. I have forgotten none of them, none at all.